D1231302

HUDSON

Refuse to compromise.

Shayne McClendon

Hudson by Shayne McClendon
Copyright © 2010-2017 Shayne McClendon

Updated Edition: July 2017

Published by Always the Good Girl LLC
www.alwaysthegoodgirl.com

All rights reserved.
This is a work of fiction. Names, characters, places, and incidents either are the product of the author's imagination or are used fictitiously, and any resemblance to actual persons, living or dead, business establishments, events, or locales is entirely coincidental.

ISBN-13: 978-0989675598
ISBN-10: 0989675599

Dedication

For the Barter Babes, who understand my bizarre fixation with a man who grew from a small piece of dialogue in my mind and has *never* let me go. Thank you for all you do, every day, to support me, to lift me up, and for all the love you give my beautiful characters.

Without you, my journey would be so much harder.

For my readers because the words mean nothing without someone to read them. Thank you for every book you purchase, every review you write, and every time you tell a friend about me.

I love you and appreciate you more than you know.

Much love,
Shayne

Table of Contents

Table of Contents (continued)

Table of Contents (continued)

Prologue

Eighteen months ago…

The Barter System Essay Directions:

Please write an essay about one intangible thing that would change your life for the better if you were in possession of it. Complete all personal information.

All essays are confidential – as is every piece of data shared by participants. Spelling, grammar, and technical writing are unimportant.

The end result is what counts. ~Riya

ESSAY
Subject Name: Hudson
Subject Age: 38
Subject Career: Real Estate
Marital Status: Single
Children (Y/N): N
Annual Income: $1M plus
Location: Manhattan

I'm not a writer.

I have everything I need.

I lack for nothing.

I'm perfectly content.

However, since I must write something, I will say that since I was a young child, I fought for everything I needed for my family and myself. I learned control. I learned tenacity. I learned discipline.

I did not learn gentleness.

I do not understand the nuances of gentle people and their behaviors. I equate the trait to weakness and do not believe I possess it.

I sometimes – rarely – wonder what it would be like to treat a woman gently, to experience her gentle treatment in return. I do not think I need this in my life, but I admit to curiosity.

Should I never have an opportunity to witness or feel gentleness that is not associated with weakness, I will not consider my life incomplete.

I have Domination.

It is a different breed of gentle. It is outside the boundaries of what most would consider tender, kind, or loving. Most are unable to understand the care, the restraint, and the force of will involved in the full application of control.

Having the *ability* to crush a woman's will, to break her spirit – yet *not* doing so – while pushing her through pleasure so intense that she is rendered incoherent: that is power.

Perhaps gentleness is not something I will know. It may not be meant for a man like me.

In any case, your research interests me. Unlocking the male psyche? A substantial goal. I wish you success. Your brilliant mind is apparent.

My curiosity is peaked.

What specific information could I impart? Would you be too different from me? Would you enjoy the darkness?

Chapter One

Hudson Winters saw her the moment he walked into the coffee house they frequented more than was probably healthy. The thought caused him to smile.

After he placed his order, he watched her.

Riya O'Connell was unaware of his attention. Just as she was unaware of the man at the table beside her or the young man behind the counter who continually looked in her direction.

She wore clothes geared more for comfort than style, a choice he commended her for considering she lived in a luxury penthouse on Fifth Avenue. Worn jeans, a soft t-shirt, and running shoes, her hair piled in a messy bun on top of her head, and dark red reading glasses perched on the end of her nose. She scribbled rapidly in a notebook beside her laptop.

Picking up his order, he approached her table. "Riya."

She glanced up distractedly and gave him a genuine smile. It was a habit of hers that never failed to surprise him.

"Hudson! What a pleasure. I need to look away from the computer for a few minutes. Your timing is perfect."

"Not something I'm accustomed to hearing." He settled in the opposite chair and placed his briefcase on the floor beside him.

The sound of her laughter was full in the small café and her hazel eyes sparkled. "I imagine not. You're rather...terse."

"You once called me terrifying."

"That, too." She grinned. He held out the second cup and she looked giddy. "Coffee! Excellent of you."

"Perhaps you've had enough?"

"Don't dare speak such a thing." He laughed. "You're not rushing off to work?"

"I don't *rush*."

"Hudson. You rush everywhere. You're a man on a mission. Worlds to conquer, empires to build, and so forth."

"Your men aren't the same?"

"Micah is more like you. It's why you're both so cranky around one another." She sipped her coffee with sincere happiness. "Max is less intense. Clients that need a softer touch prefer him."

For a long moment, he stared at her. "I see now."

Her smile was slow. "That took a while. I bet it never takes quite so long to make such connections."

"They…provide a balance for you."

"In many ways, they're very similar. In others, quite opposites." She shrugged. "They fascinate me."

Drinking his own coffee, he stared out at the street.

"Hudson? You seem…introspective."

"I turned forty."

Her smile was kind. "You're not going to buy a yellow Corvette and get a spray tan, are you?" She gave a mock shudder. "That's so *sad*."

With a chuckle, he shook his head. "You're the only woman I know who can be funny while asking someone like *me* about a mid-life crisis." He shook his head. "Nothing like that."

The way she looked at him was not as a psychiatrist analyzing a patient. Riya looked at him as if he was a wolf caught in a trap. An animal she was attempting to soothe before he chewed off his own arm in desperation.

"Why do you speak to me?" It was not the first time he wondered.

Inhaling deeply, she put down her coffee and crossed her arms on the table. "You're a man who belittles softer emotions in yourself and others. Yet, you once asked me if I'd like my attacker killed. You're far kinder than you allow anyone to see but I respect your strength and dominant will more for it. You'll never be warm and fuzzy but I hope that one day you find more reasons to smile."

Sitting back, she picked up and sipped her coffee. "In the meantime, you're successful, attractive, and in the prime of your life. I'd say the world is your oyster and you *might* want to ask for hot sauce."

This time, his laugh caused heads to turn. "Noted." He inclined his head toward her ring. "You look happy."

"I am. Thank you."

"Your wedding had little fanfare." He frowned. "Those of us who exist on the fringe of societal norms have little choice."

Riya smiled with a small shake of her head. "I was barefoot in the sand. There could have been *nothing* better. It was perfection." The silence stretched between them. "You *like* that I ended up with them." Her face broke into a broad smile.

He stood and picked up his briefcase. Leonard was parked at the curb. "I'm older. Harder for different reasons. They found peace."

"You believe they found peace with me?"

He said softly, "Even more than *you* found with *them*." With a nod, he said, "Goodbye, Riya."

"Goodbye, Hudson. Have a wonderful day and thank you for the coffee."

Without a word, he left the woman who never failed to leave him slightly rattled. As he approached his Rolls, he nodded at his driver. The two of them rarely spoke and that was the way he liked it.

Staring out the window, Hudson pondered Riya and his choices, something he'd found himself doing often since his birthday. A distant part of him felt a modicum of regret about withdrawing as one of her subjects.

Another part recognized that he would have taken too much of her spark. By nature, he would have grown territorial, unable to handle her moving on to men he knew.

Where she truly belonged.

It was better this way – having her as a friend of sorts and an unlikely one at that. No two people could be more different and it was something he liked about her.

It was out of character for him to connect to a person so...sweet. There were few women such as Riya in his sphere of existence, outside his own family.

They wouldn't survive.

He'd known Micah Chadwick and Max Scottsdale for more than a decade. They made their first million one year out of Oxford and hadn't slowed down since. Like him in many ways, the boys were different in one crucial trait.

They could be gentle.

None of their backgrounds had been either easy or safe but where it had sharpened Hudson to a razor's edge emotionally, it taught the M's to want certain things – softer and easily breakable – as part of their daily life.

Two years prior, they'd been steadily working their way to becoming like him. He observed as they used sex as nothing more than a temporary release and how they threw themselves into twenty-hour workdays to fill the void.

Then the lovely Riya appeared on their radar and life changed for them overnight.

The bastards smiled all the fucking *time* now. If Hudson didn't like their woman so much, he'd tell them to knock it the fuck off and give him a goddamn break.

He avoided the three of them in the building and at *Trois* because a man could only handle so much grinning before he wanted to punch someone in the fucking throat.

Few people understood him. Fewer still accepted him.

The thought drew his mind to Natalia. It had been *weeks* since he'd last seen his best friend. As if summoning her, his cell phone rang.

"Natalia."

"Hello, Hudson. Is this a good time?"

He grunted. "Always."

"Liar. Will you stop by the club?"

"Yes." He disconnected. "Leonard, stop at *Trois*."

"Certainly, sir." The driver changed course and soon enough they pulled to the curb in front of a mini-mansion he'd saved from demolition more than a dozen years before. As he opened the door, he asked, "Shall I park, sir?"

"Yes. I'll call."

With a nod, Leonard got back in the car and drove through the gates to the parking area along the side of the renovated structure. Hudson ascended the steps and one of the large double doors opened before he reached it.

Her eyes raked over him and she smiled. "Darling, it's a thousand degrees outside. Why in god's name are you wearing a three-piece suit?"

"Meetings."

"Naturally."

Natalia Roman was five-nine and slender. Her hair was dyed blackest black and cut in a straight bob that brushed her jaw. Her eyes were a stunning blue and surrounded by lashes he knew she turned deep black each day.

A mouth that was a bit too wide, lips that were a bit too narrow, and a figure that didn't boast curves were the source of many complaints from her over the years.

Hudson had always found her to be incredibly beautiful.

She wore lounging pants and a tank top in black, as most of her wardrobe tended to be. Her feet were bare and her toenails were painted black as well.

Leaning forward, he kissed her cheek. Stepping out of the way, she gestured for him to enter and, after locking the door, led him to her massive apartment on the second floor overlooking the front of the club.

Without asking, she made him a cup of coffee. He took it and they simply stared at one another for a long moment.

"Why have you avoided me?"

"You *know* why, Hudson." Natalia never raised her voice and rarely cursed.

He did know. His girlfriend – as much as he detested the term – hated the person who knew him better than anyone on the planet. *Jealousy.* It was a despicable trait Christina had in abundance.

"I don't give a *fuck* what she thinks."

"I realize. I was tired of the passive-aggressive bullshit. I decided to give you the space to make...whatever your thing is with her...work." She waved her hand. "That's not why I called you. However, it does involve her."

He felt his jaw clench and Natalia reached up to stroke it. "I've handled it already. I wanted you to be aware. Giving you space doesn't mean allowing the woman to carry tales."

8

Turning his face, he kissed her palm. It was like silk. "Tell me."

With a nod, she walked to her small office and used a remote to turn on the complex security system that monitored every room in the club. Ten screens lit up and she typed instructions on the computer. In seconds, several images of Christina appeared.

Hudson stepped closer with a frown. Natalia played each recorded section individually and as they ended, one by one, he felt the fury growing inside him.

"How long?" he asked abruptly.

"Unsure. My security team waited to bring it to me. Given the circumstances, they wanted to be certain before they made accusations. They went back six weeks and decided it was enough to identify that it wasn't a one-off situation. I've already spoken to the members shown with her."

His fucking *girlfriend* was dealing cocaine – substantial amounts from the looks of it – out of *his* best friend's club. A club that existed on property *he* owned. Going home to *his* building and likely storing more drugs in *his* penthouse.

"I will slit her fucking throat." He stared at the images with his hands on his hips, carefully controlling his breathing. "I leave for Chicago tonight. I'll be gone several days."

"I'll watch her."

"How did you address it?"

"It doesn't…"

"How was it *addressed*, Natalia?"

"I confronted her. She lied. When shown the footage downstairs, she started screaming and throwing things." She stood calmly, arms crossed loosely over her stomach.

Hudson walked to her, staring into her face. "What did she *say*?"

Her blue eyes met his unblinkingly. "That I set her up."

"There's more."

"Hudson…"

"Goddamn it, Natalia. Tell me or I'll have her brought here to tell me herself."

He watched her inhale deeply. "Christina said I'm of little importance in your life, which is why you threw me out of it, and that in retaliation – out of pure jealousy of everything she has that I do not – I set her up."

"You let her believe I severed ties with you?" She nodded. "Your response?"

"I told her I would address it with you directly." There was a small shrug of her shoulders. "She started begging at that point." Her mouth lifted on one side. "I found it lovely to watch."

"I'll cancel my trip and deal with this tonight."

"That's unnecessary. I've controlled it on this end. Had it been anything else, I wouldn't have bothered you with it but…this was too far. It puts both of us at risk."

"She's out on her ass when I return."

Saying nothing, Natalia turned off the screens. "I've kept you from your day long enough." He opened his mouth to speak and she shook her head. "The code, Hudson."

The silence stretched between them. He jerked her into a rough hug and kissed her temple. "I'll call you when I return."

"Travel safely."

He held her for a moment longer and then left her apartment and the building without another word. Before getting in his car, he glanced up at her window.

Then he placed his issues with Christina in a box and sealed the lid. He would deal with her in a few days. There was little she'd be able to do in the few days he'd be gone.

Winters Enterprises was about to obtain a small but successful hotel chain in the Midwest. He needed his mind focused and emotions had no place in his business empire.

* * *

From the window facing the street, Natalia watched as her best friend walked down the steps to his waiting car. He glanced up and despite the specialty glass that prevented him from having a visual of her, it was as if he *knew* she stood there.

When he disappeared inside the Rolls, she released the breath she hadn't realized she was holding.

The man was powerful, in so many ways, and he had affected her deeply from the first day they'd met.

She didn't regret one moment of their history, though she might have made different choices herself if only she'd known how.

No matter his strength, she knew the situation with his girlfriend would cause him pain. As a man who did not lie, did not waffle in his loyalty, and fought fiercely for the people he cared about, the woman's behavior would strike deeply. He would never admit the perceived weakness. He would never shed a tear. He would go on without an obvious ripple caused in his daily life.

Natalia knew him better than he knew himself. She understood what drove him and how he dealt with pain, rejection, or failure. She would help him through it in the ways she knew.

After all, Hudson was the only man with whom she'd ever felt an emotional attachment.

Chapter Two

Five days later…

When Gabriella Hernandez landed at La Guardia, she knew she would never want to live without the hustle and bustle of city life again.

After a quick call to let her parents and sister know she'd arrived safely, she slung her backpack and carry-on over her shoulders, collected her two large suitcases, and took a cab to Hudson's apartment.

Everything fascinated her and she tried to look everywhere at once.

As the yellow cab pulled to the curb of the address she still clutched in her hand, the building, the block, and Central Park across the street were almost overwhelmingly perfect.

It felt as if she was on the set of a movie.

A man wearing a full suit and white gloves opened her door. "Welcome, Miss. Allow me to help you with your bags. My name is Henry. I'm the doorman for the building."

"Thank you very much, Henry. I'm Brie."

Together, they managed to get everything inside and she paid the cabbie with a smile. He seemed taken aback by her demeanor. That made her smile even bigger.

A young man about her age stood behind the concierge desk. He was a good-looking and trim Hispanic man and she thought he had a nice smile.

"How may I help you, ma'am?"

"I'm here to see Hudson Winters. He's expecting me."

He blinked. "One moment. I don't believe he's back yet. I'll ring the penthouse." She pulled all her bags to the side of the lobby so she wasn't in anyone's way. "There's no answer, ma'am."

"Please, call me Brie. I don't mind waiting." Barely able to contain her excitement, she sat on the bench and grinned at the doorman. The older man smiled back. "This is my first trip to New York. It's wonderful and so different from Washington. That's where I'm from."

Henry nodded. "A rookie! You'll have much to see and do while you're here."

It was an exceptional late-summer day, starting to cool down but still a long way from the cold she knew was coming. Back home, the temperatures were already dropping in the evenings so a Northeastern winter didn't frighten her in the slightest. The small town where she'd grown up was situated in a deep valley. Perfect for growing grapes and even more so for catching snow in the non-growing season.

The concierge asked, "What brings you to New York, ma'am?"

"First, I'm Gabriella Hernandez. Forgive my manners. It's the excitement!" He chuckled as she stood, walked to the desk, and held out her hand. "It's so nice to meet you." Taking a deep breath, she added shyly, "I moved here for *love*, if that doesn't sound too nauseating and cliché."

The concierge came from behind the desk. "I'm sorry. Brie, right?" She nodded cheerfully. "I'm Carlo. The person you mentioned…Hudson Winters. Is that…the man you came to New York for?"

Brie nodded and felt her smile slip at the silent communication that passed between the two men. Much was said without a single word and a *feeling*, like the ones her grandmother and both of her aunts got sometimes, fluttered in the pit of her stomach.

"Why? What is it?" She controlled her breathing and tone.

Carlo parted his lips to reply when the front door opened. A group of three people entered the lobby laughing and holding hands. Two of the most attractive men she'd ever seen held a vibrant brunette between them.

"Henry! Don't worry! We *are* capable of opening the door, you know. Don't let us interrupt."

"Miss Riya. Lovely day, isn't it?"

"All of them are pretty spectacular." The brunette paused in front of Brie and held out her hand. "I'm Riya. Are you new here?"

The men on either side smiled down at her face as if she fascinated them. Unable to deny the woman's enthusiastic nature, Brie nodded and shook her hand.

"I'm Brie. I...I think *maybe*. I'm here to see Hudson Winters...?" Riya's fingers tightened subtly on Brie's and the flutter in her stomach intensified. Looking around at all of them, she said carefully, "Please. Can someone tell me what's going on?"

Without looking away, one of the men with Riya said quietly, "Carlo, please have Rodney hold the car for a bit longer." The young man nodded.

He had a lovely English accent but Brie was unable to enjoy it as she normally would. She sat down on the bench behind her with a rapidly rising sense of dread.

Riya sat beside her and took her hand. "How do you know Hudson, Brie?"

She felt foolish and inexplicably afraid. "He did a tour of the winery where I work a couple of years ago." The other woman held her gaze and she shrugged.

"He's been...coming back every few months since and we started dating. He told me to come. That's why I'm here." The lump in her throat was painful and she struggled to swallow past it. "Something's wrong, isn't it?"

"Maybe nothing. Possibly a misunderstanding. These are my husbands, Max and Micah." At the widening of Brie's eyes, she laughed. "Don't let us frighten you off. We're shockingly normal once you get to know us."

With a pat on her hand, Riya stood and tugged Brie up with her.

"Why don't you come up and have coffee while you wait? Carlo will ring the penthouse when Hudson arrives. I promise you'll be safe. I can't *leave* you standing in the lobby."

At that moment, the front door slammed wide and a powerful figure stood there with a phone to his ear and a briefcase in his hand. "Henry! I don't believe you're paid to fraternize with the fucking tenants. One job. *Door. Man.* Let's see if we can make that happen, shall we?"

He glared at Max and Micah – who returned it – but inclined his head at Riya. Brie could tell it was his attempt at civility. The woman Brie had only known for a handful of minutes laid her hand on his forearm as he neared and he stopped as if startled that she touched him.

"Wait a moment, if you don't mind, Hudson." Glancing back, her eyes met Brie's over her shoulder. "Do you recognize this man?"

Brie stood up straight and took in the big man's expensive suit, watch, and shoes with a roll of her eyes. "No. I do *not*." All the stress of the situation bubbled up and she sucked her teeth. "Money might buy many things but not *manners* apparently."

Disconnecting his call without a word, he faced her fully. He was almost as tall as Riya's men were. What he lacked in height, he made up for in a physical presence that should have intimidated her.

He glared from pure black eyes, taking her in like a mosquito he wanted to slap flat. With a slight forward lean, he cocked his head, and said in a deep voice, "What the fuck did you just say?"

Hands on her hips, she matched his glare. She enunciated each word perfectly.

"I *said*…money doesn't buy *manners*. Using your wealth…" She made a dismissive gesture at his clothing. "…and your *power* to trample on people in service positions. Poor behavior for a *child* much less a grown *man*. I suppose it would *kill you* to say *please* and *thank you*. Maybe not denigrate the staff so you can feel superior because you don't open doors for a living."

She crossed her arms over her chest and cocked her hip. Izzy called it the Mexicana *fuck you* stance. "You ought to be ashamed of yourself. I'm ashamed *for* you."

Riya's voice was quiet. "Brie. This is Hudson Winters."

The feeling became a rock in her gut instantly and she nodded once in acknowledgement. "Something told me…never mind." She laughed bitterly. "Obviously, I've been played. I've never seen this man before in my life and I don't give a damn if I never do again. I'd likely kill him inside a week."

She murmured a few choice insults in Spanish under her breath and Riya covered her mouth to hide her smile while Carlo turned away.

Stooping, she gathered her things and looked at Riya and her men. "Thank you for trying to put me at ease. Some things aren't meant to be. It was nice to meet all of you."

Desperate to escape before she had a nervous breakdown, she headed for the door.

Over her shoulder, she called, "Henry, Carlo…you were great. Thank you for being kind during a situation that must have been hellishly awkward for you considering. Have a lovely day."

* * *

Riya turned to go after Brie and Hudson grabbed her upper arm without thought.

Max stepped between them. "Hands fucking *off*, mate."

Micah moved close to her other side and there was no doubt in his mind that they would work together to beat the hell out of him if they felt their woman was being threatened.

"It's alright," she told them gently. "Hudson wouldn't hurt me."

He released his neighbor – and friend, appreciative of her defense. "My apologies, Riya."

She waved it away. "Bigger issues, everyone. Let's focus."

Hudson thought about the woman who'd dressed him down as no one dared in his life. Her ass as she walked away was a thing of beauty.

"What the *fuck* is going on?" he blurted. Riya turned her frown on him and he recognized another female with the power to make him feel bad. He watched her grind her teeth as she took a deep breath. "Excuse me, Riya. Who was that woman?"

"Jesus, you're an ass, Winters," Micah told him furiously. "If you could have been civil for a few solid minutes in a *row,* we might have been able to get more details." Irritation made his accent more pronounced.

Under other circumstances, Hudson would have provoked him because he could.

Sighing, Riya told Henry, "Please keep her in sight." The doorman nodded and she turned to her men. "I'll need Rodney to do some running around today. Will you need him?"

Max smiled and Hudson wanted to grind *his* teeth.

"Love, you *do* realize we all live to serve you, correct? We can drive ourselves but I think we'll be staying in for the afternoon." His accent was like Micah's yet gentler.

"Touching. Truly. Might we get to the fucking point?" Both men looked ready to hit him and it put him back on familiar ground. He grinned at them in silent challenge.

Henry went to the door. "She's at the entrance to the park. She looks distressed. I'll not lose her, ma'am. Mr. Winters, she said her name was Gabriella Hernandez."

Finally. Some fucking information.

Nodding curtly at the doorman, Hudson put his hands on his hips and waited for Riya to explain what was happening. His glare was known to cower businessmen around the world but it had no effect on her whatsoever.

He admitted profound respect for her fortitude.

She rolled her eyes. "I realize you like things to move at a lightning pace, Hudson. You're going to have to *wait your turn*." Gesturing to Carlo, he stepped behind his desk and handed her a pen and piece of paper. She jotted a couple of notes down. "Did she say where she was from?"

"Washington, Miss Riya."

The pen tapped her lower lip. "Definitely Washington State since she mentioned a winery." Hudson set his palm on the counter beside her and lifted his brow. "Dear *lord*, you're impatient. I'd gather Miss Hernandez has been swindled by a man impersonating you."

He drew himself up to his full height and any other woman would have taken a step back at the thunderous expression he imagined he wore. Riya didn't seem to notice.

"We don't know to what extent but the person definitely told her to come here. She arrived in New York today and came to the address she was given." Glancing up, she added sadly, "She's been dating a man calling himself Hudson Winters for two years."

Hudson said nothing. *The person would suffer for a long fucking time.*

"If she lived and worked in a small wine community in rural Washington…how did a con man even spot her?" Max wondered aloud. The blue of his eyes glowed as his mind raced to consider possible scenarios.

Not for the first time, Hudson wished the man's brain were in his employ.

Henry called out, "Oh dear! She made a phone call and now she's *overwrought*. Poor thing. Shall I bring her back, Miss Riya?"

"Riya, not that I'd dream of leaving a woman stranded alone in New York, but what exactly do you intend to do now?" Micah stroked her hair.

"I'm going to find out what happened. If she wants to stay in New York, I'll help her find a job and a place to live. Otherwise, we'll help her get back home." Raising her brows, she dared any of them to argue with her.

Max kissed her cheek. "Tell us what you need."

He was going to punch them on principle any moment. Their constant need to show affection was nauseating.

"I need her to come back." The way she rubbed her hands together made the others nervous for her safety but Hudson knew Riya was stronger than they realized. "Then I can help. You *know* how I love to help."

"She can work for the building if she doesn't think it's beneath her. I have an apartment she can rent. Anyone breathes a word that either of those offers is connected to me and I'll rescind them instantly." His announcement shocked the rest of them into silence.

Until Riya's face broke into a big smile and she patted his arm consolingly. "I know. It would be such a crime for the world to find out you're not the evil bastard you like them to think you are." Hudson grunted and she tilted her head. "I take it you'll track down the person using your name to rob unsuspecting women and stop him from doing this to anyone else?"

In a deadly quiet voice, he replied, "You can *guarantee* it."

He gave instructions to Carlo. "Pull the information on the apartment for Riya. Wait to make the job offer. I'll cover her salary since she's an addition to the approved budget. No higher than a maid. Let's see if she shows up and does the job. Understood?"

"Perfectly, sir."

"I need to make some phone calls. Keep me informed."

In the reflection of the mirror on the back wall of the elevator alcove, he watched Riya stand at attention with a mocking salute. He pretended not to notice.

Chapter Three

Hudson stepped off the elevator in his penthouse and walked to the wall of glass. Crossing his arms, he stared at the city landscape for several minutes.

His mind might not work at the pace of Scottsdale's but some things were intuitive. Two such incidents within days of each other were too bizarre to be coincidence.

Something wasn't right and he thought he knew exactly what – and *who* – it was.

He took the stairs two at a time to the upper floor, entered his office, and dialed the phone number for a man who did not exist.

"Hollow."

"Winters. I need information within the hour. Can you do it?"

"Don't insult me. My normal fee plus a little extra by way of an apology in the normal account in ten minutes. Give me names."

"Run *my* name as well as a woman named Gabriella Hernandez." With growing fury, he added between gritted teeth, "Run Christina Underton again."

Without saying goodbye, the computer hacker hung up and Hudson initiated the wire transfer from his slush account in the Caymans to an account in Switzerland. The name on that account was *not* Hollow nor anyone else who existed. The man had constructed a veritable fortress around his true identity and Hudson didn't give a damn.

He was the best. He got results. That was all that mattered.

Taking off his jacket and tie, Hudson slowly rolled up his sleeves as he considered what he knew and what he needed to know.

Walking into his bedroom, he opened the closet Christina used. It was filled with glaringly bright and revealing outfits, ungodly numbers of shoes and accessories, and a large jewelry drawer he'd been steadily filling over their time together.

Standing in the doorway, hands on his hips, he recalled how and when he'd met the woman.

He'd withdrawn from Riya's research a few weeks prior. They were having a record-breaking heat wave. Traveling all the time, he was pent up and sexually frustrated more often than not.

That day, Leonard dropped him off in front of the building and a young woman, distracted on her phone, bumped into him as he approached the door. Immediately checking for his wallet, he set her away from his body as she turned tear-filled baby blue eyes up at him.

"I'm sorry. It's not my day. Forgive me."

"Why are you crying?" He knew his words were abrupt but didn't care.

"I'm late for a job interview. I got lost…again. I don't know my way around the city yet. I'm sorry." She had an accent from some southern state, long blonde hair, and wore a business skirt suit that showed too much cleavage and leg for any legitimate company.

Pretty in the popular sense – if one preferred the polished images the media force-fed the public – she didn't seem very bright or emotionally tough.

She was still crying and her lip *trembled* for god's sake.

"I'll buy you coffee. My driver will take you where you need to go." She nodded gratefully and took fast steps in dangerously high heels to keep up with him.

An hour later, he fucked her over the back of his living room couch.

Within days of her moving in, he discovered her tendency to whine, "ooh, baby, give it to me, baby" during sex. He resorted to gagging her when they fucked.

The first time Natalia met her, Hudson watched as she nearly bit through her own tongue to stop herself from laughing aloud. Cool and sophisticated, a brilliant businesswoman in her own right, his friend had little patience for the dumb blonde persona Christina deliberately wore.

He'd walked her downstairs where Leonard waited to take her home. "Say it."

A giggle escaped and she bit her lower lip with a shake of her head. "I will not. You already know, darling. She's willing and present. It's what you require right now and with my own choices, I'm not one to judge." She winked. "However, if she'd mispronounced one more word, I might have started laughing and been unable to stop."

He laughed. "I think she plays dumb."

"She's *excellent* at it. Have fun. Call me tomorrow."

For six months, Natalia did her best to be polite. Then Hudson sponsored Christina for admittance to *Trois* and the women were soon far less amicable. His girlfriend started going to the club more and more often. She racked up enormous bar tabs and had to be carried to his car more nights than not.

In the spring, his best friend called to say, "She ran up a three-thousand-dollar bar tab last night, Hudson. She flirted openly and *physically* with Max. I thought Riya was going to kick the idiot's ass in the middle of the dance floor. Tawny walked your girl away and had a little chat I wish I could have overheard. She couldn't get out of the club fast enough."

There was a heavy sigh and he should have known it wouldn't be long before Natalia was personally tired of running interference with the latest train wreck he'd moved into his life.

"She's exhausting and I honestly don't understand how or why you bother."

It was quite simple really.

He traveled all the time. When he came home, he wanted someone to fuck that didn't want or expect conversation. In his opinion, Christina was no better than a call girl. After he got his, she expected gifts, and Hudson dutifully delivered them.

It was the main reason he didn't feel bad about using her.

She was spoiled, selfish, and cold but one thing she *didn't* do was complain about how he fucked her. The woman accepted whatever he dished out and begged for more.

He temporarily relieved the tension that rode him all the time and she scored a piece of jewelry or pair of shoes she'd hinted about wanting.

Sexual satisfaction made him generous.

A demanding professional life and high sex drive guaranteed he pretty much walked through the world hard. As a result, he didn't *think* much about his girlfriends with anything but his dick. They usually made out far better on the deal than he did.

Naturally, he'd had Christina checked out. She had a record for possession of stolen property and check fraud. As a hustler, she was a long way from her impoverished beginnings outside Birmingham.

He figured there was only so much damage she could cause so he gave her access and moved her ass in. He never considered what else she might get into with the resources he provided her. Knowing she'd likely been fucking her accomplice in the con made his head pound. Christina's circumstances were about to change drastically.

Hudson didn't share his toys.

With a small growl, he stepped into the space that smelled of too many different perfumes and was almost painful on the eyes.

It took him eight minutes to find her stash of cash and drugs divided into client-ready bags. He assumed he held tens of thousands of dollars in cocaine, if not more. Enough that a drug bust could have taken everything he'd worked all his life to build.

For that alone, he would make them pay.

Another six minutes tearing through her shoes turned up a stack of documents under the names of more than a dozen women.

Rage riding him fast and hot, Hudson removed a rubber band from the ID's with the initials "GH" on a sticky note.

It contained a passport, driver's license, social security card, and birth certificate in the name of *Gabriella Lenora Hernandez*. A photo of Christina wearing a black wig against different backgrounds was attached to each piece of forged paper.

His phone rang at the forty-one minute mark. "Winters."

"You've been *very* busy. Where did you find the time to jet set all over the country schmoozing women before stealing every dime of their money? I'm assuming Gabriella Hernandez showed up at your penthouse in the last few hours."

"What did they get from these women?" The fury that boiled through his veins made him glad Christina was not in arm's reach.

"Grand total I've found so far is around two million – nine different women in four states. Looks like they concentrated on the West coast. I'm waiting for several searches to finish and I think there will be more. The transfer was completed from Miss Hernandez's Washington account a few hours ago. The new account is now closed."

"How much?"

"They hit her for a bit more than ninety-grand combined from a small checking and substantial savings account. I'd say she's been saving practically every dime for *years*."

Classical music played in the background as Hollow dug into a stranger's life. "Otherwise, she's clean. Lived in the same small town all her life, went to college nearby, and returned after graduation. Has one older sister, both parents still living...well *hello*."

Hudson listened as Hollow typed wildly fast. Thirty seconds later, the typing suddenly stopped.

"Her parents are *loaded*. No shit. They moved from Mexico in their twenties and they've spent the last thirty years buying up small-to-medium businesses and property all over the country. Their daughters worked their asses off. Gabriella at a small but ridiculously successful winery and her sister Isabella with their fashion interests."

More typing ensued and Hudson pressed his finger and thumb into the bridge of his nose. He asked a question, already knowing the answer.

"The name of their corporation?"

"*Nuevo Día, Nuevo Comienzo* – does it ring a…never mind."

Hollow found the answer to his question as Hudson's frustration grew.

Gabriella Hernandez's parents had conducted long-distance deals with Winters Enterprises for property and other assets over the years. He'd never dealt personally with the owners, only their agents, but it was another coincidence that *meant* something.

"Threads, Winters. We'll go back to that. Okay, the girls make standard wages but…*oh yeah*…they both own major stock in the main holding company, which is kept in trust."

There was a pause. "That makes Miss Hernandez worth more than six million and these jokers only managed to grab ninety grand. Total credit card activity shows she spends about six thousand a year, most of it on custom-made bras and panties. I don't get it – she seems like a woman with few interests."

Hudson mentally recalled the curves on Gabriella Hernandez and knew why she had to order custom.

"As for Christina, she's opened accounts and safety deposit boxes in no less than six different banks over the past year. The first report that mentioned you by name was about eighteen months ago. She's not the original woman in the forged IDs. I'll run facial recognition and see if I get any hits."

"Assessment."

"I'd say she was a plant, Winters. Deliberately inserted into your life for a specific purpose. The only reason you haven't had the feds at your door is because the jurisdictions are scattered and each woman dismissed you as the man who'd robbed them based on your photo."

"Any photos of the man who used my name?"

"Not even one. That alone should have set off alarms. Some of these women reported that he was part of their lives for as much as six months."

"Gabriella Hernandez has been seeing him for two years."

"Curious." There was a long pause and more typing. "That makes her the first mark, the longest con, but the most recent victim. I'll run some searches and see what pops."

Hudson considered the fact that just days ago, Natalia confronted Christina about the drug deals in her club. It was likely the criminals were wrapping up their operation before he got involved.

Sending the last woman to his *home* was an interesting "*fuck you.*" He wondered if her partner had informed Christina about that part of the plan. Somehow, he doubted it.

"Get me paper. Through the same courier service."

"Will do."

"Thank you."

"Whoa. You're welcome, Winters. Excellent doing business with you."

They ended the call and Hudson phoned down to the concierge desk. "Yes, sir?"

"Status?"

"We're bringing Brie back now. Rodney will drive her around to see a few places from the paper. I'll tell her about the brownstone and the job in the morning. It'll start her second day far better than her first. I think she'll jump at the chance to work here."

Hudson didn't know *why* she would. Why not return to her family? Why not ask them for help?

"I don't get this woman."

"She told us she came here for love, sir." The young man cleared his throat and added quietly, "Maybe she's too embarrassed to call her family."

Instantly, he knew the concierge had it right.

A woman leaving the nest for the first time who ended up swindled and without a place to go? She hadn't struck him as the type to want people to know that.

"Keep me posted."

"Yes, sir."

"Carlo?"

"Sir?"

"I need assistance packing Christina's belongings *tonight*. I'll pay the workers in cash. Reserve a suite at the Hyatt for thirty days on my account and send up building security."

"I'll contact them and send three women up, sir."

After he hung up, he thought about the small, curvy woman who hadn't been afraid to tell him where the fuck he could go. Part of him was pissed – *no one* talked to him like that.

It made the rest of him hard.

Despite her parting words, Miss Hernandez *would* be seeing him again.

* * *

Building security showed up in less than five minutes and Hudson had Christina stripped of all clearance to his building. While they rekeyed locks and programmed new passcodes, he called his personal assistant with instructions to cancel every credit card issued in her name.

Half an hour later, three women rang for admittance. They pushed a cart laden with boxes and packing materials into his penthouse and he showed them the primary belongings being moved.

He walked through the rooms, finding odds and ends that belonged to the woman he'd lived with and fucked for more than a year...but clearly did not know.

Occasionally, he found something random and handed it to one of the women to be included in the boxes they filled. All of Christina's jewelry was sealed in a security bag.

He locked her fake IDs, drugs, and cash in his office safe. He wasn't certain how to handle the criminal aspect. He didn't need the bad press but he couldn't allow her and her partner to get away with what they'd done either.

How many other victims were out there?

He wondered at the use of his name and the connection to Gabriella's family in a business aspect. His girlfriend and her partner were going to regret the day they'd decided to fuck with him. Hudson planned to make sure of it.

He called the company driver who chauffeured Christina and asked where she was.

"She's been shopping all afternoon, sir. She's at the spa and plans to visit *Trois* later this evening."

"Don't mention my call."

"No, sir."

Three hours to get her moved out of his apartment and out of his life. More than enough time.

* * *

Hudson hadn't understood why Christina spent so many of her evenings at his best friend's private club since most of the members were in exclusive ménage relationships – hence the name.

The fact that she was dealing coke to several of the younger members – and a couple of the older ones, which had surprised him – solved the mystery.

Natalia came to him with the idea for *Trois* after spending a weekend with two men he did business with out of Dallas more than ten years before. They had been searching for the woman they could take care of and share. She'd quickly let them know she wasn't the right person for what they needed…but the idea had been born.

At first, Hudson wondered how profitable such a club would be.

"Think about Kiki's place, darling. Even people not into the lifestyle love The Playground because they can be themselves. Most self-proclaimed ménage males are stupidly rich, which provides them with gates to hide behind. I want to give them the opportunity to be in the open but still protected."

He hadn't hesitated to give her the start-up funds and use of a property he owned but hadn't decided what to do with yet. She was brilliant, the only person he trusted, and she never judged him.

Natalia accepted him for who and what he was. That gave her power she would never abuse.

Within a few years, he was proven right for never doubting her. She paid back his loan and made the club a tremendous success with members all over the world. Hudson had an apartment renovated for her on the second floor of the mini-mansion.

One of the benefits of being Natalia's silent partner was membership. Surprisingly, he used it.

Different from swinging, nowhere near as seedy as porn-popularized cuckolding, ménage existed on the fringe. Most of the relationships consisted of two men and one woman, though there were a few with the opposite configuration who frequented *Trois*.

It didn't turn him off, but Hudson knew he didn't have the personality to share a woman with another man.

His ego barely tolerated other men in his business and personal orbits – he couldn't imagine his reaction while fucking. He was too selfish, a trait he recognized and accepted in himself.

The business contacts he made through the club were beneficial and it was a good place to wind down with a drink occasionally. Natalia had provided a sound investment and a place to relax.

It was well after dark when the women Carlo sent him finished packing Christina's shit. They supervised the movers who came to pick everything up and transport it to the Hyatt. Security confirmed she'd been wiped from every level of access.

He stood alone, again in front of the glass. The skyline often drew his eye and it filled him with a sense of power to see several of his own holdings from where he stood.

Finally, he poured himself a glass of scotch and went upstairs to shower and change.

It was time to visit *Trois*.

Christina and her partner had made an extreme tactical error involving *his name* in their little scheme and he planned to show her how extreme.

He was about to dust the little bitch off his shoes.

Chapter Four

Gabriella walked quickly through the doors and out onto the sidewalk, sensing movement – probably the sweet-tempered Riya – behind her.

Without looking back, she crossed at the intersection down the block, stepped around a low wall, and dropped her bags beside it.

Staring into the park, she thought it was the prettiest she'd ever seen. She tried to pretend everything was fine. She ignored the tears on her cheeks and sat on the wall to think.

She was beyond humiliated. She didn't understand *why*…

Suddenly she remembered something "Hudson" had asked her over the phone before she'd gotten on the plane. Her blood ran cold.

"I'm going to track your location the entire time you're in the air. I can't wait to see you! I want to make sure you arrive safe and sound."

Closing her eyes, she tried to calm the panic inside her and failed. *No. That wasn't why at all.*

She stood to pace and remembered conversations they had – random questions about crazy passwords each of them had used. He volunteered several and she felt silly not doing the same.

Then she recalled the time he'd had her wallet in his hand when she came out of the shower. How he showed her the little note he was trying to sneak in there for her. After blushing and smiling about how *romantic* it was, she'd put it out of her mind.

With a rising sense of doom, she dialed the bank in her hometown.

The employee she knew personally confirmed that an account was opened in her name in New York City.

"Everything but what you requested transferred over just fine, Brie! The transaction finished a few hours ago. I bet you're excited, huh? Do you love the city as much as you thought you would?"

"Yes. I love the city. I have to run but we'll talk more soon."

"Sure thing! Have a blast, honey!"

Disconnecting, she rubbed her temple hard. Everyone back home knew she was moving to New York. As excited as she'd been, she'd told anyone who stood still for five minutes about her plans.

Receiving new bank account information from NYC wouldn't have seemed odd. She liked things neat and Brie imagined the signatures matched exactly.

The accounts she'd opened with her wages at the winery as a teenager were practically empty. In the four years since finishing college, she'd deposited most of every paycheck there.

More than a decade of earned wages…gone.

Dropping hard to the low wall, she allowed herself several minutes to break down into tears of rage, disappointment, and sadness. She covered her face and sobbed quietly.

She felt like she was shaking apart on the inside and for a little while, terror was the only emotion that made itself known.

This was *not* good. This was *nothing* like what she imagined her first day in New York would be. The worst part was how *stupid* she felt.

Obviously, the con man committed to the long game with his victims. She thought back over the past two years – to his emails, text messages, and various trips to see her. He showered her with attention and romanced her into loving him.

A bitter laugh escaped.

What had he invested *really*? A few trips out to Washington where it was unlikely she was his only victim? What had he spent? A few thousand dollars and a few weeks of his time to net more than ninety grand?

Not a bad gig if you could live with yourself.

Brie had options but she didn't want to *use* them. Returning home was not something she had any desire to do. More than anything, she'd wanted something different. Maybe an adventure.

Being conned by some asshole hadn't exactly been on her to-do list.

Fuck...she knew things were about to get bad. No one could live in New York – even in a crappy apartment – without money.

Her savings had been her "start fresh" fund. Enough to see her settled without using credit cards or asking her parents to release a portion of her inheritance. They prided themselves on the level heads they'd fostered in their girls.

She and Izzy had always been careful with money.

There was no way she was calling her parents, who would only worry and send her a plane ticket instead of help until she could find a job and a place to live. Her mother would cry and her father would be bitterly *disappointed* in her choices.

She couldn't call her older sister who would rant for an hour in rapid Spanish with a strong emphasis on, "I *told* you...didn't I *tell* you?"

The sad part was Izzy *had* told her...several times...and Brie hadn't listened. Their last conversation about the mysterious man in Brie's life had taken place the day before.

"Hudson *loves* me, Isabella. After all this time, don't you think I know him by now? He wants me to come to *Manhattan*, Izzy! He wants me to live with him and help me find a job. I can finally use my degree. Why can't you be happy for me? I'm tired of this town."

Older by two years, her sister pushed Brie's hair back from her face, smiling at the curls that wouldn't be contained without a whip and an industrial straightener. Not for the first time, she thought that the two of them couldn't look more different. Where her sister was long and lean, Brie was short and curvy enough to be a caricature. Izzy never seemed to notice.

"Brie, please listen. You don't *know* this man. In all this time, he hasn't met your family. You don't even have a picture of him. Caution, that's all I'm asking for. It seems too good to be true – can't you see that?"

Pushing away from her sister, she almost shouted, "I'm twenty-eight. I have no life and no real career. I'm pathetic. I haven't been *anywhere* and I just want to *go*." To the man she'd known as "Hudson" – who had never made her feel like the younger sister without a real future.

"Why do you always do that, Brie? Why do you think you're *less than* when you're wonderful in so many ways?"

She didn't *know* why but it had made her the perfect mark for a criminal who knew how to say all the right things. He told her all the time, "You're exactly right. I love you just as you are."

Every word he said to her, she believed because no one had ever said such things to her before.

Less than twelve hours ago, she'd headed to the airport to leave her family and small town in eastern Washington for New York City.

Her mother and father had been unable to hide their panic.

For weeks, her father had made it clear that he was not okay with her going to live with *some man* without marriage on the table. She'd had to assure both of her parents that "Hudson" wasn't like that. They'd given her three months to figure out what kind of man he was.

"Call us when you land, Brie. Don't forget."

They'd both spoken to her in Spanish, something they only did when they were nervous or stressed. Otherwise, they used perfect English. It was a fact that made them successful in a country that wasn't always accepting of their origins.

"I won't forget, *Papa*."

She hugged them again and turned to her sister. "I love you, Izzy."

"I love you, too. Be careful and call me if you need anything." As they embraced, she added, "Between us. I won't breathe a word if you need help. You're my only sister, you know?"

With a nod and tears in her eyes, she'd boarded that plane with such hopes and expectations.

Her parents loved her. They were good people but what they wanted for her was far different from what she ultimately wanted for herself. She and Izzy were close but her sister wasn't the best person to talk to right now. More world-traveled and more *with it* than Brie was, Izzy never would have fallen for something like this.

Suddenly she was fucking *furious*.

"That lying, scheming motherfucker. I'm going to find out who you are and make it my mission to fuck you up."

Chapter Five

Sick of crying, and tired of feeling sorry for herself, she stood up and wiped her face. Self-pity wasn't going to solve a damn thing.

Brie calculated how much money remained in her account. The thief was good. To make sure none of her travel expenses were declined, he'd left two thousand dollars in her Washington account.

Her card being rejected would have resulted in an instant call to the bank – where she might have been able to stop the transfer before it completed.

Thumbing through the cash in her wallet, there was no doubt that her situation was grim.

How fortunate that she'd never moved her childhood savings away from her parents' account. Absently, she wondered if there was a local branch where she could withdraw money without them finding out.

She immediately nixed the idea. If she so much as checked the *balance* on that account, her parents would know.

Bottom line: she had to figure it out on her own within the next twenty-four hours or she'd have no choice but to call home. Taking a deep breath, she considered her next step.

A hot dog vendor on the other side of the park entrance had several folded newspapers on the shelf of his cart. She asked if she could have one, pointing when she realized he didn't understand her. He handed it over happily, nodding as he said something in what she believed was Arabic. Smiling and thanking him, she returned to her stuff.

Taking a deep breath, she took a pen from her backpack and started looking for apartments and jobs. There would be no time to undergo the time-consuming interview process for marketing positions.

She needed something that started immediately and was thankful her mother and father always insisted she work. As a result, she had experience in many different areas.

Several tiny studio apartments fell within the budget she quickly worked up in her head and she called the numbers listed. Two were already rented, one man's questions included his creepy musings about if she was young and pretty, but the last three were possible.

Grabbing her bags, Brie stepped to the curb to hail a cab. A sharp whistle made her head turn. Henry the doorman waved her over. She released a heavy sigh and crossed the street, walking back to the building she'd once thought held her future.

He smiled kindly as she approached.

"Miss Riya and the M's would like a few minutes to talk to you. Their driver is going to take you wherever you need to go, miss. They'll be staying in for the night and their car is already here."

"I have to look at apartments, apply for jobs…"

"Yes, miss…but you don't know the city. Rodney can keep you safe while you do your errands." Gently, he took her bags from her hands, not attempting to take the backpack from her shoulder. "Follow me, miss. Everything is going to be fine. You'll see."

Entering the lobby, she couldn't help but smile at Riya. The woman acted as if they'd known one another forever. Getting a hug, and returning it, honestly *did* make her feel better.

She placed her hands on Brie's shoulders and asked carefully, "He robbed you, didn't he?" She nodded and started to cry silently, embarrassed at her emotional display.

The other woman hugged her close again. "It seems bad right now but this is a setback. A temporary one, Brie. You have my word on that. A month from now, it'll still sting but it won't be fresh anymore and you'll be well on the way to your new life." Tilting her head, she asked, "Do you want to go home or stay here in New York?"

Taking a deep breath, she replied, "I want to stay in New York. Despite everything, I so looked forward to living and working here."

"Alright. Then New York it is." She gestured at the newspaper in Brie's hands. "Did you find some apartments you want to look at?"

Nodding, she handed her the paper and Riya examined the circled locations with her lower lip between her teeth. Her men leaned on the concierge desk.

The leaner one…Max, she thought…said, "You're in the best hands."

"She'll have you squared away in ways that will have you thinking it was your plan all along," the bigger man told her with a wink.

"Thank you. I'm sorry to be a bother."

"Are you kidding? She *lives* to help. You've presented a challenge and she's on the case. Believe in her ability to help and you'll be right back on your feet again." The man had the loveliest blue eyes she'd ever seen and she nodded in a daze.

"They're beautiful, aren't they?" Riya snickered when Brie turned to look at her.

"I'm sorry. They're so…distracting."

The threesome laughed. "Don't dream of apologizing. I know the distraction factor well. Women *trip* when they pass. I find it hysterical." Handing back the newspaper, Riya nodded.

"This is a good place to start. Rodney knows these streets like the back of his hand. We'll check with some of the building personnel as well. Word of mouth is how you find the best places."

"You have to let me…"

"Say *one word* about paying us back for acting like human beings and you earn a spank." Eyes wide, Gabriella blushed and Riya tilted her head. "You remind me a lot of myself a year ago. My friend Tawny is going to *love* you."

Linking their arms, Riya led her back out to the street. Brie was glad for the jeans, baby doll sweater, and flat boots she'd worn. Her hair was in a tight bun but she knew it wasn't going to last much longer. It was adding to the whopper of a headache taking up residence behind her eyes.

"Here's my card. You're to call me if you need anything. When I say that…I mean it." She pressed the heavy paper stock into her hand and took out her cell. "Call me right now from your phone."

Brie glanced at the card and dialed, stunned when Riya smiled and saved a stranger's number in her contacts. Her level of trust was extraordinary.

"Henry will store your luggage and we'll be upstairs when you get back. I'm going to insist you stay in one of the temporary residences here in the building until we get you squared away. I don't want you to worry about a thing."

"I…I don't know what to say, Riya."

"That you'll see me later, of course." She smiled, winked, and returned to the two handsome men who gathered her between them as they headed back inside.

Brie felt like she was having an out-of-body experience.

"I'm Rodney." A tall and incredibly good-looking black man smiled down at her and gestured toward the car. He had an accent that reminded her of the Caribbean. "I'll run you around to the places you want to see then we'll stop at the best little deli in New York. Consider it a field trip." He opened the door with an exaggerated flourish.

It was impossible not to laugh. "I can promise, Rodney – there could *never* be a field trip that cost me quite as much as this one."

Gabriella slid into the back of the Towncar and watched Rodney jog around to the driver's door. When he was settled, she told him the addresses she'd written down in the margins of the paper and he jotted them down in a small notebook.

"The second one you mentioned is probably a bad idea. I know that block. If you were a man, it might be alright. No offense."

"None taken. I just need something small and safe."

They were quiet as he drove to the one he didn't like first. Brie's insides felt all twisted up and her head pounded unmercifully.

Traveling before dawn and the shitty events of the day were working her toward an emotional breakdown. Exhaustion made her more susceptible and she was grateful that she'd managed not to cry on the poor man so far.

As he turned on the block, he didn't slow down and she immediately realized why. A large group of rough looking men hung out in front of the run-down building where the apartment was located. A woman around her age walked rapidly down the sidewalk with her eyes averted as the group verbally harassed her.

Brie marked it off her list.

Her next listing wasn't bad but the outrageous deposit would take every dime she had available. It was reasonably clean and close to the subway but the nearest bodega was a long haul if she had to carry groceries home. Still, it would do if the last one didn't work.

The final apartment was dark and smelled as if it hadn't been aired out in a year. Just walking up the stairs and down the hallway depressed her. The interior was much worse.

Back in the car with a sigh of frustration, she started to tell Rodney to take her back to the previous listing. He turned to smile at her over the seat.

His smile was kind. "I think some food and then we break for today. I bet you're tired after traveling and everything. What do you think?"

Before she could respond, he winked and pulled into traffic. They soon arrived at a small deli that smelled fantastic and the driver insisted she not feel rushed in any way. They settled at a table by the window.

Taking a deep breath, she murmured, "I feel like I'm taking advantage. I'd hoped to find something today so I can stop being a bother."

His laugh was warm. "Nah. Once you know Riya for a while, you'll understand how her mind works. More listings come out in tomorrow's paper so we can start fresh. She's serious about getting you settled and was worried when you took off. Are you okay?"

To her complete humiliation, the words triggered tears.

She started crying and couldn't seem to stop. He handed her napkins and she turned away to get herself under control.

So much for not crying on the man.

The entire time, he talked to her gently. "It's going to be okay. You're bound to be stressed. Get it all out and you'll feel better."

Then she told the driver everything. By the time she finished her story, she felt a bit more centered and calm. It took longer than she would have liked.

It was good to talk to someone without past perceptions of who she was. "I'm just so embarrassed. I feel naïve and incredibly stupid."

He shook his head. "People like that, they trick people from all walks of life, Brie. I bet most of their victims feel just like you. The guy who took your money? He's a bottom feeder. Scum. Don't feel embarrassed. It wasn't your fault." His accent was much thicker now. "I'm sorry about your money."

Brie shrugged. "I'll work hard and grow it again. It'll take me longer to do it this time but I will." She stared through the window at the passing pedestrians on the sidewalk. "I feel worse about being *emotionally* played. My sister never believed what I told her about him." Glancing at Rodney, she tried to smile. "Izzy has more street smarts. I should have listened."

"Don't beat yourself up. It'll all work out and I bet there are good things coming that you wouldn't have found in Washington. You're in New York...*anything* is possible. Maybe this situation was just meant to get you here, yeah?"

She smiled in relief. "That's a *fantastic way* to look at it. Thanks."

They placed their orders with the patient server who had waited to approach until Brie was no longer crying. Their food quickly arrived and Rodney laughed when her eyes closed in happiness at her first taste of the fresh corned beef on rye sandwich. She was starving since she'd only had a cup of coffee since the night before.

A thought made her happy. "This is my first meal in New York."

They bumped fists. "Glad to share it with you, *mon*."

They talked and ate for more than an hour before he paid the check and they got back on the road. There was no way she'd have been able to get around so well by herself. Rodney was a good man and she felt somewhat better.

She'd think of something nice to do for him in thanks – as well as for Riya and her *husbands*. She was curious about the threesome's relationship since it wasn't something she'd ever heard of before. It was fascinating.

Admittedly, she'd been unable to find *one* honest man...she certainly wouldn't bet on *two*.

* * *

Carlo and Henry greeted Brie warmly when she returned.

Rodney shook her hand but she pulled him in for a hug. "Thank you for all your help today and for listening. I truly appreciate it."

"Hang in there. It's all going to be good. I'll see you tomorrow and we'll check out some more places. For tonight, take some deep breaths. Tomorrow is a brand-new day." With a small wave, he left to park in the underground garage.

Exhaling roughly, she tried to smile. A moment later, Riya stepped into the lobby from the penthouse elevator. "How did it go?"

"Not so well but I'll start again in the morning."

"You look exhausted, Brie. Have you eaten?" She nodded and told her how kind Rodney was. "He always seems to know when I need a coffee or a pastry. He's a wonderful man."

Taking her hand, she added, "Why don't I show you to your suite and let you get some rest tonight? A soak and a good twelve hours of hard sleep will be just the thing."

Gratefully, Brie replied, "That would be wonderful."

"I thought so." She took the key from Carlo who said he'd have her bags brought up shortly.

As Riya opened the door, she went straight to the bathroom. "Positively ginormous tub…you'll enjoy pruning in it."

"That sounds heavenly."

"Don't worry about anything. Make yourself at home, sleep, and I'm getting out of your hair. We'll be at our club but don't hesitate to call for any reason."

The valet with her luggage stood on the other side of the door when her new friend opened it. Once everything was inside, Brie found herself alone for the first time in a full day.

After indulging in a long soak punctuated with several hard cries, she showered, slipped into her typical sleepwear, and turned out all the lights. The bed called to her and she heeded it without a fight.

It had been a long day both emotionally and physically. She was sad and more than a little worried. Fortunately, her mind didn't keep her up with racing thoughts.

The moment her head hit the pillow, she was out.

Chapter Six

Hudson didn't say anything to Natalia when he entered the lobby of *Trois*. His first sight of her since they'd spoken before his trip heightened his rage at the woman he'd allowed into their lives.

His best friend took one look at his face and didn't attempt to distract him. He'd give her the details later.

Pushing the double doors wide into what had been a ballroom a century before, he paused to look around and immediately spotted Christina. She was laughing and drinking with several women who didn't seem remotely amused.

Riya and her friend Tawny were among them. Both looked ready to physically fight the blonde who giggled and chatted on without a clue. The redhead faced the door and was the first to see him make a direct line for his soon-to-be-ex-girlfriend.

Nudging the friend he respected and hoped still spoke to him after tonight, Riya glanced up and one side of her mouth lifted. Moving around Christina, she approached him and patted his arm.

"I'm always happy to see you, Hudson. Never more so than *right* now. Good luck."

Her best friend added, "I don't condone domestic violence so if you want me to smack her around for you, just give me a heads up. I'm happy to do you a solid."

Hudson barely controlled his grin.

Riya and Tawny walked away, heading up the stairs to where their men waited on the second floor. All four of whom were currently watching the dance floor from the balcony, leaned over the rail as if waiting for a boxing match to begin.

The other women drifted away in relief, leaving Christina alone. She turned to follow their looks and failed to hide her shock at his presence. The moment their eyes locked, Hudson could *see* her knowledge that she was busted.

"Hey, baby. You're back from Chicago. I missed you." Her voice was deliberately seductive and she was one woman who should've *known* that shit wouldn't work on him.

Wrapping his hand around her upper arm, he pulled her from the middle of the room to a quiet alcove. He faced her with an expression that should have terrified her. Her face was blank but her pulse was off the charts.

His voice was deadly quiet. "What have you been up to, Christina?"

The waterworks he'd expected began right on cue and Hudson internally seethed. He hated few things more than emotional terrorism. This woman used the weapon liberally.

"Why are you always so *angry*, Hudson? I haven't seen you in *days* and you walk in like this? I don't understand why you're so upset, baby."

For a long moment, he stared at her, wondering how in the fuck she'd made it through her life before she met him. How someone like *him* had let her get close enough to him and his best friend to put them at such risk. She disgusted him on every level.

"Christina, cut the bullshit." She reeled back as if he'd slapped her and one hand went to her throat. "Act as if you're abused. Do it. I have no desire to touch you in *any* capacity. Physical abuse should be the least of your worries right now."

She gave a soft gasp and her hand dropped to her side.

"Now that we understand one another, we can converse. I know *everything* and your belongings were removed from the penthouse. I cancelled your credit cards and all access to my life."

"Hudson…"

His voice was cold as he cut her off. "However, you have a suite reserved at the Hyatt and one month to make other arrangements."

"Baby, don't *do* this. Please don't do this." The fake tears slipped over her cheeks. "Whatever you're mad about…just *talk* to me. We can work through this. I'm sure I can explain."

He drew himself to his full height and put his hands on his hips. "Really? You can explain dealing illegal narcotics out of this club?"

This time, the tremble of her lip wasn't faked. "You can explain committing federal class felonies of fraud and larceny?" Her lips parted and she began to pant. "You can explain your partner in crime sending you to my door?"

If he hadn't been certain before, the look on her face verified that he'd been played from day one. The thought made him boil with rage.

Stepping closer, he allowed his size to intimidate her. "Tell me, Christina…can you explain all these things?" Her eyes were enormous. "You can't explain a motherfucking thing." Leaning back, he shook his head, awed at her greed. "You couldn't be satisfied."

"Hudson, give me a chance."

"For what purpose? To commit more crimes?"

"I'm sorry. I can change."

"You'll never change. I made a mistake allowing you – for one *instant* – to imagine you had some level of importance in my life. You *used* that assumption in a childish attempt to hurt my oldest friend…that's a mistake you'll not be allowed to repeat."

"How can you say that? After all we've been through together?"

There was no way to stop his small laugh but it was clear that there was no humor in it. "Christina, we haven't been through shit. We fucked and you spent my money. When I said that I know everything – you can fucking guarantee I know *everything*. I could have you arrested, prosecuted, and imprisoned."

"Hudson, please let me try to fix this. Please…"

He held up his hand. "Instead, in an act of unnecessary kindness and leniency, I had every item that belongs to you packed and transported to a hotel where I'll foot the bill for thirty days."

She sniffled loudly.

"Knowing that I have all the evidence needed to send you to prison…tell me, shall I change my mind?"

There was a possibility that she was in shock. Her eyes were huge in her face but she said nothing.

"The driver will transport you to your hotel and further transportation will be your fucking problem the moment he drops you off. Don't show your face at my properties, my company, or this club again. I'll have you arrested."

Not an idle threat. Hollow had fast-tracked the paperwork through his channels for restraining orders. Hudson wanted as much paper between them as possible.

"Give me another chance."

"You received every article of clothing, every piece of jewelry, and every dollar from me in trade for the exclusive use of your body. Our contract is now over." He leaned close and whispered in her ear, "The value of your pussy has dropped substantially. I suggest making wiser choices in your future."

He straightened, turned on his heel, and walked toward the exit. At the double doors leading to the lobby, Natalia waited.

In a sleek skirt, silk blouse, and heels – all in black – she looked calm and cool in a way he'd missed bitterly since taking up with Christina.

He paused and spoke quietly. "She'll leave in the next five minutes or is to be forcibly removed. Charge my card for all purchases made but don't let her back in this club. I revoke my sponsorship."

"Of course. I'll handle it personally."

Her choice of words made his eyes stroll down her body. A body he'd learned well over the years.

It had been too many days since he fucked. It made it hard for him to think clearly. With the stress of the past twelve hours, there were certain things he required.

One side of her mouth quirked up, red lipstick making the expression dramatic, and the electric blue of her eyes sparkled.

"Is there anything…*else*…I can handle for you, Hudson?"

She knew him so well. Better than any person on Earth.

"I'll send the car."

* * *

As Hudson left her club, Natalia motioned to what appeared to be nothing more than a decorative mirror. Instantly, a hidden doorway beneath the stairs opened and a member of her security team emerged.

"Stav, cover the front."

The huge man nodded and took her place as she walked into the ballroom. Christina, who'd returned to the bar, had gathered a few sympathizers and Natalia recognized several familiar faces from the security footage of the woman's drug deals.

Those that met her eyes recalled the private conversations she'd recently held with each that showed the evidence of them buying drugs in her place of business…her *home*. As she approached, they rapidly dispersed, leaving the conniving little actress alone.

Natalia would have thrown every one of them out of her club — forbidden to return — had they not made the right choice. Her livelihood was one thing.

Her friendship with Hudson was neither a secret nor negotiable. She wouldn't hesitate to destroy anyone who threatened his safety.

Part of her would enjoy it.

Walking to a sobbing Christina's side, her smile was cold. "Stop that immediately." The blonde gave a sniffle before her expression hardened and morphed to a glare.

"There's the viper I know." Folding her hands in front of her, she spoke softly but there was no doubting the indifference of her words. "It sounds as though you've been up to more than drug dealing."

Crossing her arms, Christina seethed but said nothing.

"As of now, you're considered untouchable. Your sponsorship has been revoked and future applications listing your name will be denied for admittance to *Trois*."

Christina muttered through gritted teeth, "You can't do that."

"I just did. Had Hudson not revoked his sponsorship, I would have banned you anyway. Your brand of drama is unwelcome here. I hope whatever you've done netted you enough to make it worth your while because you'll be a *pariah* in the circles you've become accustomed to."

"I didn't do anything," the blonde hissed like a petulant teenager.

Natalia held her smile and allowed the silence to draw out between them. She was rewarded when Christina took a step back. "Hudson Winters does *nothing* without proof. Though I'm not certain what crime you've committed, you can be sure that he has no doubt regarding your part in it. I can't help but wonder what you were thinking to cross such a man. You're a fool."

As if suddenly considering the consequences for her actions, Christina's eyes widened and she began to breathe rapidly through her lips.

"All the focus, all the power he wields in other areas will now be used for a specific purpose." Stepping forward, Natalia whispered, "He'll have no mercy. I wish you luck…you *will* need it."

Dusting her hands together, done with the pathetic woman in front of her, she turned and said loudly enough for nearby members to overhear, "A car will be waiting out front to take you to your hotel.

You have three minutes to vacate these premises. Attempt to return and I'll have you arrested."

In the lobby, she inclined her head at Stav. As her head of security, she brought him up to speed. Since he'd brought the video surveillance of Christina to her, he was not surprised.

He nodded and went to the double ballroom doors to watch Hudson's ex-girlfriend grab her things. Her attempt to appear the victim caused him to laugh. Furious, she slammed through the front doors and they listened to her release a blood-curdling scream on the stoop.

Chuckling, she murmured, "I'm leaving for the evening. Call me if necessary."

"Will do, boss. I'll keep an eye out for the little troublemaker."

Moments later, Natalia grabbed the overnight bag she kept in her office for evenings just like this one. It hadn't been used in over a year. She walked into the alley that ran along the club.

Hudson's Rolls waited for her and Leonard smiled as she approached. The man appeared harmless. Only a handful of people knew how deadly he could be. It was why Hudson preferred the younger man to transport his oldest friend.

When she told him several years ago that she could easily hire her own driver, he stared her into submission. "You're one of my greatest weaknesses, Natalia. I have enemies. Leonard will drive you and I'll know you're safe."

She slid across the leather seat and they made the drive in silence. As they came to a stop at the curb in front of her friend's building, she allowed the excitement to unfurl in her stomach.

It had been too long.

Chapter Seven

On Hudson's return trip to his building, there was a different kind of tension coiling inside him.

There were certain things only Natalia had ever been able to provide in his life. Christina, and the women before her, took what he dished out for a price but he never gave them the full effect of his darker side.

In that, he trusted only his oldest friend.

At the curb, he said too sharply, "Return for Natalia."

"Yes, sir."

Carlo gave him the update he requested and as he rode the elevator past the floor where Gabriella Hernandez likely slept soundly, he had the strangest urge to knock on her door but suppressed it.

Hudson entered his apartment and went to retrieve a few items from his recreation room. There would be few games. No extravagant measures that could delay his need to dominate – to exert *absolute* control. It rode him hard. His cock was so engorged it was painful.

He laid out what he needed and sat down in a chair facing the elevator to wait. She didn't keep him waiting long. Natalia never did.

As she stepped out of the elevator and came to a precise stop, he took in every detail of her form. It had been more than a year since he'd allowed himself to examine her in such a way.

Their personal code.

She was tall for a woman and everything about her was lean. Small breasts, narrow hips, and a firm ass…all of which he knew as well as his own body.

The deep black of her hair had been a difficult adjustment for him the first time she'd made the change from her natural blonde. He had to admit, it increased her air of mystery.

In looks alone, she could be any of a million women. She was lovely in an understated way and knew how to dress to accentuate her attributes but nothing about his best friend physically made her stand out in a crowd.

What made her spectacular was her need to be dominated.

It was her ability to surrender, entirely, to the right man, under the right circumstances. There were few women able to do it as well and maintain their independent will and sense of self.

Natalia would never be taken over by a Dom. She would *bend* willingly, but never break. It was a gift in the circles they'd once run in together.

As his success and financial worth grew, there was only one woman he could depend on to maintain his privacy unconditionally.

After too many *long* months, she stood across the room in his penthouse, awaiting instruction. She had not moved so much as an inch and she did not fidget. There was no impatience, no annoyance, no nervousness at being kept waiting. Her face was serene in the dim reflection of the city lights.

"Put down the bag." He paused as she did so, keeping his voice low and calm. "Take off the blouse, the skirt."

She obeyed without hesitation. Never questioning, never wondering what was going to happen next. She trusted him, he trusted her, and in this, they were *perfect* together.

In moments, she stood in nothing more than her heels, stockings, and garter belt, her posture flawless but relaxed. For him, she'd already removed her bra and panties before leaving the club. Her nipples were tight and, if he checked, her pussy would be wet.

The thought made his cock pulse painfully.

"Come here." Moving deliberately over the black marble floor, she walked toward him.

"Stop." She did so instantly. "Kneel."

Lowering gracefully to the floor, arms crossed at her back, Natalia waited with her back straight and her gaze at his feet.

He stood and walked behind her, proud that there wasn't the slightest tightening of her muscles to relay a sense of fear or anxiety. She believed in him in ways no one else did, just as he would place his life in her hands. Her breathing was faster now and he knew her pulse was likely elevated.

Anticipation was Natalia's drug of choice.

He bound her arms, her fingertips touching her opposite elbows, meticulous as he worked with the specialty rope that wouldn't abrade her skin. She'd fallen from a horse in her teens, breaking her collarbone and dislocating her shoulder. Though it healed well, it pained her if pulled too tightly and slipped from the socket easily.

No matter their play, he was always cognizant of her safety.

When he was done, he observed how the black rope done in a simple Kinbaku box tie stood out on her pale skin, and felt a shiver travel up his spine. He didn't understand his fascination with the imagery of her bound and waiting for him, but it had always affected him strongly.

Exhaling roughly, he walked around to stand in front of her. Her black hair glimmered in the low light. Her stillness was exquisite.

Reaching out, he stroked his palm over her head and watched her eyes close. Her hair was softer than silk and he allowed himself to touch her simply, to show her in one of the few ways he was able how much she meant to him.

"Open."

Her eyes opened but remained downcast as she parted her lips. The sound of his zipper lowering filled the room. He stroked the outline of her mouth with the broad head of his cock, painting it with a pearl of pre-come that quickly beaded on the tip. Somehow, he hardened further.

He was not immune to anticipation.

"Suck."

Closing her lips around the crest, Natalia explored his size and shape, curling her tongue along the underside.

It had been too long since he'd had this with her and he could feel his heart crashing against his rib cage with need. Raking his fingers through her hair, he gripped a fistful at the nape of her neck with a sharp tug. He watched as her nipples furled tighter, her breasts lifting to him in reaction to the small sting.

The way she responded to his nature – how she had *always* responded – stimulated a ferocious hunger inside him that it would take hours to satisfy.

Hudson didn't wait for her to take him at her pace, nor did Natalia expect him to.

Wrapping his fist in her hair, he pulled her forward over his cock until he touched the back of her throat. He went still, his grip ensuring she couldn't move back until he was ready.

She always seemed to know what he needed, what he wanted, and accepted it without judgment. He watched as she regulated her breathing and swallowed carefully to keep from gagging. For years, she trained her body to take what he gave.

"Excellent."

He pulled her back, let her catch her breath, and then set a hard rhythm. She rapidly adjusted and adapted to his force and guidance.

Hudson fucked her mouth for a long time because it was hot, wet, and he'd missed it with near desperation.

Not for the first time, he thought he could take Natalia like this forever and never get bored. He watched her face, awed by the complete serenity she displayed. No one he'd ever known had been capable of such calm during rough play.

The skin of his dick was incredibly tight, his balls drawn up with the desire to come down her throat, but he wanted to make it last. To draw out the pleasure only she seemed able to grant.

Three minutes.

Five minutes.

When he reached ten minutes, he said hoarsely, "Spread your legs." In a daze, she did so immediately, allowing her knees to slide apart. "You're dripping on the *floor*, Natalia."

Moaning softly, her eyes flicked up to his and down again. His mouth watered with the need to eat her but he wouldn't do that yet. His other hand lifted, both his palms cupping her skull, the silk of her hair on his skin reminding him of her fragility, her femininity.

"Take every drop and I'll let you come."

His hips thrust forward as he pulled her to his dick over and over. The impact had to hurt but she moaned around him again and he was barely hanging on as she tightened her lips.

Pulling her close and holding her still, she swallowed hard around the head of his cock as he let go of his control. The relief from orgasm was instantaneous and powerful. She consumed jet after jet rhythmically, the muscles of her throat milking the crest.

"*Fuuuccckkk…*" She gave a small whimper of need and her cheeks drew in with the pressure she applied. Her thighs flexed but she didn't close her legs. "I know. I know, Natalia."

Hudson petted her hair, pushing the short strands off her face, and loosened his grip on her as he began to stroke shallowly.

Every part of him wanted to stay like this. *Just like this.*

She told him once that she zoned out when he took her, feeling the pleasure in a way she couldn't with other lovers because she never trusted them enough to let go entirely.

He watched her catch her breath, work him, and take everything he had to give. Pumping his hips, watching the way his cock disappeared between her lips, fascinated him.

She lifted her magnetic blue eyes to his. The sight was *incredible*.

"Do you want to come?" Natalia shook her head slowly, his cock still buried in her mouth, and he smiled. "You're in the mood to be pushed."

The side of his thumb traced her cheek and he pulled his cock away, leaving the moist heat she offered with a soft sound. Bending, he lifted her carefully to her feet.

In her heels, they were the same height, their eyes level. For a moment, he let his detachment slip, let her see the pain Christina had caused him. He had *not* loved the woman but he'd tried to be good to her in the ways he understood.

His relationships never lasted. He gravitated to needy women who quickly bored him or women who couldn't handle his abruptness.

"Thank you for coming, Natalia."

"Always, darling."

He wrapped his arms around her, lightly stroking the skin of her back. "You're beautiful."

The smile she gave him was gentle. "You've always said so."

So many memories he shared with this woman. They flickered through his mind as he lifted a hand to trace her lower lip with his thumb. It was swollen and red from taking his cock. Her eyes held him mesmerized and he couldn't have said how long they stood there.

"Will you let me collar you?" To a man such as him, it was the equivalent of a marriage proposal and he knew instantly that the timing and circumstances were wrong.

Something flashed behind her eyes but was quickly gone. She kissed the tip of his finger and laughed in a way that seemed sad.

"We've known one another too long, Hudson. This part is good. It has *always* been good, between our other lovers, our other relationships." She swallowed hard as she stared at him.

Tilting her head, Hudson knew she saw more of the man he was than anyone else and accepted him without conditions or judgment. It made her unique. It made him love her.

"If we lived together day after day, I don't know that it would be good for either of us. Nursing one another through the flu, dealing with my cramps and moodiness, arguing over stupid shit."

Natalia's smile was forced and Hudson didn't understand what to say, what to do, to make it real.

"I was not cut out to be a wife and mother. I'll never symbolize home and hearth. Despite *this* aspect of my nature, I'm the most selfish person I know. I admit it and acknowledge my life as it is…not as I might sometimes wish it were."

There was pain in her words and he wanted to ease it. Emotions, gentleness, and the ability to interpret what someone needed…those things had been out of reach for him all his life.

Leaning forward, she nuzzled his cheek with hers and he hugged her against him.

"You need someone to *soothe* you, Hudson. Not someone like me who can only give in such a limited way. No more women like Christina who only understand how to take. You need a person with a generous spirit."

He grunted as an image of Gabriella Hernandez flashed unexpected and unwelcome through his mind. He was too hard, too brutal in his tastes for someone with a gentle spirit. "I'd have her in tears within hours. What would I do with someone *nice?*"

"Smile more perhaps."

The words were so similar to the ones Riya said to him that he inhaled sharply. She pulled back to meet his eyes.

After a long moment, he leaned forward and kissed her. It was deeper than he intended but her breath on his cheek was familiar, comforting, while the way she felt in his arms had been missing from his life too long. As he broke the kiss, he kissed the tip of her nose.

Enough conversation.

Stroking his palms down her arms, he stepped back. Her small smile was replaced with cool tranquility as she waited to hear his instruction. He turned to pick up the lubricant from the black box on the table and guided her around the back of the couch. His voice firmed, his cock hardened for her again, and he *needed.* She was the only one who could provide.

"Turn and bend over the back of the couch. Legs spread."

The location, the position, was not an accident. It was the first place he'd taken Christina on the day he met her. He wanted the memory of lackluster sex and porn star moaning replaced with the dark passion he always shared with Natalia.

As she moved into position, the sight of her naked and willingly vulnerable caused lust to flare in the back of his mind.

He hadn't experienced the sensation in so long he'd almost forgotten what it felt like...when the animal inside him stretched. The darkness he'd fought most of his life threatened to swamp him as he sealed his chest to her narrow back, her arms still bound between them.

"Tell me, Natalia...if it's too much. My demons are clawing at the cage."

"Purge them, Hudson. I can handle it."

He breathed in the scent of her hair for a long moment before nodding and standing upright. Uncapping the lube, he slicked a line of it down the crease of her ass with one hand as he positioned his cock at her pussy with the other.

"Don't come. I want to fill you up." He watched her ass cheeks flex and knew it was a result of her excitement. He worked his dick into her soaking wet channel with a smile. "Do you like the thought of being filled with my come?"

"My mouth is satisfied…my pussy and my ass *need* you."

Instant, visceral need made him slam to the base inside her without giving her time to adjust. As he pressed deeper, she moaned and flexed around his length. He growled, "Does it burn?"

"It burns so *good*, Hudson. More."

Taking a glass plug from the pocket of his slacks – bought long ago for his best friend – he coated it in the lube and set it at the little pucker of her ass. Her pussy spasmed around him and he inhaled carefully.

"It's been so long since I've had your ass. I can't wait to be balls-deep inside your tight hole." Pressing, he inserted the toy fully and she whimpered, rocking her hips back for more. He felt and watched her lower body tighten around him and the plug. "You're so fucking *tight*. Let's make you tighter."

Reaching down, Hudson cupped the back of her knee and set it on top of the couch. The position constricted her pussy so hard around his cock that he gasped sharply.

"Don't come." She shook her head.

Gripping her shoulders, he fucked the hot, slick channel until they both dripped with sweat. Pulling out and pushing deep again and again, he knew his hipbones would leave bruises on the back of her thighs.

The quakes along her vaginal walls told him she was fighting her own orgasm with everything she had. Then he rotated the plug, pressing it more firmly into her ass, and felt her start to tremble around him.

"Breathe through it, Natalia. Wait." She murmured incoherently in agreement.

Wrapping his hands around her hips, he held her firmly as he fucked her even harder.

She chanted his name as he drove into her body. "Please let me have it, please…*Hudson*."

He knew it was not her own release she begged for but the sensation of his seed inside her. A fistful of her hair was the anchor he used as he pulled her back to his chest.

"Take it then. Let your sweet pussy suck it from the head of my dick."

Faster. Faster. FASTER…

He went still as the orgasm stole his ability to move, to think, and for an instant, he wondered if he was having an aneurism. Her muscles milked him and there were spots in front of his eyes.

"*Mine…*" The sound of her whisper brought him back to the moment and his legs shook slightly as the last spurts of his come soaked her.

"*Natalia.*" It was all he could manage.

Her muscles quivered, her breathing was erratic, and she *needed* to come. Reaching beneath her body, he stroked her folds twice before slapping the sensitive flesh sharply. *Two strokes…slap.* By the third slap, she exploded, screaming his name.

It rattled her entire frame but nothing could have shaken him loose before he was ready. Hudson held her through it, stroking her swollen clit to drag her pleasure out. He could feel and hear their combined fluids dripping to the marble and it sent chills up his spine.

His growl broke the cadence of their heavy breathing. "I want to fuck your ass with you flat on the floor."

Her voice was weak but the genuine desire in it was clear. "*Yes.*"

Slowly, he withdrew from her pussy and removed the plug. Natalia made a small mewling sound as he lowered her smoothly.

He stretched out beside her and stroked his hand through her damp hair. Her cheeks were flushed and he knew the cool marble provided relief to her overheated skin.

Rolling her to her back, he sucked and bit at her sensitive nipples until she panted with need. Only when she begged, thrusting her hips in the air, did he return her to her stomach.

Standing, he efficiently stripped out of his clothes, his eyes never moving from her ivory body displayed against the dark stone. He felt medieval, a conqueror, a man observing his most prized possession.

Coating his cock with lube, he returned to her, straddling her hips with his knees on the floor. "I can see my come easing from your pussy."

"More. Please more, Hudson."

With a snarl, he pressed into the tiny opening and groaned as he made it past the tight ring of muscle. A tremor worked its way through her torso and he stroked his palm over her shoulders and up the column of her neck.

He planted his hand beside her head and wasted no time taking her ass as hard as he'd taken her pussy. Each thrust was designed to deliver the pleasure/pain they wanted and needed.

"When I let go and fill your third hole with my come, I'm going to carry you into our room. You'll soak in the tub and relax. Then I'll watch you wash every inch of your skin before I take my time eating you, Natalia. Getting you slick and ready for me to fuck again and again and *again*."

"Tear my ass up then. Fuck it like you own it, Hudson."

For just a moment, he wanted to stake his claim, to explain how much of her belonged to him and how much of himself he'd given to her...but he didn't.

Jerking her hips higher, Hudson tunneled deep and hard for a long time. His initial pressure was relieved so he fucked her ass until the tight heat made it impossible to hold back anymore. He didn't stop thrusting – he *couldn't* stop – until Natalia drained him dry.

Once he was sure his legs would hold him, he carried her into the room that had always been theirs alone and kept his word.

Chapter Eight

Natalia stared at Hudson for a long time when she woke the next morning.

He slept peacefully on his stomach, the thick muscles of his back drawn taut with his arms curled above him, beneath the pillow. Thick black lashes made shadows on his cheeks and she wanted to touch him but she didn't.

Subtle lines at the corners of his eyes and mouth made him more attractive than when he'd been a young man. The scattering of silver at his temples lent his features an air of sophistication.

For his fortieth birthday, she'd taken him for lunch. It was the last time she'd seen him face to face until she'd asked him to come to the club to discuss his girlfriend.

Throughout their meal, he'd been introspective. Never a rampant conversationalist, his added silence caused her to ask what was wrong.

In a rare moment of vulnerability, he admitted, "I have no idea."

As Leonard dropped her off at *Trois* shortly after, she told him, "You're my oldest and dearest friend. I want to see you happy. No one deserves it as much, Hudson."

His confession coupled with the way he'd hugged her made it impossible for Natalia to watch his interactions with Christina any longer. Knowing she was using him, knowing he allowed it, was simply too much. For weeks, every invitation was softly rejected, every call kept light, and the days passed painfully without seeing him.

The morning sunlight touched him gently and in relaxation, she saw the boy who had once mowed her yard so he could buy food for his family. Even at ten, he'd been too mature and far too intense. The persona he wore clearly on the outside of himself matched the one she hid from the world. It had endeared him to her immediately.

The connection had only grown stronger year after year.

With a sigh, she winced as she climbed from his bed. His demons had indeed been at the door. He had taken her repeatedly, harder, and harder each time, until finally he had untied her, cleaned them both up, and carried her upstairs to his bed.

They'd collapsed together in exhaustion.

She grabbed her bag and used his guest bath to keep from waking him. The full-length mirror showed the fingerprints, light bruises, scratches, and small bites he'd left all over her body.

Despite her soreness, she felt relaxed and energized. Focused for the first time in months.

Preparing herself for the distance he would put between them for a little while, she took extra care with her appearance. It provided a layer of insulation from the pain loving a man like Hudson could sometimes cause, though it was unintentional on his part.

Zipping up her bag, she readied herself to return to her isolated life.

* * *

Hudson knew the moment Natalia woke the next morning and felt when she left his bed.

She always watched him for a few minutes and despite their mutual insistence at remaining friends who sometimes fucked – and her assurance that she didn't consider him in a romantic light – he knew she could be foolishly sentimental about him.

They'd been friends so many years that neither of them seemed able to maintain distance for long.

He listened as she showered in the guest room down the hall in an effort not to wake him. Crossing his hands behind his head, he identified each sound as she moved around getting dressed to leave.

Not wanting to miss her, he sat up on the side of the bed and ran his hands over his face. Staring down at his semi-hard cock, he smirked. "Fuck...*finally* you chill the hell out."

When she stepped into the hallway, he waited for her. Leaning naked in the doorway of his bedroom, he watched her walk toward him.

The way she moved told him she was sore and probably bruised in several places. A small kernel of shame curled in Hudson's gut as he questioned the dark needs he couldn't completely live without.

"Are you alright?"

Stepping close, she kissed both his cheeks and ran her fingers through his hair. Her smile was radiant and her eyes sparkled. His best friend hadn't looked so...*happy* in a long time.

The sight moved him deeply.

"Good morning, darling. I'm better than alright, thank you. I feel like I spent a week at the spa."

Every word was sincere yet he didn't understand. The woman had *zero* survival instinct when it came to how he used her body. It made the need to hug her imperative. She and his mother were the only people he encouraged casual physical contact with, and there were times he needed the connection more than they did.

He would never admit to such a weakness.

Pulling her to him, he wrapped his arms around her slender frame to hug as much of her body as he could. She felt so fucking *delicate* in his hold. "I can be a brutal man."

Hugging him back just as hard, he felt her inhale deeply at the bend of his neck. "You're such a *good* man, Hudson. You're too rigid with yourself. I don't see you as hard or cruel. I see you as fiercely loyal to the people you care about, and the person I love most in the world."

The words sank into him, warmed him, and made him tighten his hold on her. She planted a small kiss just under his ear and leaned back. Staring into his eyes, he watched her expression change. Her cool palms lifted to smooth over his cheeks.

"If I *knew* it would work between us, I *would* try."

He doubted the words that didn't match the sadness in her eyes but pretended to believe them. Instead of asking why she didn't think it would work, he gave her a crooked grin.

"You'd be done with my bullshit in a month." *That was probably very much the truth.*

Natalia kissed him slow and deep. It made him want to drag her back to his bed. Her hands stroked back to cup his skull, massaging his scalp as her lips and tongue caressed him.

As the kiss went on and on, he pressed one palm between her shoulder blades and felt the racing of her heart. The other coasted down to hold her ass, to pull her closer to a body that could do nothing but respond to what she offered.

A long while later, she broke the kiss and rested her forehead against his. Her eyes were closed and he wondered at the tightness around her mouth.

"I'll never, ever be done with you. Not in any capacity, not for any reason, Hudson." Then she turned quickly, moving out of his arms, and headed for the stairs. "Call me. About anything, anytime."

At the elevator, she glanced up to where he watched her, his arms braced wide on the railing. She blew him a kiss and walked into the car the instant the doors opened.

He steeled himself against the usual regret he felt when they parted ways. He wasn't in love with his best friend, nor was she in love with him. They doubted they were even capable of such an emotion. Still, she was the only person who knew every sordid detail about the man he was and let him in her life anyway.

It made separation…difficult.

His appetites were not normal. It was a fact he'd been aware of for more than two decades and often caused him to question his sanity.

As sated as he was from appeasing his almost violent sexual needs with Natalia for hours on end, part of his mind wondered if Gabriella would accept an offer of breakfast.

"You're a fucking lunatic."

Verdict delivered aloud, he went to shower and put the curvy woman out of his mind. He was soaping his chest when the unexpected image of sinking his cock into her bubble-shaped ass slammed into his brain. He fought it, ashamed of his greed.

Why wasn't the satisfaction he'd found in Natalia's submission enough?

His sexuality was the one area of his life where he felt out of control. He fisted his cock and stroked himself to release, watching semen pump from the head and swirl down the drain. Out of breath, he leaned against the tile wall.

To function, he often suppressed portions of who he was and what he wanted. He wondered if he'd ever find a way to be fucking happy that didn't require the necessity.

Natalia had not been his first but she'd been the only person able to sate him, to give him peace for a little while.

What the fuck was he was going to do now?

* * *

When the elevator doors closed, Natalia took a deep breath to stabilize herself, a necessity each time they spent such time together and she had to leave him.

Hudson was unhappier every year. She wished something wonderful would happen to shake him from the rut he'd worn into his life. Endless work interrupted by the occasional girlfriend or time with her was no way to live.

He deserved so much more.

Stepping out of the elevator, she saw Riya and Max walking across the lobby with bagels and coffee in hand. They were laughing and there was whipped cream on the tip of her nose. The younger woman lit up when she saw Natalia. Quickly wiping her nose, they touched cheeks and Riya held out the bagels.

"Join us for breakfast?"

"Oh no, darling. No. If I ate that, the world would come to a screeching halt." She winked. "I refuse to exercise, you see. I get it the way I like it or not at all so…I pick my battles. I enjoy wine and chocolate far too much to sacrifice them for carbs."

"You're stunning, Natalia." Pausing, she shifted her weight. "I'm glad Christina is gone. Well done, the way you and Hudson handled it last night."

Natalia's smile was sincere. "She was causing too much trouble. I was past ready to throw her out of the club." Inclining her head at Max, she added, "The night she felt your man up, I truly believed they would have to carry her out on a stretcher."

"I was so angry and it made it difficult for me to even fake civility when I saw her here and at the club after." She shook her head. "Still…as angry as I was, I thought the top of Tawny's head was going to blow off." She snickered. "You know she's got a hair trigger anyway."

"It's one of the things I adore about her."

They chatted a few moments before two of the gorgeous threesome got into the elevator.

From his first correspondence with Riya, Hudson had been fascinated by the way she thought. He'd discussed his participation in her research at length with his best friend and she'd never seen him so animated or involved. Especially with a stranger in a virtual environment.

The moment he'd learned through club gossip that Max and Micah had applied to the last portion of her research, he'd withdrawn. Though he didn't talk about it, she knew he liked the effect the young doctor had on the men in her life.

Riya and her best friend were never boring.

The Rolls was at the curb as she passed Carlo and Henry with a small wave and walked out into the sunshine. Sliding in, she thought about her conversation with Hudson the night before. He really needed to find a woman who was better than what he'd been involved with so far, herself included.

Sitting back as they pulled away from the building, she wondered about the perfect woman for her friend. He needed someone who would be as focused on his needs as her own agenda.

He needed someone honest and kind since Natalia had seen the way Hudson watched the M's with their woman. He didn't want Riya but he genuinely *liked* her – which was unusual for him.

A woman who could provide the solace he didn't realize he needed in ways that his best friend was too damaged to convey.

Chapter Nine

For the first ten seconds after opening her eyes the next morning, Brie had no clue where she was. Disoriented, as her memories of the day before returned, anxiety rose at a fever pitch.

Sitting up on the side of the bed, she gave herself a mental smack in the face.

"Today is brand new. Today will be better...or else. Damn it."

Laughing at her ridiculous affirmations, she took a quick shower to remove the cobwebs from her brain, dressed similarly to the day before, and tackled her hair. Ten minutes later, she gave up trying to get it into another sleek chignon without Izzy's help and piled it up on her head.

Leaving the room neat behind her, she rode the elevator to the lobby.

Henry waved from the door and Carlo grinned the moment he saw her. "Brie! Good morning! How did you sleep?"

"Like the dead. I feel better, thank you." The more she said it, the more she would believe it.

"I've been waiting for you to come down."

He walked around the counter and Brie realized they were almost the same height. She was five-five and the thought that she probably outweighed the trim and attractive man by a hundred pounds almost derailed her.

Out of habit, she started to try to "shrink" herself and another mental slap in the face was issued.

His entire demeanor was welcoming. "How would you like to work here, Brie? It isn't fancy but the money is fair and your co-workers are awesome."

"Here in *this* building?" He nodded. "That would be…*so* great. Thank you." A thought made her frown. "You're not going to get in trouble, are you? I hope Riya didn't pull any strings. I don't want special treatment."

Henry laughed. "Brie, it's just a simple job and you might hate it, by the way."

"Jobs are hard to come by. I don't want to take one someone else was counting on."

Carlo assured her, "We had a woman quit a few weeks ago, but the head office hadn't said anything about replacing her. When I called to see if there were any openings, they said the timing was perfect since we'll be going into the holiday season when a lot of the residents use the floor of short-term suites for their families and friends."

He gave a small shrug. "Riya and the M's had *nothing* to do with getting you hired. Henry's right though, you might hate it. It isn't easy work."

"I'll take it – you just tell me what to do. I've scrubbed plenty of toilets. At the winery, you *really* start from the bottom and work your way up."

They gave her an application and she sat on the same bench from the day before to fill it out. Afterward, she supplied her identification for faxing to headquarters.

Rubbing his hands together, the concierge called one of the young men from the business center to cover the front desk.

"I'll take you on a quick tour then introduce you to Eleanor. She's head of housekeeping and has been running the tower for twenty years. I know she's going to like you."

Over the next hour, he took her from floor to floor. Two levels below ground were secure parking.

The main street level contained an upscale convenience store, the business center, a dining room, a restaurant that did catering for the building, a fully equipped gym, and the employee locker rooms and lounge.

The second story was where the short-term residences were. Equipped like luxurious hotel suites with kitchen and separated living space, they could be leased by the day, week, or month. Housekeeping maintained the rooms daily and took care of any guests.

The next six levels were divided into large apartments that sold in the millions and Brie was in awe at the gorgeous design of the empty apartment she toured.

Above those were three floors of extravagant two-level living spaces.

The top floor featured the two penthouse apartments on either end of the building with rooftop courtyards in the middle that those residents used in total privacy.

"Riya and the M's live in one and Mr. Winters lives in the other. They have elevators that run to those spaces exclusively and dedicated staff cleans three times a week."

They rode down to the lobby and Carlo led her to a cheery office done in various shades of green to meet Eleanor Shaughnessy, her direct supervisor. The heavyset woman had laugh lines on her laugh lines and made Brie feel comfortable immediately.

"I've been doing this a long time. I can tell the ones who figure they'll do some light dusting. You're one of the few people who could clean a bathroom flooded in shit if it came to it."

"I've done it before back home when too much rain backed up the sewage system. I have a strong stomach and I'm not afraid to work, ma'am."

"Call me Eleanor. Glad to have you with us. You start tomorrow." Brie filled out the form allowing the background check and the older woman smiled. "Carlo will introduce you to the girl who takes care of uniforms, supplies, and schedules."

They shook hands and she went to see Tammy Poi. The poor woman looked like she desperately needed a nap.

"Bear with me. I'm normally nicer. I just got back from maternity leave and I think I've had about ten hours of sleep this entire week."

"I'm in no rush. I'm happy to have a job."

The small Asian woman typed away for a few minutes. "It's going to be graveyard, which sucks, but you need to be trained and that's when everything is quiet. We have employees who specifically request those hours to coordinate with their school schedules or whatever. As soon as you finish training, we'll move you to one of the other shifts." With an exhausted smile, she added, "See you tomorrow night."

Thanking her, Brie left the woman's office with a badge, three uniforms, and a locker key. A printout of her schedule showed that she was taking graveyard shift for the first six weeks.

She found her locker and hung her uniforms inside. The lounge was like a comfortable living room and there was a long table set up for group meals. One door opened to a dorm-style sleeping area that she assumed the staff used on double shifts.

In the lobby, Brie gave Carlo and Henry a relieved smile. "I love it already."

"Riya said to send you up whenever you finished. I sent a text to Rodney with the address of an apartment for you to check out when you're ready to go."

"Thank you, Carlo. Truly. You've been so kind."

He smiled and keyed her up. Brie tucked her new employee information in her bag as the car stopped and she stepped out into an apartment with a panoramic view of Manhattan that absolutely stunned her.

Riya came across the vast space. Giddy, she blurted out, "I have a job! Here in the building! I can't explain the sense of relief."

"That's fantastic! See? Everything is going to fall into place." They hugged. "I'm so happy you're here. We decided on brunch since you need to eat before Rodney takes you out."

Leading her through the living room and around a bar, she smiled at Max and Micah in the kitchen. They both smiled and her heart stuttered a little.

"Good morning. Wow, you two are a little shocking first thing in the morning." Even with less internal angst in progress, their beauty awed her.

"Oh honey," Riya murmured beside her, "you have *no* idea." The two of them laughed and thanked her. "Tawny will be here soon because she couldn't *wait* to meet you. How did you sleep?"

"Wonderful. The soak helped."

"Always. I swear by them. I think I was a mermaid in another life."

Brie found Riya's general optimism infectious. They talked non-stop while sitting at the bar that ran around the kitchen. Not only were her men preparing brunch, they seemed to be doing a damn good job.

Unable to help herself, she realized Riya busted her staring at the two men several times. The brunette chuckled. "I can cook but they do it so much better. You're going to love Max's crepes and Micah grinds me fresh coffee beans for brew that's like nowhere else. Bonus, I get to observe them and I do love to baby-watch."

Brie asked shy questions and was pleasantly surprised when the three of them answered openly and honestly, without a trace of embarrassment. Micah and Max took turns explaining how they'd met Riya, while she inserted comic relief.

"I submitted my dissertation about six weeks ago and I'm so relieved to be done. I focus mostly on writing now and working with several charities. Ten books out so far and the next is releasing in the spring. I'm excited."

Gabriella's eyes went wide. "You still talk to…to the other men?"

Riya's laugh was warm. "Not only do I talk to them, we've had group visits. We had a staggered reunion of sorts in South Florida a few months ago and you'll get the chance to meet a couple of them over the holidays."

"I…I would love to read one of your books. I've read romance but…nothing like what you've described." She added softly, "I didn't even know that was okay now."

"Not only is it okay, I happen to have a lot of male readers as well." She winked. "Reading the racy chapters aloud is apparently all the rage." Brie's mouth dropped open at the idea. Laughing happily, Riya stood and walked into her pretty office with a solid glass wall.

From the other side of the counter, Max told her, "Brie, you've made a friend for life."

"I hope so. I don't have many friends."

Practically skipping, Riya hopped up on the stool and handed Gabriella two books. The first was *Toy with Me* and the second was *Stripped Down*. "Once I pass my boards, I'll officially be a doctor but…smart and sexy erotica is where my heart is." She shrugged and took a small sip of her coffee.

She asked more questions about the research and wondered if she would have been brave enough to attempt the journey Riya took.

The honest answer was *no*. She wasn't shy as much as *uncertain*. Men confused her, usually looked right through her, and it wasn't a lack of enthusiasm on her part. Bridging the gap and finding a relationship that satisfied her seemed beyond her ability.

Internally, she marveled that her two lovers combined hadn't given her as much casual attention as *one* of Riya's men had showered on her in the hour she'd been observing them…much less both.

Absently, she murmured, "I think you're going to be my role model, Riya."

"I'd corrupt you inside one month." When Riya realized she was sincere, she set down her coffee cup.

"I told you yesterday that you reminded me of myself before my dissertation. I was being truthful. If you ever have questions or just need someone to talk to, I'm here."

A heavy blush darkened her cheeks. "I'm not even sure what questions I'd ask but thank you."

Leaning forward, Riya grinned. "Should you decide that you want to put yourself out there, see what all the fuss is about, you let me know. I happen to know a few men who would love the opportunity to wine and dine you."

Max nodded. "I think Riya may be thinking of a few people at our club."

"I *am*, darling. We'll let you get all settled in then see if we can't coax you out to play."

"We would personally check out anyone you were interested in, Brie," Micah told her.

Blinking, she stared down at the books beside her on the bar. "I can't wait to read these."

"Just don't think too badly of me. My writing…my research isn't everyone's cup of tea."

Brie shook her head. "I don't know a lot about research like yours but…it interests me. I think you were fearless to take it on."

"It was a gamble. I loved each of my subjects for distinct reasons. I still *do* but not with the same completeness, the sense of *exactly right*, that I have with Micah and Max."

She shrugged one shoulder delicately. "The project taught me about myself, what I wanted, and what I didn't want. Never settle, Brie. If something isn't fitting…it may be the wrong puzzle piece – no matter how badly you want it to fit."

As Micah refilled their coffee cups, the elevator dinged softly.

"Bitch! We're here. I'm starving! Feed me or I tickle you until you…oh, hello. You must be Brie. Riya told me all about you. I'm

Tawny, this is Zach and Quinn. We're another dirty, filthy threesome and yes...it's *exactly* as wonderful as it sounds. Don't mind me. I'm insane." They shook hands and Tawny's smile broke slowly over her face. "I detect a kindred spirit."

Riya's eyes went wide. "Don't get her in trouble! Brie, if she asks you to moon people or – god forbid – drive any vehicle while she just *runs in somewhere for a minute*, don't fall for it."

"Slander of my good name. Every fucking word, Riya. I'll give all the juicy bits about you, Miss Goody Two-Shoes. Now, Brie! Tell me your story, start from the top, leave nothing out."

Dropping onto the stool on her other side, the redhead grinned. "No shit...and *go*."

Riya's best friend was very much like her sister Izzy, spirited and very pretty. It made her miss Izzy a little less and she felt as though she'd found a group of people she could talk to about anything.

Again, the care Zach and Quinn took with the redhead impressed her. Tawny wasted no time getting to know her in ways no one ever had before.

"I can see why Riya took to you. We're going to our club tonight if you want to come."

Brie shook her head with a smile. "It'll be a while before I feel up to being out socially again. I need to recover from this little bump in the road."

"I understand. You're keeping it together better than I would. I'd be destroying things." Her men nodded behind her and she stuck out her tongue. "We'll let you off the hook so you can get your feet back under you. Know that we *will* be dragging you out eventually. A couple of nice men to blow the top of your head off is just the thing for feeling down in the dumps as a chick."

Blushing as the others chuckled, Brie murmured, "Noted."

They sat at the formal dining table when the plates of crepes, fruit, croissants, and breakfast meats were ready.

Conversation didn't lag.

Their personalities were each so unique but they blended beautifully. Most of the time, Brie was more interested in listening to them than adding to the conversation.

Nuances of characters and backgrounds always fascinated her. She liked to *know* things, even if she was the only one. Her mother had called her Nosy Nelly when she was a child and she owned the trait, though she was better these days about *hiding* her nosiness.

Zach and Quinn ran a chain of coffee houses that were giving Starbucks a run for their money. For a good half an hour, they discussed market projections with the M's and Brie was fascinated.

Her curiosity about the behind-the-scenes decision-making spilled out and she started asking questions about the marketing aspects of their business. They answered with surprised looks on their faces.

Zach said, "You know, you could work in our corporate offices. You're obviously very bright. Did you take any college courses?"

With a smile, she nodded. "I have a master's in sales and marketing from Washington State. I'm interested because your individual businesses are on a larger scale than I'm used to."

Everyone at the table went silent.

Riya put her hand on Brie's arm. "Honey, *why* are you taking a job as a maid?"

"There was the typical worry about how long interviews and such would take. I needed something immediate. I couldn't afford to wait."

"Your interview can happen right now…" Riya began hopefully.

"No, but thank you. The people in this building are the only people I know here. I had so many hopes for what it was going to be like when I landed less than a day ago and I feel unsteady."

She sat back in her chair. "I need something simple to help me survive and acclimate. I've worked hard all my life. I'm not too good to clean until I get my confidence back."

Quinn smiled gently. "I'm sorry for what happened to you, Brie. I think I understand your reasons, but if you change your mind, the offer stands. We could use a work ethic like yours." Zach nodded his agreement.

Max added, "Micah and I both have sales and marketing departments. Should you want to stretch your legs, working for any of us would guarantee that you still know some of your co-workers."

"Thank you so much, all of you. I'll be okay for now. My mom and dad made us work our way up. We started with picking up trash and cleaning toilets at the companies where we interned. We spent enough time in each position to learn it well, then we were promoted or moved to another department. I like that method of learning."

She folded her arms on the table and looked around at each of them. "This building has a lot of moving parts and I've never lived in a city this large before. It'll give me time to stabilize, get accustomed to the city, and learn something new."

They were looking at her with a touch of pity but she knew they meant it kindly.

"I'm excited to start climbing through the various positions here. Don't think of me as settling. Don't feel sorry for me if you see me cleaning. Life works that way and I'm good with it."

Tawny grinned. "I like the way you think. If you start feeling stifled or feel like you need more earning potential, you talk to any of us."

Picking up her coffee cup, she added, "I for one, no matter the circumstances, am glad you made it to Manhattan. You're a breath of fresh air. Also, once you get this whole situation fucked out of your system, it'll be *way* better."

Everyone laughed and conversation turned to something lighter.

Glancing at her watch, she said, "I have to get downstairs. Thanks so much for letting me sidetrack Rodney for another day. I hope this apartment works out."

Riya stood and pulled her out of her chair for a big hug. "It's such a small thing."

Smiling, Brie said, "I think you know it's the small things that make the most difference."

Holding her shoulders, Riya stared at her for a long time. "I do know that. You're welcome."

* * *

She walked out on the sidewalk and took a deep breath of New York air. "Today really *is* going to be a better day."

Rodney pulled to the curb thirty seconds later and *growled* at her when she started to open her own door. He hurried around and opened it for her with a smile.

"You know, I'm not used to that. You're helping so much already."

"You'll travel in style, Brie. I like what I do. Plus, I get to look you in the eye and say good morning without straining my neck."

They laughed together and he closed her up tight in the back of the Towncar. As he settled behind the wheel, he winked. "I think you're going to like this one. I drove past it last night to see what the area is like after dark."

"You're amazing. Thanks."

"One of my girls lives near there." He shrugged. "It was on the way."

"One of your girls?" she asked with her eyes wide.

"My daughter. The relationship didn't work out but I have *her* so it's all good. My little sister lives in the other direction. My other girl. Those two are the light of my life." Meeting her eyes in the rearview mirror, he added, "Now…let's go find you an apartment."

Chapter Ten

Natalia let herself into her apartment and took a deep breath. It was good to be in familiar space, in a home that Hudson had helped to make a reality for her.

She felt unusually off-balance. It had been so long since she'd been with him and her body wasn't done.

Knowing it would be a couple of days before she saw him again made her anxious. Her skin felt too tight and her insides felt as if they were vibrating at a low frequency.

Already, she wanted more.

For sixteen years, her need for complete Domination at Hudson's hand had been a source of both intense sexual pleasure and emotional pain. She accepted her need – an edge of pain to ramp up the experience – but it was also a source of secret shame.

She kept her participation in the D/s underground to herself. It was important that she never let on to the outside world that some chafing and bruising, sustained in the heat of dark passion, were desirable.

It was not an accepted lifestyle. Total sexual submission belonged to a very small, very distinct group.

Natalia hadn't been abused. She wasn't mentally unstable. In most things, she thought the way many women thought. Others found her confident, independent, and strong-willed.

Male lovers had not inspired her trust to the level that Hudson did. Her time with them was too often unfulfilling because the pleasure was not the same without complete submersion in her submission.

Frustrated with the lack of satisfaction found with them, she'd dated women almost exclusively over the last decade. With them, she was forceful, controlling the situation and their time together.

At forty, she wondered how long she would find willing partners.

Nothing matched what her oldest friend could wring from her body every time. His relationship with Christina had been his longest, and going so long without him had been…difficult.

It was only a matter of time before he found the woman he needed, who could meet both sides of the man he was. Their code would prevent them from ever being together again.

The thought made her stomach hurt.

Rubbing her palms over her upper arms, she walked into her bedroom and removed lounging clothes in ultra-soft fabrics. Despite having showered an hour before, she felt she needed another.

Standing under the spray for a long time, she allowed her mind to see her likely future, to see the near emptiness of her life outside her friendship with Hudson and *Trois*. She could pretend that the tears on her cheeks were water.

After all, Natalia liked to tell herself that she didn't cry.

* * *

Riya was dropping off a package to Carlo in the lobby when Hudson stepped out of his elevator. She turned and smiled, walking forward to grab his hand. The casual contact jolted him.

"Good morning, Hudson. Thank you so much for helping Brie." She patted his hand and let him go. "She's on her way to see the apartment now."

"Excellent." He cleared his throat. "I'm afraid my usual charm may have given her a bad impression."

Tilting her head, she said cheerfully, "She set you straight but she'll be embarrassed the next time she sees you. Being mad doesn't come naturally to people like us. She won't hold a grudge."

"She took the job."

"Yes. She joined us for brunch after getting everything squared away." Glancing through the front windows at passersby, she murmured, "I still don't know *why* she'd take the position but she seems genuinely excited by it."

Riya's eyes met his again. "She has a master's degree in marketing." Unable to hide his surprise, she shrugged. "We tried to get her to work for one of the guys' companies but…she's been dealt a blow and says the people in this building are the only people she knows. She made it clear that we're not to feel sorry for her."

He stared down at her, unblinking and silent, and she responded with a grin. "She's another enigma, huh?" She patted his arm and walked around him to the elevator. "Good luck with figuring her out and have a wonderful day, Hudson."

In the middle of the lobby, he reevaluated his plan to go into the office. It was the weekend and Natalia had given so much, soothed him after so many months of raw need.

He should have insisted she stay with him so he could pamper her.

Internally shaking himself, he nodded at Henry and stepped outside. As Leonard pulled to the curb and came around, he said, "Change of plans. Stop by *Trois*."

"Yes, sir."

When they came to a stop in front of the club, he inhaled deeply before getting out. "I'll call. I'm unsure of the day."

Refusing to acknowledge the look of disbelief that his driver quickly masked, he walked up the steps and waited for Natalia to answer the door.

As it swung wide, there was a crinkle along her brow. "Hudson. Darling, is everything alright?"

He took in her appearance and wondered if he'd woken her. She wore a raw silk robe and short heels. Her hair was damp on the ends as if she'd showered again when she returned home.

"Were you sleeping?" She shook her head and he stared into her eyes for a long time. "Do you have plans?"

"No. Has something happened?"

He frowned. "Why would you think something happened?"

"I…" She hesitated, cleared her throat, and started again. "Generally, you put distance between us for a day or two after…our time together." His frown deepened as he thought back, certain she was incorrect. "I didn't expect to see you."

"Why in the *fuck*…" His voice trailed off, his mind in turmoil for an assumption she'd obviously had for years. "*Natalia.*"

He walked in, closed the door behind him, and locked it. Then he took her in his arms and hugged her painfully hard. After almost a minute, he released her long enough to bend and pick her up.

"Hudson, what are you doing?"

He stared down into her face. "All this time, you thought I was ashamed of you. That I thought badly of you for allowing me to dominate you."

Taking the stairs to her apartment, he kicked the door closed. "I was ashamed of *my treatment* and hesitant to face you." Setting her on her feet, he didn't let her go. "I was giving you time."

"For what?" she whispered.

"To *recover.* For bruises, scratches, and abrasions to heal." Her eyes were huge. "I hurt you. I didn't mean to. I'll make it right."

"Hudson…"

"I'll make it *right*, Natalia." Then he kissed her until she was limp in his arms. Lifting his face, he rubbed her cheek with his.

"I didn't know you thought such a thing." Pulling back, he stared into her eyes. "You weren't sleeping. You were crying."

"No…"

"You're lying. Don't lie to me." Staring up at him, her body slack, he watched her inhale deeply.

"I need it, Hudson. I've tried to live without it so many times and I can't. I've tried to duplicate it with other lovers and it was always a dismal failure. I'm ashamed of the need, the weakness. It doesn't make it less necessary to my sanity."

His hand stroked roughly through her hair, tugging the strands sharply as her lashes fluttered closed. "Then you'll have it…*without shame*, Natalia. There will never be such a misunderstanding between us again. We've known one another too long for such bullshit."

Arms wrapping tightly around his neck, she whispered, "Thank you."

They stood there, his hold on her too tight as his mind spun from the shock of knowing the person he cared for most had felt such pain. That she imagined he could *ever* be ashamed of her.

Hudson took her to her bedroom and secured her to the headboard with the tie of her robe. Naked, bound, and unafraid, she watched him undress.

"I need to be careful."

"You do *not*, Hudson."

"I used your body hard."

"I can take it. I'll tell you if it's too much."

He smiled. "No. You won't."

"Yet you've *never* harmed me in all these years. It appears my confidence is well placed."

The words sank deep and he held them close. Leaning over her, he murmured, "As is *mine*, Natalia."

He took his time kissing her and didn't mention the tears that slipped from beneath her lids.

From a box beneath her bed, he removed massage oil, lubricant, and nipple clamps.

As he placed them on the bed beside her, he felt his animal *stretch*.

Chapter Eleven

The moment Rodney turned onto the block where the apartment was located Brie was sold. The buildings and street were maintained, people walked dogs and babies, and there was a good vibe...a *safe* vibe.

He opened her door with a smile. "You like it already, yeah?" She nodded as she took in the building. "I'll come right back when you're done so take your time." He gave her his cell number and a sheepish grin. "I'll check my Facebook."

She laughed and went up the steps to the main door. From here, she could see the entire street. It must have gone through rejuvenation recently. The sidewalks were new, the trees were trimmed, and even the hydrants were repainted.

The brownstone itself was a dream come true.

A grand old building, converted to apartments at some point, the security doors at the entry featured an antique style but she suspected the glass was high impact.

The intercom had a camera above it and there was no doubt in her mind that it worked and recorded the entry and the street beyond at all times.

Remarkable, safe, and close to everything she would need.

She could see one of the subway entrances on the corner. A bodega one block down and across the street was one of the few businesses clustered in that area. The rest of the street appeared to be residential.

The door opened behind her and a lovely woman with a big smile said, "You must be Gabriella. I'm Camille Truing, the building manager."

It was impossible to tell the woman's age but Brie estimated she was probably in her early fifties like her own mother. With ash blonde hair swept into a smart chignon, an understated pantsuit in a delicate shade of blue, and camel heels, she accentuated her figure to perfection.

They shook hands and chatted as the older woman led her up a flight of stairs to the available apartment. The moment the large door swung wide, Brie fell *instantly* in love.

It was snug, clean, and bright. A little bedroom with a door was the biggest difference between this space and the others she'd seen. It was the first of many.

The walls were bright white, capturing every bit of sunshine that came through the two big windows. Original moldings or replicas, wide and carved, were around the doorways, windows, and along the ceilings.

There was a small nook with built-in bookshelves that made her heart race. She could see her workspace there already. The bathroom held an old-fashioned claw foot tub with a shower enclosure hanging above it. The tiny kitchen was plenty for her alone and featured updated appliances.

Worn but well-maintained wood floors extended through all the rooms. The fire escape was in excellent condition and the windows opened smoothly.

It was so different from the other apartments she'd seen that when the landlady – who put her immediately at ease – told her the price, Brie tilted her head in surprise.

"The other places I looked at were nowhere *near* this nice and they were more expensive."

Ms. Truing laughed. "You're adorable. Never question prices in the city, Miss Hernandez. This building has belonged to the same owner for years. The prices are regulated and the tenants are never gouged. You'll fit in perfectly."

"Please, call me Brie."

She nodded and tapped her full lips with one finger. "You know, I think I have some furniture in the basement storage room if you're interested. It was left by a former tenant and I forgot to call a charity to come get it."

"Really? Thank you so much. I'm happy to pay for it."

Waving her hand, the older woman turned for the door. "Relax here for a few minutes. I'll get the paperwork and see if there are a couple of the local boys around who can haul it up for you."

With her hand on the knob, she turned back with a smile. "I live on the top floor and I'm almost always around so if you need anything at all, don't hesitate to ask."

Glancing around at the pretty space, Gabriella knew things had just taken a turn for the better. Losing her savings was a weight on her heart. It had taken her *years* to earn it. The lesson was a tough one and she would never forget it. It would take time for her frustration and fury to cool but she had to keep going.

Fresh start from right now.

Eventually, she'd press charges. She doubted the man who conned her would ever be caught but it wasn't a stretch to imagine him doing the same thing to lots of women.

Her family would find out how dumb she'd been and the thought of that made her sick with worry but she'd deal with that *after* she was back on her feet. It would be better if she could show them, "Yes, I messed up but I'm going to deal with it and bounce back."

This little apartment was the first step into her new future. Just looking at the empty space filled her with possibilities.

She would be very happy here once she started to put her life back together again.

After filling out all the paperwork and writing a check for the deposit and first month's rent, Ms. Truing – who insisted she call her Camille – cheerfully handed her the keys.

In college, Brie lived in a dorm. Since graduation, she lived above her parents' garage. This was the very first space that was truly *hers*.

She went on a tour of the entire building. Camille chatted about trash disposal, where Brie would get her mail, and how to work the machines in the laundry room.

Like most brownstones, there was a narrow yard in the back. There were several chairs scattered among the space that would be perfect for reading or just soaking up some fresh air.

Back in the apartment, she gazed at the furniture she'd received free. She was amazed at how well the few pieces fit in the small space. The camel colored fabric was dark enough to stand out without making the rooms feel claustrophobic.

"They were cleaned before they went into storage. I've kept them covered so no need to worry."

"I love it. I can already see the throw blanket and book I'm going to use in that chair." At the front door, the women shook hands.

Brie thanked her for making a traumatic experience an absolute joy. "I can't wait to sleep here. I could probably sleep on that big, comfortable couch until I find a furniture store and buy a bed."

"I'll see what I can find locally and send you the information. I'm happy to take delivery for you if you aren't here. Now, go enjoy the city a bit. It was such a pleasure to meet you."

She was grinning from ear to ear. She called Rodney when everything was done. He was parked just down the street and told her to wait.

Less than a minute later, the car pulled to the curb and he came around to open her door. "That smile is more *like* it. It's a good place then?"

"It's more than I dared to hope for. I feel much better…about everything."

Placing her hand on top of the car, she looked down the street. "You know, I feel so good that if I had to call my parents and tell them what happened, I'd be less embarrassed because I finally know for certain that it's going to be alright."

He winked at her and she climbed in. He closed the door and got behind the wheel. Sitting back, somewhat at ease considering the last two days, and thankful for the kindness of strangers, she watched the city go by.

Brie was glad to be in New York. Despite the circumstances that brought her.

Chapter Twelve

They were exhausted after their afternoon and evening spent in the pursuits they required to remain stable. After Natalia's final orgasm, she'd held Hudson tight.

When they could breathe again, he settled them side by side. His arm around her, he told her the details about Christina and the additional crimes she was guilty of committing.

His closest friend covered her mouth in shock.

"More than a dozen victims so far. Probably many never reported what happened. She and her partner stole *everything* without a fucking ounce of compassion."

For a long time, they were silent, thinking. Then he watched a frown form across her brow. "Why send one of the women to your penthouse? I don't understand that at all."

"This woman…Gabriella Hernandez…she was a mark for two years. The others were six months or less. She was the first and they kept her on the hook. Played her emotions longer and more deeply than the rest of their victims."

"Fucking cruel." Going up on her elbow, she stared down at his face. "She's significant. Important to the impersonator for some reason."

He stared into the bright blue of her eyes. "She's…unique."

She quirked her lips. "Is there a reason you're getting a *cheating spouse* vibe, darling? We don't judge one another. Tell me why she's unique. You know I adore women."

"She told me off."

"That must have mystified you." He closed his eyes. "It made you *hard*. What does she look like?"

"Shorter than Riya. Her skin is a couple of shades darker and her hair is black, her eyes as well. I think it's really long. Hard to tell. Curvy."

Natalia rubbed her palm over his chest. "She sounds decadent."

He told her what he'd learned from Hollow and his conversation with Carlo. "I don't understand her. That she affected me is infuriating."

Cool fingers slid along his jaw, turning his face to her. "We are always taken with what we don't understand because there are few things that fascinate us anymore. There isn't a damn thing wrong with being curious, with wanting her, with wanting to unravel the mystery of who she is and how she came to be at your doorstep."

"Christina…"

Her fingertips rested over his lips. "She has nothing to do with anything because she was a distraction, a game for you. It was a game you grew bored of playing long ago. Just like so many others, darling."

Stroking her fingers through his hair, she leaned to kiss him. "I love to see you intrigued. It was much the same with Riya before you withdrew from her research."

"How have we become friends? She should be repulsed by me."

"*No one* should be repulsed by you."

Rolling to his side, he pulled her against him. "I don't need another distraction, another game."

A single fingertip traced the lines of his face. "Perhaps Gabriella won't be that. Perhaps she'll be something else altogether. Be open to possibilities, Hudson."

They continued to talk, staring at one another, until Natalia drifted to sleep. He didn't look away from her face or let her go.

For years, he'd considered their time together a necessity for him alone. He'd assumed his best friend gave him what he needed, taking what he delivered, more for his benefit than her own. He never imagined she carried a matching hunger.

Never again would he allow her to agonize over her needs.

Stretched out on his side, he watched her sleep. She was peaceful, breathing deeply, and the marks of his fingers on her hips and waist inspired less shame than ever before.

When his phone vibrated, he reached behind him, smiling when he saw the name on caller ID. He didn't get a chance to say hello.

"She's *lovely*. Nicest young woman and so grateful and enthusiastic. The moment she saw the apartment, she lit up from the inside out. She's all squared away and I think this may be the first time she's lived alone. There was a sort of awe when I handed her the keys."

While the building manager of the very first property he'd ever owned chatted away, Hudson stared at Natalia's profile.

"Hudson, are you listening? I wanted you to know I was going to charge your furniture account for a mattress set. Considering, I think it's the right thing to do. Oh! Sounds like the Asawa family across the hall just returned from their trip. I should run. She's all right and tight."

"Thanks, Mom. I appreciate your help."

"It makes me happy to help you when I can, Hudson. You do so much for me. Okay, have to go."

Hudson smiled at how cheerful his mother sounded these days. She ran his building like a well-oiled machine and the tenants adored her. She went to yoga four days a week, belonged to a book club, and donated her time and money to various charities.

There was a time when she'd been unable to get out of bed.

Hudson was particular about who lived in the brownstone because of Camille. Gabriella Hernandez would be a nice addition as another woman, and one who could become a friend for her.

Reaching down, he pulled the blankets over Natalia's body, smiling when she snuggled deeper and scooted until she was touching the warmth of his skin.

He put his phone on the nightstand and relaxed into the pillows.

He would wait for her to rest and when she woke up, they would shower and go to a late dinner.

Nothing surprised him more than opening his eyes, feeling Natalia's cheek on his shoulder, and realizing he'd slept ten hours straight. It took him a long moment to process.

"Breakfast then," he said to the quiet pre-dawn room.

Chapter Thirteen

Mid-September…

Hudson observed Gabriella Hernandez in confusion.

At first, he thought she'd quit but Carlo told him she was training during the graveyard shift. Just after midnight, he asked a member of the staff where she was currently working.

Within minutes, he walked down the hall to the open door of the temporary suite she was cleaning. Two voices came from inside.

"Brie, they vomited all over the bathroom floor. I don't understand these kids who come here on vacation and spend it wasted."

Peering around the door, Hudson saw Gabriella on her hands and knees. She backed from under the bed with a used condom in her gloved hand. "They'll probably grow out of it. If they don't, think of the millions rehab facilities will make from their parents."

The other woman laughed, rubbing her pregnant belly. She was breathing carefully through her mouth. "Give me just a minute. How many condoms have you *found* so far?"

Brie tilted the trashcan and did a quick count. "The real question is why the hell they're so far *under* the bed? I think that was fourteen but it might be fifteen. Wow. They were only here for two days." She added cheekily, "In my personal experience, *two* would have been impressive."

"That's the saddest damn thing I've ever heard, girl."

Hudson undeniably agreed.

"Tell me about it." She tilted her head and looked at the other woman. "The morning sickness is bad today, Pica. You're positively green. Go on and do the next room and I'll finish in here."

"No *way* am I leaving you to this alone. It's beyond disgusting."

Stripping off her gloves and tossing them in the trash, Brie stood. "Don't be silly. You'll get two rooms done by the time I finish in here. That's a huge help."

"You're a *horrible* liar, Brie."

She laughed. "Maybe…but no way am I having you add to that mess in there. I've got it." Gripping her shoulders, she turned the other woman toward the door. "Get some water, sit for five minutes, and breathe. You need to take care of yourself."

"Does anyone ever tell you that you're too nice?"

"All the time but I don't have a toddler at home, working full-time while seven months pregnant. It's easy to be nice to you. Get off your feet for a little while. Your man will lose it if anything happens to you."

"I told Gary all about you. He thinks you're awesome already. I promised to have you over for dinner during his next leave." She touched Brie's shoulder. "Once I have this baby and get back, I promise to make this up to you."

"Damn right. You'll get the next two-box condom room with frat boys who have too much money and no sense." The pregnant woman's eyes started to water. "Go on now. The smell in here isn't helping you. Sip water and sit before you do anything else. I'm serious."

When her co-worker left, neither of them saw Hudson standing in the opposite direction of the cleaning cart. Pica entered a room several doors down and he glanced around the door to watch the woman who randomly entered his thoughts for unknown reasons.

Gabriella put on a headset, took out her cell phone, and made a call.

"Hey, Izzy." She snapped on fresh gloves. "Well, since you asked…I'm about to scrub a bathroom splattered in puke. I know you're jealous." There was a long pause and Brie snickered. "I completely forgot about that tour. Food poisoning and alcohol…what a combination."

She smiled while talking to her sister, despite the circumstances. "You know I've got an iron stomach. I just wanted to take a quick second to check in. How's your ankle?"

Hudson heard water running and the distinct smell of cleaning products.

"You keep hurting the same damn ankle. Maybe…dare I even *suggest* it…flats for a little while?" There was a hearty laugh. "I will *not* bite my tongue!" She returned to the cart for brushes and disposable towels. "No, I'm fine. I love the apartment, the job, and the people I've met."

She stilled as she listened to her sister on the other end of the line. "Maybe after the first of the year. The thought of interviews, having to be around strangers every day, getting dressed up and feeling awkward, all of it…I'm not ready for that. Not yet. This lets me just be, pays me enough to make it, and it's honest work."

He watched her tug her lower lip between her teeth then release it with a smile.

"I love you, Izzy. I'll buzz you tomorrow when I grab breakfast. Yeah, I *am* talking about food while I scrub vomit. Later."

Grabbing her supplies, she returned to the bathroom with a few mumbled complaints in Spanish. Hudson stood there for another minute before making a note of the room number and leaving.

The next morning, he took a quick detour and called security to unlock the door of the same room remotely. Inside, there wasn't a trace of what the room had looked like hours before. He took particular care inspecting the bathroom.

He stopped to see Eleanor in housekeeping. The elderly woman looked at him strangely when he specifically asked about Brie's overall performance.

"She's really good. Dependable. The others like her. Why?"

Hudson shook his head. "Under the circumstances, I wasn't sure. I wanted to confirm I hadn't caused you any problems."

"None at all. She works hard, has a good attitude, and is always willing to pick up extra hours if we need her. She asked to work in each department so she can learn more."

"Excellent. Glad she's working out. Thank you, Eleanor."

"You're welcome, sir."

Chapter Fourteen

True to habit several days later, Hudson left the building for work wearing a dark suit and power tie. Nothing from the top of his smoothed black hair to the tips of his expensive shoes was out of place. Appearance was important to him as a man. Even more so as a businessman.

Henry held the door with a quiet, "Good morning, sir."

He inclined his head and stepped into a day that was noticeably cooler. In his peripheral vision, he caught a glimpse of Gabriella Hernandez. She was buying a pretzel from a vendor down the block. Without a word to the driver who waited for him, he turned with his coat over his arm.

As he walked toward her, he noted her easy laughter with the vendor and couldn't figure out *why*. She was completely relaxed around people, even strangers.

It was a skill he had never developed.

As a boy, he'd hidden his inability to connect to other people behind silence. As a grown man, he used intimidation. It was one of the many reasons Natalia was his only friend. Neither of them seemed able to move through the world as a natural part of it. They were always *other*…outsiders despite their money and connections.

Laughter lit Gabriella up like a beacon…and he was inexplicably drawn to the light.

Her hair was pulled snugly to her head. Judging from the size of the bun, there was a lot of it. She wore jeans and a loose top that flared over her hips. It irritated him that she hid her curves. Hiking boots covered her feet and the backpack she carried everywhere was over her shoulder.

"You're kidding me? She already plays Brahms at *seven*? That's fabulous. I'm glad you're encouraging her musical abilities. I was in band as a kid but never showed much interest or talent."

Hudson knew the moment she spotted him from the corner of her eye. He watched the blush spread over her face. She probably thought no one could see it under the rich golden hue of her skin.

"Good morning, Mr. Winters." Smiling at the vendor, she said, "I hope I see you again, Mr. Tabai. Have a wonderful day." The older man nodded and she stepped back from the cart, seeming unsure what to do with herself.

Gruffly, he asked, "Where are you going?" The question came out sounding like an accusation and a small frown appeared on her face. "Forgive me. Good morning."

He hated that they'd gotten off to such a bad start and simultaneously didn't know why he cared. She glowed with happiness until she saw him. Hudson knew he had that effect on many people but an unfamiliar part of him wanted her to see him differently.

As Riya seemed able to do.

"I…I'm going to my apartment. Running a few errands."

Her discomfort was obvious and he remembered his neighbor's prediction that Brie would be embarrassed the next time they met face to face.

"I wish to talk to you." Watching for it, he saw her blush again.

He turned, lightly crowding her, and she took a step, then another. He shortened his pace to hers. For the first block, they walked in silence.

Finally, she cleared her throat. "Are you going to work?"

"Yes. Carlo said you work in the building."

Tugging her lower lip between her teeth, she inhaled carefully. "I do. I hope that doesn't...I mean to say...I'm sorry about how I spoke to you, Mr. Winters."

"You will call me Hudson."

Narrowing her eyes at his command, especially when he had no inclination of withdrawing it, she added, "Not for *what* I said but *how* I said it. I was extremely upset at the time. I'm normally nicer."

With a sigh, she tore a small piece off her pretzel and popped it between her pillowy lips. He could picture himself sucking her full mouth while he fucked her.

You need serious help...intensive therapy.

When she licked a grain of salt off her lower lip, he found himself riveted to the movement. "Thank you for clarifying. I doubt you could be nicer. You appear to charm everyone in your path."

"Not even *close*. Obviously." It was impossible to miss the sadness in her voice.

The statement angered him on her behalf. He stopped and turned to her, looking down into a face that was both sweet and pretty. Her eyes went wide and he worked to school his expression.

"Criminals have no interest in emotions other than how they can use them against you. The purer *you* are, the bigger the dollar signs *they* see. What happened doesn't reflect on you in any way. Nor does it mean you're unattractive."

Hudson started walking again and she fell into step next to him. "Thank you for that. I hope you aren't uncomfortable with me working in the building. I didn't know anyone else in the city."

"I'm not uncomfortable. Did you find an apartment?" He watched as genuine happiness infused her face and transformed her from *pretty* to *phenomenal.*

"I did. In Washington, I lived in an apartment above my mom and dad's garage. It wasn't *mine* so I couldn't put out a statue or painting with nudity or anything because my poor mother would have been scandalized. Now, I can decorate to my tastes and no one will judge me. I like that."

Brie smiled to herself as she chewed another small piece of her pretzel.

The simplicity of her thought processes fascinated him. She came from accessible wealth yet her outlook was almost innocent. It was refreshing to meet someone lacking materialism and cynicism.

"There are original moldings, crystal doorknobs, wood floors, and the *light*…" For several minutes, she waxed poetic about the location and built-in bookshelves.

He listened with an internal smile as they steadily chewed up block after block.

It appeared she didn't notice. "The landlady is wonderful. She has that timeless look about her – she'll still be lovely when she's eighty. Do you know she found me *furniture?*" Brie gazed off into the distance and nodded her head. "I still have to think of some way to thank her."

Shaking herself, she smiled up at him. "I talk a lot, I apologize. I've gone on and on. *Bor-ing.*" A small wrinkle appeared between her eyes as she looked around. "Which direction were you headed? I think my chatter distracted you."

He gestured to the Rolls pulling along the curb. "That's my car. I wanted to know how you were adjusting to the city. Allow me to drive you."

"That's not necessary. Thank you though." She gave a small gesture with her hand. "I'm sure you have important things to do. I'm just going to buy oranges."

"I insist."

Again, it appeared Brie expected him to say more. When he didn't, she blinked. "Well, alright. Thank you." The driver held the door and she smiled before getting in. "Hello. I'm Brie. I'll be hijacking your services for a little while." She gave him the address and Hudson was proud that Leonard didn't so much as twitch at the familiar destination. "Thank you in advance."

"You're welcome, miss."

As she grinned and got in the car, Hudson watched his driver's eyes widen. Hudson slid in beside her.

She traced her fingers absently over the leather between them but when the car pulled into traffic; she folded her hands politely in her lap. He knew it was so she didn't give into her natural desire to explore her environment.

"I've rambled about me. What do *you* do for a living, mist…?" His look alone caused her to stop, swallow, and start again. "What do you do for a living, Hudson?"

An *excellent* beginning. To what, he wouldn't allow himself to imagine at the moment.

"You don't know?" There was no way to hide his astonishment. "You never looked me up?"

She shook her head. "I never even *thought* about it. Where I come from – a town with about three thousand people – everyone knows everyone. If you tell me who you are, my first response isn't to suspect you're lying."

Looking out the window, she sighed. "Which made me the *perfect* mark, I realize." The self-mocking laugh sounded *wrong* coming from her and he hoped he never heard it again.

"I can't *believe* I never thought to Google you. If there were photos of you, that would have blown his whole deal. You look *nothing* alike."

"I'm in real estate. There aren't many images of me, by design. I try to control my personal exposure."

"That makes sense."

He focused on the last part of her statement, pissed that he hadn't thought to ask her sooner so he could relay the information to Hollow. "What *did* my impersonator look like?"

Eyes closed, she took several deep breaths. "He was a couple of inches shorter than you. In general, the Hudson I knew was very much...*smaller* than you, physically and in personality. He had light blonde hair, blue eyes...pretty...which should have tipped me off."

Before he could counteract what she was indirectly saying, Brie tapped her left cheek. "He had an interesting scar right here but he never told me where he got it."

Hudson went very still, inside and out, and Gabriella noticed.

"What's wrong?" Her head tilted away from him slightly and her natural intuition roared to life. "Oh my *god*...you know who it is. You know who the fake Hudson is." Then she *blew his mind* by saying, "I...I shouldn't have said anything. I'm sorry."

"Why the devil are *you* sorry?"

Everything inside Hudson was rocked by a devastating suspicion but *her* regret did not make sense to him on any level. He did not have a single frame of reference based on past experiences.

She gripped her hands together so hard, her fingers were white. He watched her struggle with what she wanted to say. Her dark eyes lifted to his and he was amazed at the empathy he saw there.

"You...you're not very friendly. If you know who it is, that means it's probably someone close to you. Likely, someone you work with or that you're related to. If so, that would mean you'll be hurt by this situation as much as I've been and...I don't want that."

Gabriella Hernandez was very dangerous to his self-control.

For a long time, he stared at her, unsure whether his attempt to school his features was successful. Then he lied to her.

"That description fits many people I know. It simply crossed my mind that it would likely be someone I encounter regularly since I don't make a habit of leaving my identification lying around."

She smiled sadly. "I did. Some days, I suppose I'm rather naïve." Brie looked out the window.

"I don't want to suspect everyone of foul play. I don't want to expect people to mess up. I know it's not very smart in the real world."

Hudson stared at a woman in his car with fuckable lips and a perfect ass and realized she was a creature unlike anyone else he'd ever met before.

She was decent and kind. Not because she was stupid but because she wanted the world to be a place where men didn't pretend to love you until they stole all your money, or where those with power didn't insult an employee merely because they could.

Idly, the cold side of his brain wondered if she was contagious. Another part that rarely made itself known *hoped* she was.

"I'm sorry about the day you arrived. For the way I treated Henry."

She gave him a smile but it wasn't radiant like the one she'd given a humble pretzel vendor when talking to him about his child.

"You're a successful person and I'm sure it's easy to forget people – even doormen – can be hurt by things you say. Thank you for apologizing, even if you aren't sure why you should."

His world did a strange tilt to one side before righting itself. Reaching out, he unwound her hands and took one between both of his. The physical contact clearly startled her. Always able to be still and patient, he waited, watching her heart rate climb, her lips part slightly, and a light flush begin at her collarbone and spread up her neck.

The unasked question was answered without a word.

"I've been abrupt all my life. Most people call me cold. I've always been this way. Everything is a competition and there's always an end game. Kindness doesn't come naturally to me."

"It can be learned. I hope you meet someone who can teach you."

"Perhaps you'll teach me."

Her small and capable hand clenched his for one instant before she tugged it free. At the next light, she gathered her backpack, checked for traffic, and opened the door.

"I'll walk from here. Thank you for the ride."

Brie closed the door and he watched her move around the back of the car and stop beside him. He rolled down the window and she gave him her true smile. He physically felt the effect of receiving it.

"You were kind to me many times in the last hour, Hudson. Like anything else, you just have to work at it. Have a fabulous day."

She shoved her hands in her jacket pockets and walked calmly down the street. He was glad to see they were less than two blocks from her apartment.

Leonard's voice was barely audible. "Sir? Shall I follow?"

Hudson grinned. "Not this time, Leonard. Let's get to the office."

With a last look at her ass, he took out his phone and started his day. There was no doubt he needed to fuck the woman out of his system before he had a permanent imprint of his zipper on his cock.

Part of his mind wanted to focus on the description of the man who'd conned her but Hudson knew he needed to put that in a box for the time being. He had to think.

* * *

Brie couldn't get away from Hudson Winters fast enough.

She wasn't sure what was wrong with her but he made her nervous on a primal level as a woman. As someone used to ruling his universe, he'd take hard and go deep.

Being a person who gave generously would handicap her with a man like him.

He wasn't the settling down type. Not a man interested in a wife, kids, and a house in the suburbs. She couldn't picture him at a barbecue or taking his woman on a cruise to Jamaica for their anniversary. No way would he fit the type happy with birthday blowjobs and sneaking a look at whatever porn his co-workers were passing around on the sly.

A man like Hudson was into making money, acquiring power, and *fucking*, probably well and often.

The thought slowed her pace. It also tightened her nipples and made her wet. She'd never been with anyone who didn't saturate her with emotion – real or fake – and give her mediocre sex in the bargain.

Sure, she needed to keep her head down and work on growing her life in New York but maybe he'd be interested in her casually.

Shaking her head, she laughed at the course of her ridiculous thoughts and continued to the little bodega near her apartment.

Keeping her shit together, working hard, and starting fresh…that was where her head needed to be.

Thinking about playing with the enigmatic, abrupt, and sexy as all hell real estate tycoon who was *way* out of her league was sure to be counterproductive.

Chapter Fifteen

Second week of October…

Over the next few weeks, Brie finished training on the housekeeping tasks that fell to her and started cross training by request in other positions just in case someone called out.

There was nothing worse than covering for an employee and not knowing what the hell they *did* from day to day.

If she happened to catch a glimpse of Hudson coming or going, she made herself scarce. The man completely fascinated her, made her hungry for something she'd never experienced, and it didn't take a rocket scientist to know she didn't want or need the complications he'd represent in her life.

While still on graveyard, she often ended her shift when a woman with jet-black hair exited the private elevator for Hudson's penthouse. Carlo called her Miss Natalia. It was obvious she'd spent the night with him and the woman looked damned pleased with herself.

Being completely honest, Brie knew she'd probably have the same look.

She was pretty in a way that Brie could never be, no matter how much she worked out or what clothes she bought.

Tall, slender, and cosmopolitan with the sort of confidence a small-town girl from Washington didn't have a clue how to acquire.

Once she'd switched to her new daytime hours, Brie's shift started before Natalia left and finished before Hudson returned from his office.

As a result, almost a month went by without seeing him or his lover.

She concentrated on putting them – and the fantastic sex they were probably having – out of her mind.

On one of her many lunch dates with Riya and Tawny at their favorite local cafe, she happened to mention the couple, curious about what the women knew about them. She sucked at hiding how inquisitive she was and the redhead pounced.

"You have the hots for him, her, or both? That *both* thing would be kinky as fuck in a very good way. He's like a wild shapeshifter with his animal just beneath the surface, she's like a sexy vampire…they'd put you in the middle for a delicious paranormal sandwich."

Glancing at Riya, she asked gently, "Did she watch another *True Blood* marathon?" Her friend nodded. "Tawny…they aren't supernatural."

Pointing at them with her salad fork, Tawny said, "That doesn't change the fact that they're sexy, dirty, and curious about you." Brie's eyes went wide. "That's right, cupcake. Natalia thinks she's got me fooled with her questions about our *new friend* but I can smell the pheromones coming off her. Makes me want to lick her, you know, just a little bit."

With that, she sat back and returned her attention to her salad. Riya rolled her eyes lovingly and kicked her under the table. "You want to wear that salad or tell us what kind of questions Natalia asked about Brie?"

Tawny pursed her lips. "This isn't an and/or situation, is it?"

"If we were in my house? Yes. Since we're in a restaurant, I'm willing to keep the food on the table. Spill it."

"Oh! Well Natalia and I love to powwow about some of the other members. We get up to all sorts of trouble at the club and since you're a *spoiled brat wet blanket* most of the time, it's just the two of us cackling in her office. She mentioned that Hudson talks about you sometimes."

"Hudson talks about me? Why?"

"I feel like we're in high school. This is fucking awesome." She reached for her wine glass and Riya snatched it out of her reach. "Geez! He wanted to know if we had any plans to bring you to the club that she'd heard. He'd like Natalia to give him a heads up if that happens."

Brie sat back with her mouth slightly open. "I wonder why he cares."

Both her friends turned their heads to look at her. Riya shushed Tawny with a small gesture. "Brie. Sweetie. Honey. He wants to fuck your brains out, that's why. You've presented a *challenge* and there's nothing a powerful man likes more than a challenge."

She frowned. "I'm not a challenge."

Tawny rested her chin on her hand. "Have you fallen at his feet? Have you put yourself in his way? Have you dressed sexy to try to lure him to you? Have you backed through a door and accidentally impaled yourself on his dick?"

"Um...no."

"Then someone like him sees you as a challenge." Riya's voice was gentle. "There are women out there who will do *anything* to snag a rich and successful man like him. Anything, Brie. That you go out of your way to avoid him and make no effort to do anything but your job while you're in the luxury building he lives in...that makes him notice."

"Plus, Riya told me about the first time you met him and I bet he walked around hard for hours after that. I've watched him the past few months and the man is almost *always* hard."

"You stare at his...penis?" The resulting blush from the question was incendiary.

Her friends cracked up laughing. Tawny managed to say, "If we're in an after-school special, yeah, I guess I notice his penis. Since you're lucky enough to be sitting at our table – you know, with the *cool* kids – you're hereby informed that it's impossible for me not to notice his raging hard cock if it passes. I actually use the knowledge to get additional orgasms from my boy toys."

"Stop calling them that," Riya told her with a grin.

"Shut up. They love it." At Brie's confusion, she explained, "I'm two years older than Zach and Quinn. It might not seem like much but...let me tell you...first year teacher deflowering the valedictorian and president of the senior class is a role play that will go down in history."

Brie blinked.

"Tawny, stop shocking her. We have to *work her up* to our degree of moral ambiguity."

"Fuck that. She might not be used to talking about this stuff or hearing *naughty words* out loud but our girl right here is dirty, dirty, dirty...and hiding it well." The redhead winked. "I recognize a fellow all-in girl when I see one. Not a damned thing to be ashamed of either."

She picked up a forkful of her salad and glanced at Brie from beneath her lashes. "You know they're into BDSM, right? A little bit of pain with their pleasure?"

Tugging her lower lip between her teeth, she whispered, "I didn't know for sure but...something about him made me wonder."

The two lifelong friends stared at her for a long time then looked at each other. Riya smirked. "She's still interested."

"I told you...*dirty.*"

Tilting her head, Riya seemed to choose her words carefully. "Brie. I told you they've been friends since they were kids, right?" She nodded. "I'm a little worried for you. Your heart..."

"Don't worry about my heart. I need to hold on to that for a while anyway. I gave it away too easily before." It was Brie's turn to smile. "The lack of orgasms, however, can go straight to hell."

"You must be *Brie.*"

A woman's voice came from directly behind her and a quick glance at Riya and Tawny's horrified expressions confirmed visitors had approached while they weren't paying attention.

"Shit," she muttered under her breath. Turning slowly in her chair, she pretended she wasn't blushing even a little as she saw Hudson Winters and his lover standing directly behind her.

He wore another suit, this one in dark gray, with a perfectly knotted tie that matched the color of his companion's eyes. She was dressed in a black pencil skirt and a shimmering gray sweater that hugged her body.

In her heels, they were the same height.

Side by side, they were breathtaking. As if drawn there after the recent conversation with her friends, Brie's eyes settled on his cock.

The hard outline was visible beneath the fabric of his slacks.

Swallowing hard, she glanced at the two women behind her and their expressions said clearly that they'd caught her looking.

Tawny winked. "What did I *say*?"

Standing, how short Brie was couldn't have been more obvious. She held out her hand to Natalia. "Yes, I'm Brie."

Cool fingers wrapped around hers. "I'm Natalia Roman. The hostess at *Trois* – the club your friends have been trying to get you to visit."

"Yes, ma'am. It's nice to meet you."

"Call me Natalia, darling." She hadn't released her hand.

"Natalia, then. Hello, Hudson." Glancing his direction, his black eyes stared into hers for three seconds before Brie had to break the contact. The man was an open flame and she was not equipped to deal with the way he made her burn.

Instead, she focused on Natalia's face and realized she was far more beautiful up close.

"I'm happy to finally meet the young woman I've heard so much about." She tilted her head slightly. "You've made *quite* an impression on the club darlings. You're even lovelier than described." Hudson's best friend still had not released her hand and her thumb lightly petted the back.

The sensation was hypnotic. "Thank you. You have the most stunning eyes."

"You're kind to say so." Holding her gaze for a long time, she smiled. It made the electric blue sparkle. "Oh, *yes*. I can see it clearly now."

"See what?"

"How blindingly bright you are, darling. It's rather extraordinary."

She murmured, "There's nothing extraordinary about me."

Natalia stepped closer and said softly, "If you believe that, then you don't know yourself at all." She kissed the skin beneath her ear and leaned back. Brie attempted to hide the shiver the contact caused but knew she failed.

"I look forward to seeing you again. We won't keep you from your lunch." Glancing at the women seated behind her, she arched a brow. "Always lovely to see the two of you."

Looking over her shoulder, Brie snickered at the way her friends stared at the trio with their chins in their hands. Not the least concerned about appearing nosy.

Tawny said with a shooing motion, "Don't mind us. We see them all the time. I'm fucking fascinated."

Facing the dark couple in front of her, her eyes locked with Hudson's again. "You'll join us for dinner." She frowned at his insistence and started to object. "Please."

Blinking, she tried to process the flood of information in so few words. Swallowing hard, she self-consciously tugged at her top with the hand not held by Natalia's.

"I don't...go out much." Elegant fingers clenched around her hand and she looked up at the other woman.

"You will now." She smiled. "Go back to your friends. We've taken enough of your time...for today." With a final squeeze, she released Brie's hand slowly.

There was no mistaking the sensuality of it. There was no hiding her own reaction to it.

She kissed both Brie's flaming cheeks and stepped back as Hudson bent to kiss the corner of her mouth. He paused there for a long moment before he severed the contact. Then the woman winked, slipped her arm through Hudson's, and they walked away.

Brie stared at the back of their dark heads, enthralled with the predatory nature of the way they moved, until they were no longer visible. Sitting back in her chair, she steadied her breathing.

Her friends were waiting as she lifted her eyes and Tawny laughed maniacally. "You're fucked, my friend. Those two are going to *devour* you and I expect all the dirty details."

Chapter Sixteen

"She's *delicious*, darling. I can see why she distracts you. Her lips alone could be the focus of untold hours of attention." Natalia settled against the supple leather beside her friend the moment the door closed behind them. She watched as he raised the privacy glass.

The young woman clearly affected Hudson. She understood. The two of them were incredibly sexual, sensual, and greedy when it came to carnal satisfaction. They were always in harmony when it came to seeking pleasure...among other things.

Turning her head, she took in the clench of his jaw and reached up to stroke it. "From the moment you caught her checking out your cock, you were lost."

He closed his eyes with a low growl. "My apologies, Natalia."

"For what, darling? I'd personally like to see if that caramel tone is head to toe. I bet her nipples are the same color as her lips." His eyes opened and focused on her. The black held such intensity that it made her womb contract. "I want to eat her until she begs for mercy."

Watching her best friend of three decades fill with tension was much like a wolf preparing to track prey. It was a thing of beauty and something she never tired of seeing.

His hand reached out to settle on her shin and stroked up the smoky silk stockings. It was strong and warm, radiating passion in a way other lovers simply did not possess.

"You're wet for her." The natural dominance that she ached to experience flared hot.

"I am."

The heat of his palm trailed over her knee and along her bare inner thigh beneath the slim-line skirt. Two blunt-tipped fingertips trailed over the silk of her panties.

Moving them to the side, he slipped beneath the edge and dragged his fingers through her folds.

"You imagine her lips on you." She nodded, unable to form words with him pressing inside her. He watched her, barely blinking. "Sucking you as she slips her fingers in and out of your pussy."

"*Hudson...*"

"I want you taking my cock down your throat while I watch her feast on you."

Her head fell back against the seat and she gasped softly. For more than a minute, he continued to stroke her. She watched him remove his fingers and suck the slickness from them.

"You're also delicious, Natalia."

With his other hand, he smoothed her clothing back in place then sat back and twined his fingers in hers.

"We need to talk about this."

"Yes."

"I want her. I want you to have her."

"God, yes."

He gave her the smile of a conquering warrior and she smiled back. "I'm glad we talked."

* * *

Two weeks later, Hudson emerged from the back of his car in front of *Trois*, unsure if he wanted to go inside during the Halloween extravaganza Natalia threw every year. Every local member – and a few abroad – awaited the annual party with anticipation.

He was not in costume.

Before he'd left the building, a laughing Riya dressed in a naughty nurse outfit in celebration of passing her state boards stepped from the elevator flanked by Max and Micah in scrubs. Tawny, the most innocent looking Wicked Witch he'd ever seen, was inexplicably smacking her men – dressed as the Tin Man and Scarecrow – with her bag of candy.

The moment they saw him, the group tried to assume somber expressions and it made him smile.

Not that he allowed them to see it.

Riya approached and handed him a lollipop. "You don't need this. You're sweet enough already. However, it's Halloween so enjoy!"

Then he *did* smile openly as he took it. There wasn't a sweet bone in his body, as she well knew. "Have fun and try to keep your friend out of trouble."

Rolling her eyes, the brunette said in a mock whisper, "Do you know how hard that is?" She winked. "We'll see you at the club." The entire party headed for the front doors.

He marveled again that the young woman seemed intent on including him, drawing him in, being his friend. He wondered if he would ever understand her motivation. She didn't need anything from him and he offered nothing in exchange for their interactions.

It was a mystery.

After speaking to the security detail about the expected trick-or-treaters they received every year, he accepted the fact that Natalia loved it when he came to her events.

He stood in front of the club, off to the side of the broad stairs, and smoked a rare cigar after Leonard pulled away. A client had provided it at their meeting earlier. The quality was impeccable.

Always aware of his surroundings, his eyes roamed up and down the block. Movement across the street drew his attention.

"Brie…"

That he'd said her name aloud was a clear loss of control at the sight of her walking *away* from the club when he knew all her friends were inside.

She wore jeans and trail shoes, her hair in a snug bun at the back of her skull. A heavier jacket and her usual backpack told him she'd had no intention of going into *Trois*.

Puzzles had always intrigued him but this one was not difficult to figure out. Gabriella hadn't intended to celebrate Halloween with her friends and had she shown up at their *homes* to see their costumes, she would have been forced to join them. There was no way Riya or Tawny would have considered leaving her behind if there was fun to be had.

Instead, she'd apparently walked or taken a cab to the club and waited to see them arrive. He estimated they'd gone inside just a few moments before he got out of his own car.

It took everything inside him not to call out or go after her.

In his own life, he'd always felt separate from such gatherings. Despite his money and power, he recognized that he still did. He was an observer of people such as his neighbor, her best friend, and the men in their lives. Curious about their ease of moving through their environment and interactions that simply didn't compute for him.

Brie…her reasons for remaining separate were *very* different from Hudson's. She was naturally outgoing, social in any situation, able to connect to strangers and friends warmly, and a genuinely happy person.

It was the way she saw herself since arriving in New York that held her back. The blow to her self-esteem, her lack of confidence in her attractiveness, was what ensured she spent her days doing a job that was solitary for the most part and kept her at home alone despite attempts to draw her out in social situations.

"This will not fucking do." He stubbed out his cigar and headed inside to talk to Natalia.

Chapter Seventeen

Early November...

Settling into her life in New York became easier as the days passed and having Riya and Tawny as friends made the transition much more fun than it would have been. The women worked from home, often together at Riya's place, which made visiting them for lunch convenient.

The two of them could make Brie laugh until her sides hurt.

Their conversations were all over the map. They talked about everything from food to travel to the best positions for a woman to achieve orgasm – alone or with a partner – and her friends made it clear that *nothing* was off limits.

She was spellbound by the lives they led with their men. Though she typically ended up blushing furiously, Riya had no problem answering her questions and Tawny could be downright slutty.

It was wonderful.

Brie hadn't had many girlfriends growing up. With extracurricular activities such as student government, art, and band, she hadn't had a lot of free time for socializing during the school year. On academic breaks, she and Izzy worked all the time while their classmates played video games and took trips to the lake.

Sometimes their men would join them and Brie tried not to stare at the way they interacted.

On one afternoon, the four males returned from doing their Christmas shopping as the women were finishing lunch.

There was an impromptu wrestling match as Zach and Quinn tried to reach Tawny first. Max and Micah snuggled Riya between them and whispered at her ears.

Brie couldn't have looked away if she tried.

Riya laughed warmly. "I know we're ridiculous but your eyes are positively *huge*."

"Not because it's ridiculous. It's *nice*." She thought she covered her wistfulness and blushed when she realized she'd shown some of her loneliness. "I see you looking at each other. Don't feel sorry for me."

"Never, bitch. We want you to go to *Trois* with us. You should have been with us for Halloween and we'd have introduced you to all the people who are dying to meet you. You would have had a fucking blast and we'd have gotten you wasted."

Immediately the image of Hudson and Natalia slipped into her mind but that, she could hide. Picking up their plates from lunch, she shook her head. "I'm not ready to go out yet."

Halloween night had been hard. While at work, a strap had broken on her bra and she'd been incredibly self-conscious all day until she could get home to change it.

She hadn't felt good about herself and made the mistake of walking to *Trois* after her shift to see her friends' costumes without being pressured to attend the festivities.

They'd all looked wonderful and while they would have gathered her among them and made her laugh, she couldn't put herself out there socially. There were things she needed to do first that might go a long way toward improving the way she felt about her body and maybe even give her some confidence to take another shot at romance.

Riya frowned. "No one at the club would make you feel bad, Brie. All of them would love you."

She loved that her friend always wanted to make everyone around her feel better. It was impossible to explain that *other people* loving her wasn't the problem.

Pasting on a smile, she replied, "So my corruption is complete? I think not. I don't need *one* man in my life yet, much less *two*. Besides, I'd probably make a fool of myself and end up talking to the bartender all night. I do stuff like that."

When she returned to get their glasses, Riya took them from her hands.

"If you don't *stop* trying to clean up, I'm going to put you in time out." Her husbands went around them and tugged Brie's hair playfully. "They know I'm serious. You're a *friend* over for lunch. You don't clean up."

As Brie watched, the men cleared the table. "I like to help."

Micah gave her a wink. "You help by keeping these two company and by entertaining Tawny enough so she doesn't talk about streaking through the park again."

Max added, "I made cheesecake."

"Oh my god, *no*. Not another cheesecake." The last one Riya's husband made was so decadent; she wanted to weep when she bit into it. "I'll be a parade balloon if you don't stop. As it is, I watch what I eat the entire day before I come for lunch. I know you'll always have something that makes me unable to put down my fork."

Tawny scowled at her. "What the *fuck*...? You're gorgeous. I'd give anything to have your ass."

"Better in theory than in practice, I can assure you. Anyway, I've got to get downstairs. Lunch was delicious and I'll have dessert next time. Thank you for breaking up the day."

The friends kissed her cheeks and she waved at everyone as she headed for the elevator. The moment she was inside and the door shut behind her, she rubbed her temple.

It was hard to explain how she was feeling on the inside to people who genuinely cared about her. While life in New York was steadily improving, the way she felt about herself seemed to be getting worse as time went on.

Lately, she'd started dreaming about the fake "Hudson" and all the things he used to say to her about her beauty and potential. Knowing it had all been lies to make her put down her guard made her heart hurt painfully because she'd believed him so strongly at the time.

Rubbing her hand over her chest, she cursed the tears that wanted to fall and quickly rushed from the elevator when it reached the lobby.

She slammed right into the *real* Hudson.

He steadied her, his hands on her shoulders, and stared into her face with a frown. "What's wrong?"

"Nothing. I'm sorry. I wasn't looking."

Strong hands stayed on her, held her in place, and she didn't know where to look so she focused on his tie. It was a pretty violet color, something she wouldn't have pictured him picking for himself, and thought it was probably a gift from Natalia.

"Brie." She didn't respond and his fingers tightened slightly. "Look at me, Brie."

Lifting her eyes, she stared into deepest black. He was such a striking man, physically and in his overall presence. He returned her gaze for almost a minute.

"Have coffee with me."

"I can't. I've got to get back to work. I was on lunch."

Still he held her, stared at her. "You're a beautiful woman." She opened her mouth and he gave her a tiny shake. "Don't. I *will* convince you."

Swallowing past the painful lump in her throat, she said softly, "Thank you, Hudson."

One by one, his fingers lifted and he released her. Taking a step back, she felt his eyes on her while she walked across the lobby and turned toward the employee area.

As she started to work a few minutes later, she paused to think about the way Hudson looked at her, spoke to her, and asked herself if the man would ever tell a woman something for an ulterior motive. She might not know him well, but everything inside her said he didn't stroke egos.

No matter what she thought about herself, no matter how her experience with the con man made her feel, there was one thing that was undeniable and it went a long way toward making her feel better.

The knowledge made her blush. It also made her smile.

To herself, she whispered, "Hudson thinks I'm beautiful."

Chapter Eighteen

Several days later, Brie soaked up a rare warm afternoon on her day off at the coffee house she discovered her first weekend in New York. After falling in love with the place, she learned Zach and Quinn's company purchased it the year before. They'd since converted the space into one of their chain locations.

The beverages were high quality, the service was exceptional, and the atmosphere was positively Zen. Considering how much caffeine was consumed within the four walls, it was almost magical.

There was a small courtyard space enclosed with a wrought iron fence. A little gate gave the area access from the sidewalk. From her favorite table, one she wouldn't be able to use much longer, she had a perfect view of the street and the park beyond. She often took the opportunity before or after her shifts to sit there to sketch and think.

Other than her apartment, it was her favorite place.

She was consumed by a sketch of a statue across the way when her two friends dropped heavily into chairs on the other side of her table.

With a grin, she said cheekily, "Neither of you *flop*."

"We were worried about scaring you half to fucking death. Whatcha working on?" Tawny leaned over the table and her eyes went wide. "Damn girl, you're good."

Brie shrugged. "It's just a hobby." Riya was staring at her sketch with her eyes wide and she closed her notebook. "I'm an amateur. Really."

"Total bullshit." Tilting her head, the redhead asked, "Have you ever done digital graphics?"

"Sure. That's what I do on the side."

Glaring, she looked at Riya. "I'll cut this bitch. I'm not playing. Does she not realize what I *pay* for quality graphic design?"

Just then, Max and Micah appeared with a tray of coffees. They smiled warmly at Brie and she returned it. They were quickly brought up to speed but didn't contribute right away.

"What everyone we *know* pays for graphic artists?" Riya shook her head. "How did we not know this? How have you hidden this side of yourself?"

She started to reply when her phone rang. Seeing it was her mother, she internally cringed. "I've got to take this." Taking a deep breath, she answered. "Hi, Mom."

The instant the screaming started, she switched to Spanish. As far as she knew, Riya was the only one who spoke it. It would minimize the humiliation.

"How could you let this happen, Gabriella? You were *robbed* by a man who supposedly *loved* you so much. How is this possible?"

"Mom, I know it looks bad. I'm fixing it…"

"That isn't good enough! I knew you weren't ready to be out on your own! Why did I find this out from the bank? Why did you not call me yourself before I received a subpoena? It has been more than two months!"

"I just filed charges…"

"You waited all this time! That was very stupid, Gabriella."

Closing her eyes, she inhaled carefully to control the tears and hurt that always seemed to bubble up if she made the slightest misstep and her parents found out about it.

"I know. I'm sorry, Mom. I…"

"No! I'm so disappointed in you. You were foolish enough to believe this man, so stupid as to travel across the country and uproot your life, and look what happened!"

"I know." Brie kept her eyes on the park, her voice low, but there was no doubt that Riya could hear every word her mother said and, unlike the others, understood it. "I'm going to make it right."

"You can't make it right!"

Finally, she snapped. "This was my choice, my mistake, my money. It doesn't affect you at all, Mom. I waited to call you until I had a place to live, a job, and a plan to get back on my feet. This...the way you're being right now...is why I didn't call the day I found out that the man I thought loved me had stolen everything I worked so hard for. I can't talk to you anymore."

Brie disconnected the phone, shook her head when Riya tried to talk, and left the coffee house for her apartment across town.

It was best if she spent some time alone.

* * *

Hudson was coming out of the elevator when the M's intercepted him. They looked livid and while it amused him, there was a prickling at the back of his neck at their expressions.

Micah wasted no time on pleasantries. It was one of the traits he liked about the man. "We need to talk, Winters. Come upstairs."

The smile he gave them was slow, dangerous. "I think *not*. If you boys want to talk, you'll squirm in my space."

Without another word, he waited for his elevator to reopen, stepped inside, and quirked a brow until they got on with him.

He maintained his silence as the three of them walked into his living room. They had an issue; they'd be the ones to break it. It was important to establish a position of power early with Micah. The man would hit him as soon as talk to him otherwise.

Max, always the calm one, told him, "Riya and Tawny are at home. It's probably best if we speak to you alone." Hudson agreed. Tawny was a wild card on the best of days. If she was pissed, she was best left out of the equation. "We ran into Brie at the coffee house."

They had his attention.

He drew himself up to his full height. "What happened?"

The two men filled him in on the conversation Riya translated between Brie and her mother. He thought about how strong the young woman was yet fragile when it came to people she cared about. Anyone she had an emotional investment in could wound her horribly.

"Is she alright?"

"I honestly don't know, Hudson," Max said carefully. "What I want to know is what *you* plan to do about this little cluster fuck because to think we wouldn't do our own digging was...rather short-sighted on your part."

There it was. He held the bright blue eyes without blinking.

"Your ex-girlfriend was the female half of the con. In swindles like that, there are always at least two people. One to run the scam and one to impersonate the person being conned."

Surprisingly, it was Micah who murmured, "I wouldn't have been able to go to the police either, mate." Their eyes locked and Hudson understood for the first time how close the two men in front of him were. "That doesn't change the fact that she was fucked with, humiliated, and robbed."

"I know." Hands slipping into his pants pockets, he walked over to the window to stare out at the skyline. "I'm working to make it right."

The men appeared at his side. Max sighed. "The apartment was top notch, Winters. I know it normally goes for double what you're charging Brie. It was good of you. The job, too."

"It wasn't good of me. It was selfishly motivated originally to contain the fallout."

The three men said nothing for a long time.

"She'll hate me when she learns the truth." The thought caused a tightness across his chest.

"Wrong." Micah's voice contained absolute certainty. "Women like Brie…like Riya…they can't hold onto negative emotions for long. It's what makes them special."

Max turned his head with a small quirk of his mouth. "Riya wants to visit her attacker in prison." Hudson couldn't contain his growl. "We feel the same." He looked out over the city. "It keeps her up nights sometimes. That she hasn't confronted him face to face since that night. Brie will be that way, Hudson. You need to be prepared."

He gave a single nod.

"Brie pressed charges and hired a private investigator. Not the kind of people we use but someone legitimate. There's no way she'll let it go and it has nothing to do with her money." Max sighed.

"She's thinking of other women." Hudson knew that without a doubt. "I *will* find him. When I do, I'm not sure what will happen. I'll leave that up to Gabriella."

Both men's eyes went wide. Micah murmured, "You care for her."

"Right or wrong, yes."

The friends turned in his direction but he remained still, looking out over New York. Micah's smile was slow. "Good luck to you and Natalia, Winters. You may think you have Brie all figured out but…you'll see you don't know shit."

"As I'm discovering."

"We need to get back before Riya and Tawny come looking. You don't want that." Hudson couldn't hide his small smile. "Keep us posted."

He nodded and listened as they walked across his space and the elevator carried them out of his world and back to their own.

Chapter Nineteen

Brie shouldn't have been surprised when her friends showed up at her apartment but she was. Sighing, she stepped back and the two women entered as if they were ready to do battle.

Tawny held up several DVDs. "I've got action, comedy, and romance. I'll cut your ass if you choose romance. You two can watch that shit when I crash."

Riya held up a bag that had obviously been packed by her men. "Max sent that lobster salad you love and cupcakes along with a ton of other stuff. Micah sent two bottles of your favorite wine."

"I tried to get mine to come over and rub your feet but they felt it would be inappropriate and make you uncomfortable for some weird reason." She reached in her back pocket and removed an envelope, "They opted to provide cash for mani/pedis instead. Whoop!"

They walked in and laid everything out on the coffee table before walking around her apartment to explore. The books on her shelf immediately captivated Riya and Tawny flipped through one of her sketchbooks.

Brie kept herself busy by getting plates, wine glasses, and napkins from the kitchen.

The moment she'd gotten home, she took a long soak before dressing in pajamas. Her hair was clipped back from her face to dry since she had a couple of days off. As much as she scraped it into tight buns, her scalp loved the break.

"We need to talk, Brie." Riya's voice was gentle but firm.

Hands on her hips, Tawny stated, "Pretty much, you can just spill everything so we can move on to a fun night or you can keep making up bizarre excuses for not going out with us and shit. If you choose option B, we won't be leaving anytime soon. I hog the covers and leave wet towels on the bathroom floor. You've been warned."

Turning in her small kitchen, she gave them a smile she didn't feel, and knew they saw through it.

"I'm really tired of feeling like shit about myself." She poured each of them a glass of wine when Tawny handed her the bottle.

"My parents are old school. There's a trust set up in my name but it's unlikely that I'll ever see a penny because of the morality clause attached."

"Morality…wait, your folks won't let you inherit if they think you're living *immorally*?" The look on the redhead's face was priceless.

"They love me and my sister. They do. They've busted their asses to make a good life in the States and want us to be the best versions of ourselves. Unfortunately, what *defines* the best version is open to interpretation." She took a sip of wine.

"When I started dating the fake Hudson, I walked a line almost constantly. The day I told them I was moving to New York resulted in a three-day feud I never want to go through again."

"Brie…"

With a shake of her head, she murmured, "That's not the worst of it. As angry as they've been about me dating, moving away to live in sin, and being robbed in the process, nothing will make them as angry as me getting cosmetic surgery."

"You're gorgeous. Why would you need it?" Riya's expression was genuinely confused and Brie loved her for that.

Placing her wine glass on the counter, she lifted the hem of the oversized t-shirt she was wearing and pulled it over her head. Her friends' eyes went wide as she removed two tank tops with built-in support. She stood in front of them in a top of the line sport bra that clearly showed why she needed cosmetic surgery. Even it was unable to support the weight of her breasts.

"You must feel like you're suffocating under all those layers. Oh my god, Brie. I had no idea."

"At my height, these are comical. I have custom bras made because I'm a G-cup but my upper body is narrow otherwise. I've got permanent indentations of my bra straps on my shoulders. It affects my balance, my ability to find clothing that fits me, and my overall self-esteem. That's *nothing* compared to the pain. My back and neck hurt constantly."

"How long?" Tawny's face was clenched in anger.

"I've been this size since the summer before I turned fifteen."

Riya's eyes drifted closed and Tawny cursed. As women, they knew quite well what she'd endured in school. Whatever they imagined, she wouldn't tell them how much worse the reality had been.

"My mother and father believe that how we are born is a gift from God. The fact that I received a gag gift that causes me endless pain and insecurity doesn't figure into the deal. Once I receive the surgery, I can never undo it and they *will not* forgive me."

"That's why you saved so much money. You were building a safety net for surgery and to start over." Brie nodded and saw the tears in Riya's eyes. "I'm so damn sorry this happened to you."

"I feel shitty for giving you guilt all this time."

"I *love* to dance. I've only ever danced with my family because…you can imagine. If I go to places where there's music, I'll find something to distract me so I don't…jiggle."

She took a deep breath and put her layers back on.

"I don't feel strong right now. I don't feel right in my skin. I didn't before all this but…it's so much worse now." Quietly, she asked, "Do you understand?"

"Yes, Brie. Now we get it and we won't pressure you until you're ready." Riya tilted her head. "What is it about Hudson that draws your attention?"

Blushing brightly, Brie gestured down her body. "Even like this, he seems...*hungry* when he looks at me. I...think he's physically attracted to me. Wants me in a sexual way *no one* ever has. Not even the pretend Hudson." She shrugged. "It terrifies me but it...also makes me feel amazing."

Picking up her wine, she smiled into the glass. "He's not in love with me or anything and I'm *not* in love with him. I've watched him with his best friend. I don't think they understand that what they have *is* love...deep, forever love."

Introspective, she added, "I think they're...*damaged* in some way that makes it hard for them to see and embrace it. I think I could help them." Looking at her friends, she added, "He helps me without trying."

Riya smile was blinding. "That's the way I was with my subjects." She approached and smoothed Brie's hair. "You want to break down their barriers to each other."

"Do you think I could?"

Her friend nodded. "I do. I really do and I'd love that for Hudson. He's very isolated, Brie. Who better than his best friend in the world to give him a happily ever after?"

Tawny snorted. "As long as you get some screaming fucking orgasms in the process, I think you could do anything." She wiggled her brows dramatically. "You prepared to take them both on?"

"I'm fucked regarding the morality clause anyway. I might as well make it count."

"Dirty, dirty girl. I knew I loved you. Let's get Riya drunk and send her back to the M's to cluck over. It makes them crazy."

The three of them spent the evening screaming at action movies, drinking all the wine Micah sent plus Brie's stash, and sent Riya home to Max and Micah.

Apparently, she dissolved into fits of giggles that allegedly didn't ease for *hours.*

When Tawny and Brie received the quite proper lecture from a dignified Max, they shared a fist bump of victory.

Chapter Twenty

Mid-November

Hudson saw her two blocks from his office and every cell in his body was immediately on alert. Focused on the goal of soaking up her presence.

"Stop here."

Leonard didn't question the abrupt directive and within seconds, pulled to the curb. Without waiting for his driver, he stepped out on the sidewalk.

"Gabriella."

Turning in surprise, her smile sank into him. There was no hesitation as she approached. "Hudson. What a surprise."

"Where are you going?"

Her hand lifted and he followed the direction. "That little store has the best charcoal pencils. It's worth the walk."

"You walked two miles for art supplies?" If she walked from her apartment, the distance was much further.

She grinned. "The woman who owns the place is wonderful."

"Do you work today?" She shook her head. "My company isn't far. Would you like to see it?"

"I don't want to take up your time. I know you're busy." He stared at her until she answered his question. "That would be nice. Thank you, Hudson."

Side by side, they walked two blocks and crossed the street. The high-rise was older but the architecture was imposing.

The wide courtyard that spanned the front featured a fountain and several shaded seating areas.

"How pretty. You don't see many spaces like this in the middle of the city."

"I've been trying to buy the building for more than a decade." He owned many buildings but he wanted *this one* for his headquarters. Unable to convince the owner to sell, he'd rented and refurbished the top floors for his corporation.

"The owner won't let you buy it?" He shook his head and she smiled up at him. "I imagine there are few things that don't fall into line for you. You do seem to like things your way."

Meeting her eyes, he replied, "Very few things but it's usually the things I want most." There was no mistaking the fact that he considered *her* one of those things and the blush flared up her cheeks, darkening the warmth of her skin. "I'm preparing to make another offer. I travel this week to convince him of the win-win situation."

Swallowing hard, she managed, "H-how will you convince him?"

"He's heavily mortgaged on several properties. During the height of the recession, many of the other floors emptied as companies went under. I leased those as well. My company now occupies almost eighty percent of the available space."

The smile she gave him was slow. "If your company decides to vacate, all that rent money disappears. If he's spread too thin, he could lose it either way. Better to make a profit on this one and keep the others."

He enjoyed her astute evaluation. "Many call me vicious in business."

"I disagree. You're an opportunist. I'm sure you're fair in your dealings, if not sociable."

Stopping beside the fountain, he stared down at her. "I try to be."

"Do you think he'll take your offer?" He nodded. "I'm glad. Is there a reason you like this building so much?"

"Why do you ask?"

"*Hudson Winters* wouldn't wait a decade for something unless it held deep meaning. You don't have to tell me if it's personal. I'm overly curious. It's a flaw."

"There's nothing flawed about you, Gabriella." Her ability to read people and situations was a continual source of fascination for him.

He dragged his eyes away from her and inclined his head across the street. "That building belongs to my biological father's family."

He saw the questions in her eyes but she didn't ask them. Instead, she said, "This one is bigger, more striking, and better designed." Glancing up and down the street, she added, "It sits better on the block and I bet the view is awesome."

"Rated one of the ten best in Manhattan." There was no way to hold back his smirk.

"I hope you get this building, Hudson. You deserve to have it."

Such a simple thing to say yet the effect on him was powerful. "Come."

With his hand on her low back, he led her inside and the way her eyes tried to be everywhere at once was…adorable. He stopped at the security desk and the guard behind the granite surface drew himself up straight.

"Gabriella Hernandez. Put her on the list." Her eyes were wide as she looked at him.

"Yes, sir."

Then they were walking to the bank of elevators. "What list?"

"People allowed access to my floor without an appointment. They won't question your presence."

"How many people are on that list?"

"Four." The doors closed and he turned to her. "Why do you avoid me?"

"I don't..." His expression stopped her denial instantly. She swallowed and took a deep breath. "I'm attracted to you. It makes me feel juvenile and ridiculous sometimes."

"Why?"

The question seemed to genuinely confuse her. "I'm me and you're...*you*."

The doors opened and he took her hand, probably surprising her as much as himself. "Lola. This is Gabriella Hernandez."

"It's a pleasure to meet you, Miss Hernandez." The woman's expression must have told her how unusual it was for him to have guests. Certainly no one like her.

"Call me Brie." They shook hands and Brie nodded at the dozen photos clustered on one section of her massive desk setup. "What a pretty young woman. Is that your sister?"

"You're my new best friend. That's my daughter. Her name is Donna." Lola grinned.

One of the photos featured Donna in a Michigan State jersey. "You have a daughter old enough to be in college?"

"She graduates this year."

"You have great skin."

"Please don't leave this building. I'll set you up right here beside me and you can make me feel less old and boring. How's that sound?"

Hudson watched the byplay between the women, more than a little amazed at the animation of his personal assistant. Brie appeared to have that effect on many people.

"I've been Hudson's assistant forever. I'll be with him until I kick."

"Lola was the first employee I hired."

The way Gabriella's face lit up was incredible. "That's outstanding! It must have been remarkable to watch him grow his company over the years. I bet you're proud of him."

No statement could have shocked him more.

"So proud. The day he met me, I was a single mom trying to figure out how to buy my books for my last semester. He took care of Donna and me, made sure we had a place to live, and acted like I was doing him a favor by doing work whenever I could out of my apartment."

"I don't think he expects people to be loyal to him." Brie rested her arms on top of Lola's desk. "He's nicer than he lets on."

"I'm glad you see that. Donna and I adore him." Tilting her head, she added for clarification. "As does my girlfriend."

"Not shocked or dismayed." Brie pointed to another photo in the far corner. "I see two women in that photo who are deeply in love. What's her name?"

"Maria." Standing, his assistant came around her desk and stood in front of their guest. "You might be one of the most interesting and observant people I've ever met. If you need anything at all, feel free to call me personally."

The older woman handed her a business card and she tucked it into a back pocket. The movement caused Brie to lift her shirt and he barely held back his growl at the curve of her ass in her jeans.

"Thank you, Lola. It's an honor to meet the first person officially hired by Winters Enterprises. I'm blown away." Gesturing at the distressed metal sign behind Lola's desk proclaiming the company name – an identical one hung on each floor – she added, "You've come a long way from working out of your apartment when you could."

"Damn right. Anytime you're over this way, stop by for a little. I'll let security know."

"I added her to the list."

Lola's eyes went wide and then she turned a brilliant smile on Brie. "I see. Then I'm sure we'll see one another again soon." The woman who knew him better than anyone else, apart from Natalia, met his eyes. "Boss, why don't you take Brie on a tour? Show her the inner workings of what you built from nothing."

"I don't want to take up too much of your time, Hudson. I've already distracted you from your day as it is. I'll come back another time."

Without a word, he slid his hand along her lower back and guided her to his office. She waved at Lola. "I'll see you later."

Chuckling, she nodded. "Bye, Brie."

As they cleared the doorway, he closed the door and pushed the object of his obsession against the wall as gently as he was able. Her gasp sent sensation straight to his cock.

For a long time, he did nothing more than stare down into her face with his forearms holding his weight off her. The pulse in her neck was pounding and her breath panted softly between slightly parted lips.

"Your eyes aren't black. They're dark blue." He didn't give her time to nod. Dropping his mouth over hers, he *took* what he'd needed for months.

Her effect on him was a supernova in his brain.

Not opening for him probably never occurred to her and he licked between the softest lips he'd ever kissed, tasting spicy chocolate on her tongue. One hand moved to grip the base of her neck, holding her in place for what was no better than an assault.

Then she sighed into his mouth and the animal inside him wanted *out*.

Reining in, exerting a level of control he'd never had to use, he gentled the kiss. The feel of her hand lightly settling on his arm, squeezing softly, made him regret the fact that they were dressed.

He wanted her touch everywhere.

It could have been five minutes or an hour later that he broke the kiss and pulled back to look at her. She was flushed, her eyes glazed, and he wanted to know if she was wet for him.

That she didn't fill the silence impressed him. That her eyes dropped to his mouth as if waiting for another kiss filled him with desperation to take her in every way possible.

Lola's voice over his desk phone made him growl. "Hudson, I wouldn't interrupt but Harper Delkin is on the line."

Brie whispered, "About the building?" He nodded. "You have to take it." He made no move to step away from her. "You *have* to take his call, Hudson. You *need* this building."

Wrapping his arm around her waist, he took her with him to his desk. "Put him through."

A moment later, the phone rang and he put it on speaker. "Delkin."

"Winters. He wants more money."

"Does he realize I'll vacate and pick it up for one-tenth of the price in foreclosure?" There was a long silence on the other end of the line. "The price is fair, above market value. He's your friend and I've taken our professional history into consideration."

"Yeah. You're a saint, Winters."

Brie visibly bristled beside him. He wanted to kiss the intense frown between her eyes away.

Hudson needed therapy sooner rather than later.

"Unquestioned. I typically don't negotiate." That made Brie smile. "I leave tonight for Seattle. I expect to know before I step on the plane that we have a deal in place. Don't waste my time."

Another long pause was followed by, "Understood. We'll speak in an hour. One question…will Natalia be traveling with you?"

"No."

The line went dead and Brie put her hands on her hips. "It must be hard to deal with someone exactly like you, huh?" He attempted to hide his surprise. "If you can help it, keep Natalia out of his orbit."

"Why?"

She shrugged. "You want his friend's building. He wants your friend. Men like him, like *you*, don't mention women outside a business deal *in* a business call lightly." Adjusting the backpack that was still on her shoulder, she walked for the door. "Don't let him have her, Hudson. Trust me on this."

Before he could assimilate the fact that she was leaving, Brie was gone.

Chapter Twenty-One

When his plane landed in Seattle, Hudson didn't acknowledge the flight crew or driver that waited. In the back of the car, he stared out the window.

His mind was rarely chaotic. The combination of experiencing Brie's kiss at long last followed by her observations about Natalia shook the steady foundation he maintained.

The relationship he had with his best friend had always been open and honest. They both kept other lovers over the years. He'd had a couple of unfortunate choices before Christina moved in with him but Natalia *never* allowed people to cohabitate.

Why did Brie's assurance that he didn't want her near Harper Delkin resonate so strongly?

Shelving his thoughts as the car pulled to the curb in front of the high-end winery and steakhouse, Hudson blanked his features.

The low lighting and dark wood accents gave the interior an intimate feel. The hostess approached with a regal air and he followed her to a private room when he tersely gave his name.

Harper Delkin stood as he entered. They shook hands and Hudson took in the man with whom he'd maintained a friendly rivalry since college.

Since Brie's remark that it must be difficult to deal with someone so similar, he was shocked to realize how *physically* similar they were as well. Roughly the same height and build, Harper wore a perpetual frown, something his own mother frequently scolded him about. He wore his black hair longer and shaggier, his eyes were pewter gray rather than black.

Their clothing was equally expensive. Their holdings were equally imposing. Their personalities similar in ways that were not always considered positive.

The primary difference between them was that Harper was raised with money. Hunter Delkin had made money while he slept. His oldest son had inherited the skill.

Twenty years before, they'd met during a business conference for graduate students. While other men and women competed for coveted positions with established firms in various industries, Harper and Hudson were there to scout contacts, evaluate procedures, and assess their competition.

Friendship was not a word he would use regarding the man. He knew that Brie would disagree.

"Winters."

"Delkin."

"Tully's flight was delayed from San Francisco. He'll be at our meeting in the morning." Hudson said nothing and a slow smile broke over the other man's face. "I have his signed documents with me to reassure you."

"Excellent."

Gesturing to the table, they sat and placed their orders. When a scotch sat in front of him, they remained silent and he likened it to the way alpha males in the wild took the measure of one another.

"How is Natalia?"

"Well."

"I have better conversations with her."

"As do I."

"Will she attend the Valentine's gala with you?"

"She will."

At that moment, he determined that he wouldn't take Brie with them to the annual event. While Natalia could easily dissuade Harper's attention, the younger woman's natural sweetness would draw the man across from him like a magnet.

After all, she'd drawn *him*.

While she'd encouraged him to guard Natalia from Delkin's attention, he planned to follow the same plan for Brie herself.

"I look forward to seeing her again."

The silence drew out between them and Hudson sighed. "How is Harlow?"

Watching the other man bristle made him smile internally. The weekend he'd spent with Harper's younger sister more than ten years prior was still a sore point between them.

He was unsure why he'd been unable to commit to the only female Delkin in their generation. Until Brie, she was the only woman who'd gotten close enough to see the edge of his darkness and liked him anyway.

When they saw one another socially, she liked to tell Hudson that he broke her heart. Said with a wink and a smile, part of him wondered if he truly had hurt her.

If so, it was unintentional. He greatly respected her.

Jaw clenched, Harper said, "She's well. I'll tell her you inquired about her."

Messages delivered and received, both men nodded at one another and seemed to exhale. The tension dropped between them.

"Your deal for the building is beyond fair in the current market. I made that clear to Tully."

"I appreciate that."

"I also explained that the bank could give two fucks about the sentimental value he places on every fucking piece of property he buys." He shook his head. "Each one has a goddamn story behind it."

"Few things affect me in such a way."

"It's the same for me." Harper shrugged. "Tully though, he'll hang on with tears in his eyes."

"He can still *visit* the building if he starts to miss it. It isn't going anywhere." The other man's full laugh filled the space and one side of Hudson's mouth lifted. "For fuck's sake."

"Tell me about the happenings in New York. It's been too long since I visited. I miss *Trois*. Natalia aside, I've been considering opening a similar club here."

"Her business module is sound. That would make less than half a dozen in North America at the same level of exclusivity." Tilting his head, he asked, "I thought you left the lifestyle."

"It's not quite so easy."

Their eyes met and Hudson remembered the first time he'd gone to The Playground in his mid-twenties and ran into the future CEO of Delkin Acquisitions in the most unlikely scenario.

Naturally Dominant, Harper did *not* have the same hang-up about another man in his sexual orbit with a woman. It was a source of great pain throughout his life and something he'd hidden from most of the people closest to him, including his family.

The one time he'd been completely honest about who he was and what life he wished to live had ended in tragedy he almost hadn't survived.

The conversation was really about *territory*. The Delkin heir wanted to play in terrain that Hudson considered *his* and he'd shown respect in how he handled the need.

"Until you decide if you will open a club on the west coast, make more frequent trips to *Trois*." He knew well the repercussions of suppressing one's basic nature for too long.

Inhaling deeply, Harper nodded once.

For several hours, they changed the flow of conversation to common ebbs and flows of the market, property, and mutual acquaintances. As they left the restaurant, Delkin handed him fax copies of the agreement they'd make official at his office the following day.

"Read it over. I think you'll find many of your demands were met."

A few more minutes of small talk and they shook hands. Back at his hotel, Hudson spent hours going through the contract and comparing it to the original. His attorney had a copy and would be present at the meeting.

* * *

Less than twenty-four hours later, Hudson was on his plane en route to New York. He was in possession of the only building that had *personally* mattered in the grand scheme of things.

A powerful *fuck you* aimed at the people who had injured his mother when she was at her lowest.

As a young woman from North Carolina, Camille's well-to-do parents sent her to Philadelphia to go to university. The effects of the war in Vietnam found the country in turmoil. The southern states were reeling from the ongoing violence of the civil rights struggle.

Bright and naturally beautiful, she settled easily into the college environment that was rapidly becoming more accepting of female students. Good grades made her a favorite of her teachers and her charming personality won over her peers.

In her sophomore year, she began dating the captain of the rowing team. She fell in love for what she believed would be the first and last time in her life.

Noah Winters swept her off her feet and they talked often of their future together. They planned to marry when she finished her degree.

Six months after his graduation, Noah was killed in a plane crash. Three days after his funeral, Camille discovered she was pregnant.

Noah's family refused to speak to her and her own parents were so scandalized that they cut her off without a penny.

When college administration discovered she was pregnant, she was forced to leave school just four credits shy of her business degree even though her final semester was paid in advance.

She moved into a halfway house for unwed mothers on the outskirts of Philadelphia. Sunk in deep depression, Camille was unable to care for herself or her newborn child. The nun who ran the home stepped in to help.

Slowly, Sister Dana got her back on her feet and Hudson's mother tried to take back her life. She was hired as a secretary at a local accounting firm and the kindly nun watched him during the day.

When he was six, his mother's married boss raped her in his well-appointed conference room and threatened to accuse her of embezzlement if she reported her attack.

Camille became pregnant again, this time with twins. She was fired from her job when she confronted her rapist with what he'd done. He looked at her smugly and told her she was a woman known to have loose morals with one child out of wedlock and no one would ever believe her.

Once again, intense sadness overtook her, though Sister Dana did everything possible to help. When his brother and sister were born, it was Hudson and the elderly nun who cared for them.

Cami slept all the time and rarely remembered to eat or shower.

A group of churchwomen petitioned to have the halfway house shut down when the twins were less than a year old. The outraged women claimed that the home was morally bankrupt and encouraged promiscuous behavior. The city council agreed.

Hudson discovered many years later that the primary force behind the closure of the home was the wife of the man who had raped his mother. Camille was depicted as a whore by her rapist – a man who took everything from her using his reputation as an upstanding member of the community.

Dana moved them into a small home where Hudson shared a room with his siblings so he could tend to them during the night. The older woman slept on the sofa in the tiny living room. Without the stipend from the church, they were barely able to keep the power on and food on the table.

Hudson worked odd jobs to make ends meet and swore there would come a day when the people he cared about wouldn't have to worry.

Driven to succeed, he bought his first property with money saved from one of the two full-time jobs he held in college. By the time he walked away with his MBA, he owned two businesses firmly in the black and his first residential property.

He took care of Dana until her death and busted his ass to get his mother back. The corporate powerhouse he became was due to the bad hands Camille had been dealt in her life.

When he was thirty and putting his siblings through college, he tracked down their biological father. A bit of digging revealed that his mother had been neither his first victim nor his last.

Paying a personal visit to the man, Hudson explained who he was. Camille's rapist began to sputter and accuse her of lewd behavior that *drove him* to do what he did.

In silence, he listened to how his lovely, fragile mother had *asked* for her rape.

After his prey pissed himself in fear, Hudson carefully outlined how he planned to destroy him.

He left the office without once raising his voice.

Inside one year, he ruined the piece of shit financially and professionally. The day the creditors took his house, James Polton killed himself in his garage.

Hudson never said a word to his mother or the twins and he never lost one minute of sleep.

As for her parents and his father's parents, he sent them photos of a still-stunning Camille as well as newspaper clippings of his successes. He especially loved sending photos of them on vacation in exotic locations. It gave him intense satisfaction to imagine them regretting the way they'd tossed their family away.

The fact that he was the *spitting image* of his father was icing on the cake.

Several years after he bought his residential tower, Lola forwarded a letter from his paternal biological grandfather. In it, he apologized for their actions and requested an appointment to discuss Hudson's future within the family.

He'd written back a simple note that read:

It is without regret that I must decline.

The building that would now officially become the headquarters for Winters Enterprises sat in such a position to his grandfather's building that it would be a constant reminder of their choices.

Brie was right. It was bigger, better, and more architecturally imposing.

A flex of their bastard grandson's financial muscle that couldn't be ignored.

Chapter Twenty-Two

Knowing Hudson would be traveling the day after her visit gave Brie time to start a sketch she'd been itching to work on since he'd told her his reason for wanting the property. She'd switched schedules with one of the other girls to have the morning off.

Setting up her travel easel in the courtyard in front of the building that meant so much to him, she took several photographs to refer to later.

She stayed out of the way of traffic that came and went, smiling at the people who stared at her large sketchbook in surprise until she dropped into the movements and forgot where she was.

"Brie?"

Startled to hear her name, she turned and met the bright smile of Hudson's personal assistant. In the natural light, she realized that hair she thought was brown was a deep red. She stood a few feet in front of her easel and as she walked around, her gray eyes grew huge.

"That…is superb." She looked between Brie and the sketch several times. "You're incredibly talented. Did Hudson commission this?"

"No!" She almost shouted and blushed in embarrassment. "Please don't tell him about it. If he gets the building, it'll be a surprise. If the deal somehow falls through, I don't want him to know I was here."

Lola stared at her for a long time. "You're very good for him."

Shaking her head, she smiled. "Not like that. There's only one person who will ever be good for him at the level he needs in his life. I hope to see that connection."

The silence drew out between them. "You mean Natalia?" She nodded. "You see what they have?"

"I think they're the only ones who don't."

The woman's tinkling laughter carried on the cool air. "I tried to convince Natalia of that many years ago. She responded by giving me three days of the most amazing sex I'd experienced in my life." She shrugged. "I didn't bring it up again. I was worried about falling in love with her myself."

"I imagine that's something I'll have to be cautious of myself with both of them."

"You're fascinating."

Brie laughed. "Not really. I'm actually pretty average."

"I guess…I've grown unaccustomed to people without an ulterior motive." She glanced at the sketch again. "He'll love this. It'll mean more than you can imagine. You're a gifted artist."

"I like to draw." She reached out to clear a small smudge. "My primary focus is web design and graphic art but…pencil to paper is something I never tire of experiencing."

At the base of the small tripod stand was Brie's backpack. Her usual sketchpad was visible. Pointing at it, Lola asked, "May I?"

"Sure. I just…do you mind if I work?"

Grinning, the woman shook her head and sat on a bench a few feet away to flip through sketches she created almost constantly. None of her drawings were award-winners.

It was a way to pass the time and relax.

Unsure how much time had passed, Lola reappeared at her side. "You have an incredibly dramatic flair, Brie. Have you ever considered doing work for the theater district?"

"No. Most of my clients are back in Washington."

"Hmm. We might have to change that. I'm going to get you some tickets to a local Off-Broadway theater owned by old friends of mine. Natalia and Hudson know them as well. I think they would love your work. Check the place out and tell me what you think. Will you?"

"I love the theater."

"Now. You need to pack up because the temperature is dropping. Do you have enough reference points to finish indoors? I can set you up in an office where Hudson won't discover you."

Chuckling, she replied, "That's not necessary. I'll finish it at home. It's getting colder."

"Let me take you to lunch and have my driver take you home." At her obvious surprise, Lola gave her a big smile.

"Hudson takes excellent care of the people he considers his, Brie. Though we've never had a romantic relationship, I feel closer to him than my own family. His rewards for my service and the perks of working for him are beyond compare."

"You earned it. Loyalty and unwavering support seem so rare these days."

As she slipped the book into a protective cover and snapped it into a leather case, Lola smiled. "Be prepared for his care. Even if you don't end up together, it won't stop. Not when you do things like this for no other reason than to be kind."

They went to lunch and Brie was thrilled to hear her observations about New York over the forty years she'd lived and worked there. She knew fascinating behind-the-scenes information about landmarks, restaurants, and tourist attractions that couldn't be found in any book.

After securing her promise to come back soon, she closed Brie inside her Mercedes and waved as the driver carried her across town to the brownstone she loved.

Chapter Twenty-Three

Hudson stared through the window of his office. For once, he didn't focus on the view. Everything inside him was tense but satisfied. He'd acquired a piece of his fortune he chased for most of his adult life.

Lola had hugged him tight when he stepped off the elevator and said simply, "Mine."

She and the analysts were the only other inhabitants of his floor.

He'd allowed the quiet, studious types who focused all their energy on research to share space with him but they would be receiving a much bigger area in which to work now. It was their job to find him unexplored places to invest his money and grow it. If they came to him with an acquisition and he ultimately purchased it, they received a substantial bonus.

It had been his assistant's idea to hire people for such positions.

"There are so many moving parts, Hudson. Charities, struggling businesses, new entrepreneurs, and you'll never find all of them on your own. Give them parameters and you can pick and choose from what they find."

It was one of the smartest business decisions he'd ever enacted.

Inquiries for financial assistance were never answered. Instead, they went into a file and the validity of every claim was investigated. The process weeded out the "get rich quick" types from those willing to work their ass off to make their dream a reality.

The confidentiality agreements kept his name out of the press. If the world at large knew he jumpstarted artists, musicians, and wholesale paid for college degrees all over the country, he'd be flooded with far more requests than his staff could handle.

The floors below were filled with accountants, lawyers, marketing, human resources, and general administration. His staff rarely saw him personally and he was never "available" to outside visitors unless they had an appointment set by Lola herself or they were on his all-access list.

Building security knew Natalia by sight and company employees knew better than to question her presence in his life. She often stopped by simply to visit or take him to lunch.

There were times when he traveled that he would return to find a random gift on his desk. Over the years, she'd left him cufflinks, theater tickets, and small pieces of art. He reciprocated with jewelry, days at the spa, and orgasms.

The thought made him smile.

At a low whistle behind him, Hudson turned to see her looking chic in a gray pantsuit as she leaned against his doorframe.

"Natalia."

Her smile was gentle. "You were deep in thought. I didn't want to startle you." She set her purse on the chair across from his desk, shrugged her jacket from her shoulders, and walked around to stand beside him. She moved smoothly, confidently in charcoal gray suede high heels.

The silk shell top showed the tone and alabaster perfection of her skin but couldn't match the healthy shine of her hair. The slacks hugged her lean lines.

"You look lovely."

"Thank you."

"The building is mine."

Her electric blue eyes lit up. "Outstanding! I know you must be thrilled." He nodded and a small frown appeared between her eyes. "What's wrong?"

She laid her hand on his cheek, stroking back into his hair. The sensation of her short black nails on his scalp was soothing. "You look jumbled up. Tell me, darling."

Refusing to question what he needed, his hand lifted to circle her slender wrist and he pulled her into his lap. It was comforting to have her there and his arms wrapped around her waist.

The way her hands traced his shoulders, up his neck, to wrap around him was bliss. He felt calmer already, steadier holding her close as he soaked up the ease of being with her for several minutes.

Her cheek rested against his hair. Hudson breathed deeply of her body and a delicate perfume he'd had made for her when she turned thirty. It was the only one she wore.

"I kissed Gabriella."

She chuckled and hugged him against her. "She's magical. Does the experience have you anxious?"

"Something is wrong with me." She stiffened sharply and he pushed her back so he could see her face. Pure *terror* was written on her features. "Not *physically*. I'm sorry. I'm healthy as a horse."

She exhaled roughly and he hugged her to him, shocked at the way she trembled. "Natalia…"

"I'm sorry. I thought…I can't imagine day after day endlessly without your presence to remind me that I actually exist."

His arms tensed around her, holding her hard enough to bruise the skin of her back. Moving her lower, he held her head against his shoulder so he could stroke her hair and she could listen to his heart beating strongly in his chest.

Her palm rested along the side of his neck.

They sat like that, in silence, as he considered her words. Suddenly, his own worry seemed less. Her focus didn't waver.

Finally, she inhaled slowly and deeply several times before sitting up to look in his eyes. "What do you mean something's wrong? Try not to give me a heart attack this time."

He smoothed her hair away from her cheek and thought about withholding what he considered a weakness but knew he couldn't. She was his closest friend and the only person who would understand.

"You and I were together just three days ago. The relief isn't lasting as long as it once did. I become… tense more quickly. I *need* all the fucking *time* and it distracts me."

"Sexually, you mean?" He nodded. "It wasn't so bad before?" Closing his eyes, he shook his head slowly. "You think this makes you abnormal or something?"

Hudson grimaced painfully.

"You think there's something wrong with you because you need sex more often?"

"I can't *concentrate*. That isn't normal."

She grinned. "Name one thing about either of us that's *normal*, Hudson." He gave her a sharp chuckle and she held his face in her palms. "You have a lot of weight on your shoulders. Your daily life is hectic and millions of dollars move in and out of your businesses in minutes. I can't imagine the pressure you must be under all the time."

With a shrug, he responded, "I've always been busy. Stress doesn't factor into it."

"You've never had much time to enjoy your success. Maybe that's the problem. You work seven days a week. You travel all the time but not for pleasure. Even on supposed vacation, you work almost constantly." She gave him a delicate shrug of her own. "If you can't enjoy it, what's the point?"

"You think…I need to slow down?"

"I think you need to ask yourself why you're still pushing so damn hard." Slipping her hands along his jaw, she kissed him gently.

"You've beaten every statistic, laid waste to every preconceived notion of who you would become. You're powerful, the master of your world, Hudson. I'm so proud of everything you've accomplished. I'm so proud of *you*, of the man you are."

Exhaling roughly, unable to tell her how deeply the words affected him, he ran his fingers through her silken hair. "You're a magnificent woman, Natalia. Thank you."

The moment hung between them, heavy with importance neither of them knew how to translate. She returned her head to his shoulder and he held her, rubbing her back.

"I feel the same urgency." His hand stilled but he said nothing. "You aren't alone in feeling that it's never enough. I didn't want to tell you. I didn't want to remind you of those needy women whose hands must be held at all times."

"I would never think that."

There was a long pause before she said softly. "I dream about Brie. She's so *warm*, Hudson." Sitting up, she gazed into his eyes. "I feel as if she could thaw the ice around us."

Her hand lifted to trace his lips. "She's so unlike the women I've been with in the past. Vibrant and kind, unaware of her allure and uncomfortable in her own skin. She draws me."

He watched her breathe deeply.

"I want to kiss her, too."

Chapter Twenty-Four

The admission was not an easy one.

Natalia moved her arm around Hudson's shoulders and played with the hair at the nape of his neck. For a moment, she was preoccupied by the softness that was always so unexpected on a man the world viewed as anything *but* soft.

His eyes watched her closely. "There's something about her."

"Yes. I listen to stories from Riya and Tawny, even their men find her fascinating. Brie is *radiant*, Hudson. In a way I've never been, a way I wouldn't know *how* to be." She shrugged. "It makes me want to be with her, soak her up."

"I'm glad you share the attraction."

"Does it bother you that I want her?"

"It makes me hard."

It felt as though her smile came from her sternum. "You're always hard. I like that about you." He laughed and her fingertips touched the dimples that rarely showed themselves.

"I'm greedy, Natalia."

"You're human, darling. If you need more sex, you'll *get* more sex. That's *not* a hardship…for either of us. I need more as well. I'm willing as I've *always* been willing."

Hudson's hand tightened on her, another coming up to palm her skull, and he took her mouth destructively. Only when her heart was pounding and her breath coming in rapid pants did he break the kiss.

She watched her friend, wondering for the hundredth time why women didn't throw themselves at him. He was such a good-looking man. His good looks were ramped up even higher with the aggressive sexuality that blazed from him.

Sweet anticipation…

His black eyes lowered to take in the flush over her chest before returning to stare at her. He stroked over her hip through her slacks.

"Lock the door. Undress. Everything. Even the shoes."

Without a word, she stood and moved to close and lock the door to his office. She turned and began removing her clothing piece by piece. She laid each item over the couch in his sitting area.

She was careful not to rush. Hudson enjoyed watching her slowly reveal herself to him.

He sat in his chair with his chin between his thumb and forefinger. He traced back and forth over his lower lip and she felt the overwhelming desire to kiss him again.

When she was fully naked, she stood with her shoulders back and waited for his instruction.

"Come here."

In her bare feet, she walked to him. As she came around the side of his desk, he stood and pushed the few papers aside before simply staring down at her.

Natalia was unaccustomed to being barefoot with him. She felt smaller, more vulnerable. Her heart rate sped up and he noticed.

Hudson rarely missed anything.

Large hands wrapped around her waist and lifted her to the desk surface. The glass over the wood was cool on her ass. She'd be thankful for it by the time he was done.

As he poised to move, she said, "Kiss me first."

161

The whispered words were out of her mouth before she knew she intended to say them. They were both surprised at the request.

"You never ask me for *anything*. Why have I never noticed?"

It wasn't a question she knew the answer to so she remained silent.

He nudged her knees apart and stepped between her legs, cupping her face. His hands were huge, strong, and she'd always loved the way they felt on her body. The warmth of his palms as he cupped her face felt as though it sank to the core of her.

For almost a minute, he stayed like that, his deep black eyes sparking with something she didn't recognize and she didn't know why.

She knew everything about him.

Then he dropped his mouth over hers. The kiss was hot, wet, and tinged with a hint of his natural aggression. It made her heart race and a small moan escaped her. She thought he was breaking it when he changed his mind and kissed her again.

Against her lips, he murmured, "Your *mouth*, Natalia."

Another kiss, far more devastating to her sense of balance than the others. Her fingers curled into his shoulders and she wanted him to crawl inside her body with her. The ache in her nipples was intense and her clit pulsed in need.

Pulling back, he stared into her eyes. Raking his fingertips roughly through her hair, he said, "I forget your hair is naturally blond. I haven't seen it in years."

He could probably hear the pounding of her heart, it was so loud. The words reminded her of so many things between them.

"Hudson?"

"Yes?"

"I…" Her mind went sideways and the thought that floated to the surface for a single instant drifted away. She raked her hands down his chest and the crisp dress shirt was warm from the heat of his body.

Their eyes locked.

She wanted to be certain that this man never doubted himself again when she could ease his mind.

"If you ever find yourself unsure again, ever feel distracted by what you need, call me. We can figure it out together." With one more kiss to his jaw, she whispered, "I'm yours to command."

His hand stroked from her face, down her neck, to the center of her chest. Supporting her, he ordered, "Lie back."

The directive surprised her but she schooled her expression and lowered to the surface of his desk. His hand splayed over her torso as he lifted her leg behind the knee and placed her heel on the edge. He repeated the position with her other leg.

"Keep your heels there."

He tugged her forward until her ass touched the back of her ankles. Slight pressure on the inside of each leg pushed them wide. She was fully open to him, visible to him, ready for him.

"Breathtaking." He rubbed the flat of his hand over her mound and she worried for her control. "Are you alright?"

Thankful for yoga for making such a spread position possible, she nodded. Lightly slapping her mound, he stepped back and walked around his desk to take her in from another angle.

She may have imagined the growl but she did not imagine the way his fingers plumped her breasts from above her head.

"Stay like that."

Returning behind his desk, he sat in his chair. Natalia heard him pick up the phone and smiled. If having her on display while he worked settled his thoughts, she could stay in this position all day.

A few seconds later, she listened while he finalized a joint venture with Spencer Bishop the Third for charity.

The young billionaire had recently married and his new wife used a hefty portion of his fortune to fund cancer research. Shania had been very close to her mother and lost her to pancreatic cancer.

The Bishops were one of those adorable couples she liked to watch sometimes, but didn't understand in the slightest.

Happy, in love, with stars in their eyes.

They were stunningly attractive, even more so in person, and carried a powerful presence despite the fact that Spencer was barely five-seven and Shania was a tiny five-three.

Philanthropy was a driving force in their marriage and their energy levels were to be envied.

The large messenger bag she carried everywhere gave her a reputation for eccentricity but Natalia found her charming.

At a women's luncheon she'd been invited to by Mrs. Bishop, she'd glanced down, and gasped at the quick sketch the young woman had done of her.

Carefully removing the piece of paper from the sketchpad she traveled everywhere with, she'd handed it to Natalia with a gentle smile.

"I don't know what you were thinking about but it made you even lovelier than usual. You have such lovely bone structure."

The sketch had Shania Murphy-Bishop's tiny signature at the bottom with the words, "Keep thinking beautiful thoughts."

It was framed in her office at *Trois*. Hudson asked about it sometimes but she would just shake her head. How could she explain that she'd been thinking of the first time he kissed her?

Hudson brought her back to the moment when his hand stroked over her stomach and down to the bare folds of her pussy. It took all her control to hold back the moan.

Nothing was able to stop her full-body tremor.

He never paused in his conversation. "I agree. Put me down for another quarter million. I like her involvement with the foundation, Bishop. Bright woman."

Two fingers raked between her lips and the muscles in her thighs flexed against her will.

"I'll call him. The rich bastard needs to open his wallet and we have a deal on the table. You'll hear from him." He circled the entrance of her pussy, gathering moisture to slick over her clit. "I'll be there and bring Natalia as well. Regards to Mrs. Bishop."

The call disconnected but Hudson still didn't speak. A moment later, she heard him demand to speak to Harper Delkin.

With a small gasp, she held in her laugh. His reason for having her like this was immediately clear.

Both alpha males, the two men could have been brothers. The way they looked, their powerful personalities, and the same intolerance for bullshit were just a few markers they shared.

Hudson had engaged in a long weekend with Harper's younger sister years prior and Harper had been trying to even the score with Natalia ever since.

Though *he* wouldn't know that her pussy was being viewed and played with by his friendly rival, *Hudson* would know and that was what mattered. She found their feuds very entertaining and beneficial.

Her best friend leaned forward and dragged his tongue over her. She pressed her hand to her mouth to hold back the sounds her body wanted to make. Realizing she'd moved without permission, she returned it to the desk and willed her body to calm.

"Delkin. Spoke with Bishop. I don't *care*. Put up a hundred." Hudson listened for almost a minute and spent the time licking her pussy lazily. His palm stroked her inner thigh as if to soothe her.

"We're about to sign the contract for the hotel chain. Are you fucking kidding me? You stand to make millions on that deal."

As the other man's voice got loud enough for her to hear through the handset, Hudson's mouth returned to sucking and licking her.

Natalia was so turned on that she was struggling to hold back her climax. He fucked into her body with his tongue then nibbled her outer lips with his teeth. Two fingers drove deep as he resumed his conversation. There was no change in the tone or volume of his voice.

"Don't be a stingy fuck. Call Bishop and make the additional donation. You know he'll make every dollar we contribute quadruple inside three months or less."

He turned his hand and curled his fingers upward to hit the oh-so-sensitive spot behind her clit as he sucked the little bundle of nerves between his lips.

Natalia lost control of her orgasm.

Hudson stroked her through it and planted open-mouthed kisses all over her without making a sound. Only when her tremors eased did he pull back.

"Bishop has his hands in just about every industry in New York. The cause is a good one. I'll see you in Houston to sign the contracts after the first of the year. Hmm. I'll certainly let her know."

He disconnected and rested his head in his hand, his elbow propped on the desk between her legs. "Delkin said to tell you hello and that he looks forward to seeing you at the Valentine's gala."

Planting a sucking kiss on her clit, he added, "Too bad he won't see you like *this*." He winked at her. "You look so fucking gorgeous splayed out for me to feast."

No way was she able to respond.

Casually petting her, he added, "I love your pussy, Natalia. It's always so hot and slick. I'd have to say it's my favorite snack."

She went up on her elbows and stared at him down the length of her body. He usually made her wait for her pleasure a long time and he looked ready to go back to eating her.

He was in a strange mood and getting her pleasure first had her feeling shaky on the inside. Sitting up fully, she took his face in her hands and kissed her essence off his lips.

"I was supposed to make *you* feel better, not the other way around."

Chapter Twenty-Five

Suddenly Natalia was scooped off the desk and straddled his lap. Hudson's mouth ate at hers with his fingers fisted in her hair.

His cock was hot and hard beneath his slacks and she knew she was getting the expensive fabric wet with the fluids that eased from her pussy. Uncaring, knowing he always had another suit in his office, she ground herself against him, and he snarled.

Hot palms gripped her ass cheeks, separating them and squeezing as he worked her on his length. The stimulation to the little pucker made her hot all over.

She wanted him everywhere instantly and didn't mind begging. Shaking fingers loosened his tie and worked at the buttons of his shirt. She needed his skin against her.

He murmured, "You make me feel better by *breathing*."

One skip and her heart resumed. Putting that in a little box and locking it tight, she returned to kissing him, pulling the sides of his shirt from his pants.

He was iron-hard and she gyrated her hips up then down the length. His grip on her tightened.

Leaning back, he told her, "Raise yourself up." With her knees on the leather along his thighs, she did.

"Gorgeous nipples."

He sucked them *hard* and she slid her hands under the material of his shirt to use his shoulders for balance. The pleasure was exquisite. Moving to the other peak, she moaned as he repeated the attention.

Her eyes closed.

"Look at me." It was an unusual request since submission typically required she keep her gaze lowered. "Look at me, Natalia."

Their eyes met and she thought she could have fallen into the deep pools of black. One of his hands slipped between her legs and he stroked inside her, coating his fingers with her come.

His thumb worked over her clit and she wasn't sure how long she could hold herself up.

"Pinch your nipples." Breathing too fast, her hands settled around the modest mounds and her fingers worked the pebbled tips roughly. "I'm glad you never fucked with your perfect breasts."

Only *he* had ever thought them perfect. He saw her insecurity and smiled. "I could lick and suck them for hours."

She told him quietly, "You *have*."

"Because they're exactly right and so fucking sensitive."

Blinking rapidly against ridiculous tears, she leaned down to kiss him. Then she pulled back and stared into the raging hunger he had for her.

"Take out my cock."

Bending, she reached between them and unbuckled his belt, loosened the button, and lowered the zipper carefully. Her fingertips brushed the tip and he hissed through his teeth. Natalia pulled him free of the boxer briefs and held the throbbing shaft in her hands. Her thumb slicked over the head, spreading the pearl of pre-cum she found there.

"Put me in your pussy."

Lifting slightly, she positioned him at the soaked entrance and lowered until she'd taken him halfway. At that point, he held her still.

"Brace yourself." She had enough time to inhale as he adjusted his hold on her hips and slammed up into her body so hard she whimpered. One hand held his hair, the other gripped the leather back of the chair.

He powered into her pussy and she didn't know she was moaning his name softly until his mouth stopped the sound.

Hudson stood and took her with him. Her upper back met the cool leather of his couch. With his elbows holding her knees, her back on the seat, he pushed them to her chest and gripped her shoulders in his palms. Half of her body was suspended while he fucked her harder than he ever had before.

"More…"

"Natalia…"

Before he could speak, worry for her, she met his eyes and nodded. He continued to pound her into the cushion and she zoned out, taking in every nuance of this experience with him.

Sweat beaded the skin of his forehead. His eyes were focused on watching his cock disappear inside her. His mouth was set in a firm line as his nostrils flared with every breath.

The tap of his dick deeper than any man had ever gone with each stroke echoed throughout her body and she felt the climax building too fast to stop it. She tightened around him.

He groaned, "Fuck, that's it. Show me I'm not just *hurting* you."

Natalia didn't think he intended to speak aloud. Then she was coming and thought was beyond her ability.

Hudson didn't stop, didn't slow, just powered harder and faster into a pussy that needed what only *he* had ever been able to give her.

The first climax quickly built into a second. "Cream all over my dick and then I'll fill you up."

She was shaking, moaning, and gripping his forearms for an anchor that had never let her down. As the wave of pleasure rolled through her body, he slammed balls-deep and went still. Hot semen left the head of his cock with astonishing force.

"Yes, Hudson, *yes.*"

A thought drifted through her satiated brain that she had only ever allowed Hudson to take her bare. The belief in her he showed by *taking* her bare made her heart ache.

Hudson's wealth was unbelievable and highly coveted. Women had tried to trap him before.

If she were ever to become pregnant…

She slammed her mind shut against the thought and focused on holding tight to the total body happiness her best friend caused.

When the last of his come spurted inside her, he exhaled roughly and gathered her in his arms. He collapsed on the couch, palming the back of her skull and holding her to his chest.

She straddled him, his heart pounding beneath her ear. Only when she was confident she could move, Natalia sat up and lifted her body from his, slipping to the floor between his feet.

Assuming the submissive posture with her ass on her heels that drove him crazy, she waited. Their combined fluids dripped to the carpet beneath her.

"Suck my cock."

The command made her body hum in response. It was what she'd hoped for and she wasted no time in rising and taking his half-hard dick in her mouth. She was able to take him to the root and she sucked their combined slickness from him.

"You like the way we taste."

It wasn't a question but she moaned around him anyway. She was too busy enjoying the salty-sweetness they created together.

"I love the taste of your pussy. Watching you suck me after fucking you so hard is unbelievable."

For good measure, she held his cock in her fist and sucked each of his balls. There was no doubt he would be ready again quickly.

Hudson wasn't abnormal in his appetites but he produced more semen than any man she'd ever known. Part of her wondered if that might be linked to his alpha personality and then she didn't care because he rocked his hips, fucking between her lips.

"I like seeing your lips around me. Seeing them stretch to take me. Watching you enjoy something so many women hate." He was hardening again and he paused as the head touched the back of her throat. "Your mouth is a fucking furnace. It feels amazing."

He stopped with a small grunt and pulled back. She released him with a soft sucking sound and a small frown.

"Stand."

She stood up and waited naked in front of him. Her toes curled into the carpet and he tugged her between his knees.

A taut pink nipple was sucked firmly to the roof of his mouth and her hands drifted through his hair. He pulled back and stared at her face as he placed his palm on her mound.

"I want to know our come is dripping from you when I take you to lunch. I want it to soak your panties. To remind you."

"I could never forget time with you."

Pushing two fingers inside her, he gathered their come and smeared it over her clit and through her folds. When he sucked his fingers, her breath caught.

"I see why you like it."

"You make me crazy."

He winked and the dimpled grin he gave her reminded her of the boy she'd met so long ago.

"Get dressed and let's have lunch." He stood and kissed her cheeks, forehead, nose, and finally her lips. "I feel better. I'm fucking grateful for you, Natalia. Every single goddamn day."

The vague thought drifted over her brain again but was gone instantly.

Instead of trying to catch it, she smiled. "I'm fucking grateful for you. Especially when you give me mad orgasms then feed me. I want a steak. A big one, and wine." As she moved to go around him, she added shamelessly, "Then you can fuck my brains out again."

He slapped her naked ass sharply and she moaned. He grabbed her by the waist to hold her still. From behind, he slicked his fingers inside her pussy and smoothed the moisture back to the pucker of her ass. His other hand squeezed her breasts before trailing down her stomach and working over her clit.

Fingers deep in both entrances, he fucked her and whispered at her ear, "I'm going to bury your vibrator in your pussy before I take your ass. I want to make you scream."

"Always. You always do, Hudson."

He devoured her mouth, matching the rhythm of his tongue to his fingers inside her. He made her wait a long time before giving her permission to come. The intensity, the location, the fact that he was still dressed combined to push her over the edge with a painful gasp.

There was no way to miss the hunger in his eyes and she hoped she'd always have a place in this man's life. No one had cared so much, done so much for her in all her life.

In his bathroom, he changed his suit after they cleaned up and he slapped her ass again as she turned to dress. "Later, I'll take all the licks you want to give me. Every single one, darling"

"Dress or we won't be *having* lunch, Natalia."

Laughing, she went and did exactly as he bid. Lunch extended to a bit of shopping for wines and then a light dinner several hours later.

When he suspended her and striped the back of her body hot, she didn't think the day could get any better. Then he fucked her exactly as he promised he would and proved her wrong.

Natalia didn't mind.

Chapter Twenty-Six

Gabriella was expected to return home for Thanksgiving.

When she calmly explained, once again, that employees who'd been working at her job for years had scheduled the time off months in advance, her mother hung up on her.

Things had been tense between them for weeks and only their phone calls in the last few days had started to be civil again.

Brie thought her sister might have had something to do with that.

The next evening, she opened the front door of her building to find her parents and Izzy standing in the downstairs foyer with Camille. She was shocked as the three of them surrounded her.

"If our girl can't come to *us* for Thanksgiving, we come to *her.*"

Knowing they'd given up annual plans with dozens of extended family and friends just to see her, inspired tears. "Thank you. It means so much that you came."

Her family spent three days sightseeing while Brie was at work. When she arrived home in the evenings, her mother and father *smothered* her with attention.

They made enough food to fill her freezer, bought enough dry goods to fill her pantry, found gadgets for her apartment that she didn't need, and generally staged a full invasion of her usually peaceful space.

She and Izzy slept in the living room and her parents slept in her bed at her insistence. It reminded her of when they were very small before her parents bought their first house.

Back then, every dime they made went back into the business and their girls were raised to understand what had to take priority.

The first night, Isabella looked weary, sad almost, but wouldn't tell her what was wrong. "I can't talk about it yet but when I'm ready, you're the one I need to tell." Giving her a soft smile, she added, "You look so pretty, Brie. As if just being here has given you a new lease on life."

"The beginning was horrible but it all worked out. You were right and I promise to listen with more logic than emotion in the future."

"I'm so sorry about everything. I wish I'd been *wrong*." Her fingers reached out to push wayward curls behind her ear. "Don't try to change your heart. It's what makes you wonderful. I wish I could be less logical sometimes. My brain makes choices that my spirit pays for when it's too late."

Brie opened her mouth to speak and Izzy shook her head. "Not yet, little sister. I'm not ready just yet."

"Alright. I love you. I'll wait."

Not long after, she watched as her older sister fell asleep. Her heart clenched in pain when silent tears slipped from beneath her lids.

Isabella was one of the strongest people she'd ever known. Whatever was weighing on her mind was hurting her intensely.

She would give her the time she needed. It wouldn't be easy.

* * *

Gabriella loved her family deeply but after days of having them in her home, she felt awkward and irritable. Irritability did not sit well on her and she needed to walk.

Leaving their parents at the apartment, the sisters headed out together and Brie took her sister to her favorite coffee shop near the building where she worked.

"This is a long ass walk for coffee, Brie. Damn."

With a laugh, she let Izzy find them a table and went to place their order, adding muffins since they were the exercise fanatic's weakness.

Izzy grinned over the edge of the cup. "I can't believe you got me a banana nut, you evil bitch."

"You're welcome. You can obsess over the caloric content later."

Strangely, she shook her head. "I don't have to do that anymore." Pasting a smile on her face, she added, "Hang in there. It's almost over and then they'll be back on the other side of the country."

"I feel, I don't know, like I can't do anything right."

"That's your insecurity talking. You do so *many* things right, Brie. Take a deep breath and stop expecting them to change. They're old and set in their ways. Just be you and they'll either learn to deal or they won't."

Brie's eyes went huge. "But…"

"You wouldn't be the first child to put distance in place with overwhelming parents." Isabella sipped her coffee and waited for Brie to make connections she probably should have made a long time ago.

She stared at her sister as if seeing her for the first time. "You don't care, do you? How they are?"

"No, I don't. I knew when I was fourteen that I'd likely never see my inheritance. Their idea of morality is *far* different from mine." Glancing out at the pedestrians bundled for rapidly cooling weather, she shrugged. "I knew for so long that when it came time to make choices, I chose the ones I thought were best for me."

"What do you mean?"

"I mean, I'm not perfect but I live the life I want. I make no apologies for that. You shouldn't either."

"I want to be like that."

Leaning her arms on the table, she grinned. "You can. Stop giving them so much power. They're just people. No more, no less."

They took their time walking back and when they started up the steps of her brownstone, Izzy touched her arm to stop her.

"I'm really proud of how you handled a situation that probably would have crippled other people. You look great and I love the life you're making for yourself here."

She'd always looked up to her older sister. Her words meant more than she probably realized. "Thanks."

"Stop being a crybaby," Izzy said with a grin. "When they act crazy, just breathe through it, nod, and smile." She shrugged. "That's what I do. It's why they think I conform. I smile and then do whatever the fuck I want because *my* happiness relies on *my* choices, not theirs."

Their conversation stayed with her through the rest of her family's visit. It made her stronger.

The issue of her being robbed was brought up repeatedly and she'd simply tell them that the police were working on her case. No matter how many times they asked, her answer was always the same.

Naturally, *men* were a common theme since they now believed their youngest daughter was unable to distinguish the *good* ones from the *bad* ones without intervention.

Their mother started listing the *appropriate* men she knew who would be *perfect* for Brie. One family name caused her to glance up in surprise but she quickly hid it.

"The Delkin boys are wonderful. Hard working young men though their sister is a little wild. Poor dear lost her mother so that could explain it. The youngest boy – Harrison – doesn't seem *right* to me. I think he's living with a man. He might be one of *those*."

Bristling on principle, Brie prepared for a verbal battle of epic proportions. Rapidly working up her speech about equality, that Washington was pro-gay rights, and that her mother needed to step into the current world and throw down her pitchfork.

She was disappointed when Izzy smoothly changed the subject. Later, she said, "Pick your battles. Gay rights with our parents is not one you can win. It sucks but it's the truth. Live the life right for you, see them when you can, and keep the two worlds separate if possible."

As frustrated as her parents could make her, she still cried a little when she saw them off at the airport. They boarded their flight for Seattle a couple of hours before Izzy's left for Chicago.

"You need to lose weight, Gabriella. Your weight and your posture is why your back hurts, not the girls up front. Practice good posture and get some exercise. That will fix it all up."

Brie smiled and nodded but didn't reply. The words cut as they had when she was eight, fourteen, and twenty…but not as deep, because her sister was right.

They were never going to change. If she wanted change, it had to come from herself.

As the elder Hernandez's walked into the line for security, Izzy bumped her shoulder. "Better, right?"

"Better. Much better."

They had lunch and made plans for Izzy to visit again alone. Only when her sister disappeared from view did Brie walk back outside and hail a cab.

By the time she turned onto the street where she lived, she was smiling again. She'd survived her first visit with her parents despite lectures about money, men, how naïve she was, her weight, and why she was working as a maid.

She was stronger than when she'd left Washington three months before, and the next time she saw them, she'd be stronger still.

Chapter Twenty-Seven

Over the next month, Brie's routine was calm and steady. She picked up a lot of extra shifts at the building, which increased her allowed time off. Since she'd started with two weeks of vacation, she was hoping to accrue at least three more to use as recovery time after her surgery.

She didn't hang out with her co-workers outside of work, but she was well-liked and openly considered one of the hardest working members of the staff.

The night she filled in at the concierge desk after Donald came down with food poisoning, she thought Hudson was going to have a coronary when he walked through the door.

Approaching the desk, his annoyance was obvious. "What are you doing here?"

"Working."

The poor man ground his teeth. "Brie."

"Yes, Hudson?"

"Why are you at the front desk?"

"Donald has food poisoning."

"Why didn't they find someone else?"

Brie leaned toward him and crossed her arms on top of the desk. "I was here, I volunteered, I've cross-trained on the position, and with the holidays almost here, everyone is already overwhelmed."

"I don't like you behind the desk."

She blinked once before asking carefully, "Hudson, are you ashamed to be my friend if people know I work here?"

He reared back and came forward with a growl. "I'll spank your *ass*, Brie." Her face went hot. Staring at her, satisfied with her reaction, he explained, "We've had issues once or twice. I don't like you visible to the *street*. You're a woman and you're too fucking tempting."

"Chubby Mexican women are pretty common so the odds are in my favor. I should be fine." His eyes narrowed and he moved as if to come around the desk. "Don't get me fired from my job. I mean it."

Matching her position on the other side of the desk, they stared at each other for a long moment.

"You make me hard," he murmured.

Face blazing, she replied, "I've got it on good authority that you're always hard."

"Tawny?"

"Yup."

"No shame. One of her best traits."

"I think so, too." She grinned. "I really am fine, Hudson."

"Are you going home for Christmas with your family?"

The question surprised her and she shook her head. "Working and helping Riya. I had to promise my mother I'd go to Christmas morning Mass. The weather is too bad for travel."

"You'll be careful up here." It wasn't a question.

"I will. Thank you for your concern, Hudson."

"Selfishness on my part." Turning to go, he paused. "I get hard for power and fucking. Your curvy body and smart mouth inspire both." She gulped and he inclined his head. "Goodnight, Brie."

She wouldn't remember later if she responded since her entire body had gone on red alert at his words. Her heart pounded, her nipples pebbled, and her folds were instantly damp.

Only when he disappeared behind his elevator doors did she realize she was holding her breath.

* * *

Brie's first Christmas in New York was the first she'd ever spent by herself, but her friends kept her from feeling lonely.

She worked a ton of hours at the building in various departments and when she wasn't on the clock or sleeping, she was helping Riya with her Christmas Eve party.

Due to her schedule, Riya and Tawny insisted she have a sleepover the night before so they could take their time with last minute details and get ready together before the first guests arrived the following night.

Straight off a double shift, she helped Tawny assemble gift bags for each invitee. Around midnight, with most of the preparations ready to go, the redhead started encouraging Riya to relax and have a drink...or six.

They laughed their asses off as the brilliant doctor attempted to make sense of nonsensical things.

"I've never seen anyone get drunk so fast, or so thoroughly," Brie said in awe. Riya was standing beside the bed in the guest room, dancing to music that played low as she gave them a twenty-minute lecture on why ribbons were better than bows.

"It's all in the *presentation*." It took her four attempts to get the word out properly and she high-fived herself in celebration.

Tawny snickered. "I love this shit. Usually I record her ridiculousness and share it among our mutual friends. She's so fucking perfect all the time that I don't have a choice."

"That's just *mean*, clever, but mean."

The redhead shrugged. "It's all part of my charm."

When Riya started trying to do the Macarena – to a Christmas carol - Tawny went in the hall and whistled for the M's.

"She's toast. My work is done."

They appeared in sleep pants and t-shirts, a sight Brie considered an early Christmas present.

Micah's brow arched and he stared at the redhead. "Please tell me you didn't record her like this…*again*."

"Nah. Everyone is still laughing from the last time when I convinced her to try hula-hooping while intoxicated and she broke every bottle on your bar cart." She shook her head, looking disappointed in him. "You have to leave them wanting *more*, dude."

"I'm not even a little bit drunk. Not even a *little*," Riya told her husbands with her hands on her hips. She swayed like she was on a boat and Brie hid her smile behind her hand.

Max laughed as he scooped her up. "I know, love. You're *completely* sober. Still, I'd feel better if you let me carry you so you don't fall down the stairs."

A pout appeared on her face. "I can *walk*, Max. I wouldn't fall *down* the stairs because I'd be going *up* them."

"Then I won't point out the fact that you're quite adept at falling *up* the stairs as well." Max winked at his wife's friends and left with Riya in his arms.

They heard her mumble, "It was just that one, two times."

Micah watched them go with a shake of his head and grinned. "Can I get you ladies anything before I turn in?"

"We're all set. Give her the magic potion because we kept telling her she wasn't actually drinking." Tawny was not remotely ashamed.

"You're fucking diabolical." His tone of respect was obvious. "I hope you never turn completely to the dark side or we're fucked."

"Silly bitch won't let me take Satan's deal…and he keeps adding to the comp plan. It gets harder and harder to say no." The big man laughed and it lit up his honey eyes beautifully. Tawny shrugged. "It's why you *lo-o-o-ve* me, Micah. It's my job to remind her that she isn't *really* a fairy princess. Otherwise, she'd get a fat head. I take my job seriously."

"Understood. Stay out of trouble for a few hours. Goodnight, ladies." Chuckling, Micah followed the others upstairs.

The redhead went to the door to listen and after a minute, she nodded. "Coast is clear. I'm going for baby cheesecakes."

"Aren't those for the party?"

"I'm a party guest, here *very* early. Max made them special with eighty-percent cacao. *Mine.* Be Bonnie to my Clyde and let's get a couple of those destroyed. Almost everything is being catered but those are here *now.* They've been calling my name for hours."

They ended up with Patrón and cheesecakes on a tray between them on the bed. Brie admitted that the combination was delicious.

"I love the relationship you guys have. You remind me of my sister."

"She's totally awesome then, obviously." She popped a mini-cheesecake in her mouth and moaned happily. "You know, Riya was the only chick friend I had until you. I normally can't stand women. You're like Riya without the halo."

Brie couldn't help the laughter that bubbled up. "Uh, no. No halo."

Tawny grinned. "Things come easy to her. She's naturally *good* at shit. If she weren't such a great human, I would have punched her out when we were teenagers. Until her dissertation, Riya was so fucking sweet it could make your teeth hurt."

"I read a couple of her books and it was an education."

"Right? She has some dings in that halo now, I tell you what. I'm glad she took to you. You're a good fit. A halfway point between us."

"Thanks."

"Alright, I'm going to pull out all your deep dirty shit now. Time for some *Truth or Dare*."

The next couple of hours were spent acting like teenagers and Brie knew she'd never had so much fun with another person besides Izzy.

After a three-hour nap, they were up again, making pancakes.

The trio was awakened to the sounds of them singing *Here Comes the Sun* at top volume. Max and Micah appeared at the top of the stairs.

"Ladies," Micah said carefully. "Good morning. Is something the matter?" His voice was still scratchy from sleep.

Tawny blew them kisses. "Nope! Just want you to get a sample of what holiday mornings will be like when you have kids. Up, up, *up*! Lots of stuff to do today!"

Max mumbled, "She's *not* serious."

Behind them, Riya yawned. "Oh yeah, she is. Best to go with it or she'll get worse."

Brie laughed quietly as Tawny nodded somberly. "You can totally bank on that. She's a *doctor*. Come on! We made pancakes!" Then she dashed back to the kitchen.

Stopping in front of Brie, Riya took her shoulders. "She got to you."

"Sorry."

"Liar. You'll never be the same now."

"I know. We have coffee and mimosas."

"I smell the coffee. It's the only thing currently keeping her *alive*, Brie."

The five of them sat around the dining table and Brie felt warm on the inside as the threesome slowly woke up.

Riya announced that this was her first Christmas as a married woman and Tawny made fake gagging motions. Conversation was constant as they planned the day.

"I have a half shift this morning so I'll be back to help with last-minute stuff a few hours before the party. Do you need me to bring anything?" Brie steadily cleaned up their mess from breakfast.

Suddenly, Tawny was behind her, lips pressed to her ear as she whispered loudly. "Don't clean one more dish. I don't want to have to choke you out."

Without missing a beat, Brie replied, "Bring it, red."

"Fine. I'll go get the tarp and the baby oil." Then she slapped Brie's ass and went to shower.

Chapter Twenty-Eight

Christmas Eve day was perfect. By the time Brie finished her half-shift and returned to the penthouse, the light streaming through the floor-to-ceiling windows was truly dazzling.

Carols played through the rooms while they finished last minute preparations.

The caterers arrived at the same time as Zach and Quinn, and Tawny said she was going to get more wine from the cooler. Dragging her men behind her, they passed the wine and entered the gym.

Riya snickered and leaned up to kiss Micah soundly.

At Brie's questioning glance, she said, "She's been here for two days. She likes to make them insane."

"Are they married like you guys?"

"Nope. She tells them she's only using them for their bodies."

"She's really in love, huh?"

"Head over heels. They'll run her to ground eventually. She likes to be the badass in every relationship but with two of them, they might have a fighting fucking chance."

Micah winked. "Or not." He held a tray of candles while Riya placed them around the room. "If Tawny's involved, always place your money on her. She fights dirty."

Reaching up, Riya stroked his face. "That's one of the nicest things you've ever said about her. I love that you get that." She kissed him again and he made a funny face at Brie.

Max carried all the gift bags from the guest room and Brie helped him display them on the table just inside the foyer. When they were done, she put out several bowls of gourmet chocolate.

Riya came over and wrapped her arm around her waist. "Let's go get ready. I picked up the dresses yesterday." Over her shoulder, she screamed across the penthouse, "Bitch, we're getting ready! Remove all male parts from your body and hustle your ass!"

To Max and Micah, she whispered, "Check the gym when they come out. They accidentally left a condom in the half bath last time. How the three of them fit in that tiny fucking space, I have no idea."

Max leaned down and rubbed noses with his wife. "Already planned on it. Thank goodness we're all mature and in control of *our* impulses."

"Um, right. In control is *exactly* how I'd describe the three of us. You nailed it, babe."

From the other side of the room, Micah mumbled, "Nailed something but control was not fucking it."

Brie was laughing so hard she could barely walk up the stairs. Less than a minute after they entered Riya's gorgeous bedroom, Tawny came in at a full run.

"Skank. Your thong is over your sweater and above your jeans." Riya's hand was on her hip.

"At least I have them *on* which is more than I can say for you three hours into the Halloween party, slut."

"True that. Go shower so we can all get dressed. You smell like semen and bad decisions."

"My favorite perfume, bitch." Tawny skipped into the master bathroom and slammed the door.

Walking into a closet that was bigger than her bedroom at the brownstone, Riya emerged with three dresses covered in plastic.

Several weeks before, Riya had suggested they visit a seamstress.

Despite her embarrassment, the woman had put her immediately at ease. They'd struck up a conversation and the older woman said, "After you get your surgery, you bring this dress back to me and I'll alter it for you. It's going to be gorgeous on your figure."

The three cocktail dresses were the same fabric but varied colors and styles. All of them fell just above the knee. Tawny's was a gorgeous green that matched her eyes and Riya's was a delicate bronze that made her skin glow.

Brie's was custom-tailored for her odd shape and had substantial built-in support that her own bras usually failed to provide. The dark blue made it more obvious that her eyes were not black.

Now, Riya could barely contain her excitement. "You're going to love how it turned out. I'm so excited."

The finished product was almost unreal. When she realized her friend had splurged on shoes and silver jewelry for her to wear, Brie started crying.

"Get it out now. Once we do your makeup, I'll kick your ass if you start bawling." With that statement, Tawny stripped the towel off her body and walked naked across the room to step into her own dress. "Panties or...?"

"Don't make me cut you."

"Fine. Smother me with your *rules!*"

Riya zipped her up as Brie went in the bathroom. As much as she loved them, *she* could barely handle the sight of her own body naked. Allowing them to see her wasn't something she could do.

She'd brought the panties she had to order special to fit her ass and slipped them on before removing her upper body layers. That was the primary reason she loved winter. She never stood out in the winter.

She stepped out with her arms crossed beneath her breasts to hold up the bodice and Tawny zipped her up.

"You can let your girls go. Tonight, those babies get to breathe."

Dropping her arms, she stared at her reflection in the mirror. Riya straightened her straps while Tawny smoothed the skirt.

"You look fucking stunning, Brie."

She *felt* stunning and wondered why ordering *all* custom clothing had never occurred to her before. The gown accentuated her skin and narrow waist without making her ass look ridiculous.

Her breasts were still obviously too huge for her but they were at the right level due to the boned corset-style bodice and it made them appear less bulging.

They took her hair out of the big clip and it fell to the middle of her back. Tawny grabbed a lock and watched the tight curl spring back.

"I want to see what it looks like flat-ironed."

"Ha! Your arms will get tired *way* before you finish. *Next time.* We don't have time to fuck with my hair right now. I promise."

Grumbling, they settled for doing her makeup and a casual up-do with sparkling silver combs she never would have accomplished on her own. The sterling silver earrings resembled chain mail and were accompanied by a matching necklace, the lowest point dropping into her cleavage.

Based on the quality, she knew Riya had spent a fortune. Stepping into the matching high heels, she took in her reflection with a smile.

"Thank you both. So much."

"Merry Christmas, Brie. In a few days, you'll start your first official year in New York. I'm so glad you came here."

Blotting her eyes, Tawny said, "Fuck you, Riya. Just, fuck you with the sappy shit. *God!*"

She went in the bathroom to touch up her makeup while Brie gave Riya a hug. As she pulled back, she stared into the other woman's eyes. "I'm so glad I met you. Thanks, Riya. For so many things."

* * *

It seemed that everyone arrived around the same time. She discovered that many of the guests were staying in the temporary residences available on the building's lower floors.

The space quickly filled with talking, laughter, and eclectic music. The friends and family who arrived were very different from the people Brie knew growing up in her small town in Washington.

They were wonderful.

Tawny's mother and Riya's father arrived together. The older woman immediately made Brie feel welcome by asking her rapid-fire questions about where she grew up, her family, and her interests.

Maggie was lovely and loved to laugh, but it was her obvious acceptance of the young women's ménage relationships that blew Brie's mind.

Even Riya's father seemed somewhat okay with everything. Tawny told her things hadn't always been peaceful but it was getting better every day as Archer saw how much Max and Micah loved his daughter.

"That's something to remember, Brie. If your family wants you in their life badly enough, they'll accept you for who you *are*, not who they *want* you to be." She bumped their hips together. "You're pure awesome so anyone who doesn't think so can get fucked."

"You have such a gentle way about you, Tawny." She was unable to hide her grin.

"I know, right? I'm working on toning it down so I don't get a reputation as a sappy spreader of sunshine but I think it's too late."

Riya's father was a nice man with a booming voice. Archer shook her hand and held it between his two big ones. "My girls filled me in on what happened with your money. I'd be happy to look into things, maybe speed the process along for you."

"Thank you, Mr. O'Connell. The investigation is ongoing but I try not to think about it too much. It'll either get resolved or it won't but it won't affect my life from this point."

"Damn good attitude, young lady. If you change your mind, just let me know, and call me Archer. Mr. O'Connell makes me feel old and I'm convinced I'm still in my prime."

"Understood."

Food was consumed and alcohol flowed freely. When the deejay put the holiday music on hold and started playing dance hits, the open space along the windows became an impromptu dance floor.

Though she tried to decline the invitation several times, Riya's father insisted on dancing with her.

"It's not natural for young people not to dance. I danced all the time when I was your age."

All the dancing she'd ever done in her life was at family gatherings. Mexican celebrations were *filled* with music and dancing. She was ready to panic at the thought of dancing around other people.

"Sir, I've never danced with anyone who wasn't a relative. I'm self-conscious." She knew there were tears shimmering in her eyes. "I'm so embarrassed."

"Oh, honey. Let's talk to Maggie."

He led her to Tawny's mother and repeated her words. Tawny and Riya huddled close. Brie stared at the floor.

The older woman nudged her chin up with her fingertip. "You're a vibrant young woman. This is your *youth* and you deserve to enjoy yourself among friends, Brie. Everyone needs to have fun. Dancing brings joy whether you're good at it or not."

Stroking her knuckles along her cheek, she added in a whisper, "Archer will keep you safe, darling. You can count on him."

These are friends. They won't judge me.

Without another word, Archer led her out. The man had to be in his sixties but he was an excellent dancer. Blushing brightly, Brie soon found the rhythm and began to relax.

It wasn't that she didn't know *how* to dance; it was her fear of appearing comical with her large breasts and ass.

Archer led her around the floor, his smile brilliant as she began to allow herself to focus on the music. He kept up a steady stream of conversation and before she knew it, she forgot to wonder what other people would think of her.

As the song came to an end, Max tapped on Archer's shoulder and took Brie in his arms. She blushed brightly.

In his proper British accent, he told her, "When Riya first arrived, she believed that it was her clothing that made her attractive."

Her eyes went wide. "She's exquisite."

"Yes, that's what I said. It took a long time to convince her, Brie. I don't know what it is about being a woman that makes so many of you blind to your signature beauty but it saddens me as a man to see it. Just like Riya, you need convincing. I hope one day there's someone in your life who makes you *feel* it, so you'll finally *see* it."

"You're a poet, Max."

His smile made him even more gorgeous and she almost stumbled. "I've heard that a time or two."

As the song ended, he kissed the back of her hand before placing it in Zach's. Tawny's man grinned. "I'm a horrible, god-awful bad dancer, Brie and that puts me at a disadvantage with my girl. I swear to try not to step on your feet."

They laughed together and when there was a pause in the music, he exhaled roughly. "No accidents." At her laugh, he shook his head sadly. "I so wish I was kidding."

Quinn was the next to dance with her and he was rather good. "Did Zach tell you about the dance we went to in high school where he pulled down the entire conga line?" She bit her lower lip to keep from laughing. "True story. Another time, he tried to dip his date to mimic something he saw on television and gave the girl a concussion when she smacked her head into one of the tables."

"Oh lord…"

"My point is that he does it anyway, Brie. He's horrible at it, he has no rhythm whatsoever, but he gets out there when Tawny takes his hand because he loves her and wants to make her happy." He tilted his head. "You're an excellent dancer and a truly pretty woman inside and out. There's nothing that should keep you off the floor when music is playing. Alright?"

"Thank you, Quinn."

He twirled her and Micah stood waiting. Quinn kissed her cheek and said, "We waited to pull out the big guns on you." Then he walked to Tawny's side.

The tall man nodded at the deejay and she heard the first notes of a salsa. She immediately started to panic.

"I've been watching you, Brie. You damn well *know* how to dance so pull your distinctive bravery around you and show me."

Tugging her lower lip between her teeth, she gave him a nod.

"Good girl." Then he proceeded to make her exhibit every single move she'd ever learned. Around and around the floor, he spun her, forcing her to keep up because he knew she could.

On the last note, he twirled her and kissed her hand.

"You must never doubt yourself again. If you can keep up with me when I'm not taking it easy on you, you can keep up with anyone. Don't let insecurity hold you back from the life you're meant to live."

She inhaled deeply. "Thank you for simplifying it."

"It happens to be a particular skill of mine." He grinned and led her to her friends. "Someone has been keeping her mad dance skills a secret. Brie, don't you know we *always* need partners?"

"Thank you all for helping me feel less awkward." Horrified, she realized she was on the verge of tears.

Tawny shook her shoulders roughly. "I'll kick your hermit ass." She handed her a shot of Patrón. "Don't make me drink alone."

Brie took it gratefully, clinked glasses with the redhead, and drank it down. "I didn't know I could have fun…the way I am now."

"Fun is universal. We should have pushed you harder," Riya grinned. "You're an *amazing* dancer and you need to do it often. The more you do, the better you're going to feel."

Quirking her brow, Tawny added, "We go out, we dance, we drink, and we make *Riya* drink so we can record the chaos."

Laughter erased the last of her *almost* tears.

Chapter Twenty-Nine

Gabriella alternately danced and mingled with the other guests. The more she moved through the crowd, the more comfortable she was.

She was *thrilled* when she discovered a couple of Riya's dissertation subjects were among them.

Joshua was a few years younger than she was, and during *Beautiful Liar*, he pulled her out on the dance floor. He held her close and she thought the man was ripped like no one she'd ever touched.

In her heels, they were almost the same height. She was painfully aware of the fact that her breasts filled the few inches of space between them.

"I was Riya's third subject and we had a blast. My girl and I love the *hell* out of that woman. You know we both work for Max and Micah's companies, don't you?" Brie shook her head slowly. "It's great. We do what we can to provoke the M's around Riya. They should never forget how awesome she is."

As the song changed, he didn't let her go. "When we graduated, New York was our first choice. There's no place like it."

"I love it here, too."

He stared into her eyes and his smile was incredibly sexy. "Jess and I don't stand out so much here as we did in Texas."

"What do you mean? You're both gorgeous."

"We work hard and we play hard." He paused and his fingers smoothed over her waist. "You should hang out with my girl and me, Brie. We would show you an amazing time."

For a quick moment, she wondered if he was hitting on her then dismissed the thought as beyond ridiculous. "You don't want to hang out with me. I'm dull."

A moment later, Jessica joined them. By *joined*, the pixie blonde stood behind Joshua and held Brie's hands against the man's perfect sculpted ass as he watched her face.

Laughing nervously, she supposed the woman couldn't mind her boyfriend being felt up if she facilitated it. They kept talking as if there was nothing unusual about Brie's hands all over her man's ass and she admitted that she really liked the way it felt.

Then Jessica moved around them, standing behind Brie with her hands on her hips. She nuzzled their cheeks together and said at her ear, "Did I hear you call yourself dull, pretty girl?"

"I mostly work and sketch. There's *nothing* very exciting about me."

The couple nudged in closer. They settled their faces on either side of hers and she tried not to think about how much of her chest Joshua felt against his own.

"I think that's bullshit." He nibbled her earlobe and her entire body responded. "You have excitement simmering just beneath the surface, waiting to claw its way out."

"We could help you with that, Brie." Jessica's hand smoothed around her hip, stroking up and down her thigh. "Your skin is so warm and soft. Joshua and I love curves…just love them. We're both so lean and it feels real good to touch someone silky like you."

Glancing at Riya, she saw that both her friends stood with their mouths hanging open, their men in shock beside them. Brie swallowed and let the couple do whatever it was they were doing.

Joshua's hands cupped her ass and she was amazed at the strength in them. "We would spend hours on your body, Brie. You wouldn't regret letting us get to know you."

A silken palm slid up the column of her neck and turned her face. Jessica took her mouth in a kiss that Brie probably should have been shocked at receiving. She was too busy absorbing the sensations.

After almost a minute, the blonde broke the kiss with a moan and licked her lips. "I bet all of you tastes just as good. Let Joshua taste, pretty girl. We'll fantasize about it until you agree to play."

With that, he cupped her jaw and brought her mouth to his. She received the kiss and sighed as he licked between her lips. Other than Hudson, no one had ever kissed her with such focus.

To have two people, one of them a woman, doing it in the middle of a party was nothing short of glorious.

The music slowed to a stop and they hugged her, delivering additional kisses before Jessica withdrew a business card and tucked it – *slowly* – beneath the bodice of her dress.

Stroking his fingers beneath her necklace, the tops of Joshua's hands grazed her chest. His whiskey brown eyes lifted to hers when he felt her tremble. "Call us, Brie. Let us pour some pleasure on you."

Jessica smoothed a tendril of her hair behind her ear. "Don't be shy. I'd be so gentle with you and it would be our little secret." They stroked their fingers down her arms. "Warm caramel, and I bet all of you is the same shade. I would love to taste you everywhere."

With a wink, Jessica led her man away as Gabriella stared after them feeling too warm and struggling not to call them back. The experience had been so *tactile*.

Riya and Tawny appeared at her side. "Just in case you're offended, I'm sorry. I should have warned you about Joshua and Jessica. They can come on a little strong."

Brie stared at the retreating couple. "Offended? Not even close. I've never been so flattered in my life. His ass is like marble and she smelled fantastic." She fanned her face.

The three of them started giggling and couldn't stop. She patted their card under the material of the dress.

"If I ever get the nerve." That started a fresh round of laughter as Zach brought them drinks.

"You'd take them both on, wouldn't you?" Tawny shot her tequila.

"I'd feel self-conscious, to be honest. They have like twelve-percent body fat." She cupped her breasts. "With these I come in at around forty and it isn't a *good* forty."

"Bullshit. Those two would crawl all over you until you forgot what the fuck body fat percentage meant."

Brie absently took her hair down and tugged her lower lip between her teeth. "Maybe *after* the surgery."

"Do it. You won't regret it." Riya had a little frown between her eyes. "It doesn't freak you out that they were part of my research, does it?"

"Not even a little." Her fingertips stroked the necklace over her upper chest. "They're so pretty, Riya."

"The experience would be memorable."

They settled in one of the seating areas and the three of them slipped off their heels. Being introduced to Riya's fifth subject was surreal.

"I'm Ricardo and this is my wife Malina."

The man was stupid gorgeous and his wife laughed as Brie took in the man's physique. "That's why I'm pregnant again when I just had our first in the summer."

She congratulated the couple in Spanish and soon they were talking like old friends.

Leaning heavily on Tawny, Riya said, "I wish you could have met Lucas and Victor. They can't travel until summer because of their businesses. You'll get to meet Sean and his ladylove next week when you bring in the New Year with us."

A song began to play in Spanish and it was one of Brie's favorites. She sang along, clapping at the right spots, and Riya joined in when she learned the chorus.

Ricardo and Malina settled on the other couch, talking until the song changed again. Gathering Brie's hands, he tugged her up and danced with her to *Lloralas* as they sang the words.

He complimented her in Spanish and twirled her back to sit. "I like this new friend of yours, Riya. You need more heat like Brie around you so you don't forget, yeah?"

Tawny seconded the motion.

Riya laughed and a moment later, Micah and Max collapsed beside her. Max raked his fingers through his damp hair. "Tawny, your mom kicks ass on the dance floor."

The friends grinned. A waiter came by with drinks and each of them took one. Tawny and Brie chuckled as the M's exchanged a look.

The redhead whispered, "I'm going to get my phone just in case. You know I *live* for the half dozen times a year I can get her wasted."

She stood and made her way across the room. As she approached the stairs, she was waylaid by her men and pulled into the den. They had her in their arms before the door closed.

Gabriella sipped her tequila and listened to Ricardo and Malina talk to Max and Micah with part of her brain while the rest of her truly enjoyed a party for the first time. Stretching her legs out and crossing her ankles, Brie sang along to the music with her eyes closed.

When someone sat down beside her, she turned to find herself staring into Hudson's black eyes. A full body shiver followed the shock as he murmured, "A Patrón woman."

"I only drink when I'm around people I know." Carefully, she cleared her throat. "Merry Christmas, Hudson."

"Merry Christmas, Brie." He placed a wrapped box on her lap. "I knew you'd be here." She tilted her head as he motioned to the gift. "I didn't forget what you said."

Brie opened the paper carefully then the box inside and exhaled slowly at the small but exquisite statue inside. It was tastefully done in jade, a nude man and woman wrapped around one another in passion.

"Hudson, it's perfect, enthralling. Thank you so much."

Holding it in one hand, she hugged him with the other. His arms slid around her and Brie thought Hudson's hug might be one of the best she'd ever received.

He whispered at her ear, "You don't need to avoid me outside the building. I don't bite unless you ask. Should that happen, I can assure you I've had all my shots." Then he nipped her earlobe lightly.

Heat flooded her system instantly and she gasped softly.

"Dance with me, Brie."

Chapter Thirty

The first strains of *Feeling Good* began to play and Hudson lifted Brie to her feet. She resisted and he almost growled.

"One second." He held her hand as she stepped into her heels and placed the statue carefully in the box on the side table.

Taking her in his arms felt beyond incredible.

The tailored dress she wore accented the curves she always strived to cover and made her eyes sparkle. The expanse of warm skin it bared was marvelous. He idly wondered at the ability of her small frame to support the weight of her breasts.

She looked gorgeous and he wished Natalia were here.

He'd arrived earlier than anyone realized. He found himself spellbound watching her dance with a young couple – a man and a woman – as they casually touched and kissed her.

Brie's responses, the way she allowed them both to caress her, had him hard as steel. Such a display made it necessary to get his own body under control before approaching her. He didn't want to risk dragging her to his own home like a fucking caveman.

As they danced, he gradually guided them away from the other guests.

Her light blush intrigued him and as he stroked his fingers through her loose hair, her eyes fluttered closed. The mass of curls was softer than silk and shimmered in the low lighting.

"You never wear it down. It's lovely."

"Thank you, Hudson."

He wanted to hear his name from her lips while he fucked her incoherent. "You're so goddamn beautiful."

The words spoken through gritted teeth sounded more like an insult than a compliment but Brie seemed to read him easily.

Her smile made his cock pulse. "I feel beautiful right now."

"You should feel it *all* the time." He stroked the back of his knuckles over the bodice of her dress, the outline of the business card beneath the fabric. "Did the couple you danced with make you feel that way?"

She swallowed hard. "They helped. It isn't common for me to provoke that kind of reaction. It's the dress. Riya and Tawny did my makeup." There was a tiny shrug of her shoulders. "Not things I generally do so I feel pretty."

He said nothing but knew she could feel his eyes on her. Finally, she lifted her face. "It isn't the clothes or the makeup, your body, or your experience." Sliding his hand along the back of her neck, he told her, "It's that you're incandescent. You draw those with a touch of darkness to you like a moth to flame."

"Do you believe you're dark, Hudson?"

"I *know* I am, Brie."

One shoulder lifted in a delicate shrug. "To me, you shimmer."

No one had ever said such a thing to Hudson Winters in his lifetime. That this small woman with honeyed skin and hair his hands itched to fist had been the first caused a potent reaction to ripple through every cell in his body.

* * *

Brie tugged her lower lip between her teeth, her eyes on his. "I didn't get you a gift." The moment the words were out of her mouth, they both knew what she wanted.

She tried to steady her heart rate and failed. Everything about Hudson screamed *dirty sex* in a way she really wanted to listen to.

His eyes never broke contact, hard hands tightened, and he pulled her closer. "I could say dancing with you *is* my gift." He smiled the smile of a man who knew how powerful he was, how sexual he was, and *reveled* in the knowledge. "I'm not that selfless."

Warm fingers flexed on the nape of her neck when she remained silent. "You're afraid to ask me."

"I don't know what you'd say." She could think of nothing but the man in front of her, watching how he watched her.

His other hand lifted and he traced her lower lip with his thumb. "You have exotic lips, Brie. I remember the way they felt." Pools of black flicked up and she was entranced. "I want to kiss them again. Now."

She tried to stay calm but it was wasted effort.

Pressing his body forward, she felt a wall behind her and realized he'd maneuvered them into the small alcove on the other side of Riya's kitchen. She hadn't even noticed they were no longer dancing.

It was a struggle to silence the self-conscious voice inside her.

Hudson moved his hand beneath her chin, tilted her face upward as his lowered, and she inhaled the *mind-blowing* smell of him. A combination of expensive cologne and a trace of something that reminded her of the forests back home.

He kissed one corner of her mouth, then the other, before his tongue traced over her lower lip. He sipped at her with tiny open-mouthed kisses that threw her entire body into heat.

Needing air, her lips parted slightly, and he darted inside for an instant before he planted more kisses along her lips and nuzzled her cheek. His breath on her ear was warm and she pressed against him.

"I'm not polite or gentle. I want nothing more than to fuck you until you're aware of nothing but my name."

A small moan slipped past her control and he growled.

Nothing registered in her brain but the feel of him. He was big and hard pressed against her body and she wanted to have sex with Hudson more than she wanted her next breath.

His rigid cock nestled against her lower belly and she tried to feel more of him without seeming obvious. As she rocked her hips, his entire body stiffened in response.

"You make me come and I'll get revenge from your sweet ass, Brie."

Her sharp inhale could have been shock or excitement. Possibly a little bit of both. Hudson slid his palm along the back of her neck beneath her hair, lifted her jaw with his thumb, and held her still.

Since the day he'd kissed her in his office, she'd dreamed of this. Her memories of what he could do to her did not disappoint. He delivered sexual destruction with his mouth.

It was a kiss that conquered, that made her question every man who'd ever touched her. Where her previous lovers had been a simmer, Hudson was a four-alarm wildfire.

What he gave her was passion.

One of her hands touched his face, the other slid beneath his jacket and around to his back. He kissed her until she felt more drunk from him than the alcohol she'd consumed. His tongue coiled and played over hers while she learned how to return what he gave.

Bending his knees, Hudson positioned his cock against the cradle of her body through her dress and *rocked* against her firmly. She'd never wanted anything as much as she wanted him inside her.

There would be no lovemaking in his arms. No gentle copulation filled with sweetness and soft words. She'd known that from the very start.

Hudson Winters *fucked*. Brie wanted that experience and she wanted it with him. *Right damn now before she lost her mind.*

She could feel the head of his cock raking across her clit and she wanted nothing in the way.

As if he read her mind, his fingers gathered her dress at the back until his hands gripped the cheeks of her ass through the diaphanous material of her panties.

Barely utilized strength worked her center over the length of his dick. She was beyond involved in the sensations he provided and she was still dressed. On and on, he took her sanity with his kiss as he pushed his cock over her most sensitive flesh.

Then she fell apart in his arms.

He kissed her possessively as she rode the unexpected climax. Gripping her ass, he separated the cheeks, the tips of his fingers stroking between her legs from behind. Even over the thin fabric, she felt as if she was shaking apart.

There was no way to hold back her whimper of need. She felt him inhale several times before he carefully released her, lowered her dress, and smoothed his palms up and down her back. He pressed his cock more firmly against her, holding her hard.

"I want to fuck you, Brie. To be buried inside you when you come for me again." She almost sobbed and crushed herself against him, uncaring how easy it was for him to read her desperation. "You're *hell* on my control. Absolute hell."

For several minutes, he held her. Only when she stopped shaking did he lean back to look at her.

"I have to do things differently. I must *be* different. The man I usually am isn't good for you." Delivering another kiss that tried to drag her beneath a sensual haze, he stroked her, fingers tightening on her ass again. Then he suddenly stepped back and let her go.

Brie was instantly chilled.

Unable to process the change of pace, not understanding what had happened to alter the direction of where she'd thought his attention was headed; she stared at him in confusion.

Somehow, she managed to murmur, "Alright."

Lightheaded and unsure of herself, the past few minutes took on a dreamlike quality and she shook her head to clear it. As her logic returned, so did her insecurities.

What did a man like Hudson want from a woman like her?

"What are you thinking, Brie?"

"That I don't know anything about anything." She moved to pass him and he caught her hand. The simple touch was almost her undoing.

"I don't want to *take* from you. My entire existence revolves around getting what I want. You deserve better."

"I don't understand taking. I only understand giving. I guess that's my problem. Merry Christmas, Hudson and thank you for the gift."

She tugged her hand and he let it go.

* * *

Hudson watched Gabriella walk quickly around the wall that separated them from the main living spaces with a frown.

For almost a minute, he examined what he'd said, his thoughts tangled up at the clear sadness he'd seen on her face. Suddenly, he knew he'd hurt her unintentionally.

She thought he didn't want her.

He followed in her wake and examined the faces of every guest. Within thirty seconds, he knew she had gone off by herself to gather her composure.

Unable to find her without causing a scene, he hissed, "*Fuck.*"

When she hadn't reappeared five minutes later, he knew he had to get back to his space before he started searching Riya's home room-by-room for her friend. In the elevator, he called Natalia.

Chapter Thirty-One

Plastering a smile on her face, Brie quickly entered the guest room she'd shared with Tawny the night before. Closing the door and locking it, she walked to the bed and sat down.

Her mind was in utter chaos.

She wasn't in love with Hudson but she genuinely *liked* him. It had never occurred to her that he wouldn't take what she willingly offered if given the chance.

Embarrassment flamed over her body and she fought the urge to cry with everything inside herself.

Somehow, she'd misread the situation, misinterpreted what Hudson wanted from her, placed too much importance on it.

For a long time, she sat there trying to understand but ultimately, she realized she didn't know nearly enough about the opposite sex – or even the same sex – to decipher the messages.

With a heavy sigh, she shook her head with a bitter laugh.

She changed out of her dress and hung it in the closet. She placed the shoes beneath it on the floor. In the attached bathroom, she carefully removed as much of the makeup as she could and gathered her hair into a heavy pile on top of her head. The silver jewelry went on a shelf in the closet because she didn't feel right about taking it.

Familiar with mountain winters, she'd brought extra layers in her backpack. She put on leggings, jeans, two long-sleeve shirts, and a sweater. She picked up her heavy coat and backpack.

The small jade statue was tucked safely inside.

In the main room, she hugged her way through everyone and Riya pulled her aside. Her friend wasn't steady on her feet.

"Stay here, Brie. It's *freezing* outside and you've been drinking."

"I love the cold, I'm dressed warmly, and unlike you, *lightweight*, I can actually handle alcohol. I have less than the slightest buzz now."

"Are you sure? Why don't you just stay?"

Hands on her friend's shoulders, she smiled brightly. A sober Riya would have seen right through it and Brie was glad her intuitiveness was compromised.

"I have Mass in the morning, remember? I promised my mom. You need to wake up Christmas morning without guests so you can give proper thanks for the gift of Micah and Max in your life. You don't understand right now because you're drunk off your ass."

She pouted. "Let me call Rodney to take you."

"It's Christmas Eve and the woman he's dating would *hate* you. I'll have the guys call me a cab. It isn't a problem, I promise. Merry Christmas, Riya. Thank you so much for including me." They hugged tightly and Brie was genuinely thankful to have met these people.

Tawny walked her to the elevator. "Something happened."

"You're right. I got *really* tired and want my bed. Someone who shall remain nameless made sure I only got about six hours of sleep in the last two days."

She grinned but Tawny didn't buy it. "Hmm. I call bullshit."

"Go soak up some more attention from your men. Despite your earlier appetizer, they're looking at you like a steak." Tilting her head to the side, she added, "They love you, Tawny. So much that you can see it on their faces."

Zach and Quinn leaned against the mantle across the room, watching the woman they worshipped together.

She watched as Tawny's eyes closed and when they opened, she was shockingly on the verge of tears. "I know," she whispered.

"*Tawny...*"

Shaking her head sharply, she pulled her usual personality around herself. Planting her hand on her hip, she said, "You need to let us drop you off or I'm liable to fuck them in the car on the way home."

Weighing what she wanted to do and what her friend needed at that moment, Brie took a deep breath and grinned. "I'm not being accused of cock blocking. Thank you for everything. I mean it."

She hugged Tawny tight. At her ear, she murmured, "You can talk to me when you're ready. I'll listen and I won't judge, Tawny."

The redhead's arms tightened hard for an instant before they broke apart. As she got on the elevator, the other woman watched her with her arms crossed over her chest.

"Merry Christmas, Tawny." She blew her a kiss as the doors closed.

Downstairs, Donald called her a cab and they chatted while she waited.

From the corner of her eye, she saw Hudson's Rolls pull up out front and Leonard get out. Brie said she needed to get something from her locker and went around the corner to wait in the hallway.

Thirty seconds later, she heard, "Good evening, Miss Natalia."

"Hello, Donald."

She peeked around the wall and watched Natalia walk to the elevators wearing a calf-length fur coat and high heels.

Brie wondered if she was naked beneath it.

She wanted out and away. Rushing past the desk, she said softly, "Forget the cab. Merry Christmas. Give my love to your girl, Donald."

"Brie, wait, it's *freezing* out there!"

Pretending not to hear, Brie nodded at the night doorman. She kept her eyes on the sidewalk as she stepped into the New York winter night. A block away, she shrugged into her big coat and wrapped her scarf up to cover her ears.

She tugged on her gloves as she walked. It was at the halfway point between the building and her apartment across town that she suddenly stopped.

"Brie, you're an asshole."

Of *course,* Hudson and Natalia had plans. It was Christmas Eve and they loved each other. Even if they couldn't figure that out, they'd been friends for three decades. Who better to spend the holiday with?

Natalia was the woman he was meant to be with and Brie was a person he liked, might even be attracted to, but not in the same way.

It soothed her pride to think that he'd rejected her out of loyalty to his oldest friend than because he found her hideous.

With renewed energy, she started to walk. Her smile was finally sincere and she didn't care if a cab appeared or not.

* * *

Natalia rushed to the door and watched Gabriella walk rapidly down the street. She frowned and contemplated calling Leonard to pick her up and take her where she needed to go.

Something told her that Brie was upset and wouldn't appreciate the gesture in the slightest.

"Donald, please call the penthouse after you confirm that Miss Hernandez has arrived home safely. Don't mention me."

"Yes, ma'am. It's twenty degrees outside. No one should be walking in it. I'll check on her every few minutes."

"Thank you."

With that, she returned to the elevator alcove. She stepped into the living room and knew instantly that something had happened between the two of them.

Hudson stood at the window, his arms crossed over his chest. She went to his side and her heart clenched at the expression on his face.

"What happened, darling?"

For ten minutes, her friend explained his time with Brie.

Wide-eyed, she shrugged off the coat and he took in the cocktail dress she wore beneath it. It was made of the finest raw silk and hugged her from her shoulders to just above her knees.

Every year, she hosted a party for the club staff on Christmas Eve. Hudson had attended but excused himself early to make sure he didn't miss seeing Brie.

"Did I tell you how gorgeous you look tonight?"

"Several times. Thank you." Her fingers stroked through his hair and he leaned into the touch. "It was a misunderstanding. It can be fixed."

He put his hand over hers and sighed. "I don't understand why I'm obsessed with this woman."

"First, she isn't falling all over you and the life you could give her. That must be a wonderfully unique experience for you." He grunted in agreement. "Second, she's our polar opposite. From the many things I've heard about her over the last few months, she couldn't be more different in the way she views the world."

Hudson turned to look at her. "I need to stop this."

"Why? Few things hold your interest for so long. I'm enjoying myself immensely." Her head tilted slightly and she asked, "How are you feeling otherwise?"

"Much more relaxed. Thank you for last night."

"Stop thanking me for accepting orgasms, Hudson."

Stepping closer to him, she wrapped her arm around his waist and laid her head on his shoulder as they stared out at the city together. "I don't want to split your focus more than I already do."

"You don't split my focus. What are you talking about?"

"Hudson. Darling, I adore you but you can be a trial on my peace of mind." Angling her body in front of his, she held his hand in hers. "Don't you ever wonder why you can't keep long-term relationships?"

"I've had them."

"Killing time. It's the sex between us that holds you back." She shook her head. "Any woman would have an issue with a friend such as me in your life. Our sexual history is obvious even to those who haven't known us long."

The look on his face was fierce. "Natalia, what are you saying to me right now?"

"I have *no* idea." It was absolute truth. "All I know is that our relationship makes lasting relationships with other people impossible. What we're doing isn't working."

"Then we *make* it work." The vehemence of the words shocked them both. "I…"

She smoothly interrupted him. "What about Gabriella?"

"Explain."

"I shouldn't have to but I will. I love women almost as much as I love men. Maybe she's the answer. The *home-and-hearth* type neither of us will never be." Her heart slammed against her ribs as she broached the subject that had haunted her for weeks. "We could *share* her."

Most of the ménage relationships among the members of *Trois* were two men and one woman. Hudson stared at her. "How did my mind conveniently skip over the *other* alternative?"

Two women and one man.

Specifically, Natalia, Gabriella, and *him*.

"You get what you need, what you want from me openly and honestly. You also gain a woman who represents what you need most, a wife and mother type that might not be able to provide the same benefits that I do."

"You've considered this."

"I have."

"You've been watching her, following her."

"Yes."

"You're a little in love with her already, aren't you?" She nodded carefully and a slow smile broke over her face. "Natalia, I've always known you were smarter than me, I just didn't know how much."

With a snort, she faced forward, and he kissed the top of her head. "I could have told you, had you thought to ask."

"We need to go after her together."

"There's still a chance she won't…"

"She will." Then he told her about the couple who danced with Brie at Riya's gathering. "Her nature is inquisitive and open. There have been experiences in her past but nothing compared to what she wants to know, to feel." He tilted her face up with a finger under her chin. "She'll be open to both of us, Natalia."

"A coordinated effort," she murmured. A few minutes later, a call from Donald at the concierge desk confirmed that Gabriella made it home safely. "She's alright."

"Excellent."

Then Hudson took her in his arms and made her forget everything but the feel of his hands, the taste of his kiss, and the hardness of his cock.

She received exactly what she wanted for Christmas.

Chapter Thirty-Two

To say New York was a mob scene during the holiday season was an understatement. Brie absolutely loved it.

After attending Mass on Christmas morning and spending several hours on the phone with her family, she straightened her apartment and worked on her painting for Hudson of his building.

The original sketch was clipped to the corner of her canvas and she had several photos printed that she sometimes referred to on her bulletin board.

Despite her confusion and initial hurt about being rejected, she gave herself a firm shake and recognized that it wasn't the first time she'd read a man wrong and he didn't belong to her anyway.

Putting the experience in perspective, understanding that he was a sexual man who often acted on what he wanted rather than what he needed, she felt better.

Later that evening, she received an emergency call from Eleanor Shaughnessy. The young woman who ran the tower business center was rushed to the hospital for an emergency appendectomy.

"I've tried everyone and I'm desperate, Brie."

"I'll come in. Give me about an hour to get there."

"You're an angel. Just so you know, the hours you pick up this week earn you double the comp time. You'll have what you need as of the first of the year. Though I admit those few weeks without you are going to be hell."

Thrilled, Brie told her happily, "Thank you so much, Eleanor!"

Rushing to get herself together, she stood her easel in the unused closet beside the front door. She put away her supplies, changed clothes, and rushed out of the building, hoping she'd be able to find a cab but willing to take the subway.

She was surprised to see Riya and Tawny getting out of the Towncar in front of her building. The brunette frowned. "Brie! Why are you dressed for work?"

"They called me in. Can I ride back with you?" The three of them slid inside and the warmth was wonderful. "Your timing was perfect."

Turning in the seat, her friends stared at her. "I know what you're thinking but my manager just told me that all the hours over my regular shift that I work this week count double. That means I can schedule my surgery and know I'll have the paid time off for recovery."

"That's wonderful, Brie. Now, why the hell did you leave last night and why didn't you take the clothes and stuff with you?"

Faced with a sober Riya, she knew she had to tell the truth. Releasing a heavy sigh, she tried to explain. "I made out with Hudson last night." Both women gasped and then snickered. "It was intense. So fucking good I wanted to crawl inside his body." She shrugged. "I definitely wanted him to crawl inside mine."

That made them laugh harder.

"When he stopped everything, my feelings were hurt. I immediately thought it was me and I was horribly embarrassed." She told them what he'd said to her as her face flamed.

"Oh, Brie, he wasn't rejecting you."

"He kind of was but I can understand." She paused and folded her hands together in her lap. "Natalia arrived as I was leaving."

"That motherfucker…" Tawny began.

"No. It's not like that and I realized as I was walking home…"

"You *walked* all the way home last night?" Riya shouted.

"Yes, but Donald from the front desk kept calling to check on me. It would have taken forever for a cab to get there anyway." She looked back and forth between them, wanting them to understand as she did. "As for Hudson, he *belongs* with Natalia. It makes sense that they'd spend the holiday together, don't you think?"

"Well, yes, it does actually."

"They probably had plans together before he came to give me my present and he got caught up in the moment."

"What present?"

She'd taken a photo of the statue for her sister and she pulled it up on her phone. "He remembered something I told him the first time we talked. After I started working for the building. He's so busy, it kind of amazed me that he'd remember something small like that."

"That's gorgeous. It's also hella expensive," Tawny told her.

"So, you're okay?" Riya asked gently.

"I really am. Part of it was being so ramped up from dancing with Joshua and Jessica then getting fondled by Hudson. I was needy. I took care of business and got some sleep."

Tawny snorted. "Damn right." They shared a laugh.

"Why didn't you take the stuff we got you?"

Turning to look into Riya's eyes, she said, "Have you ever had someone look at you funny for owning something expensive? That happened to me a lot in college. Most of the kids in my first semester classes assumed I was there on scholarship. The diamond earrings my aunt gave me for my eighteenth birthday were obviously fake. Boys only dated me, they assumed, because I put out."

Riya's eyes closed. "You didn't want to take what belonged to you when Tawny and I weren't with you." She sighed heavily. "You didn't want anyone to think you were stealing it."

"The world is fucking *fucked up* and I'll cut any bitch that treats either of you like that in front of me. Slice and fucking dice."

With her furious outburst, Tawny threw herself back against the seat and stared out of the window.

"It sucks and it's wrong but bad shit happens whether you pick fruit as an illegal or own a multi-million-dollar corporation. The only difference is racists hide it if they *know* you have money and power."

"I'm sorry, Brie."

"Don't be. I don't live my life based on those things but sometimes I do have to think about it in regard to safety and stuff. Stop and frisk is real and I walk everywhere. I didn't want to have obviously expensive jewelry in my bag."

They pulled up to the building and Rodney came around to open the door. As Brie stood in front of him, he gave her a fist bump. "Keep smilin', yeah?"

"Yeah, Rodney. Always."

The three of them went inside and she hugged her friends. They'd managed to remove any last remnants of her self-doubt and sadness.

It was time to get to work.

* * *

The next several days were spent working double shifts. Brie filled in for the business center manager and worked her own shift as well. Her comp time racked up and she kept her mind off thoughts of Hudson, Natalia, and how much she wanted to touch them.

Knowing she had three days of doubles remaining before several members of the staff returned from vacation, she decided to pack a bag and stay in the employee dorm instead of going back and forth.

Riya offered repeatedly for her to stay with them but she felt it was inappropriate. She and the M's didn't have children and they didn't need a week-long houseguest making it impossible for them to run around their house naked.

The thought always made her grin.

As she came off the graveyard shift at the business center, she was overtired and in desperate need of coffee.

Izzy didn't understand why the business center was open around the clock but though it was generally quiet overnight, Brie had seen the value for residents who needed last-minute presentations prepared, business cards printed, or postcards created.

She used the downtime to work on ideas of her own while playing with a few of the websites she'd designed.

Grabbing her backpack after changing into street clothes, she headed out to say goodbye to the next shift coming in. Henry showed her pictures of his new grandchild on his cell phone.

"He's gorgeous. What did they name him?"

The proud grandfather put his chest out and his shoulders back. "Henry Jacob."

"An excellent name! I know you must be thrilled!" She hugged him tightly.

"They've been trying for three *years*." He smiled at the photo. "It finally happened for them." Henry shook himself. "Look at me keeping you! You've worked all night. I'll see you later, Brie."

She gave him another hug and waved to Carlo as she crossed the lobby.

A voice behind her said, "Good morning, Brie."

Turning slowly, she faced Hudson's lover less than three feet away. "Good morning, Natalia. Did you need something? I'll be happy to grab one of the girls for you."

"Oh no. I need coffee. Will you join me?" Brie opened her mouth to object. "Please."

A lifetime of manners made it impossible to refuse. "Alright."

The much taller woman motioned for her to proceed through the door Henry held with an unreadable expression and she slipped through it to the sidewalk.

Natalia walked in the direction of her favorite café and silence stretched between them since Brie was unsure about what to say. She felt self-conscious in her jeans and trail runners. The height of the chic woman wearing heels beside her highlighted how short she was.

Inside the warm and familiar coffee house, Natalia insisted on purchasing their coffees. They settled at a small corner table and her electric blue eyes seeming to see *everything*.

"You really are *quite* lovely."

"Thank you. Very different from you, I know."

She smiled. "What does that mean?"

"You remind me of my sister. Everything in the right proportion. You look like you belong in the city, with a-a life like the one you have." She almost said *man* instead but caught herself. "I take after my grandmother. I look like I should have eight kids and start dinner at nine in the morning."

"Yet I find myself wishing my hair was naturally as black as yours, my skin as warm as yours, and my lips as full. I've always felt too tall and I have no curves to speak of." The admission surprised her. "We women are endlessly hard on ourselves."

For the first time, Brie smiled sincerely. "I guess you're right."

"I often am. You're a beautiful woman, Gabriella."

Taking a deep breath, she said simply, "Thank you."

"Better. Eventually, you'll see it yourself because you'll feel it. That's what makes all the difference."

"Max told me that at the party." She lifted her gaze and saw clearly that Natalia knew what had happened.

"Hudson is abrupt and often misunderstood. In all the years I've known him, he's never been interested in a woman who's gentle and kind like you. Hurting you was not his intention."

"I was embarrassed more than hurt. Confused. I felt like I was going to vibrate out of my skin. I don't normally do things like that. I felt better after I gave it some thought."

"You thought he didn't want you."

"I've had that happen before." She looked out at the passing traffic. "The experience was so different from anything I had to compare it to that I was vulnerable and immediately assumed the worst." She turned back with a small shrug and stared at her coffee cup.

"He desires you to distraction, Gabriella."

"I'm sorry." Hearing Hudson's best friend, the woman he was meant to love, say the words made her heart hurt.

"Why are you sorry? I *also* desire you to distraction." She was unable to hide her shock and Natalia smiled. Sitting forward, she crossed her slender arms on the table. Brie saw faint indents on her skin.

The other woman *let* her see them.

"Do you know what these marks mean, Brie?"

She considered lying and immediately changed her mind. "BDSM. You like to be tied up. Hudson likes to do the tying."

"A simplified explanation but close enough. There's an aspect of my nature and his that *needs* the feelings the ropes inspire."

"Like an addiction."

"Sometimes, it feels that way." She traced the lines with the tip of her finger. "Has anyone ever tied you up before?"

"No. I've never trusted anyone enough to do that."

Sleek black hair swung forward as she nodded. "Trust is crucial. I've always trusted Hudson with my body and my safety." There was a pause as their eyes met. "You could, too."

"I know." She was breathing too fast.

Natalia stared at her for a long time. "You fascinate me."

There were so many things she wanted to say to the woman across from her but she was still confused, still vulnerable from a hurt that – while unintentional – had cut her deeply.

"You and Hudson are best friends. You sync well with one another but I think you're both missing the big picture. I may seem like a quasi-virgin from the sticks but I read people pretty well."

She inhaled deeply, prepared to let go of her hopes to experience every dirty thing Hudson – and Natalia – could show her. At the end of the day, she knew the excitement, the edge of darkness, did not belong to her and she didn't *want* to be a distraction to them.

If they were focused on her, they wouldn't see each other.

"Right now, I interest you because I'm different. I'm not greedy or cold like the women you're both probably used to. It makes me a game and while it might be something that fills the time for you and Hudson, it could ultimately hurt me deeply to let you toy with me."

She stood and picked up her backpack. "No matter his present desire for me – just like Christmas Eve – only you will ever be able to give him what he really needs. That isn't fair to you, Natalia and it certainly isn't fair to me."

Pushing in her chair, she murmured, "Thank you for the coffee. I have to go."

The chilly air felt wonderful on her overheated skin. A block away, she was furious at the tears on her cheeks and grateful that the streets were all but empty at this hour on the weekend.

Gabriella knew she'd done the right thing but she was so fucking *tired* of being good all the time. Making all the decisions best for everyone else while taking nothing for herself.

Selfishly, she wanted Hudson and Natalia to see her as a grown woman with needs. She wanted them to give her memories of sex that didn't make her cringe when she remembered them – unlike those she had with the lovers in her past.

She wanted someone to show her the *good* things about sex and think she was enough. No one had ever considered her enough and the pain of that grew every year.

The only thing that shocked Gabriella more than having her hand grabbed and being spun around was the insanity of Natalia Roman claiming her mouth in a kiss that was every bit as destructive as Hudson's had been.

Everything inside her reached for what was offered and Brie realized something crucial about herself.

She might be greedy after all.

Chapter Thirty-Three

The first ten seconds were fierce as Natalia backed Brie into the narrow gap between two buildings, gripped her head in her hands, and completely devoured lips she'd *dreamed* of kissing.

Awed the smaller woman wasn't resisting, she gentled the sensual attack. Nothing less than rejection could have made her stop. Blood roared in her ears and she understood Hudson's obsession with this woman more than ever before.

Then Brie began to kiss her back.

The taste of *her* mixed with coffee was rich and smooth. Her tongue was small and silken, wrapping over and around Natalia's until she felt it in her breasts and clit.

She never wanted to let Gabriella go.

A loud sound down the street startled Brie and Natalia broke the kiss, pulling back to gaze into dark blue eyes.

"I'm sorry I hurt you, even unknowingly." Using her thumbs, she wiped away the tears a woman such as her should never have to cry. "You're so naturally passionate, Brie."

"I just want to *know*. To understand without games, guilt, or ulterior motives. I don't want to be ashamed of *wanting*."

Then she covered her face and Natalia knew that she would do everything in her power to never be the cause of her tears again. She hugged her, understanding what feeling *less* was like.

"There's no shame in wanting, Gabriella."

Leaning her head against the wall behind her, she stared at Natalia in a way no one ever had before. "Everyone thinks that because I'm nice, because I'm gentle, that all I care about is finding some nice man to love me, take care of me, and give me babies."

She shook her head. "I'm twenty-eight. I've felt nothing with lovers because they bored me and I could have been anyone at all. I faked my orgasms, made sure they were happy, then cooked for them."

"It wasn't like that with Hudson."

"It's not like that with either of you, Natalia." She wiped her face. "I know what both of you think. Someone like *sweet little Brie* is obviously looking for love. You think I'm in love with Hudson but I'm not. I'm in lust with both of you."

Natalia smoothed her palms down Brie's arms to her hands, lifting them over her head and holding them there with one of her own. Her breath came in pants that were visible on the cold air.

"Lust is new for you, isn't it?" She nodded. "It makes you feel confused because you haven't had a way to learn. Do you touch yourself often?"

"Yes. Too much, I think."

"Hmm, I would love to see that."

Brie's eyes widened and Natalia smoothed one hand over skin that was so soft and warm beneath her upper body layers that all she wanted to do was take her home and spend days crawling all over her.

Pressing her thigh between Brie's legs, she could feel the heat of her pussy through their clothes. With a small roll of her hips, Brie worked herself on what promised to relieve the pressure.

"That's it. Take what you want, Brie. I want to make you come right here in this alley, just a few feet from where we could be discovered. Would you like to come?"

"Desperately."

"Have you ever been with a woman?" She shook her head and Natalia pressed her thigh more firmly against her mound. A small moan escaped. "I would lick you everywhere and suckle your little clit until you begged to come. I would let you so I could taste your cream."

She gripped a perfect ass, increasing the force of Brie's hip movements, pulling her folds up and down her thigh. Sliding her hand around and under her shirt, Natalia flattened her palm on Brie's belly. Unsnapping her jeans made dark blue eyes open.

"I need to touch you."

"Yes, please yes."

Sliding beneath the low band of her jeans, Natalia took her time stroking back and forth over Brie's low belly above her panties. Then she pushed the panties aside and found her clit swollen and slick.

"You're soaked for me, Brie." As her fingertip made small circles, Brie thrust her hips against the pressure. Dipping lower, she pressed just inside. "I want to feel you come. That's it. Your pussy is so hot. I'd love to feel it while I fuck you with my tongue."

"*Natalia…*"

Rocking more quickly, Brie drew in air as the climax slammed into her. Natalia sealed their mouths together to capture the sound, fucking her mouth as she drew the orgasm out as long as possible. She continued to stroke, pressing a second finger deep in her pussy as she used her thumb on the little bundle of nerves.

Breaking the kiss, Brie whispered, "Coming again."

Arching off the wall, she pushed herself more firmly into Natalia's hands and groaned low in her throat. Her entire body was shaking.

As she came back to herself, Natalia lifted away and took her hand from under her clothes. Brie watched, breath sawing between her lips, as she sucked her flavor from them.

"Exactly as I thought. *Delicious.*"

Taking a single step back, she straightened Brie's clothing and took her hand. Distantly, Brie registered being led to the sidewalk and dazedly watched Natalia raise her hand, followed quickly by Leonard pulling to the curb in front of them and coming around to open the door.

"Where do you need to go, Brie?"

It took a moment to organize her thoughts. "I need to pick up a few things and go back to the building. I'm staying in the employee dorms for a couple of days."

"Yes, ma'am."

Natalia raised the privacy glass and pulled Brie to her for another kiss. Warm hands lifted to cup her face and it almost startled her because she was so unaccustomed to anyone's touch but Hudson's.

Resting their foreheads against one another, she murmured, "You're so tactile and warm, Gabriella. I enjoy your touch."

As if she'd only been seeking permission, Brie's fingers combed through her hair before her palms slid down her neck, lightly massaging the muscles of her shoulders.

"I never know if I should touch. I always want to."

The simple confession made Natalia realize how careful she and Hudson had to be with this woman's heart. The first person to give her absolute freedom would also have the power to destroy her.

They needed to move slowly, showing her all the things she wanted to know without rushing her emotions.

The sexual knowledge...*that*, they could rush.

"Did you not touch Hudson?" Brie shook her head. "Why?"

"I didn't want to do anything to make it stop."

As Brie's hands glided over her shoulders and back again, Natalia inhaled sharply when they settled on the outsides of her breasts.

"I'd give absolutely *anything* to be so perfectly sized, Natalia."

The words had her blinking back tears and she wrapped her fingers around the nape of Brie's neck to hold her still for a brutal kiss. Only when she was moaning into her mouth did she release her lips.

Small tremors vibrated over her skin and she tugged her pillowy lip between her teeth.

"You need to come again." Without waiting for an answer, she opened Brie's jeans and returned her fingers to the warm wetness of her body. "I need you to come again."

Wrapping her arm around Natalia's neck, she whispered, "I'm selfish."

It made her smile. "You're not selfish, Brie. There will come a day that you'll give me orgasms and I believe they'll be some of the most powerful of my life. Today, the *first* day I'm given the privilege of touching you, you'll receive the pleasure you deserve."

"You smell so good, Natalia."

"So do you. I look forward to being naked with you, touching and kissing your body. I want to learn all the things that make you sigh, moan, and scream."

Lifting her head, she added, "I look forward to watching you with Hudson, Brie. To seeing him fuck you until you can't stand up."

She watched the idea take root in Brie's mind and her hips moved urgently beneath her hand.

"Your lips wrapped around his cock as I eat you." She nuzzled their cheeks together. "You eating my pussy as he fucks my mouth. So many things I want to show you. To give you so that you're never afraid you aren't enough again."

Then she was coming, moaning, and gasping for air as she tried to get as close to Natalia's hand as possible.

Stroking her through it, Natalia watched Brie's body gradually settle, and then kissed her several times before withdrawing her hand and putting the younger woman back together.

When she spoke, her voice was firm. "The next time I make you come, it will be with my mouth. I'll drink you down like fine wine."

Brie released a shuddering breath.

"You're naturally sensual and that makes you curious." She planted a gentle kiss on her lips. "There's nothing wrong with that. There's nothing wrong with taking what you want. We will give you all the sexual memories you wish to have, Brie. All you have to do is trust us and know that we will never intentionally hurt you."

As they turned on her street, Brie murmured, "I can't believe he remembered the address from so many months ago." Glancing at Natalia, she added, "You don't have to wait for me. I'm sure you have lots to do every day with your business."

"I'm taking you back." The firm tone made the pulse in Brie's neck race and that made her smile. "You have no idea how much you're going to enjoy Hudson."

The car stopped in front of her building and before Leonard opened the door, she said, "No matter what, I'll never doubt that it is the two of you who belong together, Natalia. You shouldn't forget that either because anything I can do to make you both see it, I'll do."

Glad for a few minutes alone while they waited for Brie, Natalia steadied her breathing and calmed her heart.

She wondered how much power Gabriella would hold over *their* hearts when all was said and done.

It was at once alarming and exciting to consider.

Chapter Thirty-Four

After a day of meetings in Houston to close on the hotel chain, Hudson paced his suite, filled with tension and unable to release it.

The woman Hudson wanted to fuck lived in his old apartment and worked in his building but Brie might as well have been on another planet. Since the party, she'd reached ninja status in her ability to avoid him, and he was well aware that he'd handled the situation wrong.

The only thought that played in a pounding rhythm that night was fucking her in every way imaginable. He wanted to show her all the sinful acts her body was created to commit.

Instead, he'd managed to hurt her feelings. Deciphering her mindset was almost impossible for someone like him.

They were different at their cores.

Much of his psyche told him to leave her in peace and stop trying to fit her into his world. A small portion told the majority to *fuck off*.

It kept him awake at night and made him hard at unexpected times.

His cell rang and he picked it up with a smile. "Natalia."

"Hello, darling. How was your day?"

With a bark of laughter at the domesticity of the question, he filled her in on the end results of his meetings.

"Delkin said hello again."

"Hmm. I wonder why his interest is suddenly engaged."

"You *know* why. He knows you, that you would accept his darkness along with the little extras. He's hunting again."

"I've experienced it before and while it was exciting, I don't have the relationship with him that I do with you. It would never work."

His heart slammed hard against his ribs and he breathed through the territorial growl that wanted to escape.

Instead, he asked her, "How was your day?"

"Actually, that's why I'm calling. I ran into Brie this morning." There was a pause. "By *ran into*, I mean that I waited by the concierge desk to waylay her when she was finished with another ridiculous sixteen-hour shift and invited her for coffee. She was too polite to refuse."

"How is she?" The gruffness of his voice couldn't be helped.

"She's much more open than we thought."

On the other end of the line, he heard her sigh softly and his entire body went rigid in response.

"Are you naked, Natalia?"

"Yes."

"Are you spread out on your bed?"

"Yes."

"Are you touching yourself?"

"I'm remembering and trying *not* to touch myself."

"Wait."

Putting the phone down, Hudson quickly removed his shoes and clothing. Piling up the pillows on the bed, he sat with his back against the headboard and returned the phone to his ear.

"Are you naked, Hudson?"

"Yes."

"Are you on the bed?"

"Yes."

"Are you touching yourself?"

"Not yet. Tell me. Every second, Natalia."

"We talked at the coffee shop and she said she was embarrassed because she thought she'd misread the situation. She thought you didn't want her."

"Fuck."

"She saw me arrive when she was leaving that night and it hurt her to know you played with her but fucked me."

"How do I fix it?"

"More on that later." There was a rustling sound. "She left the coffee shop after we talked for a bit and she was upset. I went after her. I wanted to sample her perfect lips so I kissed her."

"Was it all you imagined?"

"Better. I want to feel them on my pussy. I want to watch them sucking your cock."

"Touch your breasts." He knew she obeyed instantly without needing to be in the same room or even the same time zone. His cock throbbed against his lower belly. "Did she enjoy the kiss?"

"She was surprised at first but then, *oh god*, she kissed me back."

The memory of eating at Brie's mouth while pressing his cock against her body made his balls tighten painfully.

"Pinch your nipples, Natalia." A low moan came through their connection and he did not want to be in Houston anymore. "Tell me."

"I pulled her between the buildings. I knew I needed more. I wanted to make her come. I *needed* to make her come."

Natalia's breathing sped up.

"I showed her how to work herself on my thigh. I could feel how hot she was through our clothes. So *hot*, Hudson. I told her I needed to touch her."

"Did she want you to touch her?" Every cell in his body wanted to be balls deep in Gabriella's body in that moment. Scenarios flashed rapidly through his mind that included the three of them naked, sweaty, and moaning as they found forbidden pleasure in one another.

"She did. She gave me permission so I slipped my hand inside her clothes and her pussy was *drenched* for me."

It was the image that forced him to fist his cock. "Slick and hot?"

"Yes. I played with her swollen clit and pushed two fingers inside her. I ate at her mouth and wanted to crawl inside her. She came hard but it wasn't enough. I wanted so much more."

"Did you taste her?"

"I did. Hudson, please."

"Stroke your clit. Don't come. How did she taste?"

"Warm, salty, musky. Hers is a flavor I could easily become addicted to. Clean and delicious. You'll love eating her pussy."

His fist tightened on his dick, stroked up and down once, twice.

"When she was back together, I took her home. I put up the privacy glass so I could touch her more. I couldn't get enough."

"Did you make her come again?"

"God, yes. She worried she was being selfish and I told her I'd get orgasms from her later, not to worry, to focus on her pleasure."

"What pushed her over the edge?"

"I talked about watching her lips around your cock while I ate her pussy. How I wanted her to eat me while you fucked me in the mouth." She moaned on the other end of the phone. "The thought of the three of us made her come so *explosively*, Hudson."

"*Natalia…fuck!*"

He lost control of his body at the same time Natalia lost control of hers and he listened to her moaning, whispering, and inhaling deeply as jets of his seed splattered on his stomach and chest.

For a long time, he continued to stroke in silence, watching his release pump from the head of his cock. Stroking his hand down, he cupped his balls roughly and realized they were completely depleted.

It was not something that happened to him often and never because of masturbation. Only Natalia had ever accomplished it.

His mind and body were calm.

In New York, where he wanted to be, Natalia whispered, "That felt so good, Hudson." There was a long pause. "I *want* her. If you don't share her, I'll *take her* for myself."

He told his best friend, his only *true* friend, "You're the only person who could snatch her from my grasp."

They cleaned up and talked for hours. She told him about things Brie had said and some of them made his chest hurt.

"We have to be careful with her. She thinks to use *us* as she believes we are using *her* and that's what we need to let her have. She wants to know everything. You and I can show her that and more."

It was near midnight when Hudson turned off the lights in the hotel room and laid down. He and Natalia continued to talk.

When she told him about her fantasy of tying Brie down and teaching her about submission, he countered with his own fantasy of tying Natalia down and teaching her about Domination.

Talking one another through another orgasm, they crashed.

Neither remembered to hang up.

Chapter Thirty-Five

First week in January…

A rewarding soak with a well-written book was the *only* plan Brie had for the evening. Finally past the New Year and with the rest of the building staff back on the clock, she'd pulled her last double the night before.

She'd been in the tub for over an hour, periodically refreshing the hot water, when her phone rang. Careful not to get it wet, she picked it up. Since she didn't recognize the number, the voice on the other end of the line shocked her.

"Gabriella."

"Hello, Hudson." Her face flamed. His call was so unexpected.

"I'm taking you to dinner." Struggling to calm her heart, she heard him exhale heavily. "I'd like to take you to dinner."

"Do you mean tonight?" She swallowed hard. "I just pulled eight double shifts in a row. I'm not at my best, Hudson."

She wondered if he heard what she *wasn't* saying. She was overtired and sore. A woman did not willingly subject herself to a powerful man without plenty of reserves.

"You work too much."

That made her smile. "Says the man who pulls fifteen-hour workdays seven days a week."

"Touché." There was a long pause. "I'll give you a few days to rest. You'll go to dinner with me." Another pause and exhale. "When you're rested, will you *agree* to go to dinner with me?"

"Yes, Hudson. I'd love to go to dinner with you." Truth.

"Excellent." She sat up and water sloshed along the side. The man never missed anything. "Are you in your bathtub?"

"Yes."

Growling, he told her, "You can't imagine what I would give to see that, Gabriella."

"I promise, it isn't nearly as exciting as you're imagining. As a matter of fact, I can guarantee it isn't."

For almost a minute, he said nothing. "I can guarantee it would make me hard."

"What doesn't?" she quipped.

"You're in a playful mood. I like you relaxed, Brie."

"Thank you. I enjoy playing with you."

After several heartbeats, he said, "You will. Another guarantee."

"All my witty comebacks just died an undignified death, Hudson." His laugh made her inner walls clench in need.

"You're refreshing. I enjoy you."

"I hope so."

There was another pause. "There's no doubt in my mind. There won't be in yours." Her breathing came in small pants. "Natalia called me while I was away."

"I thought she might." In the three days since she'd allowed Natalia to give her multiple orgasms, there was no doubt that the best friends would have talked.

"Does that bother you?"

"Not at all. I enjoyed our time together. She's lovely in many ways."

"You're an honest woman."

"I try to be."

"You realize we both want you."

"Yes."

"You *will* be safe, Brie."

"I know." She swallowed hard. "It surprises me that you're having this conversation over the phone."

"I have no control around you. I needed to keep my hands off your body long enough to talk."

"I'm *stupidly* flattered by that."

"Good. Talking to you is difficult for me." He cleared his throat. "I'm sorry about Christmas Eve. I didn't intend to hurt you, Brie."

"Thank you, Hudson. It was wonderful, despite the way we parted."

"I overheard Riya talking to Carlo. You're taking time off?"

"I work for the next few days then I'll be off for several weeks. A small thing. Nothing to worry about. I worked hard to accrue the paid time I would need."

"You won't avoid me anymore."

"I won't."

"Enjoy your relaxation, Brie. Rest while you can." There was no mistaking his meaning.

"I'll take vitamin supplements as well."

The smile in his voice was clear. "Not a bad idea."

"Goodnight, Hudson."

"Goodnight, Brie."

After she hung up, she stared at the ceiling for a long time. Hudson and Natalia had starring roles in her wandering thoughts.

More than once, she'd witnessed his abrupt rudeness. He said and did things without thinking.

Her overall impression was that of a man who found it difficult to connect to others but didn't obsess over the flaw. He fucked women and did business but maintained no lasting relationships.

The one exception was Natalia Roman.

She was the only woman who consistently pulled emotion from Hudson. They were lovers but mostly, they seemed like friends who found something in one another – above and beyond the BDSM lifestyle they shared – that the other people in their lives didn't provide.

The days following their nights together, Hudson was visibly calmer. The barely suppressed rage that seemed to burn just beneath his skin settled for a day or two. Because she provided him peace, Brie would have liked the other woman no matter what.

The fact that Natalia had played *her* body so easily made her want to spend more time with her.

All her adult life, Brie had suppressed her sexual nature but the walls wouldn't stand against the two friends. Hudson provided kindling, Natalia lit a match, and between the two of them, it came roaring to life in a way that could be hellishly inconvenient.

Before them, lovers barely made her warm. She used to convince herself that the *emotional* connection was all that mattered. After her time with them separately, she now knew that was bullshit.

She would never settle again.

She reclined in her tub and imagined him. As her fingers drifted down her stomach and over her mound, the most farfetched series of thoughts popped into her head. Once there, they *wouldn't* leave.

What did he look like when he fisted his cock?

Did he move fast or slow?

Did he concentrate on stroking the shaft or rub his palm over the head?

Did he cup his balls while he jacked off?

Would he let a woman watch him do it?

She took her time stroking herself, rubbing her clit, and let the climax build slowly. She imagined herself in a chair, touching herself like this for him, her legs over the arms so she was completely open.

Hudson would stand over her while he fisted his cock and watch her play with her pussy. He would tell her exactly what to do.

The thought turned her on in a way few things ever had.

The sound of his voice in her head was now common while she masturbated. She neither questioned his presence nor felt shame at the sexual response it caused.

He'd move closer when he sensed she was about to come. "Your little clit is so hard and red. Slip two fingers inside. Fuck, yes. I can see how good that makes you feel. Keep going."

His eyes would lock on hers, filled with too much power, and it would make her breath catch in her throat an instant before her body snatched away her control.

The climax would be extreme, almost painful.

Triumph would be clearly written on his face. Then he would let his own pleasure go, pumping stream after stream of warm semen on her belly and the folds of her pussy with a primal growl.

Maybe he'd lean over her, with his hand on the back of the chair, and let her take the final drops left on the tip of his cock with her tongue.

With a whimper, Brie came so hard she was lightheaded. When the image of Natalia massaging Hudson's come into Brie's pussy as she helped suck his cock clean popped into her brain, it slammed her over the cliff again.

She wasn't sure she maintained consciousness throughout.

Without a doubt, they were the best fantasy material she'd ever had in her sexual history. She wanted *more*.

When her breathing returned to normal and she was sure her legs would hold her, Brie stood and drained the tub. Pulling the shower curtain closed, she quickly showered and washed her hair.

Since she had a couple of days off, she let the heavy mass air dry to give it a break from being tightly bound.

Standing in front of the mirror, she examined her body. She was her toughest critic but she tried to see the good things. Her hair was thick and healthy, her eyes bright.

Her skin was golden all over and it was soft and clear from regular sugar scrubs and moisturizers her mother made and sent her. Her stomach was slightly rounded, no matter what she tried. She'd never been able to flatten it.

Her hips and thighs flared out but if her big ass didn't have hips to go with it, she'd look ridiculous. Going up on her tiptoes, she pronounced her calves thick but shapely. Her legs looked so much longer and leaner in heels, which she loved.

Then there was the bane of her existence.

Enormous breasts too big for her body, too heavy to hold back the effects of gravity. They drooped as if she'd breast-fed half a dozen children. Her brown nipples were lost in what looked like partially filled water balloons.

Her mouth firmed and there was no doubt anywhere inside her about the surgery. She'd stopped by the cosmetic surgeon's office immediately after her shift ended. They did her paperwork and took blood for a full workup to be done. They sent her home with a huge stack of pamphlets to read.

In less than two weeks, she would be free.

Pulling on her cotton pajama bottoms and two tank tops with built-in bras, she crawled under the covers with her book.

Turning her head, she stared at the small statue Hudson gave her. It was her favorite possession because it spoke to the hidden part of herself. *The part no one before him had ever cared to see.*

Brie wasn't naïve. There was no long-term future for her with Hudson or Natalia. The two of them were perfect for one another, already shared a sexual relationship, and were hunting her separately for a mutual purpose that she wanted to experience.

They were too close to see that they were meant to be together. It was the only explanation she could come up with. She remembered reading once that if you married anyone other than your best friend, you were marrying the wrong person.

She'd make sure they didn't make such a mistake. It was the least she could do for awe-inspiring orgasms.

Chapter Thirty-Six

Saturdays in the city were wonderful. After weeks of severe cold, it was almost mild outside and the citizens of New York took to the streets. The flow was different from during the business week.

It was the city that never slept but there was an ebb and flow Brie loved more every day she lived here.

She wore a pair of high heels styled after hiking boots that her sister purchased and hated. The jeans, two fresh bra tanks over her "bulletproof" bra, and a white button-down shirt gave her enough layers to feel confident.

With her heavy jacket, scarf, and backpack in hand, she was ready to spend some time outside herself.

Gabriella walked without a specific destination in mind, but it was no surprise when she ended up at the coffee shop she visited most often on the days she worked.

She accepted her order, waved to the familiar barista, and found a table by the window to people watch.

She settled in happily before opening her backpack. A notebook and pen helped her to relax while she soaked up the day and sipped her coffee.

A man and woman laughed together on the other side of the coffee house and she sketched the way their heads leaned together. Signing her name below it, she added a tiny heart above the "I" and grinned at her silliness.

For a long while, she soaked up the sounds and smells and movements going on around her. She ordered a Chai tea and Greek yogurt cup with fresh strawberries.

Flipping to an earlier page, she worked on one of her favorite sketches with a set of charcoals.

The coffee shop was one of the best places to hang out. It was peaceful and the customers provided an endless source of inspiration.

An elderly woman with a small child captured her attention as they walked to the counter and ordered hot chocolate and muffins.

When they sat together at the table beside her, she sketched as fast as she could while they ate and laughed together. As they started to clean up, Brie removed the page.

They came alongside her table, moving slowly because the child had very little legs and the woman was very old.

Careful not to startle the woman, Brie spoke softly, "Excuse me. Excuse me please. I don't mean to bother you. You both looked so happy I had to sketch you. I'd like you to have it."

The woman looked suspicious. "How much?"

"Oh no! I don't want you to *buy* it! I thought you'd like the memory." Brie held it out. "Here."

She handed the woman the sketch and the wariness faded away, replaced with a soft expression as she lowered it so her grandson could see. His face broke into a gap-toothed grin.

"That's *me*, *Savta*!" he shouted.

"Yes, it is. Your mother will love it." The woman beamed.

"I'm glad you like it. Have a lovely day." She returned to her book and smiled as they continued on their way, talking animatedly.

"Do you do that a lot?" asked a familiar voice from a table away.

Closing her eyes and gathering her composure, she turned her head to face the always-fierce gaze of Hudson Winters. It was the first time she'd seen him out of a suit.

With an inner chuckle, she hoped it wasn't the last.

He wore jeans and an untucked dress shirt with stylish leather shoes on his feet. Positively casual. A large coffee cup sat empty beside him.

How long has he been sitting there?

She tucked a stray strand of hair behind her ear and concentrated on forming words. The man looked edible. "Do what? Sketch?"

His long legs were stretched out in front of him and his hands were clasped loosely over his firm stomach. "No. Do you often give away portraits you do of strangers?"

The man had her flustered.

"I, well, they're *in* it." She busily straightened the items on her table. "It's just doodles anyway."

"May I?"

Moving silently for a big man, he appeared at her side, and held his hand out for her notebook. She stared up, frozen with him so close. Her mind went blank.

"Brie?"

She wanted to melt into the floor. Her entire body was molten.

What the fuck is wrong with you?

Hudson stared at her without speaking and she got the distinct feeling a mouse probably felt when faced with a snake. Not that he was a snake. She knew he wasn't. More the predator/prey thing. The man wasn't *reptilian*, for god's sake.

Again, what the fuck is wrong with you?

Without a word, he sat at her table and stared at her across the short distance. "May I see your sketches, Brie?"

She swallowed hard and pushed her notebook toward him.

The moment he started flipping through the pages, she realized her mistake. She knew the instant he found the sketch of him and Natalia. He went completely still and lifted his eyes to hers.

"I sketch *everyone*. I always have."

The excuse sounded weak, even to her own ears. The difference between most of her sketches and the one featuring the best friends was the detail.

It was a sketch she frequently returned to and it showed.

His eyes shifted past her and a crinkle of annoyance appeared between his eyes. She understood why when she heard Riya call her name.

"I can't *believe* you get up early enough to be clear across town. You're possessed with the fearsome demon my men call the *morning person*." Micah gave a mock shudder beside her. "*Hudson*. What a surprise."

Her friend came around to kiss her cheek as Micah held her hand.

"Riya. Chadwick."

Riya rolled her eyes. "You can call each other by your first names. Men often confuse me. If they confuse me, imagine the plight of the women out there that haven't done my research." Tilting her head, she said, "Did you come over to meet Hudson for coffee?"

Oh shit. "I was out walking. I like to walk without a place in mind. I- I like to watch people. The coffee here is my favorite."

You're a babbling idiot and should seek professional help.

Laughing, her friend asked, "You're walking the city in *Azzedines?*"

"Walking in what?"

"You're wearing a twelve-hundred-dollar pair of designer shoes, Brie, to go for a walk."

Brie knocked her empty coffee cup off the table, tried to grab it, and succeeded in knocking the empty yogurt cup over as well.

Stopping her frantic movements, she calmly picked up the items then cleared her throat and turned to Riya.

"Are you telling me these shoes cost more than one thousand *dollars*? My sister paid more than a thousand *dollars* for them and gave them to me instead of returning them when she didn't like them?"

"That's exactly what I'm telling you. I bet Izzy bought them for you and made up the story about hating them." Riya let go of Micah's hand and crouched, lifting Brie's foot in her hand. "These are the real deal. Very hot on you, honey."

"I can't *wear*…I'm going to *kill* her."

Riya stood and slipped her arm around her man's waist. "Yes, you *can* and don't you *dare* kill a woman who buys Azzedines as gifts."

Hudson had returned to flipping through the other sketches, ignoring their unexpected visitors. When her friend noticed, her eyes got wide.

"Oh my god, I love these! Babe, look!" She tugged Micah closer and they stood looking over Hudson's shoulder. He was unhappy.

Brie kept it together for thirty seconds.

The moment they neared the sketch of Hudson and Natalia, she cracked. "I have to get back to my apartment, Riya. Lots to do today. Errands and…stuff. I'm going to go. I'll call you later."

She stood and picked up her trash, moving around them to throw it away. On the way by, she grabbed Hudson's empty cup as well. When she leaned over to pick up her backpack, she took the opportunity to tug her tank tops firmly into place.

"I'll drive you." Hudson's *offer* was really a command as he handed her back her notebook.

"No. I can walk. I like to walk. It's alright, thank you."

Brie touched cheeks with Riya and Micah, shoved the notebook in her bag, and grabbed a hair tie out while she was in there. She roughly gathered all her hair and somewhat secured it in a messy bun.

"Great to see you guys. Okay, bye, everyone." She shrugged on her jacket as she walked between tables, slipping cheap shades on as she made her escape.

Two blocks later, she remembered she was walking in shoes that cost more than the rest of her wardrobe combined.

A sharp whistle hailed a cab.

She gave him her address and pulled out her phone to call Izzy. It went to voicemail. The message she left was succinct.

"You are *toast*, sister."

At her building, she paid the cabbie and got out. As she closed the door, her phone rang and she leaned against the banister.

"How could you give me shoes that are so expensive and not tell me? I wear them to get *groceries* and pick up my *laundry*. Yes, I realize they're meant to be worn. That's not the *point* and you *know* it."

Turning to face the street, Hudson stood less than ten feet away, leaning casually against the light post. She screamed and bobbled her phone, barely managing to hold on to it.

"Izzy, I'll call you back."

Chapter Thirty-Seven

Disconnecting, Brie stared at Hudson for a long moment. "Did you follow me?"

"Leonard has been here."

"Duh. Of course."

"I'm not a stalker but if I were, I would rejoice in the fact that you don't pay very close attention to your surroundings." She blinked, unsure how to respond. "We were talking. We were interrupted. I want to finish our conversation."

"I-I don't...what?"

"For such an eloquent woman, you seem to be having trouble today."

Pushing her sunglasses on top of her head, she waited a beat but couldn't fight the smile that wanted out. The initial awkwardness she'd felt *seeing* him for the first time since Christmas Eve dissipated.

"Did you just make a *joke*, Hudson?"

"You're extraordinarily pretty when you smile."

There was no doubt in Brie's mind that the man planned to fuck her and the logical half of her brain couldn't come up with a single reason that wasn't an excellent plan.

Clearing her throat carefully, she asked, "Would you like tea?"

"I would."

Brie nodded and walked up the steps, feeling awkward and clumsy as she pulled out her keys to unlock the entry door. As she glanced up, she saw him watching her in the door's reflection. Hiding the shaking of her hand, she pushed it open and waited as he walked through.

It was disconcerting to have him behind her on the stairs because she was distinctly aware of the size of her ass. She was never so thankful to get to her door. Accomplishing another lock, Brie put her bag down on the little foyer table and headed into her kitchen.

"You've done remarkable things with the color and light in this space."

Turning, she looked out over her apartment and smiled. "Thank you. I love this apartment. The owner maintains the building so well and they preserved a lot of the old detail."

Moving to a small door set in the wall, she opened it to show him a shallow spice rack. "Behind this is the original dumbwaiter. Instead of taking it out, the space was repurposed."

She ran her fingers over the carved shelves. "The detail is amazing. It's just a *cabinet*, you know? You wouldn't think the edging would have mattered." Closing the door with a shrug, she went to the sink to fill the kettle. "Most people would slap a piece of plywood in there and call it done."

"You have a good eye for detail."

From the corner of her eye, she watched as he roamed her living room, touching fabrics she'd decorated with, leafing through books on the shelves.

Hudson was a big man but moved gracefully through her space without overwhelming it. He glanced through the door to her bedroom but didn't go inside.

At her desk, he stopped and stared at something. After she turned on the water to boil, she joined him and saw he was looking at the pamphlet the doctor gave her to prepare for surgery.

Mortified, her entire body hot, she was instantly on the verge of tears.

Reaching past him, she grabbed the stack of information and shoved it in the top drawer. Her hands were shaking violently. The silence went on and on for almost a minute.

"Now I understand," he said softly.

"I-I…" She couldn't look at his face and had no idea what to say.

"Turn around, Brie." Thankful for an excuse to avoid his face, she did so instantly. His hands touched her shoulders and she jumped. "I won't hurt you."

He began to massage the muscles of her neck, shoulders, and upper back and it felt *incredible*. The weight of her breasts put constant stress on her upper torso.

"You must hurt all the time."

She nodded but knew it was impossible to answer him. His forearm moved across her upper chest and gripped the opposite shoulder. She stiffened in embarrassment.

"It's alright. Don't be afraid."

With his other palm, he pressed at the center of her back between her shoulder blades and it eased a burning pressure she lived with almost constantly. She wanted to sob at the momentary relief.

"My mother is built like you. When I sold my first company, I found the best doctor in the country and she had the surgery done. She was in her late forties and said it changed her life."

Hudson didn't rush, working the muscles that ached as if he had all the time in the world. It was one of the kindest things she'd ever had happen to her and she would never forget it.

"When are you going?"

Her voice was low. "I get my final lab work done next week. If everything is good, they'll put me on the schedule within a couple of days. I already scheduled the time at work."

"Do you have help? Someone who can stay with you?"

"The girl across the hall. I helped her with some schoolwork so she's happy to be able to return the favor."

The teakettle whistled and his hands stilled after one final stroke over her back through her clothing.

"Thank you, Hudson."

She walked into the kitchen and tried to get her breathing under control as she made a tray. Hudson sat in her large chair.

He looked perfect there.

Shaking herself, Brie put the tray down between them on the side table. He picked up a triangle of baklava and bit into it, his eyes drifting closed. She watched as he chewed slowly. Only when he swallowed did he open them.

"Where did you get this? It's the best baklava I've ever tasted."

Her eyes went wide and she laughed. "The wife of the man who owns the bodega, Mrs. Stoermer, gave me the recipe. I'll tell her it was a hit."

The man glanced at the dessert and back at her. "You made this?" She nodded with a grin. "Do you like to cook?"

"I do but I only cook on the weekends. I make my meals for the weekdays. It's silly to cook for one person after work."

Brie sipped her tea and watched him finish the pastry with a look of pure pleasure on his face. She held out the tray and he took another.

"What are you making this weekend?"

"I'm beginning to stockpile finished meals for-for after my procedure so I just have to heat things up. It'll make it easier." She looked through the sheer curtains, focused on the bright sunlight.

"Tonight, I'm making a pot roast. It's been marinating all morning." The silence dragged out because she was terrified. She wasn't sure she could handle Hudson rejecting her a second time.

"Brie." She met his gaze. "Ask me."

She loved the way the man gave orders. His black eyes never looked away from her face. He didn't even blink.

"Would you like to stay for dinner?"

"Yes."

"It needs to cook for several hours. I'll start it." Standing, she moved to her bedroom and took off the heels. She'd finish yelling at Izzy about them later. In the meantime, she stepped into sneakers and went to the kitchen.

All the ingredients were prepped and waiting in the refrigerator. Hudson stood there as she closed the door. She almost dropped everything. His hands steadied her.

"Thank you. You move silently for a big man."

He tucked a curl behind her ear. "I would never hurt you."

"I know."

She stayed busy and avoided his eyes as she prepared the meat to go into the oven. It gave her time to collect her thoughts. When she'd set the timer to slow-cook the roast and vegetables, she washed her hands and turned to him.

"You fascinate me, Hudson. I'm highly susceptible to you."

His eyes stared at her so fixedly that she almost couldn't find the courage to say what she needed to say to him in person. There could be no doubts about what she wanted, what she needed from him.

"I'm susceptible to Natalia as well."

"Did you enjoy what you experienced with her?" He wanted to see her face when he asked the question and she respected him for it.

"I did. Far more than I would have thought possible." She pulled her lower lip between her teeth. "She's beautiful and passionate." A small pause. "I want you both but I won't cause issues between you."

"You intrigue me on so many levels."

He stepped closer, gathered her hair to one side, and bent to kiss the skin along her neck. The shiver that worked through her in response didn't go unnoticed.

Nudging her face up, he stared at her. "I want you. That's all I know, all I can think about."

The choice to take whatever Hudson could give her *right now* was a no-brainer. Always, she'd have the memories he gave her.

"Alright." Before she finished saying the word, Hudson had her in his arms, his mouth covering hers.

He took her *apart* and she invited him in to do as much damage as possible because she didn't know if she'd get another chance. She had no intention of questioning a fucking thing. It would all work out.

Thinking was the fucking enemy.

He gripped her ass and sealed her to his body. Walking backwards, he guided her into the living room and sat in the large chair. He brought her down on his lap, cradled her head in the bend of one arm, and used the other to push back her curls.

"The blue of your eyes in amazing in this light." Stroking his palm along the outside of one breast, he asked gently, "Tell me honestly, Brie, do you want me to leave you covered? I want you to feel pleasure – not nervousness."

Unwelcome tears slipped from the corners of her eyes as she nodded.

"Don't cry." It wasn't an order despite the way it sounded. He lifted and hugged her, rubbing her back.

"No one has ever asked me that before." She wrapped her arms tightly around his neck and straddled his lap. He inhaled sharply and crushed his arms across her back.

The man gave the best hugs ever.

With a deep breath, she sat back. She didn't look at his face. Instead, she focused on touching him. It was something she'd missed the first two times he'd kissed her.

Brie wanted to explore him so badly.

She trailed her hands over his shoulders and chest. Her eyes followed the movements, memorizing him. Both palms flowed down the center of his torso and she pressed, her lips slightly parted.

Her heart was beating hard and fast. Letting her hands slide apart, she cupped his sides and stroked back up to examine his pecs, scratching lightly with her short nails.

The freedom to touch him was *intoxicating.*

"Brie, if you don't stop kneading me like a kitten, I'm going to have you stripped and fucked within three minutes."

She blinked, landing back in the moment. "Hudson…?"

"Yes?"

"I like touching you so much. I want to touch you *more.*"

His hands clenched hard on her hips. "Brie." She met his eyes and licked her lips. "Fuck it. We'll go slow next time."

Chapter Thirty-Eight

Hudson stood and took Brie with him. She gasped and wrapped her legs around his waist. He took long strides to her room where he tossed her on the bed.

Her sneakers, socks, and jeans were gone in under a minute.

He tried not to focus on the green silk panties that formed to her like a layer of skin or the head to toe golden flesh he planned to know up close and personal very soon.

Lifting her into a sitting position, Hudson took her shirt and tank tops off, leaving the bra that matched her panties. He lightly cupped the sides of breasts that must have made her a target for every adolescent penis in her town since the day they appeared.

He took her lips as he unbuttoned the top two buttons and started to pull his shirt up his body. He thought she was reaching to help take it off but she flattened her palms on him with a low moan.

Brie again kneaded his skin like a fucking *kitten* and every nerve in his body fired to life as he broke the kiss and ripped the material over his head.

With a firm grip on the hair at the back of her head, he held her still for an all-out assault on her mouth while he worked to remove his shoes with the other hand. He managed to get his wallet from his back pocket and throw a condom on the bed beside her.

When he reached for his belt, she pushed his hands away and dragged the leather through the buckle. The tips of her fingers slipped into the waist of his jeans to unbutton him, brushed the head of his dick, and he thought he was going to embarrass himself. Lowering the zipper with one hand, she used the other to stroke him. She was shaking.

"Hudson, now. *Now.* I need you inside me."

He growled as Brie shoved his jeans and boxer briefs to his hips and ran both hands over his cock and balls. Her touch was careful and unsure but her need and enthusiasm were obvious.

It ramped his own need to a fever pitch he'd never experienced with anyone other than Natalia and *never* in "vanilla" pursuits.

Placing his hand in the center of her chest, he forced her to lay back on the bed. He traced the band of her panties, leaning forward to kiss her smooth belly as he pulled them over her hips and down her legs. Unlacing his other shoe, he toed it off and sank to his knees.

"Look at this pretty pussy." Hudson nuzzled her inner thighs, inhaling the clean, musky scent of her. He gripped her ankles and pushed them back, leaving her feet flat on the bed before he pressed her knees out. "Keep your legs wide, Brie."

He slid his palms under the cheeks of her ass and brought her to his mouth. She jerked with a gasp and exhaled his name. The taste of her exploded over his taste buds and he lightly bit her folds.

He dragged his tongue through the sweet syrup gathered there. Blood pounded through his veins and his cock throbbed hard and heavy with the ache to take her.

Instead, he focused on licking away every slick drop before circling his tongue around the entrance to her pussy and pushing inside. He fucked her with it, watching as she arched off the bed to the rhythm he set but never moved her legs from where he'd placed them.

With open-mouthed kisses from her pussy to her clit, he sucked the swollen little bundle of nerves into his mouth and flicked it with his tongue.

"Oh god, Hudson…*yes.*"

One finger penetrated her deeply and he laid his palm over her low abdomen, feeling her womb spasm as her climax started. Increasing his attention, his strokes inside her, he shoved her over the edge and watched her embrace the moment.

Give herself to the pleasure.

He dragged it out with firm suckles and she bit into her lower lip with incoherent moans. He stroked her clit and reached past her leg to grab the condom. It was rolled on in desperation as he stood.

Notching his cock against the entrance of her wet heat, it sucked at the head, trying to pull him deeper. He felt lightheaded when he leaned over her body.

"You taste amazing, Brie. Taste yourself so you know why I plan to have my tongue buried in your pussy as often as possible."

She moaned and lifted shaking hands to his cheeks, rising slightly from the bed to get closer. Tentative licks across his lips and then she kissed him deeply, curling her tongue around his, and sucking it between her soft lips.

The shaft of sensation it shot to his cock had him thrusting forward harder than he intended. She inhaled sharply and Hudson pulled back to look at her face.

Her eyes were closed and she whispered, "Yes."

The word brought him into sharp focus. "Brie, open your eyes." She did instantly and he told her firmly, "Tell me if I hurt you. Do you understand?" She nodded.

Only when he was fully buried could he think again. He stared down at her. "Are you alright?"

She smiled and reached up to stroke her fingers through his hair. "Yes, Hudson. I'm wonderful." One finger trailed from his temple to his chin and she smiled. "You're *so* beautiful."

He felt his heart thump hard against his sternum and took in the image of Brie letting him *take* her.

From her wild hair to her bright smile to her willingness to please him, he drank in the sight, and found himself lowering until their upper bodies were sealed together. Sliding one hand under her back, he scooted them higher on the bed and went still.

Reaching down, he pushed his jeans and boxers further down his legs. She helped by shoving them the rest of the way off with her feet.

He was fully naked with her, holding her, and letting her hold him. It was a closeness, an intimacy, he wasn't accustomed to, and he would be lying to himself if he pretended not to be affected.

Hudson *never* lied to himself.

She took immediate advantage of their new position by stroking her legs along his and touching his skin wherever she could reach. Warm, soft hands coasted over his skin and he let himself *feel* it.

His ex-girlfriends were greedy sociopaths. They did what they considered their *job* and random touches were not encouraged on either side. Business arrangements were cold and impersonal.

Not that Hudson had wanted anything from them other than to get off. He admitted that.

His relationship with Natalia went from drunk and playful encounters to D/s. Their interactions were controlled and they weren't outwardly affectionate. She was careful to minimize her touches, always reinforcing distance when she felt she'd crossed some imaginary line.

He dominated every aspect of their sexual relationship and, as far as he knew, they both preferred it that way.

Watching Brie's face, he knew one thing without a doubt. She was not in love with him yet but she *could* be so easily.

Everything about her was soft and welcoming.

She was vulnerable to him in a way no one had ever been and the knowledge humbled him in a way few things could.

As he started to move, stroking deep and strong into her body, Hudson pulled her knee up to rest along his hip, and ran his palm up her side to her face.

"You feel fucking amazing." He thrust harder and her breathing quickened. He growled deep in his chest.

"More please."

One hand slid under her back to her opposite shoulder and he held her firmly as he drove hard into her willing body. She wrapped her legs around him and closed her eyes. Panting now, her upper body slowly rose from the bed, and her short nails dug into his back.

"Your pussy sucks at me." Brie bit her lip. "Fuck yes. Tighten on me." Getting close to her ear, he murmured, "Make my cock slick with your sweet cream."

She moaned and thrashed, clawed at him, her muscles locked inside and out while he fucked her through her first orgasm with him buried in her body. It held her for a long time and he watched her face, amazed at how openly she expressed her pleasure.

When she came down, she lifted to kiss him again, her hand sliding into his hair. Small tugs as she licked and bit at his lips. Her other hand stroked his chest, scratched over his nipple, and he grunted into the silken heat of her mouth.

The touches, the kisses, the *attention* she gave awed him.

Jerking her into his arms, he sat back on his heels, and brought her hard against his chest. He spread his knees, opened her, tightened her further around him, and her head dropped back on her shoulders with a moan.

He hit deeper this way and fully controlled her body and the rhythm. Wrapping his arms around her, holding her completely still, he drove up into her body.

"Yes. Please *don't stop.*"

He watched the impact of his thrusts on the upper swells of her breasts and knew he was probably being too harsh with her. She wasn't used to it and rough sex would take its toll on her later.

There was no way he could pull back now. He had to mark her, give her something no other lover had ever given her. "Hold on, Brie."

She obeyed instantly, happy to hug him with her arms. He felt her breathe in the scent of him at the bend of his neck and shoulder.

His hands drifted down her back to her stunning ass. Grabbing a cheek in each hand, he separated them and pushed them back together, stimulating the little pucker without touching it.

The sounds she made told him she felt the pleasure that could be found there. He had to prepare her for the fact that he *would* take her ass. Burying his cock deep in her tight heat while he held her round cheeks in his hands was necessary to his continued sanity.

Just as having her lips spread to take him while he fucked her mouth was on his agenda.

Her head came up and their gazes locked. Her curly black hair was everywhere. She was naturally sensual, freely taking what he gave her.

When her hands moved from his shoulders to his face, holding it while she stared into his eyes, he almost came. Reining in his focus, he drove his cock hard and deep and watched her orgasm rise.

"Better than I imagined, Hudson...being with you. Thank you."

The kiss she gave him held an emotional connection different from any he'd allowed a woman to show him before. In response, he held her tight enough to steal her breath as he returned it.

The climax rolled over her like a freight train and she broke the kiss to inhale hard, his name a chant on her lips until he claimed her mouth again. He didn't fuck her as hard as he took Natalia but harder than any *other* women he'd been with and she soaked it up.

Pushing her higher and keeping her there until her entire body went limp, he knew there was no way to hold back another moment.

His own orgasm felt like someone had his balls in a vise and then release, release, *release*. "Fuck *yes*, Brie."

They held one another, his strokes shallow as he pumped every drop of come from his balls. He lowered them to the bed and Brie sighed as the linens touched her back.

Hudson stared into her face. They were breathing hard but she had a grip on his shoulder and his hair that he didn't want to lose.

He wasn't surprised when she began to drift off.

"That erased so many sad memories. Thank you, Hudson."

A soft sigh and her entire body relaxed within seconds. He'd never seen anyone fall asleep so fast. Rolling them to their sides, he watched her for a long time.

He didn't think he'd fall asleep, but he did.

Chapter Thirty-Nine

The sound of the oven timer woke Brie from her nap. She felt pleasantly sore and a little sticky. Having Hudson curled around her body was a bonus she hadn't expected.

Slipping from underneath him, she made her way into the bathroom to wash up. Clean panties and a shirt were fine to check the roast. After she washed her hands and gathered up her hair, she walked to her kitchen.

She took a loaf of her homemade bread from the freezer. Everything she needed for salad was spread out on the counter and she started prepping it. This time, she heard him move up behind her.

Likely because he wanted her to.

"It smells amazing in here." His arms wrapped around her stomach and he nuzzled her neck.

"Thank you." She couldn't stop smiling. "You realize it's just pot roast? Nothing fancy?"

"I've never actually *cooked* in my kitchen – though caterers have used it. My mother never cooked so, I look forward to it."

She turned in his arms. "You don't have someone to cook for you?"

He shrugged. "I don't like too many people in my personal space. I eat out or order something."

She grinned. "Then you're likely to go into shock. There's pot roast, vegetables, homemade bread, a tossed salad, and more baklava."

"I need baklava now to hold me over."

His expression was grave and it made her chuckle. She reached past him and lifted the top off the cake plate, holding the base between them. Hudson took a piece with each hand.

"You're a dangerous woman."

With a wink, she put the dish back, and returned to chopping veggies. She could feel him watching her while he savored the dessert.

"Spit it out."

"I'm watching your ass in those panties. I considered dropping to my knees and biting the fuck out of it but you're holding a knife. I didn't want to risk it."

"You're sweet."

"No one has *ever* called me sweet. Not even my own *mother* calls me sweet, Brie."

"You hide it but you're *definitely* sweet." She smiled at him. "As for my ass, it leaves the room a few seconds after I do. It's the true trait I received from my mother's mother. Hard to find jeans that fit."

Moving behind her, he grabbed a cheek in both hands and squeezed.

"Round, firm, bitable." Nudging stray hairs out of the way, he kissed her neck and ground his cock against her ass. "You have a perfect ass. It leads into curvy hips just the right size for my hands."

He demonstrated and she put down the knife.

"Which leads to these silky thighs that took a hard fucking without bruising." His palms slid between her legs and pressed her thighs until she stepped out. "Framing this perfect pussy that sucked my ability to think out through my cock."

When his fingers slid beneath the line of her panties and stroked her, Brie dropped her head back on his shoulder. Two fingers worked into her pussy while his thumb circled over her clit. He took his time.

"Give me another sample. Soak my fingers." She worried about staying on her feet when the orgasm took her. "You come so pretty."

Reaching up to grip her chin, he turned her face to the side and held her in place while he ate at her mouth.

The man was a fucking force of nature.

When her muscles relaxed, he pulled his fingers from inside her and gave her clit a light tap. He used the tips to paint her lips before he licked them clean. He broke the kiss and locked his eyes on hers. She couldn't fight the tremor that worked over her body.

He used his thumb to open her mouth and rubbed the pads of his fingers over her tongue.

"Suck." Brie closed her lips, drew on them, and stroked her tongue around the length. "Jesus. That hits the root of my dick."

She turned her body and stroked her hand down his torso. Before she could take him in her hand, he stopped her and pulled his fingers from between her lips.

"I shouldn't have distracted you. I'll behave." She quirked her brow and he added with a small laugh, "For now."

He gave her ass a sharp smack and turned her back to the counter. His hands settled on her shoulders. She couldn't contain her sigh when he began to massage her again.

"You'll let me hire someone to help you in addition to the teenager."

Glancing up and back, she shook her head. "Hudson…"

"It wasn't a question. You're having major surgery. I'd feel better knowing you had someone checking your bandages and making sure you don't overdo it."

"I'll hire someone then. I promise."

"I choose to ignore you." The words made her smile. He continued massaging her and relieved the pressure again between her shoulder blades. "Why the fuck didn't your parents have this surgery done years ago? I can't imagine it hurt less as a teenager."

"More actually since I was still growing. They didn't do it because they're devout Catholics who don't believe in cosmetic surgery." She diced tomatoes. "I was fourteen, just over five feet tall, and the butt of every locker room joke in my school."

Tossing ingredients into a large wooden bowl, she rinsed and dried her hands. "My parents love me but they'll never understand the person I'm on the inside and I'm tired of pretending to be someone else."

She moved around the kitchen getting plates and made a dipping sauce for the bread. "That's why I've worked and saved so hard. I have a trust fund. I'll never receive it. Relief of the pain is worth every cent."

"You may never get back what was stolen from you, Brie. Let me write you a check."

She laughed. "No, Hudson." She stretched up on tiptoes to get wine glasses. "You've already tried that." He said nothing and she gave him a soft smile. "When the detective in charge of my case called me down to the station last week and handed me an untraceable check, I knew it was you. People rarely get their money back in situations like mine."

He simply stared at her.

"It's only money. I really *will* be just fine." She tilted her head. "I appreciate the gesture but it isn't your responsibility to help me." Walking past him, she took the envelope from her safe box and handed it to him before returning to the kitchen.

He opened it, his eyes widened, and he stared at her. "You didn't deposit it." She shook her head. "Why won't you take help from me?"

"That isn't *help*, Hudson. That's almost a hundred grand." With her hands on her hips, her answer was gentle. "I won't take it because it isn't your job to take care of me."

"This amount is nothing to me, Brie."

"It's a lot to *me* and I'm not a whore, Hudson." She watched him go still and wondered if she should have rephrased the statement.

His voice was deadly quiet. "That wouldn't make you a whore, Brie."

"If we're having sex and I take substantial amounts of money from you, yes, that makes me a whore. I don't need jewelry. I don't need fancy vacations or designer clothes. I'm partial to Reese's peanut butter cups when I'm on my period."

She leaned against her counter and he blocked her in. The expression on his face should have frightened her but instead, it made her inner walls clench in need.

"Don't *ever* refer to yourself as a whore again. You won't sit for a week." He reached up and gripped the back of her neck to hold her still. "I should spank your ass red for daring to *suggest* you could *be* that. If I buy you jewelry and clothes and take you places – that *still* doesn't make you my whore. That makes you my *woman*."

Tempting but that wasn't possible and he would see that soon enough.

"I'm not…"

"Don't lie to either of us." He stared down at her and she glimpsed the animal that lived inside him. She wanted to pet and nuzzle it. "Who do you belong to?"

"I don't…"

"Brie, I'll put you over my lap." He was going to make this difficult and her body didn't care about semantics, it just wanted him to fuck her. She fidgeted on her feet. "I won't hurt you. I can be hard. You need gentle as well. I'll work on it."

His other hand moved between her legs, massaging her through her panties. Her response was immediate and undeniable.

"Don't pretend you don't know. Don't pretend this soft, wet pussy isn't mine to eat and play with and fuck." Sliding under the fabric, he rubbed her slow and easy until her legs opened and she began to shake. "Who do you belong to, Brie?"

"You, Hudson." *Until you see, and feel, the love that waits for you.*

He let her come and held her close to him, bringing her down slowly until her breathing steadied.

She held herself up on the counter and he went to her bathroom, returning with a warm washcloth. He tugged her panties down, wiped away the evidence of her orgasms, and settled them back in place.

Lifting her chin with the side of his hand, he stared into her eyes. "Sleepy?"

"A little." She smiled. "I'm not used to so many orgasms."

He probably didn't realize how gentle the smile was that he gave her before he kissed her forehead. Brie had to hug him and was happy when he returned it.

"I'm hungry and I imagine you are, too. I'll finish the food."

Twenty minutes later, they sat at her small dinette in front of one of the large windows. He wasted no time digging in.

"This is, dear lord, Brie."

"I'm glad you think it's good."

"Oh yeah. Good."

She realized it was the first time she'd fed a man after sex and felt as if he deserved every bite.

He said very little as he demolished the first plate and she refilled it as she sat back with her glass of wine to watch him.

There was an ease with him she'd never found with other lovers. She enjoyed Hudson as a person and she thought that probably made all the difference.

"You're easing me into it. Aren't you?"

Hudson picked up his wine glass. He didn't pretend to misunderstand and she liked that he didn't underestimate her intelligence. Certain things he said and did couldn't be mistaken for vanilla sexuality.

"A bit. I'll keep you safe." Taking a drink of wine gave him a moment to think and she let him have it without the hundred questions she wanted to ask.

"I never doubted that for one moment, Hudson." She could tell the words pleased him.

"You're sexually giving, Brie. It's your heart. You need to make the people around you happy. With a Dominant who will keep your safety paramount at all times, that's an amazing gift."

"I trust you to do that."

"Trust is incredibly important. I'm going to start you slow and work you as high as you're comfortable."

"What happens then?"

The lifestyle made her curious. She imagined being a good fit for someone *like* Hudson, though not *him* specifically since he already had the *ideal* submissive.

"That's where we stay until you feel comfortable to go further. I'll push your comfort zones. Things I do to you or ask you to do may embarrass you, be physically uncomfortable, or truly hurt and I need you to know the difference. Do you understand?"

"Tell you about pain but if I'm just embarrassed, power through it." Her time with him had already been an exercise in pushing her comfort zones.

"Exactly."

He pulled her from her seat and led her over to the large chair in her seating area. She draped her legs on either side of his and leaned back against his shoulder. They sat like that, in silence, and watched the sun move across the wood floor.

Without a single doubt in her mind, it was the best day she'd ever spent with a man and she would never forget how he'd made her feel.

Despite their conversation, she knew she couldn't keep him.

Chapter Forty

It was fully dark when Brie opened her eyes and realized she'd slept *on* Hudson. Glancing up, she smiled at the power even sleep couldn't fully erase. She badly wanted to touch him but didn't.

Long black lashes created smudged shadows beneath his eyes. His black hair was beginning to silver, the hairline along his temple shimmered in the low light. A broad mouth and full lips were almost too sensual for a man. She found it sad that he smiled so rarely.

Built like an oak, not overly tall but thick and strong, Hudson had an air of capability to him that most men simply didn't possess.

She *wanted* him in many ways but knew to guard her heart from him and his best friend. No matter what they thought, she was not – nor would she ever be – the right fit for either of them.

Moving carefully to avoid waking him up, she lifted away and stood up. Leaning forward, she inhaled the scent of him and brushed her lips lightly over his jaw before she walked into the bathroom. Only when the door was closed did she turn on the light.

After starting the water for her shower, she caught a glimpse of her reflection across the room and turned to examine herself more closely.

Her hair was loose and falling around her. Her lips were swollen and red. Her body was sore yet rested. Every part of her felt relaxed and comfortable for the first time in a long time.

She felt pretty, maybe even desirable.

She unbuttoned her shirt and let it fall. The industrial strength bra followed and she found herself thankful when steam overtook the small space.

No matter how wonderful Hudson made her feel, nothing would change how she felt when she saw herself naked.

Clipping her hair to the top of her head, she showered and dried off. When the towel was secured around her upper body, she moved into the bedroom and found clothing as quietly as possible.

Only when she was fully dressed in multiple tops and yoga pants did she feel as though she could face Hudson.

The moment she stepped into the living room, she knew he was awake. His black eyes glittered at her from across the space. She wanted to climb back in his lap.

Silly girl. Follow the rules.

She curled up in the corner of the couch – close enough to touch him if she reached out but with enough distance to give her confidence.

Hudson leaned forward with his elbows on his knees. The half-smile he gave her made her heart hurt because he didn't understand yet why she had to remain detached as much as possible.

"As much as you think you *should* put distance between us, you can't quite manage it." One hand reached out to stroke her hair and she didn't stop herself from leaning into the touch. "I want you more than I did before I had you."

Turning her face, she kissed his palm. No one in her world had prepared her for a man like Hudson or a woman like Natalia.

She wasn't surprised when he moved to crouch beside her, both of his hands cupping her skull. He kissed her ferociously and every cell in her body strained toward him.

It was not a gentle kiss. It was a *claiming* and there was no doubt in her mind that he meant it as exactly that.

Hudson pulled back to stare into her eyes. "You're lovely and intuitive, Brie. I'm not releasing my claim on you. Are we clear?"

She started to shake her head and he stilled her with another kiss. Only when she was panting with need did he break it.

"Nod." Brie did so in a daze. He was very good at negotiations. "Excellent. A woman will come tomorrow to introduce herself and assess your needs after the surgery. You're not to discuss payment with her. Do you understand?"

The denial that rose to her lips was kissed away by Hudson and she found her upper body cradled in his arms by the time he pulled away.

"Things will be simple between us, Brie. This is not a gray area. You need professional care. I know this from experience. I'll provide it with no strings attached. In other areas, you may argue, not about your health. Speaking to Riya would obtain the same result."

She knew he was right about that.

He kissed the tip of her nose. "Let's try again. A woman will come to help you. You won't discuss her fee. Do you understand?"

"Yes, Hudson. Thank you."

"Better." He kissed her again and settled her against the couch cushions. One finger traced along the side of her face, down her neck, and along her collarbone.

"When you're healed, I plan to remain buried in your body for days. I want to sample your nipples – which I suspect are the same cocoa shade as your lips."

"*Hudson...*" She arched into his hand as he circled her nipple through her layers of clothing.

"Let your body heat for me." He leaned down and nuzzled her ear. "I want you to touch yourself. Imagine that your fingers are my tongue and when you come, think about me lapping up every...silken...drop."

She trembled and Hudson ground his teeth. He delivered a final kiss that included a firm tap to her mound through her clothing and then he headed for the door.

It clicked shut and automatically locked behind the most primal sexual being Brie had ever met.

In seconds, she had her hand inside her clothes, working her fingertips over her folds. The orgasm was almost instantaneous and it was Hudson's name she moaned into the empty apartment.

Emotions be damned. Sexually, the man had her tied in knots. She was still shaking and panting when her cell phone rang.

"Did you come hard, Brie?"

"I…yes," she stammered.

"Did you think of me?"

"Yes, Hudson."

"Put two fingers in your pussy."

"W-what?" It reminded her so much of her fantasy that she quivered.

"Do it now."

She leaned back on the cushions, holding the phone in one hand. The other stroked over her rounded tummy and beneath the fabric of her clothing once again. Her breath caught as she brushed over her swollen clit.

"That's it, touch yourself for me. Slip two fingers in, Brie." She did and was shocked at how *wet* she sounded and felt. "I bet your pussy is just *dripping* for me, isn't it?"

"Yes."

"Stroke in and out, slowly."

She obeyed him without saying a word and knew that *alone* was enough to turn him on. There was no way to stifle the sounds that bubbled up in her throat and she gripped the phone more tightly to keep from dropping it.

"Everything in me screams to come back to you, Brie. To return and fuck you until all you know is the feel of my cock inside you."

"*Hudson...*" She gasped at the force of the orgasm that took her.

"Yes, Brie. God yes."

She could hear the strain in his voice. She wanted to tell him to come back, just *come back,* and *take her* again.

"Sleep. You're going to be sore. I'm sorry."

"Don't be, please don't be." Her voice was quiet because she meant it in so many ways.

"Thank you for dinner and a very memorable evening."

"You're welcome and thank *you* for the orgasms." She was smiling as she ended the call.

Without moving more than it took to pull the throw blanket over her from the back of the couch, Gabriella slept where she was. Her thoughts drifted as she neared sleep.

She had agreed to be his and for a little while, she would be. However long she might have him, there was no doubt in her mind that he would rule her sexually. It was guaranteed to be an education.

She also realized Hudson was right.

She *was* sore, and she *liked* it.

Chapter Forty-One

The next morning, Hudson fisted his dick for the *third* time since leaving Brie. He could think of nothing but burying his cock deep inside her again. Her pussy, her ass, her mouth.

Already he felt as if he hadn't fucked in days.

He knew exactly how to bring her into full agreement. Gabriella was much more sexual and sensual than anyone – including her – gave her credit for being.

He knew how to use those traits against her, and ultimately *for* her.

Not that he wouldn't benefit as well. For a moment, he questioned his motives, his greed – and then he remembered how willingly she'd let Natalia touch her, how she'd allowed him to take her body.

He knew she was innocent compared to him, but not too innocent to what a sexual relationship with him and his best friend would entail.

Once he was dressed, he wasted no time arranging for a home care nurse. He made his requests clear and paid their fee in advance. Their care would commence when Brie's surgery was done.

When his phone rang at noon, he picked it up knowing who it was. "Natalia."

"Good morning, darling. Brunch?"

"I'll pick you up. Be ready in thirty minutes." He hung up knowing she wouldn't be offended.

Dressed in dark slacks and a lightweight sweater, he called for the car. It was waiting out front by the time he made it downstairs.

Natalia appeared at the curb near her building as they pulled to a stop. She climbed in looking tired and a little hung over.

"Late night?" He couldn't help the grin.

"Coffee. Get me coffee and then you can mock me."

She rested her head on the back of the seat and said nothing more until they were ensconced in a private alcove at their favorite restaurant.

When a large cup of coffee was in her hands, she sighed happily.

"Alright. There's a new girl on the scene at the club who was sponsored by the lovely Blythe. Fantastic figure, like Brie actually."

"Sounds fascinating."

"I knew you planned to woo our girl yesterday and needed a playful distraction. She was very energetic. I feel like I've run the fucking marathon. There's a small possibility I'm getting too old for this shit."

Hudson laughed. "Young?"

"Twenty-two if that. She's fun but rather silly." Natalia focused on him for the first time since getting in the car. "You look different." She cocked her head to the side and smiled.

"Hudson. You look almost relaxed." He said nothing, allowing her to scrutinize him while he drank his coffee.

"You fucked Brie at last." They grinned at one another. "Lucky, lucky darling. Is she everything you hoped?" Hudson closed his eyes and she laughed. "Never mind. I withdraw the question."

"The woman has the survival instinct of a baby lemming, Natalia." He pulled out the information of the surgical facility she planned to use and her brows shot up.

"Cosmetic surgery? She does *not* seem the type, not at all."

"Breast reduction."

Natalia's eyes widened and she looked through the windows for a moment. "I wondered. So many clothes, no matter the weather." Glancing back at him, she nodded. "I'll check them out."

"She has an appointment. The last series of lab work before her procedure. Her surgery would be a day or so after the tests come back solid. I wrote it down."

"Are you putting me in front of her, Hudson?"

"She *wants* you in front of her, Natalia. She couldn't have made that clearer. She said she's *susceptible* to both of us. She called you beautiful and passionate."

"I worried that I'd *frightened* her." Tapping her perfect nail on the tabletop, she said carefully, "This could blow up in your face."

"It could blow up in *yours*, Natalia. What would you do without your nightly romps? You've grown accustomed to variety."

Hudson knew his friend wouldn't consider his words judgment. They'd known one another long enough to understand what was said and left *unsaid*.

"You'd spend more time with me, Natalia. It might be too much."

Their food arrived and neither spoke as they ate. Only when she pushed her plate away did Natalia address his concerns.

"You and I alone. It could be too much. I can never be the woman you really need, Hudson. I'd never do your laundry or have dinner on the table. My own ninety-hour work weeks prevent that."

She shrugged lightly. "Still, as much *variety* as you think I have, I spend most nights alone. The girl last night was the first in more than six months." He was unable to hide his surprise. "I eat alone. I sleep alone. You're my only true friend."

"I love you, Natalia. Since I was ten years old, I've loved you. I don't know that it will ever be what love is supposed to be."

"I know you love me. I love you deeply." She paused. "We could break her. I don't want to break her."

"We won't. She's strong. Stronger than she thinks she is." He leaned forward and took Natalia's hand. "I'm greedy. I've never been more so. I think she's soft enough to temper the rough edges of who we've become."

"I feel like we're using her. Hudson, we *are* selfish. That woman doesn't have a selfish bone in her body."

"Then we have to make it what she needs."

"How in the *hell* do we figure out what she needs?"

"Natalia. We *ask* her."

* * *

Her best friend's grin was so sincere, so warm, and so unlike most of the smiles Natalia had ever seen on his face that she was taken aback by the beauty of it.

"You're in love with her, Hudson."

"I feel protective of her. I want her, even after having her within the last twenty-four hours. Even after getting myself off multiple times this morning to temper the sexual insanity she inspires."

"*Hudson...*" Natalia closed her eyes against the erotic image.

His hand tightened around hers, his voice was low. "I know the thought of fucking you while you feast on her was the primary thought in my mind while I stroked my cock. The thought of introducing her to the fine delicacy that is your pussy while I take her hypnotic ass is almost more than I can handle and remain in control."

Natalia's breath came in small pants and Hudson could see the pulse pounding along the pale column of her neck.

"Sit back, Natalia."

It was a command and both of them knew it. She obeyed without question and slipped her hand from his.

"After I left Brie, I called her. She'd given herself another orgasm. She was breathless." Natalia brushed her wrist over her nipple, pretending to straighten her napkin.

"I made her put her fingers in her pussy and I could hear how wet she was. You know how she tastes. Sweet and musky."

Natalia slid her hand under her sweater and into the soft waist of her skirt. She knew he saw the moment she touched her clit.

"I told her to fuck herself and she *did*, Natalia. She played with her pussy while I listened. As my mouth watered and my dick throbbed."

The linen napkin on Natalia's lap hid the position of her hand as she stroked herself. Hudson had seen her do it often enough, commanded it countless times. Even if their server appeared, he would never realize what was happening right in front of him.

"Her folds were wet and warm and it took every ounce of my control not to return and fuck her until she *could not* walk." Flicking his eyes to her lap and back again, he gave her the permission she wanted. "Come."

Only years of training in self-control made it possible for Natalia to hide her orgasm. Orgasms involving Brie seemed so much more powerful and she didn't understand why it was that way.

She doubted Hudson understood it either.

He alone was aware of the way her entire body vibrated, the pounding pulse at her throat, the shallow panting sounds she made and she knew he *wanted* her, he *wanted* Brie, he wanted them *both*.

The thought made her womb tighten.

It was important that they understood Brie would take finesse. Bending her to their will without losing the qualities that made her so unique. It was a delicate endeavor.

He watched from across the table as she came down from her climax and she knew his cock was iron hard behind the fabric of his slacks.

She hadn't seen him so determined, so focused, since they were fresh out of college and he started buying and selling millions in assets.

Natalia and Brie each had something he needed. He wouldn't stop until he had them and she wanted it to work just as badly.

"You're even more beautiful when you come, Natalia." He took a sip of his coffee. She lifted her wet fingers to her lips and licked the tips. Hudson's grip tightened on the mug until his knuckles were white.

"Hudson, you look beautiful when you talk about us being with Brie together. It's a look I could become accustomed to seeing."

He set down the cup and grabbed her wrist, pulling it close so he could suck her fingers himself. A hard tremor rocked her body and she knew he felt it. Releasing them with a soft *pop*, he sat back.

"Meet me in the restroom in one minute."

Without another word, he stood and made his way to the dim hallway leading to the alley behind the restaurant, turning at the last moment to enter the men's room.

Timing it exactly, she stood to follow. As she entered, Hudson wrapped his hand around her upper arm and walked quickly to the handicapped stall at the back of the space.

Closing and locking the door, he ordered, "Turn around."

Natalia turned and he pressed the center of her back with his palm. She bent, gripping the small sink in front of her, as he slid her slim skirt up her thighs. His eyes held hers in the mirror.

When it was gathered at her waist, he pulled her panties low enough to expose her and stroked a single finger through the cleft of her body.

"Dripping wet."

He licked his fingertips and placed them over her clit. She moaned softly while his other hand worked to release his cock.

"I want your pussy wrapped around me, Natalia."

"Yes."

"I've never taken you in a bathroom."

"One more item to check off my list." She meant it literally, though she would never tell him so.

Not soon enough, he notched himself at the entrance of her and wrapped his forearm around her waist. "Put your foot up on the toilet." She did, balancing carefully.

There was no time for finesse. Urgency was unavoidable.

He thrust hard and deep, his fingers never slowing on her clit. Hudson bent over and sealed himself to her back.

At her ear, he whispered, "Brie is standing against the wall, watching me fuck you while she plays with herself."

Natalia bit her lower lip, moaned softly, and held his gaze.

"She's waiting her turn. Waiting for us to fuck her."

She was unable to control the way her body clenched and shook around him. He tunneled harder and faster.

"After I take you, after I fill you, she wants to taste us. Sample our blended flavor direct from your body. She wants to stroke her tongue over you, in you, before sucking your little clit between her lips."

With a low keening wail, she rocked back, coming even as she knew she also took his control.

"Yes. Fuck yes."

He inhaled deeply of her hair as they struggled to keep the sounds they made quiet. He continued to hold her, stroking inside her, long after he'd emptied his balls.

Their eye contact remained.

"You get the same look when we talk about her, Natalia. Now we need to show Brie what we have to offer."

She tightened around him. "I want her badly. I want to watch you with her. I hope you know what you're doing, darling."

They straightened their clothing, cleaned up, and returned separately to their table. When they sat across from one another once again, he motioned to their server for more coffee.

Meeting her eyes, he murmured, "I don't have a choice."

"There's always a choice, Hudson."

"I *need* you. I can *never* lose you. She'll accept us both." His hand clenched on the table. "She craves the sex, the passion, and will willingly submit to receive attention no one has ever paid her. I don't know *why* they haven't but she has grown desperate for it."

Folding her hands on the table, Natalia told him quietly, "You strategize to capture a woman so different from us. It's her *heart* that should terrify you, Hudson. It's warm and fragile. She'll fall in love if we push her. In love with you, in love with me. Be certain you want that. Be certain you won't tire of her *emotional* needs."

Even as she said the words, she knew her friend did not understand. She knew him well.

It would be up to her to protect Brie's heart.

Chapter Forty-Two

Second week of January…

Brie waited quietly for her doctor on Monday morning for the final physical and lab work before her procedure.

She was nervous but excited. When the nurse left her alone to change, she stripped and slipped on the hospital gown.

It was freezing in the exam room and she knew she was shaking from a combination of nerves and the cold.

The door opened and a man who was *not* her doctor walked in.

"I'm sorry – who are you?"

"Dr. Tavin had an emergency. I'll be doing your final workup."

"Oh, alright then. Who are you?"

Sighing, the man answered impatiently, "Dr. Bilk. I fill in for Dr. Tavin here and at the hospital."

Brie pushed down her nervousness. It was always hard to get comfortable with new doctors. She took a calming breath as the good-looking doctor glanced over her chart.

"I see you'll be having reduction surgery. Hmm." His eyes cut to her and she nodded. He took her in from head to toe. "Nothing else?"

"I don't…what do you mean?"

"Let's take a look, shall we? Stand up."

Brie did so and the doctor opened the hospital gown, exposing her panties and nothing else beneath as he crouched in front of her.

Every part of her wanted to recoil but she didn't. Instead, she stared straight ahead and waited for him to be done.

"I'd suggest here, here, and here as well."

Something cold on her torso made her look down. He was making lines on her skin with a marker and moving around her hips to her ass.

"Excuse me. No. I don't *want* all that. The surgery is for my back. That's all I'm here for."

He stood up and capped the marker with a smile. "In for a penny, in for a pound, that's what I always say. You have to go through the recovery anyway. Why not come out looking good all over? You could be pretty."

For a moment, she stared at him in shock and complete humiliation. Then her temper kicked in.

"Fuck *you*. You don't even *know* me. How dare you try to make me feel bad about the *rest* of my body? As if I don't feel bad enough about myself already. Get the hell out of here. I'm getting dressed."

"No need to get overly *emotional*. We'll just do the *reduction* if you…"

"Get *out*! I'm not staying here another minute. I'm going to start screaming if you don't leave. I'll scream this fucking place down."

He scrambled backwards to the door and slammed it behind him.

Brie pulled on her clothes as fast as she could and ignored the nurses calling her name as she ran for the elevator.

Once inside, she collapsed against the back wall in tears that made her even more *furious*. As she neared the lobby, she did her best to wipe her face but when the doors slid open and she came face to face with Natalia, her effort was useless. She started crying uncontrollably again.

Without a word, she pulled Brie from the elevator and out of the lobby to the street while making a call on her cell phone.

"Come back. Quickly."

Moments later, Hudson's car pulled up and Brie found herself in the back seat with Natalia beside her, holding her close. Her head on the narrow shoulder, she felt stupid, small, and ugly.

"It's alright, Brie. Tell me what happened. We'll fix whatever it is."

Between gasping breaths and brutal tears, she got the story out and was mortified that it made her sob even harder.

"Fucking *men*. Brie, you're perfect, just as you are. *Yes*. You can't let that asshole ruin what you want for yourself. I'll get another doctor for you, but let me take you home and make you some tea first."

She nodded and Leonard made the turn toward her apartment.

During the drive, she worked to get her crying jag under control. Natalia said nothing, simply held her, and smoothed her hair.

Fifteen minutes later, Brie opened the door to her apartment and Natalia smiled. "Definitely you." Turning and closing the door, she took Brie's shoulders in her hands. "Go change. Something soft and comfortable. I'll make tea."

Then she leaned forward and kissed her forehead and both cheeks. Another kiss was placed lightly on her lips before she was turned toward her bedroom.

* * *

Brie returned with her face washed and her clothing changed to find Natalia making tea and plating cookies.

The woman was striking in very high gator heels, a slim-line cashmere skirt, and silk blouse. Her hair glistened smooth and blue-black in the morning sun from the kitchen window.

She was long and lean…*gorgeous.*

Natalia turned as she appeared and gave her a warm smile. "There you are. I'm waiting for a call-back from the cosmetic surgeon who handled some scars for me a few years ago."

"Maybe I-I should just forget it."

Tray in one hand, the other sliding around Brie's shoulders, she led her into the living room. When she was settled on the couch, Natalia perched on the edge of her coffee table with a gentle smile.

"That would be a mistake, Brie. You know the pain will only get worse. Right now, you're young enough to avoid long-term damage but what about another five years or ten. Can your back and shoulders take *years* more of this?"

The thought alone made her want to start crying again.

She handed Brie a cup of tea and her cell phone rang. "Yes, I'm here with her. She's better now, Hudson. Positively adorable in jammies, in fact."

Natalia winked at her and Brie blushed. "No need to rush. I made tea." She listened for a moment with a little wrinkle between her eyes. "As a matter of fact, I *do* know how to make tea. You incinerated a pot holding nothing but water so one must not cast stones."

Glancing over, she rolled her electric blue eyes.

"Settle, darling. Brie's feelings were hurt but I've assured her she's absolutely perfect and that the doctor was a fuck-wad." Natalia chuckled as she reached over to play with a long curl. "No, she isn't crying anymore. Fresh and lovely, our Brie."

The words shouldn't have made her feel warm inside, but they did. *Our Brie.* It was salve on a very hurt part of herself.

"Yes. I called him." A pause. "I would entrust her to no one else. I'd have suggested him from the start had I known." Natalia smiled and handed her a cookie, which made Brie laugh softly.

Putting her fingers over the phone, she murmured, "I could get good at this nurturing thing. You'll have to teach me."

Her hand rested casually on Brie's knee and after staring at the perfect manicure for a long time, she set down her mug of tea, reached out, and traced her fingertip over the smooth lacquer polish. It was glossy black, the nails short and squared, and made her slender fingers appear longer and more delicate.

Turning her palm over, they held hands as Natalia answered Hudson's questions. When Natalia's thumb smoothed back and forth over inside of her palm, Brie leaned her head back and listened to the easy banter between old friends. There was a warm rhythm to it.

* * *

"Brie."

Her name spoken by Hudson pulled her from a quiet pool where she'd been swimming. Opening her eyes, she stared into his black ones and gave him a smile.

He was crouched in front of her; Natalia still perched on the coffee table behind him. Brie realized she still held the other woman's hand but made no effort to pull away.

"You alright?"

She nodded. "Yes. Thank you, Hudson. Why did you come?"

"To assure myself that you weren't going to let some fucking quack mess with your head."

She didn't try to stop him when he lifted the edge of her t-shirt and scowled at the faded marks she'd been unable to wash away completely.

The cosmetic surgeon had narrowed her waist by several inches, made lines for a tummy tuck, and shaved off substantial portions of her hips on either side. Hudson saw those when he pulled her stretchy sleep pants away. His palm was warm as he cupped her side.

His voice was quiet. "None of this bullshit. Not *ever*. The reduction will help you with the pain I *know* you have. The rest of you doesn't need to be fucked with."

Leaning over, he kissed her tummy and nuzzled the warm skin with his cheek. "You're gorgeous and soft and warm. Just as you're meant to be. Exactly right."

The tears that slipped into her hair brought him over her. "Don't cry. Ssh, everything will be fine, Brie."

He gathered her up and hugged her hard and she hoped, no matter what happened, that she would never have to do without his hugs.

Natalia had received the *hurt and angry* tears – understanding what it was like to be a woman in a world that expected perfection.

Hudson received the *quiet* tears that had accumulated over a lifetime – first from boys and later from men – of never thinking she was good enough, pretty enough, or thin enough.

Always comparing her to her sister. The hurtful suggestions of diets, exercise, and now plastic surgery to "fix" what was "wrong" with her.

Brie was *exhausted.*

Chapter Forty-Three

Complete disorientation confronted Brie when she opened her eyes. She hadn't realized she'd fallen asleep, had no idea how she'd gotten to her bed, and was staring into the lovely eyes of a woman who affected her in ways no woman had before.

"Natalia."

"I love that your eyes seem black but in reality, they're a dark blue. Summer midnight," said the ethereal creature stretched out beside her.

"How...?"

"Hudson carried you." Brie's eyes widened in instant embarrassment and she stiffened. "One word, Gabriella, just one and I promise he'll spank your ass." Natalia followed the words with a grin. "Not that I wouldn't like to see that, but still."

"She speaks the truth," came the throaty reply just behind her ear. "Not a word, Brie."

Strong arms tightened around her midsection as the fact that she was stretched out in her own bed with the two people on the planet she was most physically attracted to sank in.

It wasn't the fact that Hudson then licked along the shell of her ear. It was more that she was unable to hide her reaction to it. She stared into Natalia's eyes as her entire body responded to the moist heat she wanted *everywhere*.

"My first boyfriend told me I looked more like a boy than his little brother," Natalia told her as she entwined their hands.

She couldn't stop her gasp of outrage.

"My second boyfriend requested I keep my padded bra on during sex so he could at least *pretend* I had some tits."

Brie's heart hurt and she knew the other woman had felt much worse when the words were said to her.

"The first man I seriously dated, who I thought was different, offered to pay for a *rack* because I needed to take my *hotness* up a level. Hudson got there before I could go through with it." Natalia went quiet as she watched Brie's tears fall into her hair. "Are you crying for me, Brie?"

"The first time I saw you, I thought, I'll *never* be that beautiful and sophisticated. Every part of you is in perfect symmetry while I feel like I was stuck with the wrong puzzle pieces. You're stunning and those men were *wrong*, Natalia. So very wrong."

Brie reached out, her knuckles stroked along the fine cheekbone and down her jaw.

"You touch so easily, Brie." Thinking it was unwelcome, Brie moved to lift her hand away but Natalia pressed it closer. "Please don't stop. No one touches us. No one *ever* touches us."

"*Why?*" Her confusion was honest. "All I want to *do* is touch you. I could overdose on the pleasure of touching you."

Natalia got closer, placed her forehead against Brie's, and sighed as she was hugged warmly, naturally. "We're cold, Brie. I don't know why but we are. We don't know how to connect, to touch, without payment of some kind. We're selfish, both of us, but we refuse to take without compensation."

Stroking her narrow back, Brie smiled.

"My compensation is in the giving, Natalia. Consider us even. I wish you and Hudson could see what I see when I look at you. Understand that you're worthy of love and affection, and far from cold. These things take time, I guess. Maybe there will be enough."

"Why wouldn't there be enough time, Brie?"

Her smile held a touch of sadness. She wouldn't burden them with the truth. *It wasn't time. Not yet.*

"You sparkle. The two of you together are elegant and striking; people notice you and move aside to watch you." She shrugged one shoulder. "My family has money. I *know* how to behave in formal situations, how to act at a cocktail party, and which stocks to invest in, but those things don't come *naturally* to me."

She nuzzled their cheeks together and gave Natalia a light kiss.

"I'm more likely to be found chatting with the coat-check girl or the valet." Brie ran her fingers through Natalia's hair and smiled. "It's like silk." She traced her brow with the tip of her finger. "What's your natural color?"

"Blonde."

"Will you tell me why you changed it?"

She watched as the other woman swallowed hard. "The jokes, the misconceptions. Then I started to like that it matched my insides."

"You think your insides are dark?"

"I think, I *know* I'm not like most people and I don't know why."

"What makes you different?"

"I'm afraid of children. I have no interest in things women are supposed to care about. I go through my life on autopilot. The black, the club, the people I take to my bed, it all enforces a distance so no one ever knows."

Brie cupped her skull. "What don't you want them to know?"

"How alone I feel. Isolated. As if I could snuff out like a light and only a few people on the planet would even notice." She smiled sadly.

Behind her, Brie was aware of Hudson's complete stillness. Without asking, she knew Natalia was saying things he had never heard.

She knew he *needed* to hear them.

"Do you want to know what I see?" She nodded. "I see a woman who may not love easily but who loves fiercely. A woman who would leave her home in the middle of the night to help a friend who needed her, in whatever capacity."

She kissed her forehead lightly. "I see a woman who has so much passion but may be stuck in stasis, because it's the way it has always been, and isn't certain how to change it."

Another kiss on her cheek. "Being different doesn't make you dark or cold. It means you're meticulous about who you have in your life and how much of your heart will be invested. You're meticulous; likely because of hurts and disappointments in your past." Her fingers raked softly through the dark strands.

"I see a woman who may mistake *reserve* with *coldness* yet knew just what to say to a woman she barely knows to make her hurt less." Her smile was gentle. "Even made her tea."

"You're easy to care for, Brie. Easier than anyone I've ever met."

She shook her head. "No. It's all about the timing. Whatever you needed twenty, ten, or even two years ago may not be the same as what you need *now*." With a small shrug, she added, "There isn't anything wrong with that. It's alright to change, to grow."

"You make it sound so simple."

A small laugh bubbled up. "That's because it *is* simple. If you don't want to be the person you've been, you change." Her smile was warm. "You can't get much simpler than that."

They rolled her to her back and moved closer to her, their bodies wrapped along her sides, draping over her torso. The touch of their shoulders made the moment more intimate.

Each of them had a hand in her hair but Hudson's was firm where Natalia's was gentle. They lowered their mouths to kiss the corners of hers, then her cheeks, and along either side of her jaw to her ears. Hudson lightly nipped her lobe and Natalia sucked it between her lips.

The effect was powerful and immediate. Brie's hands rose to wrap around their backs. She loved to be touched and these two people were very good at it.

Kisses followed to her neck, the bend of her shoulder, and her collarbone above her t-shirt until she was straining toward them, wanting more.

Hudson dropped his forehead on the pillow beside hers and tightened his hands on her.

"We have to wait. You can't go in for your procedure with marks all over you, Brie." He inhaled the scent of her hair with a small groan. "You already have my fingerprints on your ass. I don't want you to be embarrassed."

While she struggled to settle her breathing, Natalia petted her stomach, hips, and thighs. Their arms encircled her.

Brie slowly came down, running her fingers through their hair softly, gently. "Past those gruff exteriors you wear for the world, my god, you're so very warm."

She turned her face and kissed Natalia's lips then did the same to Hudson. They pressed closer and she smiled. There was another fifteen minutes of silent snuggles before she heard a sound from Hudson that made her chuckle.

He cleared his throat. "Do you have leftovers?"

"I do, Hudson." Giving him another kiss, she shimmied out from between them and pulled her slippers on. They were super-soft and shaped like floppy bunnies. "Don't judge the slippers."

At the door to the bedroom, she glanced over her shoulder. Hudson and Natalia were sitting up, staring at her, and they were *breathtaking*. Moments before, she'd been nestled between them.

"Wow. Just...*wow*."

She headed for the kitchen without another word, putting her hair up in a messy bun on the way.

Brie was pulling dishes from the refrigerator when she heard the click of Natalia's heels approaching from behind and turned. Glancing up, she was again reminded of how short she was. Normally five-nine, the other woman cleared six feet in her shoes.

Natalia said nothing as she gathered Brie against her, one hand along her back and the other at the base of her skull.

The kiss she delivered was one that Brie thought came with an unspoken message. "*I want you just as much.*"

She couldn't stop herself from responding. It seemed a lot of time had passed when she broke the kiss and laid her forehead against Brie's.

"I really like the slippers."

Breathless, she replied, "A gag gift from my sister. She's mortified that I wear them." Hudson leaned in the doorway, arms crossed over his chest, watching them with a look of intense hunger on his face. "I have a question."

"Anything, Brie."

"I don't want to cause problems between you. I would hate that. Can you promise me that I won't?"

The blush crept up her chest and neck, warming her face and making her eyes bright. She wanted them physically but ultimately, *their* relationship was far more important.

Even if they didn't see that yet.

Hudson moved into the kitchen and Brie felt like her heart was going to pound out of her chest. He stepped behind Natalia. In her shoes, they were the same height, though he was much broader.

"Nothing will come between us, Brie. Before anything, beyond anything, we're friends. That will never change." He put his hands on her shoulders and Natalia kept her eyes on Brie.

"It's obvious that we both want you. There are qualities you possess that draw us, inflame us, and make us want to crawl all over you until you can't remember your own name."

Brie watched as his hands stroked down the other woman's arms to her hands. "We are willing, anxious even, to share you between us."

He lifted her arms, crossing them behind her. She left them in the position he placed them, lightly gripping her elbows.

"There are things I provide to Natalia – and that she provides to me – that we've been unable to find in other lovers, Brie. Neither of us knows yet how you'll react to those darker sides of our sexuality."

Hudson's palms moved over her narrow hips, up her flat stomach, to cup her breasts. She was so lean that his palms covered a large portion of her ribcage as his thumbs stroked back and forth over her nipples.

As they pebbled under her clothing, Brie unconsciously licked her lips.

"What we've talked about endlessly, is whether *you* will be open to sharing *Natalia* with me, and open to sharing *me* with Natalia." Keeping his eyes on Brie, he placed his lips at Natalia's ear and said firmly, "Spread your legs."

She did so instantly and Brie watched as Hudson began to work the soft skirt up her thighs. The length of Natalia's legs was even more pronounced in the heels and silk thigh-high stockings she wore. The silk that covered her mound was damp.

Brie wanted to touch her.

His palm traced over the bare skin between the stockings and the panties and Natalia's breathing picked up.

When his fingertips brushed over the damp fabric, Brie pressed her thighs together. As he slipped his hand inside Natalia's panties, she bit her lower lip to keep from moaning.

"You're not to come until Brie gives you permission." His fingers began a lazy circle and Brie knew he was working over her clit.

Natalia's breathing sped up again and the muscles in her thighs tightened and released several times. Unable to stop herself, she reached up to smooth Natalia's hair from her cheek.

"Does it bother you for me to be here, watching you?"

"No, Brie. It makes it harder to hold back. The effect you have on me is very strong." She inhaled carefully. "Does it bother you that Hudson is touching me like this?" Brie shook her head slowly as Natalia clenched her jaw. "Tell me what you're thinking."

"That I want to touch you, too."

She released a gasp followed by a low moan. "Please touch me."

Brie placed her hands on Natalia's sides and stroked up to curve around the sides of her breasts. She didn't wonder at her blush, she'd never touched another woman intimately.

"I want to feel your skin." Moving to the buttons of the silk blouse, Brie separated them with shaking hands. The pink lace of her bra was revealed and Brie kissed the flush above the scalloped edge.

Enthralled by breasts that were so different from her own, she unsnapped the center clasp and slowly peeled the lace away. Bright pink nipples drew her fingertips and furled tightly.

"Don't stop. Take anything you want." The permission made her mouth water. "I'm begging you."

"You never need to beg me, Natalia. You deserve every good thing. I'd love to give you good things."

Stroking her palms gently along the outer curves, Brie leaned forward and took a taut nipple between her lips. Both Hudson and Natalia groaned instantly in response. The texture and flavor was surreal.

Brie wrapped one arm around her body and the other as far as she could reach around Hudson. As she began to suck, Natalia's head dropped to Hudson's shoulder and her entire body began to shake.

"Don't come. Hold it back. She hasn't given you permission."

The strain in Hudson's voice as his fingers continued to work over folds that were now *audibly* wet slammed into Brie's brain and she released the first nipple with a soft *pop* before moving to the other.

This time, she tugged the tight peak with her teeth before she sucked it and felt Natalia's legs begin to lose their ability to hold her up.

Leaving open-mouthed kisses between the two points, Brie sighed. "Please come for us, Natalia."

There was an instant tightening of the other woman's entire body then a sharp gasp as she let the orgasm claim her. Back and forth, she sucked the peaks firmly until the climax eased and Natalia exhaled hard.

Letting go, she licked over the tip with her tongue and planted kisses up her chest and neck. Pulling her face down, she claimed lips that were the same perfect pink as her nipples. Her hold tightened around her torso and the kiss went on and on.

Hudson's warm hand cupped her head and tugged her to one side. Keeping Natalia between them, he kissed Brie aggressively.

When he broke the kiss, he lifted the fingers that were slick with Natalia's essence and painted her lips with her own flavor before kissing it away. Brie clasped his hand, wanting to sample what another woman tasted like.

Growling, Hudson's face jerked sideways to stare at her. "Suck."

With wide eyes, she took the tips of both fingers into the heat of her mouth. His thumb gripped the underside of her jaw and he stroked his fingers slowly in and out between her lips as she sucked the sweet tang from them.

Natalia's eyes concentrated on the interaction. "Brie, you have such perfect lips."

She didn't realize her eyes had drifted closed until Hudson said, "We need to stop before I insist on having them wrapped around my cock." He pulled his fingers away and watched as a little frown appeared between Brie's eyes. "Tell me, Brie."

Her eyes flicked down and she took in the sight of Natalia's breasts again. She still hadn't moved from the position Hudson put her in. Reaching up, she cupped them in her hands, her thumbs smoothing gently over the still-tight nipples.

Natalia moaned softly and Hudson said her name.

Meeting his eyes, she said, "I enjoy sharing Natalia with you, Hudson." She continued massaging the modest mounds as she spoke. "She's so different from my own body. I like the way she looks, smells, sounds, feels, tastes. I never even considered…"

Her voice trailed away.

Hudson provided, "That you'd be sexually attracted to a woman? I doubt it would be the same with just any woman."

Meeting Natalia's eyes, she said softly, "I *know* it wouldn't be."

Brie lifted one hand to comb through her hair. "Will you stay this way until he gives you permission to move?" She nodded with a small smile. "It makes it more intense for you, doesn't it?"

"Yes. More than anything, placing my pleasure in someone else's hands gives me the freedom to take in, to do nothing more than experience."

"Are you ever the dominant?"

"Many times, with women," she said.

"Have you been with a lot of women?"

"Never anyone like you, Brie. Never anyone who even came close."

Still caressing, she asked what she wanted to know. "How would you be with me?"

"I think we need to learn what you like, Brie. You're open, honest in your reactions. There may be times, like today, where you prefer a more dominant role where I'm concerned but I can see definite submissive tendencies with Hudson."

"I've only been with two people other than Hudson and…now you. I don't know anything."

"You know so much more than you think, Brie. You're one of the most naturally sensual people I've ever known."

Hudson's hands covered Brie's. "Natalia will always tell you if you go too far. Try alternating a soft touch with a firmer one." Squeezing the nipples between their combined hands, Natalia responded by rocking her hips forward.

Experimentally, Brie pressed with her own hips and Natalia moaned. "I want to see you."

Kissing her way down the other woman's torso, she pulled her panties away as she lowered to her knees. She was so wet that her release was visible on her inner thighs. Her folds were pink and free of hair.

"You're so compact, so perfect."

Unsure what to do, she leaned forward and planted a kiss at the very top of the glistening cleft. The long legs almost buckled.

Lifting her hand, she smoothed through the shimmering moisture and licked her fingertips. Trailing her hands up the back of Natalia's legs, she moved around to frame her pelvis. Using her thumbs, she opened the folds and exposed her clit.

"Pink and pretty." Unaware that she'd spoken aloud, she took her first female lover's clit between her lips and sucked.

Natalia bucked in Hudson's grasp and he held her up as she moaned and rocked her hips.

Brie's hands didn't stop moving, exploring her legs, her ass, and finally stroking between her legs. Leaning back, she slipped one finger inside a pussy that was just as hot and wet as her own. Adding another finger, she stroked in and out, fascinated at the fluids that dripped over her palm from Natalia's body.

Glancing up the length of her, she saw that Hudson had her nipples squeezed tightly between his thumbs and forefingers. He stood slightly to the side so he could watch. "What do you want to do, Brie?"

"I want Natalia to come for my mouth."

Whimpering, she glanced down. "Brie, oh my god."

Sticking out her tongue, she stroked it through the syrup-covered flesh without taking her eyes off Natalia. "I want to make you feel good."

"My clit...please, Brie. Suck it."

She mimicked the motions Natalia had performed with her hands using her tongue. Within moments, she was bucking and gasping. Hudson supported her, watched Brie, his jaw clenched tight.

Remembering that she liked an edge of pain, she sucked the sensitive nub harder, fucked her with her fingers more forcefully.

She was rewarded by an orgasm that seemed to go on forever as she drank down the release of the only woman she'd ever wanted.

As her body calmed and the moans faded, Brie sat back on her heels with a happy smile.

Hudson stared at her for a long moment. "We'll try for some gentle play." To Natalia, he added, "Relax."

He kissed her neck and she brought her feet together while dropping her arms. The moment she stepped away from his chest, Hudson pulled Brie roughly to her feet between them.

"Did you enjoy that?"

"Very much." She slid her hand around his neck. "Taste." Their kiss was hot and demanding. She shared the flavor of his best friend's body and he gave her his tongue to suck.

Finally pulling back, he murmured, "I have no control when it comes to you, Brie. You shred it." He rested his forehead on hers with a sigh. "You're wet from sucking her nipples and clit, aren't you?"

"Yes, Hudson." She stroked over his shoulders. Natalia was pressed against her back, her hands smoothing along Brie's hips. Raising her face, she met his eyes. "I want to learn what *you* taste like now."

"*Jesus.*"

Chapter Forty-Four

Hudson's eyes were black flame. "Natalia. Spot me. Make sure I'm not too rough with her."

She nodded and nuzzled against her ear. "Have you ever sucked a man's cock, Brie?"

Blushing hot at the explicit words, she closed her eyes against the memory. "I tried once but I didn't do it right."

"Why would you think that?" The warmth of her voice caressed the sensitive skin.

Swallowing hard, she repeated what she'd been told. Her first lover had often criticized how she touched him. "It was too fast."

She felt Natalia smile against her. "That was *his* fault, Brie. The sight of your lips wrapped around his cock caused him to lose it." She sucked Brie's earlobe and her heart pounded in her chest.

"There's no doubt in my mind that you did it right. Did he give you time to take the length or just the head before he lost control?"

She could barely get the words out. "The...just the head."

Natalia took one of Brie's hands and placed it over Hudson's cock.

It was thick and hard behind his slacks. Her fingers automatically curled around the heated length with a whimper of need.

"Hudson lasts a long time. His control will give you plenty of time to see what the fuss is about." She tightened her hand over Brie's. "I'm going to show you *all* the tricks."

She kissed a line down her neck and up again. "That way, every time you suck a man's cock with your perfect mouth, you'll know, without a doubt, that you're doing it *exactly* right. Then we're going to show you all the things people can do for *you* in return."

Squeezing her fingers, Hudson rocked his dick against her hand. "I want to know all of it."

Natalia's hand followed the stroking motion Brie began without conscious thought.

"Slide down and cup his balls. Feel how tight they are. He wants to come but he'll wait. He wants your mouth on him when he comes so you can swallow him down."

She zoned out with the feel of him in her palm. Her other hand unbuttoned his shirt. When it was open, she used both hands to caress him everywhere.

"You're *so* hard. I need you in my mouth." Brie settled over his belt and pushed his hand away when he tried to help. "I'll do everything."

His hands dropped to his sides and she felt their eyes as she lowered to her knees in the middle of her cheerful kitchen.

Separating the fabric of his slacks, she pushed it to his hips then carefully lifted the waistband of his boxer briefs and lowered it away from the cock she hadn't had a chance to fully examine when they'd been together.

"You're beautiful, Hudson." The worshipful tone in her voice couldn't be helped. Leaning forward, she kissed the ridge that ran along the underside and he inhaled sharply.

Behind her, Natalia knelt and pressed the flats of her hands against the inside of Brie's thighs. "Keep your thighs apart. Let the tension build in your clit by not pressing there."

She stroked over her center and moaned. "I can feel how wet you are even through your clothes. Thinking about lapping up your sweet cream makes my mouth water."

Hudson took his cock in his hand and traced the head over Brie's lips, slicking them. Seeing him hold the rigid shaft made her breath catch.

"Open." She did and he stroked over her tongue. "So fucking hot." Without being told, she closed her lips around him and his head dropped back on his shoulders.

"Take him a little deeper. Nice and slow. Breathe through your nose; it helps control gagging, just like that. Hudson, oh my *god*, her lips are gorgeous." She released the long curls and watched as they fell down Brie's back.

Taking several deep breaths, Hudson lowered his head to watch and she wanted *all of him* in her mouth.

"Fuck." One hand went into her hair and gripped it tight at the back of her neck. "Slower, *fuck*, let yourself adjust." Her eyes started to tear up and he pulled back. "Brie. Slow. Don't push."

"Having your mouth anywhere near his cock feels incredible. You can't compete with porn overnight and you don't have to. Just steady, that's it, and keep taking shallow breaths between strokes through your nose." She pressed at her inner thighs. "Keep these apart."

Brie whimpered and Hudson's hand tightened in her hair. "You're so giving." Her eyes locked with his. "Sweet lord, look at you."

Both hands held her still as he began to pump his hips carefully, thrusting his length in and out of her mouth. "Watching my dick disappear between your lips is unreal."

Natalia nuzzled her face against Brie's hair and inhaled deeply. "You're doing so well...I told you it wasn't you. You needed a man who was more interested in watching you suck him than popping his nut." She scraped her nails along her inner thighs and Brie shivered. "Yes..."

She kept her eyes on Hudson, letting him gently fuck her mouth.

"He wants to come but he wants to wait. He wants to draw it out but watching you suck him is too much. He's wanted it for so long." She paused and added softly, "Do you want him to come, Brie?"

In answer, she moaned around his flesh. "Your entire body is trembling. Just the *act* of sucking him is bringing you close to orgasm."

Gathering her hair and putting it over one shoulder, Natalia nibbled up the column of her throat. "You're the most generous lover. I'm going to enjoy giving back, feeling you come apart in my arms, watching you come apart in Hudson's." Brie whimpered.

"Each time he's deep, swallow around him."

The first time she did it, Hudson bucked and almost came. The second time, he ground out, "Fuck, Brie, yes."

He held her head in place while he shot his seed down her throat. Her eyes began to water but she didn't pull away, holding Hudson's hips and keeping him lodged halfway, swallowing the hot jets as smoothly as she could.

The expression of painful pleasure on his face was captivating. Only when the tightness released from his muscles did Hudson pull back, stroking shallowly as Brie caught her breath.

Then she pulled away and tangled her hand in Natalia's hair. As their lips touched she whispered, "Taste."

Hudson crouched in front of them, his dick only slightly less hard than moments before. He watched them share the taste of his come and she imagined he had a million different scenarios for the three of them.

When their mouths broke apart, Brie licked her lips.

"Thank you for taking the edge off my hunger for you." He ran his knuckles over her cheek. "We've taken when we should have given."

Her smile was gentle and sincere. "I'm not keeping score, Hudson."

"You should be."

"No. Keeping score while giving of yourself defeats the purpose. Sort of like the difference between listening to others and waiting for your turn to talk." She shrugged, knowing they didn't completely understand. "There's no score and there are no conditions."

The concept was foreign when spoken aloud but Brie knew they already embraced the concept with one another and with her.

They were so wrapped up in their own bad press.

Wrapping his arms around them, Hudson lifted the two of them to their feet in a show of strength that was incredibly impressive. Not as much as when he hugged them and kissed their foreheads.

That made her heart break a little.

Exhaling, he begged, "Food, Brie. I need food."

She laughed, planting light kisses on their lips before turning to make the poor man nourishment. They'd been playing in her kitchen for more than an hour.

As she worked, she thought about all the things she could do for them before they had to let her go. If they weren't able to do it, she knew she'd have to be the one to walk away.

A threesome would work for sunny afternoons but it would *never* work for them long term. They'd known one another too long, shared too much, to include an outsider for any length of time.

Hudson and Natalia didn't know that yet. She had to show them.

* * *

Pulling her hair back into a messy bun, Brie turned to the refrigerator and noticed her bunny slippers.

Meeting Hudson's eyes, she said with a straight face, "Under most unusual sexual encounters, you can truthfully say that you once received oral sex from a woman wearing bunny slippers."

She laughed with her entire body and they stared at her as if seeing and hearing laughter for the first time, unable to avoid joining in.

"Oh my god, *sex-ay!*" Then she was off on another round that lasted almost a minute before she could count on herself to be calm. After she washed and dried her hands, she moved around the small kitchen, microwaving and plating food.

Occasionally, she'd get the giggles again and have to catch her breath before she could continue. When they offered to help, she waved them away, still snickering.

"No, no. If I interact with other humans in any way right now, I will *not* be able to stop. I'll be laughing for another hour. I can't even look either of you in the eye until the bubbles stop."

"Bubbles?"

"Bubbles of laughter just trying to escape. It's *awful*. I get this at the most inappropriate times. Another reason my parents limit my public exposure. I can't be serious for long periods of time."

She started to giggle again when Hudson spun her around, backed her against the refrigerator, and kissed her stupid.

His palms gripped her ass as he ground his cock into the cradle of her thighs in a slow, rocking rhythm.

Brie couldn't have sworn how much time passed but when her lips were released and she opened her eyes, Natalia was leaning against the fridge with a huge grin.

"It's a miracle cure."

"The answer is not to limit your exposure. It's to *divert* your attention. However, laugh as much as you like. Your laugh is lovely."

His mouth dropped over hers again and she moaned.

He kissed along her jaw to her ear. "For the record, you could have been wearing an entire fucking bunny costume and the feel of your mouth around my cock would have been my entire focus, Brie."

With a final kiss to the tip of her nose, he stepped back and she handed him a plate in a daze.

They sat at her little table to eat and for the first time in four months of watching them, the pair was completely at ease. They talked and she wondered at the questions they had for her. From her very first job for her parents to what she thought about television.

Brie found great pleasure in making them laugh and her observations about strangers succeeded every time.

She talked for hours and they avoided touching her too much. Hudson wasn't kidding about waiting to take her again until she was healed.

A little part of her wanted to growl in frustration.

He asked about her sketches and she allowed them to look through her books. The detailed drawing of the two of them was conspicuously absent but he didn't mention it and she didn't offer an explanation.

She was happy that the painting of his building was secured in the closet. That was a surprise that she hoped made him happy.

In a book by itself were a series of burlesque-style caricatures. She'd used vibrant markers to shade in certain aspects.

"Brie, these are fantastic. You need to do some stuff for the club."

"In a few months, I'd love to." She didn't mention that she'd already researched several things to do for both of their companies. In that way, she'd *happily* take Hudson's money.

"A while back, Lola introduced me to some friends in the theater district." To Hudson, she said, "I adore her, by the way." He grinned.

"She couldn't stop gushing about *you*, Brie." The two women shared a look and she knew the assistant had told Natalia about the painting.

"When I walk the city, I like to sketch the gargoyles and old buildings. At the little theaters, if they let me, sometimes I'll watch rehearsals. These are from one of the scenes in *Not that Desperate*. I gave the cast a few as well. I've seen the play thirteen times now, I think."

Hudson flipped back and forth between them. "I *know* this theater. The Zelder brothers?"

"Yes. They're both very nice."

"You *met* Isaiah?" Natalia asked in surprise.

"He's coming out of isolation now."

The friends looked at one another and Hudson said, "It's been years. We'll make an evening of it."

Brie smiled. "The play is in its second run now. Everyone involved is wonderful. I laughed until my sides hurt. You won't be sorry."

"You'll go with us." It was not a request but she smiled and gave him a small nod anyway.

Natalia's phone rang and she stepped a few feet away to speak with the caller. When she hung up, she came to crouch beside Brie's chair.

"Dr. Geldin would like you to come in very early tomorrow morning and they'll complete your labs onsite. You could have your surgery done by tomorrow evening. What do you think?"

"You like him?"

"He is *nothing* like that asshole you dealt with today. He's going to love you, Brie. I would never send you to someone who wouldn't be good to you. I've known him for years."

"Alright."

As the sun started going down, they tucked her in and stretched out beside her. For almost an hour, they talked to her and stroked their hands over her body.

Gradually, they worked in tandem to play with her gently, in a relaxed way that pushed her over the edge of several orgasms. When she tried to reciprocate, they shook their heads.

"You've done so much already, Brie. Rest. Relax."

Their attention calmed her nerves about the procedure.

They continued to touch her casually, almost innocently, and she marveled at the love they desperately wanted to share, and their inability to share it fully with one another.

She drifted in a dreamlike space between fully awake and light sleep. They whispered to her about all the things they were going to show her and the experiences they would have together.

"I'll be your bridge. A way to get from where you are to where you want and need to be." She could feel them looking down at her but she was exhausted from an emotional morning and the sexual experiences she'd had. "Once you cross over, you don't need the bridge anymore but that's alright."

"No, Brie. That isn't your role." Natalia's voice was gentle as she stroked fingers through her hair. It felt lovely.

"Bridges are so important when you don't know how to get where you need to go. I *love* being your bridge and I'll keep you safe. It doesn't make me sad. Not even a little."

Her last memory before sinking fully into sleep was the sensation of their clasped hands over her tummy.

Many years in her future, whenever Brie was asked about one of her happiest memories – though she might not confess it – she would remember the first day she spent with Hudson and Natalia.

It would always make her smile.

Chapter Forty-Five

Brie planned to call a cab to take her to the clinic but Natalia made it clear that she was picking her up and bringing her home. It wasn't even light out when she slid in the back of Hudson's car.

They held hands. "It's all going to be just fine. I promise." She smoothed her fingers over her cheek. "I know you're nervous. I'll be right there waiting for you when you wake up."

"You don't have to stay, Natalia. I know you probably have so much to do with the club and everything. I don't want to be a bother."

"You couldn't be a bother if you tried. I'll wait."

Half an hour later, as a doctor she'd never met came in personally to arrange for her labs to be taken, Natalia explained that Brie was a close personal friend who needed as much tender care as possible.

"She's not a bitch like me, Abraham. She's sweet and gentle. The facility she almost used tried to shape her into a mannequin."

Dr. Abraham Geldin looked Brie over from head to toe. Only a couple of inches taller than her, he had a German accent and a trimmed silver beard and mustache.

"This one? No, no. That would be a *crime*." He approached Brie with a smile. "Gabriella, yes darling?"

She nodded shyly and he gave her a warm smile.

"Your figure, the classic hourglass, will come back into fashion one day, God willing, and women such as you will gain the popularity you deserve." He put the side of his finger under her chin and she stared into kind gray eyes.

"My own wife, may she never hear a better offer and leave me, is shaped like you. I know her curves better than my own hand and don't regret the learning."

Turning to Natalia, he grinned. "We will take good care of her, Natalia. Don't worry." He clapped his hands together. "Now! We will get this pain resolved. What cup size are we going down to, Gabriella?"

"The other doctor said a C cup. I just want to look in proportion and take pressure off my back."

"Right now you're a G-cup which is far too large for your bones. I think C may be too much of a change. We want to keep the balance with your bottom. I think a full D-cup is a better choice. The weight difference to your back and shoulders will be significant." He tucked a curl behind her ear. "What do you think?"

"If you think I-I won't still look too top heavy, that's fine."

He nodded happily. "Once you heal, I suggest several chiropractic adjustments and regular massage. You will also want to do lightweight upper body exercises to keep the strength that the weight of your breasts always gave you. Yes?"

"Yes. I do yoga several times a week. I'll have better balance now."

"Many good changes. Your little bones should have been relieved of this weight long ago. We fix it now and I'm excited to get started." He kissed Natalia on both cheeks. "You made a wise choice to bring her to me. I'll have Mala call you when she wakes up."

"No. I'll wait, Abraham."

Abraham gave her a wink. "Ah, she is that important to you. Very well, you may use my office. You know where it is."

Natalia moved around him and bent to kiss Brie's cheek.

As she stood, she smoothed her hair back. "I'll be here the whole time. Abraham is the best surgeon on the East Coast and he only employs the best. Don't be afraid and I'll see you when you wake up."

At the door, she turned one last time and gave her a bright smile.

Brie looked up at the doctor who was smiling down at her. "I've known Natalia *many* years. Never has she seemed so relaxed. I can tell it is you. Have you met Hudson?"

She blushed from every cell in her body. "They're growing into what they were meant to be now."

He stared at her silently then nodded with a small smile. "I always wondered what it would take to bring them together. You seem to have been the key. I'll get you through this safely."

"Thank you, doctor." An hour later, Brie was counted backwards into peaceful darkness and she wasn't afraid.

* * *

The recovery room was pale green and flooded with sunlight as Brie opened her eyes. A sharp exhale drew her attention and Hudson came into her line of sight.

"There you are."

"I told you, Hudson," Natalia said. "Some people take a little longer to shake the anesthesia." Brie felt unbelievably heavy but managed to turn her face slightly on the pillow to locate the woman on the other side of the bed. "How are you feeling, honey?"

"Weird. Like I weigh a million pounds. I've never had surgery before."

"Hope it's *never* fucking necessary again," Hudson said firmly.

Natalia laughed. "He was like this when I had my appendix removed. He's not very patient and tends to worry."

She felt his hand in her hair a moment before his lips were on her forehead. "I thought you weren't going to wake up."

"I'm sorry. I'm alright." Glancing down her body, she scowled. "I look like a Macy's Thanksgiving Day parade balloon."

Natalia kissed her cheek. "You're swollen from the procedure but Abraham said you'll be very happy once the initial swelling goes down. It will all be wonderful, you'll see."

Over the next several hours, the medical staff continued to monitor Brie while the anesthesia slowly worked its way out of her system.

It was almost dark when they took her home. They insisted on waiting while the hired nurse organized her prescriptions and helped her change clothes. The drugs lagged for a long time, making her feel sluggish, then wore off quickly.

As she went in the bathroom to brush her teeth, the strain was apparent around her mouth and eyes.

They tucked her in her bed, the nurse brought her water and pain medication but she didn't really want to take it. It was going to knock her back out.

"Take the damn painkillers so you can *rest*. Don't be stubborn, Brie." He helped her sit up and held the glass while she did as she was told. Then he leaned over and brushed kisses over her cheeks, forehead, and lips. "Call me for any reason."

"I would never bother you at work."

His eyes stared into hers for a long moment. "You've been important to us for months. We will always answer your call, Gabriella. The sooner you understand that, the better."

Part of her wanted to ask him to stay but she wondered at her right to make such a request. Instead, she nodded with a small smile.

"Thank you, Hudson. I'll call."

Natalia bent over the bed and kissed the tip of her nose. "This is going to be the worst part but once it's over, you'll feel better in a million small ways. Be strong and call me if you need anything at all."

"You were wonderful to stay with me today. I felt better knowing you were waiting."

"Rest now, darling. We'll see you tomorrow." One more kiss on the lips and the two friends left her to sleep.

* * *

The first week after surgery, Brie gritted her teeth through the pain she hadn't been as prepared for as she thought. It felt as if it went clear to the *bone* and she was ashamed that she had to lean so heavily on the painkillers Dr. Geldin prescribed.

Lydia, her home care nurse, was awesome. She was so grateful for Hudson's insistence on hiring someone to be with her.

Within the first hour of arriving, she'd made it clear that she was *happy* to help, *hired* to help, and Brie was to stop apologizing as if she was a burden.

The nurse was in her mid-thirties and very strong with healthy skin that reminded her of dark chocolate. Short hair, trimmed nails, and a no-nonsense attitude competed with cheerful scrubs in bright colors that made Brie feel better just looking at them.

Her teenaged neighbor Sita came by every day to visit, check her mail, and run errands for Lydia with a smile.

The three of them sat together in the afternoons and enjoyed lunches at her small table. Sometimes, they ate the meals Brie prepared before her surgery and sometimes Lydia would cook food she'd learned to make as a little girl growing up in Mississippi.

When she tasted the nurse's crawfish, beans, and rice, she begged for the recipe. The pineapple upside-down cake she baked was better than any version of the dessert Brie had ever had. A cup of her chicory blend coffee was the perfect accompaniment.

The two of them kept her smiling and distracted from the pain and the grossness of the healing process.

* * *

Riya and Tawny came almost daily with breakfast and coffee from her favorite little café by the building.

When the redhead wouldn't stop staring at her, she finally caved. "What? You sense something, know something, suspect…what?"

"You got laid. It's written all over you, dirty girl. Despite the pain, you're relaxed and more confident than you've been since we met. You have three seconds to spill it or I'm taking your coffee away."

"You really do fight dirty."

"Damn right. Quit stalling."

For the first time in her entire life, she gave intimate details of a sexual encounter, telling them about her time individually with Natalia and Hudson as well as the afternoon the three of them spent together. She *tried* to be vague but Tawny wasn't having it.

Riya's eyes were wide and her lips were parted in surprise.

Finally, she just started laughing and couldn't stop. "You're going to twist those two up like no one else, Brie!" Taking her hand, she asked, "How's your heart?"

"Still strong and beating in my own chest. I like them intensely. They're genuinely kind and good people. Right now, they think they need what I bring to the table." She shrugged. "I definitely needed some of what *they* bring to the table, but they only need each other."

"They'll be slow to learn. They're set in their ways."

Brie smiled. "I'm patient."

When her friends couldn't come by, they talked on the phone. There were times the calls lasted hours as Riya traveled with one of her men or they ran errands. She loved their energy and easy laughter.

* * *

Natalia stopped by most afternoons. She worked until the middle of the night and generally slept until noon. One visit, she brought a woman with her who did her nails and toes.

"You can't go to the salon yet and I imagine you're getting tired of being cooped up as much as you usually walk."

Brie hugged her for a long time after the nail technician left with a smile. "That was so thoughtful, Natalia. Thank you."

"Such little things please you. I rather enjoy seeing your face light up, darling. I'll take you to see Bibi soon. She's traveling for a few weeks but she's going to *love* you. Now, what would you like for lunch? We'll beg Lydia to make us some of her coffee after we all stuff our faces."

* * *

Hudson had several trips he hadn't been able to reschedule and he would enter her apartment upon each return grinding his teeth.

After several kisses, he would crouch beside her so she could touch him while they talked. "The swelling is much better. How's the pain?"

"Lessening all the time. I'm down to one pill at night, when I have nothing to distract me. All psychological, of course."

"Or, it's pain from surgery and when you lie down, it's more obvious."

She grinned. "So logical. You look gorgeous, Hudson. I don't think I've ever seen you wear the same tie twice." She smoothed her fingertips over the dark gray tie with silver accents.

"I have hundreds. You look dazzling, Brie."

"Thank you."

"What do you want for dinner?"

"Everyone keeps trying to feed me." He laughed. "I'm not hungry but there are leftovers from earlier." With a wink, she added, "I took out a tin of homemade fudge and left it on the counter for you."

Leaning forward, he kissed her for a long time and it made her breathless and needy.

She was glad that Lydia always went for a walk when Hudson or Natalia stopped by. She wondered if that was prearranged.

Day by day, she was beginning to see the physical changes in her body. The figure she presented in the bathroom mirror wasn't comical anymore and each day she grew more excited to see the results.

She wore the special bra Dr. Geldin gave her and didn't mind because her breasts ached otherwise.

Ten days after her surgery, she decided to take her trash out before Lydia arrived. She was doing so much and being a maid was not part of the deal.

As she stepped out on the landing, a small patch of ice sent her flying and only the quick reflexes of a man beside her kept her from falling. Being jarred caused agony across her stitches and she sat on the steps to catch her breath, ashamed of her tears.

"Are you alright, miss?"

"I just had surgery. Thank you for stopping the fall. It could have been much worse."

Glancing up, she met the pretty green eyes of a man in his late fifties. Hair that might have been dark red once was peppered with silver and cut close to his scalp. He seemed formidable for a man of his age.

"I'm Brie. It's a pleasure to meet you."

"Glenn."

Just then, Lydia got out of her cab and came up the walk giving Brie hell. "You're the most stubborn patient! Why do you have to make it harder on yourself? Mm, you know who's gonna be pissed so I don't have to say one word. Let's get you inside before your butt freezes to the concrete."

"Thank you again, Glenn." He nodded and jogged away. "Lydia. We don't need to tell Hudson about this."

At the look the nurse gave her, she knew she should prepare herself.

* * *

When Hudson entered her apartment later that night, Brie held her breath. His smile was calculating.

Then Riya and her men walked in behind him and she knew shit just got real. Her friend bustled around like a mama bird.

"Brie, tell me what you're going to need for the next few weeks. Pick your favorite sketchbooks and things but I'll get you more supplies if you need them. Lydia, you're going to be coming to this address. I'm happy to send our driver to get you if that's a problem."

Mouth hanging open, Brie watched Riya pull her suitcase from the bedroom closet and talk to herself as she packed it.

"Um. Riya?"

"Say just one word when I know you almost fell today and could have reopened your stitches, making your recovery so much worse. You'll be close, Tawny and I can see you more, and no *stairs* while you're healing since you're one of the most stubborn people I know."

She gave Hudson a healthy glare and he continued to smile.

"I promise not to use the stairs."

Riya came over and sat on the coffee table. "I have so few real friends, Brie. No one like you. You're irreplaceable and if it makes me feel better to have you closer for just a little while, until you *heal* from a surgical procedure, then you should give me that peace of mind."

Sniffling, she whispered, "Don't you *want* to give me that peace of mind if you have it within your power?"

Releasing a heavy sigh, she said, "You're absolutely playing me right now. Since our minds think alike, you know I'm going to give in because it'll make you happy. It infuriates me that you know that."

"Yay! I know you love your privacy so I'm putting you in one of the suites. Close, taken care of, and I'll be thrilled." Then her friend was off packing again.

To Hudson, she mouthed, "I'll get you for this."

He mouthed back, "I hope so."

The M's stood together in front of her bookshelf, and Max said, "You have some great titles, Brie. I'm impressed."

"I like your lack of clutter," Micah added.

"I can't believe you let her come here and bully me like this, guys."

Micah shook his head. "Either that or she said she was staying with you until you were one hundred percent and I think you know we'd have had to be here, too. No way can we be separated that long."

Hudson pretended like he was going to be sick and it made Brie laugh.

"Then you're off the hook. I know where to exact my revenge." She wiggled her brows at the powerful man who hadn't said a word since walking in her door and he winked at her. "Thanks."

He nodded and an hour later, she found herself ensconced in one of the temporary suites in the building.

Her co-workers were thrilled to see her and she knew staying here would be nice. She could go downstairs to visit. She was also closer to Hudson and Natalia by association.

There were definite upsides.

* * *

Though Brie was early for her follow up appointment, one of Dr. Geldin's nurses took her back right away. A gentle exam of the incision sites found they were healing well.

After she was dressed, the elderly doctor returned and patted her cheek. "Healing is good, your body is strong, and I'm pleased." He tilted his head. "You feel better, yes?"

"Yes. So much better, doctor. Thank you."

"This makes my heart glad. You will take it easy for another two weeks. I want to see you again. After that, very light activity for one more week. Then! You shall be all better and have less pain for the rest of your life."

There were a few new instructions, another prescription for cream to prevent infection, and he kissed both of her cheeks before she left.

Life was positively wonderful.

Chapter Forty-Six

Second week of February…

Hudson had no choice but to attend a Valentine's Day charity gala for a foundation for which he quietly provided substantial funding.

"We can find something extra soft for you to wear, Brie," Natalia pleaded. "It isn't right to leave you here and go have fun."

"There's no way I can handle anything on my breasts yet and this bra is the size of a tank top so there's no hiding it. This has been planned for months. You have to go."

"I can stay here and keep you company…"

"Absolutely not. I *forbid* you to remove that dress before at least five hundred people see you in it."

Natalia was splendid in a custom dark gray gown that hugged her figure like a second skin before flaring at the knee and dropping delicately to the floor.

The silver threads throughout brought out the sparkle in her eyes. Combs in her hair with smoky gray crystals made the black shimmer even more. Her jewelry featured the same soft gray stones.

Brie was surprised to learn that Natalia straightened her hair every day. The natural curls made her appear younger, almost carefree.

"You look glorious. You *have* to go and you can tell me all about it tomorrow. I need a photo of you and Hudson before you leave."

As Natalia approached the couch where she was sitting, Brie held up her hand. "Not one thing to mess up your hair or makeup. Make Hudson kiss you stupid for me and I'll give you extra tomorrow."

Hudson arrived and she wasn't the least bit embarrassed at the way her jaw dropped.

"You're both so, just absolutely, oh my god, I'm speechless."

Hudson in a suit was a lovely thing to see. Hudson in a tuxedo with his hair swept back made her womb tighten.

The two of them laughed. "Get together so I can get a photo. Holy shit, I can't even verbalize how breathtaking the two of you are." Frowning, she looked away from the camera.

"Hug, get closer, act like you're going to fucking prom or something and I'm the sentimental mom."

"We didn't go to our prom," Natalia told her. "We were too intellectually advanced for such things."

"Hmm. I bet you felt weird around the masses because you guys think differently than other people and I doubt it was less obvious as teens." She shrugged. "I didn't go to mine either. I wasn't shoving my ten gallon boobs in a five-gallon dress." Winking, she added, "Looking forward to the reunions though."

Considering, she suggested, "Tonight, pretend like you're going to prom. It'll make you feel young and silly. Before the businesses, the fancy lives, and the years passed. Will you? For me?"

They nodded, seeming introspective. "I wish I'd thought to get you a corsage and whatnot. That would have been a riot. Okay. Get together so I can take like a dozen photos and then you can hustle. I know poor Leonard is grinding his teeth."

This time, they wrapped their arms around one another, their bodies snug together. When Hudson kissed Natalia's hair, her eyes closed.

Brie's phone silently clicked away.

"These are lovely. I'll send you copies." They gave her massive amounts of attention before they left but she finally got them moving. As the door closed behind them, she scrolled through the photos.

"How can you not *see* it?" she asked the empty suite. "How can you not *feel* how much you love each other? I want that for you so much. Something has to shake you up."

Grabbing her sketchbook, she played with a few ideas. When she got tired, she put everything away and crawled into bed.

She smiled to herself and knew Tawny would be hella impressed with her ideas to start pushing the couple together. She might even enlist the redhead's help if they were too stubborn.

* * *

In the car, Hudson took Natalia's hand and kissed the back before placing it on his leg, covered with his.

"Gabriella is right. You look beyond gorgeous."

"As do you. Thank you, darling." She glanced out of the window. "Do you remember why we didn't go to prom?"

For a long moment, he didn't respond. His thumb stroked the delicate skin on the back of her hand.

"We didn't want to go with anyone else but hesitated to go together."

"We thought people would talk about us."

"They did that already." He remembered well.

"I was the uptight ice queen with no tits and attitude to spare."

"I was the kid with the chip on his shoulder who fought faster than I talked and thought I was better than everyone else."

She turned her head to look at him. "You *were* better than everyone else. From the very beginning."

"I've always loved your attitude and your tits." That made her grin. "We aren't like Brie and Riya. We can't be that open and relaxed."

"I think Brie's right though. Maybe we aren't cold as much as reserved." She squeezed his hand. "You've always been warm to me, Hudson. We show that aspect of ourselves differently."

He stared at her for a long time and saw that it made her squirm.

"You're lovely. Inside and out. From the day I met you. If I don't tell you enough, show you enough, I'm sorry. I *always* feel it."

"Thank you, Hudson." She reached up to stroke his face. "You're still and always have been the best man I know." The slow smile she gave him made his heart give a hard thump. "I should have made you take me to prom a million years ago."

"I should have insisted we go." Tilting his head, he kissed the skin beneath her ear and she trembled in response. "I'll make up for it."

"You already have, darling. Many times over."

"It didn't count. We didn't realize the error until tonight."

His hand lifted and his fingers coasted over her nipples through her bodice. He growled when the car came to a stop. Pulling back, he watched Natalia's eyes flutter open.

"More later. Right now, you have to make me appear to be human."

The statement held more truth than he usually admitted. Small talk was not his strength. Natalia was a social facilitator.

She enabled him to avoid ruffling too many feathers. It was another aspect of their relationship that had never been so glaringly obvious.

Before the door opened, she leaned up and pressed her cheek to his. "You're the most *amazing* human, Hudson. I adore you, exactly as you are – in every light."

Then Leonard was there and he stepped out to assist Natalia to the red carpet. Her hand tucked into the bend of his, he led her inside and noticed how many appreciative glances his best friend received. Strangely, he wanted to take her back to the car.

* * *

Caught up with Spencer Bishop, Hudson kept his eye on Natalia in his peripheral vision. She was brilliant and gorgeous, an asset to him on many levels at functions such as this.

She circulated, familiar with many of the same people, able to remember details of their personal lives that he couldn't give half a fuck about. She smiled, laughed, and conversed with dozens of people and didn't look remotely unhappy.

He would have been miserable.

"Ah, here's Shania. Hello, love." The diminutive woman wrapped her arm around her husband's waist. In her heels, they were almost the same height.

"Hudson. How *wonderful* to see you again." That she sounded sincere surprised him. "At a luncheon for one of the foundations I chair, your name was mentioned in awe."

Unsure how to respond, he remained silent.

The woman smiled at him. "You're a man of few words. I imagine it must make you uncomfortable around chatterboxes." That made him laugh. "Your donation of contracting assistance – everything they needed to bring the building up to code – kept the home from closing. I heard it from a little bird that you and Natalia made a personal appearance to help with the work."

"I…"

"Your secret is safe with me, of course." Resting her hand on his arm, she added, "Those women and children are so thankful, Hudson. You kept them from being shuffled back out on the street to face God only knows what. Thank you."

"You're welcome."

Her grin made her green eyes glow from her face. "Spencer and I like the fact that one always knows where they stand with you. No frills, all results. I wish more people had the same personality."

"It would have been better if Natalia was here to respond."

"You're a darling man. I understand so you don't need to say a word." She put her hand on his shoulder to bring him down to her level. Pressing her cheek to his, she hugged him.

"Enjoy the party and I'm so happy you're part of our little family whether you see it that way or not. Don't change a single thing."

Stepping back, she winked and said to her husband, "The banker I don't like was asking for you. I wasn't talking to him alone for one more second. You can take that one, Spencer. He creeps me out."

Laughing, the couple said their goodbyes and disappeared into the crowd. He glanced around and spotted Natalia across the room.

She was chatting animatedly with Harper Delkin. The man whose agenda for almost two years had been sweeping Natalia off her feet.

Circling the room, he took in their body language and the fact that they were standing too close. The way the man looked at her made Hudson's hackles rise. The obvious flirting made him want to piss on his rival's thousand-dollar shoes.

For several minutes, he watched them interact, ignoring the servers who approached. Finally, he'd had enough. Moving through the crowd, he appeared a few feet behind her.

"Natalia."

The word was said quietly, almost softly, but there was no mistaking the power behind it. She glanced up, surprised to hear a *command* in the middle of a gala that charged twenty-thousand dollars a plate.

"Yes?"

"Come here."

A small frown of confusion appeared between her eyes but she didn't hesitate to turn from Delkin and walk to his side. He stared at the other man – so similar to him – and gave him a slow smile.

"The Bishops were looking for you."

The men stared at one another across several feet of space and the tension between them was palpable.

Natalia stood silently, glancing back and forth as if unsure what to do.

Hudson knew she was shocked at his territorial behavior but for some reason, *he couldn't fucking stop himself.*

After a long moment, Harper's pewter eyes cut quickly to Natalia before returning to Hudson. "Always a pleasure to see you, Winters. You're the only man who's as big of a bastard as I am. Finally, you made yourself clear. It's about fucking time."

Approaching Natalia, he lifted her hand and kissed the back. "You're a stunning and captivating woman. It's important that a man not only *tell* you but *show* you where you belong. Tonight, you've been shown. To men such as us, it's no small thing."

Inclining his head to them both, he turned and walked away.

Hudson slowly exhaled before turning his gaze on Natalia. Her expression showed that she didn't understand why he'd behaved in such a way. In all their years of friendship, it was a first.

"Hudson...?"

"Don't."

Taking her hand, he led her through the crowd to a quiet alcove behind the DJ table. Dropping the thick drapes, his hand slid around her waist to pull her against him.

He tried to be gentle but he knew he gripped her too hard. Closing his eyes, he pressed his face to hers. The feel, the smell of her calmed him.

"Don't ask me, Natalia. I don't know."

How long they stood like that, he was unsure. Hudson held her close, trying to understand why she was trembling, wanting to reassure her, but unable to find the words.

Her arms were wrapped around his torso under his jacket and he didn't want clothes between them. He didn't want to *be* here.

"We're leaving."

"Alright."

He led her through the crowd, ignoring requests for a moment of his time, and they got in his car. The moment the door closed behind them, he raised the partition and brought her to him for a kiss he couldn't deliver when others would have seen evidence of it.

They didn't speak one word until they exited the elevator in his living room. Leading her upstairs, he stopped beside his bed and his hand went to his tie.

"Undress. Quickly."

Practically ripping his own clothes from his body, he helped with hers until they were finally naked together.

For hours, he took Natalia, fucking her, *marking* her inside and out with an aggressiveness that worried him. Only when they crashed from fatigue near dawn did he feel as if he could breathe.

Watching her sleep, he rubbed his hand roughly over his chest. It was then that he realized that he'd never once thought about Gabriella.

Chapter Forty-Seven

There was no doubt that something pivotal had happened between Hudson and Natalia the night of the gala.

They looked ready to crawl out of their own skin.

Brie knew that whatever they were feeling, it was unfamiliar and frightening. Neither of them would admit to weakness and she knew the time was coming for her to gracefully exit their lives.

In an effort to pretend they weren't reeling from their epiphany, they positively *poured* attention on their ingénue. Though she appreciated it, things simply couldn't continue as they were.

Hudson had two trips back to back and Natalia was monitoring several construction projects at *Trois*. Brie was admittedly happy to have some time alone.

Lydia's time as her nurse ended but they still chatted every couple of days and shared recipes. They'd gotten hooked on watching *The Tonight Show* on YouTube and would send each other funny videos of Jimmy Fallon and his guests.

The woman was another connection, another friend in New York, and Brie didn't take the gift for granted.

During the day, she visited her apartment and worked on the painting for Hudson. She was anxious to commemorate the most important acquisition in his professional history.

Taking the original sketch, she'd transferred it to a much larger canvas that barely fit in her foyer closet. She hoped the result would be as physically imposing as the building – and the man – was to her.

The day she finally finished it, the sight brought her to tears. She compared it to the photos she'd taken the first day and found herself incredibly proud of the final product.

She took a photo with her phone and sent it to Lola. Less than thirty seconds later, the personal assistant called her crying.

"It's even better than I dreamed it would be. He's going to love it."

Once it cured, she would have it professionally framed for him so he could put it in one of his conference rooms or something.

Each article of her clothing was sorted. Her old tops fell lower and hung loosely in the chest. Many were so stretched out that she'd never be able to wear them again.

It felt good to remove the items she'd hidden in, piling each item on the bed to make room for clothes that would fit her properly.

The final appointment with Dr. Geldin was moving. The man held her face after he pronounced her fully healed and told her she glowed.

"Now you will be happier. You're lovely." He grinned. "Since I knew you were coming today, I asked my wife to stop by. She so wanted to meet you."

Mrs. Geldin was a lovely woman who was the same height and shape as Brie. She kissed both her cheeks and squeezed her shoulders.

"As lovely as you said, Abraham." Smoothing her hand over Brie's hair, she said, "He has told me much about your gentle nature. I had to meet the woman able to pull emotion from our Natalia and the formidable Hudson. You must allow us to take you to lunch."

The three of them sat for a long time at the little bistro near the doctor's clinic and Brie sketched the couple while they talked. When she handed it to them, their eyes went wide and they cuddled together. They stared at it, speaking softly to one another in German.

It made Brie feel amazing.

She walked them back to the building and they all said goodbye out front. They kissed her cheeks and held her hands.

"I find myself so happy that we met, Gabriella. I feel it was destined and it will become clear one day. In the meantime, take care of your lovely self and know that you have made two old people happy with your talent."

Leonard waited behind her and she waved at the couple as she slid in the back of the car. As the door closed, she glanced to the side and was badly startled.

She could have *sworn* she saw Hudson's impersonator passing in another car. The idea was ridiculous, of course.

The man had gotten what he wanted from her. There was no reason for him to be in New York.

Brushing it off, she called Tawny. "I need you and Riya to sex me out with clothes and whatnot. Are you up to the challenge?"

"Oh, bitch. Bring your ass into my clutches. We're leaving for Florida day after tomorrow and I know you have plans that include hard-core dirty fucking. I don't get a call with the deets and you're getting *cut*."

"Um, okay. I'll meet you at Riya's." Tawny hung up but her final evil cackle made Brie laugh. Glancing up front, she smiled at the driver in the mirror who took her everywhere these days.

"Leonard. You honestly don't have to drive me. Every time I ask the guys to call me a cab, I'm told you're waiting for me. I feel like you must never have time off."

"I'm happy to, miss. You're an absolute pleasure and no trouble at all. Also, I have particular skills that my fearsome employer wants to cover you until further notice."

She blinked. "You're like Liam Neeson in *Taken*, huh?" He nodded with a small smile. "That's so awesome, I feel like a kid."

He laughed. "My sister speaks highly of you. Since you're important to many people important to me, I'll gladly drive you wherever you need to go."

"Your sister...?"

"Lola. Mr. Winters' personal assistant."

"Oh my god! How did I not know this?" Sitting forward on the seat, she leaned on the rear facing seat back. "Tell me about being brother and sister. I want to hear all about your childhood."

They spent the drive chatting and before she knew it, they'd arrived at the building. Grabbing her bag, she grinned. "I know I'm nosey but it adds another layer to you now and I find that fascinating. Now that I realize, I can see the resemblance."

She squeezed his shoulder and told him she'd see him later.

"When you're ready to go shopping, I'll be waiting." She started to object. "Miss, I have my orders directly from Mr. Winters and nothing will happen to you on my watch."

Laughing, she shook her head. "Alright then. I promise it won't be necessary much longer."

Upstairs, she quickly showered. She'd asked Lydia to pick up a few sport bras and smaller t-shirts for her until she could get proper clothing and she dressed in casual clothes before heading upstairs.

Her friends took in her figure and Riya instantly started crying.

Tawny put her hands on her hips, looked her up and down, and pronounced, "Oh girl, I'd fuck you."

The laughter started and *did not stop* for the rest of the afternoon.

The first stop was a custom lingerie store and the goods inside were heavenly. After she was fitted, she stood staring at her reflection for so long that her friends busted inside the dressing room and scared the shit out of her.

"Fuck. Look at you."

"Oh god, Brie. You look so good."

The material of the bra and boy short panty was delicate and hugged her body as underthings were meant to. Her breasts were at the right level and it was strange that her ass didn't seem as big now that she'd had the reduction.

The deep burgundy stood out against her skin. All she could think about was having Hudson and Natalia take it off.

She bought a dozen matching sets in assorted colors – wearing the one she'd tried on out of the store – and when she tried to pay, the redhead *slapped* her credit card out of her hand.

"I use this card for underwear, you know? I usually have to spend way more than this on custom-created stuff so…"

"I've been waiting for this opportunity for *months* and you're not going to ruin it for me!" she shrieked.

The poor saleswoman looked ready to call the cops. You had to know their friend to get that she was *violently* affectionate.

"Chill, Red. Damn." Staring at her friends, she sighed. "Fine. You get the tab. I have ways of paying you back."

Tawny grinned and after that, she was off the chain.

They dragged her from store to store, picking tops, dresses, and jackets that fit her perfectly.

In one casual store, the girl behind the counter took in Brie's figure as the door closed behind them.

"With that Latina ass, you came to the right place. Our jeans are going to hug those curves like nothing you've ever seen."

It was a claim she promptly backed up.

Their last stop was at a day spa and she felt marvelous being massaged, buffed, waxed, and basically *girled out* in ways she'd never considered.

Her hair was washed and trimmed. The stylist thinned out some of the thickness, gave her long layers, and gave her a product that would help her curls relax a bit.

The result was a look she'd never accomplished in her life.

Afterward, they reclined in massage chairs while their nails and toes were done. All of them fell asleep.

Having a good time was *exhausting*.

They enjoyed dinner together and it was getting dark when Leonard dropped them off in front of the building. She kissed his cheek and thanked him for his patience. He actually blushed.

They hauled all the stuff to her suite and she made it clear that she was returning to her apartment two days later.

"We *love* having you so close." They pouted at her.

"I love my apartment. It's mine and I miss it."

"You should come to Florida with us! You'll fucking love it."

"First, I go back to work in a few days and I need my shit. Second, I'm going to need a little time to recover from my date."

Tawny nodded sagely. "I hear you. Your ass and shit are probably gonna be sore. Recovery day. Want us to wait an extra day for you?"

Brie blinked and Riya snickered. "When are you going to start looking for another job?"

"The building management has been so good to me. I want to give them a year and plenty of notice to find and train someone. After the time off they allowed me to accrue, I can't do any less." Tilting her head, she laughed. "It's not like I'm not already doing contracting work for *all* your men anyway."

"You work too fucking much and you need to play more. We're scheduling that shit."

The moment her friends left, she organized everything in the suite. She packed her personal belongings, including her clothing, leaving out two outfits for the following day.

A casual one as well as one to inspire lust in the two people she desperately wanted to crawl all over – completely, blissfully naked for the first time with them.

Hudson and Natalia would be available the following day and she had a clear plan of action. An element of surprise, a pleasant conversation, and a night she would never forget.

After she took a quick shower, she climbed into bed and thought about the way they would touch her. It wasn't long before her fingers were slipping over her freshly denuded skin, the sensations especially intense without hair to distract.

The vision of them taking her was almost too much, too powerful, and she slept deeply.

* * *

The following evening, she took care with her hair, using the conditioner, and pleased that she could recreate the effect. Tawny planned to do her makeup and Riya told her in no uncertain terms that she was wearing the jewelry they'd given her for Christmas.

Slipping into one of her new outfits, choosing simple black from her underthings to her dress to compliment her lovers, she stepped into the gorgeous black heels and took in her appearance.

She felt pretty. Confident. Ready to take on the world. She'd settle for taking on two of the most sexual people she'd ever met.

Half an hour later, she stopped in the lobby to let Carlo know that she'd be at Riya's, to buzz her when Hudson or Natalia arrived.

Joining her friends upstairs for drinks, the reactions of their men when they saw her was good for her ego.

Micah handed her a glass of wine and announced. "We're dancing. It'll get you ready for our club whenever you give us the green light."

She laughed and nodded. They drank and nibbled on the delicious foods Max laid out and conversation was manic considering Tawny was involved.

When they put on music, Zach waved them off when they tried to include him. "We don't need any emergency room visits. The numbers are ideal to get me off the hook."

Quinn, Max, and Micah danced and kept trading partners for almost an hour. Zach watched, tapping his foot off-rhythm, which Brie found fucking *adorable.*

When the elevator dinged, they all glanced up in surprise.

The appearance of Hudson and Natalia sucked all the air out of Brie's body. They looked *magnificent.*

"Sorry to interrupt, darlings. We're stealing Gabriella away now. I know you understand. Have a safe trip. See you when you get back." Natalia approached, wrapped her arm around Brie's waist, and tugged her toward a waiting Hudson.

Tawny and Riya were in fits of laughter as the door closed.

Instantly, they were on her.

Chapter Forty-Eight

First week in March…

Their hands were *everywhere* and Brie was spinning from the sensation.

"We're taking you to dinner like civilized people," Natalia murmured at her neck as her fingers smoothed back and forth under her breasts.

"Then we're fucking you until you pass out." Hudson's palm had a hold on her ass that was beyond erotic as his lips traced her shoulder.

The doors opened in the lobby and she allowed them to lead her to the car in a daze. It was cold but her overheated skin appreciated it. Leonard grinned as he closed the door behind them.

"The way you look right now is making it difficult to remember that we need to feed you."

She'd never imagined that the simple black dress and heels would have such an effect on them. The wraparound style hugged her curves and the two of them traced the outlines of her figure with clear hunger on their faces.

"You smell so good, Brie."

Natalia turned her face and delivered a kiss that stole her ability to think. Maybe when they arrived at the restaurant, she'd get it back. She truly needed to talk to them.

"I'm hard for you."

"You're always hard, Hudson. It makes you something of a machine and I can tell you, it's pretty awesome."

He laughed and claimed her lips in the rough way she liked and it took a moment to realize their hands were gliding up her inner thighs beneath the dress.

"These panties feel decadent. I can't wait to see them...and promptly take them off so I can feast on you." Natalia's lips parted and she placed her teeth over the muscle at the bend of her neck and shoulder, biting lightly. "I want to devour all of you."

Then their fingers were stroking over the silk, gliding over her and finally beneath the fabric. Their heads came up at the same time.

"You waxed your pussy." Hudson's voice was barely recognizable. Brie nodded. "You're *fucked*, Brie. I hope you rested."

She had to laugh but it ended on a sigh. The feel of their fingers on flesh that had never been hairless before was extraordinary. They explored her everywhere, playing with her clit and stroking inside her.

"If it was your first time, it will be sensitive for a couple of days. I'll soothe it with my tongue, Brie. Licking and sucking you until you come in my mouth."

Then the climax rose and shattered out of nowhere. She gasped and dropped her head to the seat. Still they stroked her, whispered to her, and brought her down gently.

As one, she watched them remove their hands and suck her slickness from their fingers. Then they leaned over her and kissed deeply before taking turns kissing her.

When her heart settled and she could breathe again, they straightened her clothing and held her between them.

They helped her from the car when Leonard stopped at one of the most exclusive restaurants in the city. She was shocked when they were led to a private room. The single expense probably rivaled the cost of her first car.

Hudson gave the server instructions and placed their orders. They asked her about her day out with the girls, what she'd bought, and how it made her feel.

Constantly, they petted her.

When their drinks arrived, Hudson told the young man to give them privacy for half an hour. He nodded and quickly left.

She sat back in her seat and smiled at them. "I adore the two of you, do you know that?"

They nodded.

"I've thought of nothing else for weeks but being able to touch you and have you touch me. I masturbate constantly." Their expressions and forward movement made her laugh. "Wait. You keep touching me now and I won't be able to create coherent sentences."

Taking a sip of her wine, she took them in. Natalia wore a supple black leather skirt and silk blouse with heels that clasped around her ankles in a way that made Brie want to lick her way up her legs.

Hudson was resplendent in a black suit, gray shirt, and matching tie. She couldn't wait to peel away all his layers.

"I know you have the idea that we'll be a long-term threesome and while that sounds lovely, I think we all know it won't work." She crossed her arms on the table.

"I *lust* for you but I'm *not* in love with either of you. You feel the same way about me. Too much time spent in your company will *change* that for me...but you'll *not* grow to love me and that will get increasingly difficult as time goes on."

"Perhaps..."

Brie shook her head. "No, Hudson. It won't happen and I understand. It doesn't hurt me *now* but can you imagine how I'll feel in six months? A year? You don't want to hurt me but you can't *force* emotion that isn't there."

"We love you, Brie."

"Not in the way I mean and you truly *do* know the difference. You think to keep me as a buffer, to play it safe. While I understand, I can't allow you to do it because I'd end up shattered."

She sipped her wine. "With that said, you both made promises to me about what you would do after I recovered and I find myself an absolute glutton for the knowledge, the experience."

Hudson couldn't hide his surprise and it made her smile.

"I'd like us to have tonight. One night where my heart is not yet involved despite how deep my affection runs for both of you."

She looked back and forth between them. "Time for you to touch me, for me to touch you, to learn so many things I want to know."

Inhaling carefully, she added, "Then you have to let me go before my heart *is* involved and the stakes are too high. It would be too easy to fall in love with either of you separately. I've had to guard myself against it from the beginning. Together, my pain would be far worse."

Meeting their eyes, she whispered, "Do you understand?"

Leaning forward, Hudson took her hand and guided her from her chair. She was surprised when he settled her in his lap. Natalia sat on his other side and they stared at her.

"You'll have what you want."

"Thank you, Hudson."

"Nothing, *ever*, will release you from our protection."

She smiled softly and ran her fingers through his hair. "The two of you are loyal to a fault, generous, and achingly attractive. Though I have no choice but to protect my heart, I want you to know that I can't imagine my life without the two of you in it, in whatever capacity you choose."

Her fingers traced over their faces. "Where you'll always have my back, know that I'll always have yours. I may not seem very imposing but I can be an asset in my own way. I'm an excellent listener, give soothing hugs, and I'm a great cook."

She shrugged. "Not so important in big business but a soft place to land if you need to breathe for a little."

"How lovely your soul is, Brie." Natalia held her hand. "How I wish I had your ability to brighten the lives of those around you." She kissed the inside of her wrist. "As for your night, it's yours."

They took turns kissing her, stroking her, loving her in their way and it was heartbreaking to a small piece of herself.

She *would* take from them…she hoped to also give back.

* * *

Dinner was delicious and after their talk, it seemed that the tension between Hudson and Natalia was better than it had been in weeks.

They left the restaurant and drove by his office building. They got out and walked the courtyard.

"I can see slight changes you've made already to the seating areas, the planters, and the fountain. It's just lovely, Hudson."

"I want you to work for me, Gabriella. In any position you like. I want you to have a place, a group of co-workers that helps you grow into your various talents."

She repeated what she'd told her friends and noted the pained expression that crossed his face.

Inhaling deeply, he told her, "I own the building."

One blink. "This building…? I know."

"The building you currently work in. I own it."

She sat down hard on one of the benches facing the fountain and Natalia settled beside her, taking her hand. "You *own* the building where I work?" He nodded. "Why didn't anyone tell me?"

"The day we met, you thought badly of me. I handled things wrong. I had to get to the bottom of what brought you here but I needed to know you would be alright. It was my responsibility."

Absolute shock. "It wasn't your…"

"My *name*. Your con artist brought you to New York using *my name*." She understood how hard that must have been for someone like him. "I didn't know if you'd stay or return home. I was a dick at first and I knew you wouldn't accept my help."

Hudson gave her a small smile. "I wouldn't have, in your position. Then I didn't know how to tell you without it seeming like I *expected* something from you."

Tiny things clicked together in her mind. "You own my apartment building, too. Don't you?"

"I keep the first building I ever purchased because I've seen people lose everything with one bad investment. It's my insurance policy. My apartment there sat empty, just in case. Apartments in some parts of the city can be dangerous. I wanted you to have somewhere safe to live."

Brie's eyes stayed on his for almost a minute and he didn't look away. "Thank you for your help, Hudson. I didn't want to leave New York."

"If I hadn't done anything, you would have taken an apartment you hated, a job you hated, and you *still* would have made it, Brie. You're a fighter and you were *hungry* for a new life. Nothing would have stopped you from getting what you wanted."

"You have no idea how much that means coming from you."

The words pleased him immensely and he settled on her other side. They kissed her repeatedly and she absorbed the shock of so much additional information.

As they returned to the car, another connection was made and she blushed hot. "Camille is your *mother*, isn't she?" He nodded and she laughed nervously. "Well, that's awkward. She *might* have brought something in while I was away and seen a sketch I was working on of- of the two of you." She cleared her throat. "You weren't dressed."

Keeping her eyes forward, the friends burst out laughing on either side of her. Soon, the three of them were hysterical.

It was a singular way to begin a night of carnal excess.

Chapter Forty-Nine

As the trio entered Hudson's penthouse, they led her to the bar and he poured each of them a glass of wine.

Natalia smoothed her hand over her hair. "Since you've made it clear what you want and need from us, we'd like to spend the night with you in the downstairs bedroom. It's not a regular guest room, you see. It has a few *perks*. If one night is our parameter, we'd like to show you as much as possible."

Planting a kiss beneath her ear, she went to turn on the house stereo system and within moments, a sensual bass-filled instrumental replaced the silence.

Hudson watched her and she knew he saw the way her nipples tightened. "So *responsive* to stimulus. In preparation, we purchased a few things with you in mind. Gifts, but nothing you're accustomed to." He winked. "We wanted to be ready as you grew to trust us."

"I already do, both of you, implicitly." His eyes were hungry as they stared at her. "If I know I'm pleasing *you*, I'm happy to place the use of my body completely in your care."

Natalia stood behind her, hands sliding from her shoulders to her hands. At her ear, she whispered, "Your safe word is chocolate."

She nodded and murmured, "I doubt I'll need it but thank you."

He stepped closer, the friends boxing her in, and leaned down to kiss her lips. "You don't know what we're going to do yet."

"It doesn't matter. I'll enjoy it. You're the only two people to ever affect me in such a sexual way."

His expression was surprised. "Ever?"

"I always *knew* he wasn't sexually attracted to me." She smiled sadly. "I thought he liked my personality, the way I treated him. I let it be enough. With every relationship, I let it be enough."

Lifting her hand, she loosened his tie.

"Every look, every word either of you have given me for months shows that how you feel about me is not the same. Not just *anyone* would be here with the two of you like this."

"Brie, no one has *ever* been with us like this."

She met his black eyes and saw the truth of the statement. Her own filled with tears. "Thank you for giving me such a gift."

"No, darling. We are selfishly *taking* what we've grown desperate to have. We will sensually gorge ourselves on you, indulging every lustful thought we've entertained. By morning, you'll be covered in our fluids as well as your own. You'll feel debauched yet free in ways that will change everything."

Resting her head on Natalia's shoulder, she whispered, "*Please.*"

"Come."

Natalia took her hand and turned toward the guest room. Taking a key from his pocket, Hudson unlocked the door and stood to one side.

She entered and her entire body went hot. "God *yes.*"

The walls were painted deep purple. The ceiling and floor were black. Her heels sounded loud on the marble.

Glass shelves held sculptures in different mediums. Upon closer inspection, she realized they were all erotic. There was a conspicuously empty space and she smiled.

"You gave me one of *yours.* I'm honored, Hudson."

There was a glass shelf that held various clamps covered in velvet. Some were attached to chains while others had rings. A flat case displayed whips, crops, and floggers.

She stroked her fingertip over them, learning the textures.

An assortment of glass toys, meant to be inserted in the pussy or the ass, filled a cabinet and were artwork in their own right.

Oils, lubricants, and sanitary wipes. Every style of cuff, rope, or binding. Blindfolds, spreaders, and low-heat candles. Erotic books and paintings.

There were hooks in the ceiling and she saw the leather straps used to suspend a willing submissive. One corner held two black leather chairs with a small table between them.

A bed took up one end of the room, covered in black satin sheets.

A metal bar that resembled something found in a dance studio stretched along the back of it. There were hooks at all four corners on the ceiling and floor.

Turning back to them, she could see the nervousness they felt at exposing their innermost sanctuary to her.

"I should have negotiated for more days."

Then she untied her dress and let it slide from her shoulders. The door slammed and they were walking in her direction before it fully settled at her feet. She kicked it away and didn't care where it ended up.

Hudson shrugged off his jacket, removed his tie, and rolled up his shirtsleeves. Natalia stepped behind her, her hands coasting over the exposed skin between her bra and panties.

"Are you frightened?" She shook her head slowly. "Are you trembling from excitement?" She moaned and managed to nod.

"Your skin is so soft and warm, Gabriella. This lingerie set looks so good, I almost hesitate to remove it. *Almost.*"

With that, she unclasped the bra and gently lowered the straps. As her rebuilt breasts came into view for the first time to anyone but her and her doctor, they both groaned.

"Perfect cocoa nipples. I knew it," she said with a kiss to her shoulder.

Thumbs hooked in the waist of her panties and Natalia lowered one side, put it back, and lowered the other, teasing before committing to taking them off. She slid down the back of her body, kissing her ass cheek.

Brie stepped out of the panties and her shoes were removed as well.

Standing on the marble floor, completely naked while they were dressed felt wicked in a delicious way. Her toes curled but she remained still and waited to be told what they wanted her to do.

Hudson hadn't taken his eyes off her since she dropped her dress. After a full minute, he gave her a slow smile.

"You're a natural, Brie. Excellent."

"Spread your legs, darling." She walked her feet out. Cool silk brushed her back and then was placed over her eyes. "Just for a little, to help you let go completely."

She nodded and when it was tied snugly in place, they stroked her skin for several minutes, simply petting her, squeezing her, learning her. Kisses were given until she was lightheaded. Thick fingers stroked through her damp folds and there was a sigh of satisfaction.

"You're wet for us."

"Usually."

He lightly slapped her mound and her breath panted between her lips.

She was carefully guided across the floor. Natalia stood in front of her and took her wrists. "What's your safe word, Brie?"

"Chocolate."

"You're to say it if you pass excitement to fear or if there's pain you can't handle. Do you understand?"

"Yes, Natalia. Thank you."

Her palm slid along her neck, holding Brie immobile for a destructive kiss that drew her nipples painfully tight.

Then her arms were lifted above her head and held there. Supple leather circled her wrists and within moments, she was suspended from the ceiling.

There was no give. She experienced a moment of panic at being bound but she breathed through it.

"Very good," Hudson breathed at her ear. "Your body in this position is a feast for the eyes."

His strong hands cupped her breasts and she moaned as his thumbs flicked nipples that she'd never allowed lovers to touch. He offered them to Natalia who took her time sucking them.

Brie tried to get closer and when she realized how close the other woman was to her, she balanced on one foot and stroked her toes along the outside of her leg.

"How much you enjoy giving and receiving touch is fascinating to me." Cool fingers stroked from her breasts, over her sides, to squeeze her hip and around to her ass.

"Are you ready, Gabriella?" His breath was warm on her cheek.

"Yes, Hudson. I'm ready."

Her hair was gathered and dropped over one shoulder, covering the breast on that side.

Four hands smoothed over her body, massaging her with an oil that tingled. From the back of her neck to below her ass.

When she was completely covered, Natalia stood in front of her, naked as well, and cupped her breasts.

The first lash across her back made her arch forward, pushing her more firmly into the other woman's hands. She moaned, exhaled slowly, and evaluated the sensation without her vision to distract her.

Sharp, but it had surprised her more than hurt. It was bearable.

The second found Natalia's hand between her legs. The combination of pleasure and pain was disorienting. Each time the leather landed on her skin, she received another stroke over her clit. By the tenth, she was trying to hold back an orgasm that surprised her.

Then she lost count of how many times her back and ass were strapped and narrowed her focus on the pleasure. She found that if she went up on the balls of her feet, she could move her legs further apart.

Fingers instantly entered her pussy and stroked deep. "Yes, Brie. Your instincts are powerful. Don't doubt them."

All she could manage was a whispered, "*More.*"

"As much as you can take, darling."

Again and again, the whip landed on her skin and she understood why they referred to their needs as dark. She felt it, embraced it, and knew it wouldn't change her.

She was glad for the knowledge.

The next time the leather connected, her body took over. Her head dropped back on her shoulders and she gasped at the force of an orgasm she did not expect.

Hudson was suddenly naked at her back, lifting her leg and placing it over a now-kneeling Natalia's shoulder. She planted a soft kiss on her inner thigh and Brie's orgasm continued to travel her body.

He thrust hard and fast into her pussy. It should have been painful but she was wet, aching.

"Don't come again." Nothing less than a command.

"I won't."

Holding her in place, he fucked her brutally hard and it felt too good to be real. It was even better when Natalia's mouth settled over her clit and sucked firmly.

With each stroke, Hudson's chest brushed against the skin of her back, the sting left by the whip added another layer to the experience.

They drove her, showed no mercy, and she knew she neither wanted nor needed mercy. Still, she couldn't contain her whimpers of need.

"Hold it back, Brie."

His palm rested over her stomach above her womb. She wondered if he could feel how hard her denied orgasm caused it to quiver.

On and on, he fucked her and she dropped into a place where there was nothing but the feel of them touching her. Natalia alternated between licking her and rubbing the flat of her fingers over flesh that was hypersensitive and slick.

"Fuck, *fuck*, Gabriella." He drove harder and faster half a dozen times and stilled.

She felt the way his cock throbbed inside her, filling the condom, and she dropped her head back on his shoulder, controlling her breathing as he stroked shallowly in and out of her body.

The sense of triumph she felt that she'd held back her climax turned to a sob when they were suddenly gone.

"We're here. Let me fill you, darling. We know you ache. You're doing so well."

Natalia slowly inserted a fake cock that was so like the size and shape of Hudson's, she knew it must have been purposeful. Her hips worked on it instinctively.

"It's bewitching to watch you fuck this cock."

Holding it just far enough away to keep her from taking it deep, she knew they watched her take as much of it as she could in the current position.

She tightened her leg on Natalia's back, bringing her closer. A sigh of relief filled the room when she settled her lips over Brie's folds. She continued to roll her hips, grinding herself against her face as the cock shuttled in and out.

"Your mouth feels like heaven."

"We're going to prepare your ass. Do you want me to leave the fake cock in place? It will be very tight, darling."

"Leave it. Please leave it."

"A telling answer." With that, she inserted the cock to the base and ribbons were tied around her waist and hips to hold it in place.

Hudson's lips kissed each of her ass cheeks as his slick fingers slid along the cleft. "Such a perfect ass. I've dreamed of fucking it."

"I've dreamed of you fucking it. Usually with Natalia performing her magic. It's a fantasy that makes me come forever."

Natalia licked her clit above the base of the dildo. "Mm, have you had other fantasies about us, Brie?"

Moaning, she whispered, "Yes."

"Tell us about them. Which one is your favorite?"

"I'm in a chair…"

The feel of Hudson pushing two lubricated fingers in her ass made her cry out. Then he started to move them and she gradually relaxed.

"I can take you now. Please don't make me wait."

"It will burn…"

"I don't care. I *need* it. I want to remember, to feel you both on me and in me when our night is over."

He stood and she knew he was already hard again. Hudson was always hard. He kissed the back of her neck, holding his lips there for a long moment before moving away.

The lubricant that coated him was chilly as he placed the head of his cock against the pucker of her ass. "Brie…"

"Fuck me, please." Then he drove deep and she screamed. She was so full and it was almost too much but still she wanted more. She wanted to experience all of it. "Don't stop…"

Natalia stood at her front and they held her between them, the back of her knee held in her deceptively strong hands. She planted kisses over her face as Hudson fucked her into a trance state.

His palms held her hips and he tunneled into her ass as hard as he'd taken her pussy and she was glad. She was sincere about wanting to take all of it with her. Memories to soothe her after weeks of their physical attention.

Each moment would remind her.

Her body hummed for them. Time had no meaning so he could have fucked her for ten minutes or an hour. She moaned against Natalia's shoulder, her entire body vibrating violently.

"We need to let you come, darling."

"Not yet. Not yet. I can wait."

"You're unbelievably calm. I've seen women enter the lifestyle who'd already be in tears."

"You won't hurt me. I *know* you won't."

Hudson kissed her neck. "Thank you, Brie." His strokes slowed but didn't stop. "For trusting us."

"I've *always* trusted you. If someone told me six months ago that I'd be suspended from the ceiling getting naked time attention from the two of you, I'd have told them they were high."

Their arms crossed at the front and back of her torso. Each thrust of Hudson's hips went deep and it didn't burn anymore.

Natalia told her gently, "If someone told me six months ago that a woman with such a beautiful heart would accept us, care for us as you do, I *also* would have told them they were high, Gabriella."

She felt disconnected from reality, floating in a place of so many new sensations that she couldn't have sworn whether or not she spoke aloud. "You're so easy to care for. It's hard for me to let you go but as much as you care for me, and I know you do, I need someone to *love* me. Really *love* me for the first time in my life."

He pushed forward until he was completely buried inside her and stilled. She whispered, "I want to be the reason someone gets up in the morning. I want to still *be* that reason thirty years later."

Their arms tightened hard around her. "Do you think that will happen for me? That it's possible? Sometimes I don't think so but I hope because I want to know the way it feels. It's so very beautiful."

"Gabriella…"

He carefully pulled from her body, making her whimper.

"Ssh, darling. We'll make it better."

She heard water running and then he was behind her again. Natalia untied the ribbons and removed the cock from inside her.

His forearm went across her ribcage, just under her breasts and then her arms were released. Her legs wouldn't have held her up but she needn't have worried.

Hudson picked her up easily and walked into the bathroom.

He lowered her in the tub and the water made her skin prickle in a strange but wonderful way. Natalia gathered her hair and used chopsticks to fix it to the top of her head. She guided her back to recline.

"Stay here for a few minutes, just like this, and we'll join you."

Though her womb was spasming painfully, the water soothed the skin of her back and the tender muscles of her ass.

So far, her evening with Hudson and Natalia had been so much more than she dreamed. The soreness of her body, the slight ache in her heart, was well worth the memories they would leave her with.

She had *no* regrets.

Chapter Fifty

Hudson stood just outside the bathroom door holding a shaking Natalia. Barefoot, the top of her head was just beneath his chin and she rested her head on his shoulder as she cried in silence.

They *had not* spoken but as Gabriella talked about the emotional connection she hoped to have one day, their eyes met over the body they were *using* and they knew they'd made a mistake.

Though she might not be in love with them, she *would* hurt.

It was something they'd never intended. They forgot about her giving nature. How much she would allow them to take from her, expecting nothing in return.

Gabriella was instinctively submissive. It was a natural part of her sexuality and one that would serve her well if she pursued the lifestyle.

Hudson would carefully vet any man or woman who thought to touch her. Anyone with impure motives wouldn't get near her. He wouldn't allow her to be hurt or used.

The relief they'd felt when she talked to them at the restaurant had been a tangible thing. In the weeks since the gala, they'd known they were out of their element when it came to the gentle woman who'd become such a fixture in their lives.

They cared for her deeply and that wouldn't change. Natalia's warnings several weeks ago about Brie's *emotional* needs could suddenly be seen and felt.

That they *did not* love her in the way she needed frustrated them.

If there was ever a person who deserved it, who *earned* it with every thought, every word, and every gesture since the day she'd arrived in New York – it was Gabriella.

He smoothed Natalia's hair, stroked her back, and her arms left his waist and circled his neck.

At his ear, she whispered, "I don't want to hurt her."

With a nod, his arms tightened around her. He fisted her hair at the nape of her neck and pulled her head back to look into her face. The electric blue of her eyes was brilliant, made more so with the tears that sparkled in them.

Connections happened in the back of his mind, suddenly there. Now was not the time to talk about it.

Instead, he kissed her. Took her mouth in a kiss that was familiar, necessary to every part of his life. His tongue stroked deep and she coiled hers around it, her hands cupping his skull to hold him to her.

When it broke, they stared at one another. He stroked his fingers through her hair, raking it back from her face. With his eyes open, he planted another kiss on her lips.

Nuzzling her ear, he said softly, "Help me show Brie what she wants to know. The knowledge best for *her* to take from this experience."

"Yes."

It would be different from what they were accustomed to. It was the least they could do for the woman who'd given them so much.

One final kiss, a hug, and together they walked into the bathroom.

She hadn't moved from where they placed her and she startled as they climbed in beside her.

Hudson lifted her into his lap with Natalia beside him. She removed the blindfold and they watched Brie blink against the light.

Her smile was brilliant as she looked at them. Without a word, she maneuvered her body so she could wrap her arms around their necks.

"Thank you." She planted a soft kiss on Natalia's lips and another on Hudson's. Cupping Natalia's face, she stared at her intently. "You've been crying." A pause. "You think you're using *me* when I feel as though I'm using *you*."

"You couldn't use someone if you had a step-by-step handbook."

That made her laugh and it relieved the ache he felt in his chest. "What do you want to learn? We've shown you a taste of our sexuality but there's so much more than that. What are you curious about?"

She blushed hot as she idly stroked the backs of their necks but didn't say anything.

Natalia smiled. "You want to touch us."

Her blush spread. "I never had a chance to see anyone naked before my first day with Hudson." They were shocked and it must have showed. "The-the lights were always off."

She swallowed and they could see her embarrassment. "I'd seen pictures but it wasn't the same. The two men who came before, *they* used me. You aren't using me because I'm a real person to you."

The idea that men had taken her body without her ever *seeing* them infuriated him. Natalia was equally livid.

"You're the most splendid person I know, darling. I mean that."

"Thank you." Brie cleared her throat and took a deep breath. "I'd really like, if you wouldn't mind, to give you a massage from head to toe so I can see and feel everything. So I'm not shy." Her smile was sad. "I don't want anyone to ever know I was twenty-eight the first time I saw a man naked."

They hugged her hard between them and it was suddenly clear that darkness came in many different guises.

With Hudson and Natalia, they'd always felt it came from inside. For Brie, it had been pushed into her from outside.

Maybe they could take some of that away.

"First, we're going to give you a glass of wine to take with you on a tour of the house." They worked together to wash her skin.

Her eyes lit up. "You're going to show me your house?" He nodded, confused. "I would *love* that. I've never seen where either of you lived before and it makes me happy to see spaces. It adds a layer of information to a person I care about. If you tell me you're in your kitchen or office, I can picture you there."

"Jesus. I'm sorry, Brie."

"Don't be sorry. You're both very private. I understand." She was visibly giddy about seeing where he lived. It was humbling. "Soon, I'll get to see *Trois* and that will be fabulous since the girls talk about it all the time. I'm excited."

"I live above the club."

"I didn't know that. Your commute to work is awesome." Natalia grinned as she rinsed the soap away. "I imagine that isn't common knowledge for safety reasons. I'll keep the secret."

"I look forward to showing you. There are renovations being done off hours to space that was previously unused and locked off from the rest. You'll get the first tour."

"The girls have been trying to get me to go for months but I was embarrassed. I feel better now."

They lifted her from the tub and dried her together. They stood pressed against her and it was easy to see her pleasure in the touch.

"Gabriella, you're gorgeous right this moment but you were no less stunning the first day I met you." Natalia placed her palm over her heart. "This always made you beyond enchanting."

They led her to the kitchen and she sipped her wine. Walking to the refrigerator, she opened it and her mouth dropped in shock.

The interior held bottles of water and wine. The freezer was completely empty.

"You need *food*. Hudson, you should get a housekeeper. Someone to come in every day and cook for you. They can leave before you indulge in kink. They'll never know the naughty and you'll get real meals."

He laughed loudly. Natalia said, "I told him he needed someone to take care of him."

"You already take care of each *other*. All you need is someone to cook, clean, and run errands. You don't need a soccer mom type to live with you. You can *hire* people to do the crap you want but hate to do." She tilted her head and her smile told them she'd figured out more than they'd ever said.

Walking around the bar, she grinned up at them. "It doesn't matter what the movies and shit show. You don't need it. All you need is to feel like you're *home*. The person you love is what makes that feeling possible. Love and care come in so many different forms."

They held her, took turns kissing her, and encouraged her to ask questions. The ones that interested her surprised them both.

She raked her fingers through Hudson's hair and said, "Your mother is lovely but you look nothing alike. Do you look like your father?" He nodded. "He must have been a handsome man."

He told her the story of his parents and Brie was silent throughout.

When he was done, she wrapped her arms around him and whispered, "I'm glad you got that building. They have no idea what they missed and they deserve to have a daily reminder shoved up their ass." Leaning back, there were tears on her face. "No wonder you're so strong, Hudson. I understand now."

How easily she wrecked them. They hugged her back so hard that they worried they would hurt her.

They showed her the penthouse and were glad that she didn't seem to have a problem taking the tour naked.

Everything fascinated her. Two of the bedrooms upstairs were completely empty but she walked them anyway.

His office gave her goosebumps and she refused to go inside. She stood at the door and stared at everything for a long time. "I'm not messing with the power mojo in that space. You need it."

"The way your mind works fascinates me, Brie."

Her same reaction at his bedroom surprised them both.

"I can't leave my imprint in there. I bet you changed the mattress set after your last girlfriend." He nodded. "Bad vibes. You probably regret every person who's slept in that room other than Natalia."

Her ability to verbalize things that consistently escaped him was something he'd never tire of.

She turned. "You can't have a memory of *me* in that room. It's not the same downstairs. That room was created for pleasure and there's a sort of disconnect there. Purposeful, I think." Her smile was gentle.

"This is where you *sleep*. Where you let down your guard. When you haven't been with other people, I bet you've fallen asleep here together many times. You can't have a memory of the three of us together here. It wouldn't be right."

"You're sensational."

"I still want orgasms. Just not here." She winked as she sipped her wine and it made them smile. Stepping close to Natalia, she stroked through her hair. "You haven't climaxed even once. You're due."

"I don't mind waiting."

"I imagine not. I'm sure it makes it more powerful."

Placing his palm over her rounded tummy, he felt the low vibration in her womb. "Are you in pain, Brie?"

"Not really. I find I rather like the waiting as well."

Back downstairs, he refilled their glasses and returned to the converted guest room. They'd quickly straightened while she was in the tub. Her clothing was neatly folded on top of one of the cases.

They watched her eyes land on the chairs in the corner and watched her nipples pebble, the pulse in her neck began to race.

"I never told you my favorite fantasy, the one I masturbate to." They tensed, turning in her direction. "It might relax you. If you're relaxed, I can take my time learning you."

"Tell us."

"I'd like to change it up. Put Natalia in my place and take the place she always had in my mind."

With that, she led his best friend across the room to one of the chairs. She settled her on the seat, pulled her ass to the edge, lifted her leg and placed it over one of the arms, and knelt between her thighs.

For several minutes, they watched her stroke her palms over the front of Natalia's body. She took her time, starting with a deep kiss as her hands plumped modest breasts and rolled nipples that were drawn incredibly tight.

Using the flat of her hand, she rubbed up and down the pale folds he knew so well.

Looking at her face, she murmured, "It felt really amazing when you did this to me." Natalia nodded, her breath panting between her lips. "You're so wet."

She carefully inserted two fingers into her pussy, turning her palm up. He knew she curled them when Natalia gasped. "Hudson did that to me. I thought the top of my head would pop off."

"He has often made me feel the same, darling."

"I imagine. I mean, look at him." Natalia did exactly that. "You have to tell us what to do, Hudson. That's always the best part. Hearing your instructions. I u-usually pretend you're, um, stroking yourself while you do it."

His cock pulsed painfully. "Do you?"

"For a long time, I didn't even *know* other people masturbated. I thought I was doing something wrong so I asked my sister. She told me not to be embarrassed because everyone does."

She swallowed hard. "The two of you are the first people who ever made me wonder...what you *looked* like when you did it."

"That you're so innocent yet so sexually destructive is more effective than you probably realize, Gabriella."

For the compliment, Brie lifted herself to deliver a long kiss. The movement of her fingers never stopped.

When she settled back on her heels, she looked up at him and tugged her lower lip between her teeth.

"When I imagine it, you always come. You have to come *on* her so I can rub it into her skin."

"Jesus. You're going to *annihilate* a man one day, Brie."

"Wouldn't that be nice? I'll have the two of you to thank for the chance to learn." She winked. "Who knows? I might need two people for the rest of my life. The dynamic is so interesting."

"Darling, the hunters at *Trois* are going to love you."

That made her laugh. "I doubt it but I'll enjoy watching everyone interact. I didn't even know people *did* stuff like this in real life."

They watched her lean forward and drag her tongue through the cleft of Natalia's body, planting a sucking kiss on her clit. A full-body chill worked its way over her alabaster skin.

Lifting her hand, she cupped the back of his thigh and brought him closer. The side of Natalia's extended leg brushed his other hip.

He needed.

"Play with your nipples." Instantly, her slender hands curved around her breasts and she worked the pink tips between her fingers. He wrapped his fist around his cock.

"Pull them out from your body." The more she worked them, the more distended they became. Glancing down, he observed the way Brie studied him, enthralled by the movements. "Add another finger. Fuck her harder."

There wasn't an ounce of hesitation as she followed his instructions. With her other hand, she smoothed the natural lubrication over the tiny pucker of Natalia's ass.

"Yes. Do it." He watched as she pressed gently into the tiny hole, pushing until her finger was deep.

"You're so hot, Natalia. It feels different from your pussy. I can see why Hudson's cock feels so good when he fucks you here."

She moved more quickly with her three fingers, allowing the slickness to gather so she could add a second finger to an ass he'd never tire of fucking.

Leaning over the chair, his knee resting beside Natalia's on the arm, he told her, "Get me wet."

Her mouth opened and she took him deep, swallowing around the head as he struggled to remember the plan.

The additional sensation of Brie lifting to take his balls in her mouth almost caused him to lose control. They worked together to suck him and the sound of Natalia's wet pussy made the skin on the back of his neck feel too tight.

"Fuck." He pulled back and Brie dropped her mouth over Natalia's clit. "God yes. Suck it hard." He bent and licked a pink nipple between her fingers, sucking it to the roof of his mouth.

"Please, oh god, please." She rarely begged.

Releasing her, he stood straight and worked his fist faster and harder over his length. Brie unconsciously matched his rhythm, driving in and out of Natalia's body as she ate her.

Then he knew he couldn't hold back. "Come."

Brie slammed her fingers to her palms and sucked the swollen clit hard. Natalia shattered, her entire body going tight, arching from the chair, struggling to get closer to the source of her pleasure. The licking and finger fucking didn't stop until her body stopped shaking.

With a final kiss, she carefully removed her fingers from Natalia's pussy and lifted her hand to him in offering.

"She's delicious."

He took her three fingers in his mouth and sucked every trace of come from them. She pulled her fingers from the tight hole and kissed the top of her mound before standing.

"One second." She ran into the bathroom and washed her hands, back in seconds. "I want to be careful with your body but I'm not very smooth about it."

She returned to her knees and dragged her tongue from the swollen clit, down to push her tongue deep in the first pussy she'd ever eaten.

"I can't…" Natalia came again without warning and Hudson was at the limit of what he could take.

"Sit back, Brie." She did so and watched him stroke his cock. She was gasping for breath. "Where?"

"Her pussy. All over her pussy."

"Fuck." Brie used her fingers to separate the lips. "Fuck yes, yes covering your sweet pussy."

Jet after jet of his come splashed over Natalia's folds and he watched as Brie's fingers rubbed it everywhere, gathering some to fuck inside a pussy that was dripping to the leather. More was rubbed into her nipples and he wasn't certain he would be able to keep standing up.

Air sawed in and out of his lungs as they watched the most giving woman they'd ever known suck the pink nipples she'd painted clean before kissing her way down the lean torso and lapping the combined taste of them from her body.

Then she sat back and said, "I knew you wouldn't be completely soft. We have to clean you." She smiled. "I like that part, too."

So saying, she leaned up and took his cock as deep as she could and sucked *hard*. When his eyes met Natalia's, she sat up and wrapped her arm around Brie's shoulders.

Releasing him with a small pop, the two of them kissed for a long time. Then they took turns sucking his cock, trading between his balls, and cleaning the length.

Finally, she sat back and smiled at them with a rough exhale. "See why I use that when I masturbate?" Her eyes were over-bright and her skin was incredibly flushed.

One heartbeat, a second, and he scooped her up from the floor. Natalia stood and they hugged her from the front and back of her body. They traded her mouth between them.

"You can continue to learn us…after we make you come."

Moving away, he rolled on a condom and added lubricant to avoid chafing her. He sat in the chair and pulled Brie closer. At the last moment, he faced her away from him and lifted her over his lap.

It was Natalia who placed the head of his cock at her pussy. The sensation was unlike anything he'd ever felt.

Carefully, he lowered Brie until he was fully seated. She was already shaking violently. He brought her back to his chest and Natalia spread her legs even wider as she knelt between them.

"Don't hold back. This is about giving you pleasure you deserve to feel. We want to make you come." The instant Natalia's fingers settled on her clit, she exploded around him, tightening like a vise.

Her head lowered to his shoulder and he slipped over her skin, up to take her full breasts in his palms. "That's better. You held it back for so long, Brie. I'm proud of you."

They held her between them, Natalia stretched out over her upper body as she reclined on him. The climax went on for a long time.

She positioned her folds over Brie's, one of her knees on the arm of the chair. Working their pelvises together, their slickness was audible. The imagery, one light, one tan, was stunning.

That he'd never watched Natalia with another woman struck him and he took in every detail.

"Hudson's cock is buried so deep in your pussy. It feels good, doesn't it?" Brie nodded. "Filling you while your muscles milk him."

She kissed her deeply. "I've wanted to rub my body against yours for months, Gabriella. To feel your firm little clit stroking mine. Knowing your wet pussy is holding his cock makes it so much better than I imagined."

Rolling hip movements maintained pressure on the little bundle of nerves. They were so slick that the friction was smooth and gentle.

There was a hard tremor and she came for them again.

"That's it, darling. Nothing but pleasure. All the good things you deserve to feel. How desperate we've been to touch you, to kiss you, taste you, and fuck you. Your generosity makes us want to drown you in orgasms."

Another long kiss and Natalia stood.

From a drawer, she removed one of the plugs they'd purchased for Brie. She opened the package and carried it to the bathroom to rinse it thoroughly.

"I can't believe you're still hard, Hudson. What a fucking skill." She chuckled. "See what I did there?"

He hugged her from behind and kissed the skin beneath her ear. "How do you feel?"

"Like I'm on the pain meds again. So high."

Natalia returned and covered the plug heavily in lube. "Put your feet on the floor and bend forward, darling."

She managed it with her limbs trembling. With his cock still buried in her pussy, he watched as the plug was carefully inserted in Brie's ass. Natalia turned on the vibration and the walls of her pussy spasmed around him. He buckled down his control.

"*Oh my god…*"

They returned her to Hudson's chest, spreading her legs, and Natalia bent at the waist. Her tongue dragged from Hudson's balls to where they were joined and finally swirled around Brie's clit.

Stretching over her body, Natalia gripped the back of Hudson's neck and fucked her tongue into his mouth so he could taste. The expression on his face when she pulled back was one she knew well.

"Fuck her, Hudson. Make her scream."

Standing, he turned and placed Brie on her knees, facing the wall. "Sit on the back." He could tell the command surprised her but still he *needed*. "I want to watch her eat your pussy again."

Brie's voice was shaky. "The cock shaped like Hudson. I want to fuck you with it." When Natalia returned, climbed on the back of the chair, and spread her legs with her feet on the arms, she smiled.

"We'll trade places. I want to watch him fuck you, too."

Gripping her hips, Hudson proceeded to fuck her until she was incoherent with pleasure.

By morning, they'd all be dehydrated.

Chapter Fifty-One

Brie's eyes opened and she was confused for a moment.

Pressed to the front of Natalia's sleeping body, she saw Hudson curled behind her ivory body with his arm wrapped over the two of them.

Every moment from the night before rushed back and made her smile.

They took her in every position, in every combination. She'd eventually gotten the chance she wanted to learn them by sight, feel, and touch.

They set no conditions on her exploration but she was gentle, reverent of the opportunity and didn't want to waste it.

For more than an hour near dawn, she alternated back and forth between their bodies, massaging them with oil, planting small kisses on the flesh she touched.

That it pushed them into deep slumber had pleased her more than she could have explained. It showed a level of trust she would never take for granted.

For a few minutes, she was still, watching them sleep. She loved the way their faces looked in the soft morning light that streamed through the bank of windows on one side of the room.

Carefully, she slipped from the bed and grabbed her clothes. Tiptoeing into the living room, she dressed in silence. She wouldn't put her shoes on until she got in the elevator.

After she opened several empty drawers in the kitchen, she found a notepad that had probably been there for *years*. Two drawers later, she found a pen and was shocked that the ink was still good.

It struck her again how different their lives were from most people.

> *Good morning!*
>
> *I didn't want to wake either of you so I'm going downstairs to shower and dress. I need coffee like a crackhead but I'll be back in a little while.*
>
> *I'm going back to my (your) apartment today but I thought we could have brunch together if you guys are in the mood.*
>
> *Thank you for every minute of our night together. Just so you know, I don't feel the least bit debauched…but definitely educated at last. I adore you both. I'm so glad that I met you. No one else would have treated me so well.*
>
> *Muah!*
> *Brie*

She left it on the bar beneath her wine glass and picked up her shoes. As the elevator opened, she took a deep breath and stepped inside.

* * *

Downstairs, she showered and washed her hair. Her body was sore but there were no signs of the night she'd enjoyed.

She'd never bruised or marked easily. Izzy liked to joke that after generations of hard labor in the sun, Mexicans could take anything.

"We're practically indestructible."

Chuckling as she examined the flawless skin of her back, Brie murmured, "Girl, I think you're right."

Quickly pulling on one of her new lingerie sets – peach this time – she dressed in her new jeans, a t-shirt, trail runners, and a hoodie. With her phone and slim wallet tucked in her pockets, she pulled her hair on top of her head and went downstairs.

She asked Carlo if he wanted coffee and he nodded gratefully. Henry showed her a new photo of his grandson and she told him to print a couple and she'd make him a painting for his son and daughter-in-law.

"You don't have to do that, Brie. Where you find the time and energy, I don't know but I'd love if you shared some with this old man."

She winked. "Your missus says different, Henry."

He blushed and practically giggled. His wife was the head of the catering department, a fact she hadn't learned until she'd been at the building for several weeks.

"I don't like to brag," he'd told her when she'd asked him directly.

Remembering made her smile. "Get the business center to print a couple of your favorites. I'll enjoy every moment." Turning, she started down the block. "Do you want coffee?"

"Will you get me one of those scones with the berries in it?"

"Sure thing. I won't even tattle!" He laughed behind her.

She took five at one of the planters and did a few deep stretches. Riya once talked to her about running and it sounded wonderful. With the breasts she'd been born with, the thought *alone* caused her pain.

Now, she thought she might try it.

The entire world felt different, brighter with far more possibilities. In that way, Natalia had been correct.

No part of her felt corrupted or ashamed. They'd given her so much without leaving anything negative behind.

As she approached the intersection, she stopped at the corner. It was still early and the city was slower to wake on Sunday mornings.

An elderly couple stood beside her and she chatted with them as they waited for the signal to cross. Then the light changed, she waved goodbye, and stepped off the curb and into the street.

Drivers in New York paid attention to pedestrians because there were too many not to. Even the most reckless cabbies knew that hitting a person would see them put away for a long time.

She was halfway through the crosswalk when the sound of an engine accelerating drew her attention. Glancing to the side, she saw Hudson's impersonator behind the wheel of a dark sedan.

This time there was no doubt.

Her mind had no time to process what she was seeing, what was happening. Coming too fast, already too close, and it was too late.

Their eyes met through the windshield, there was the sound of brakes squealing, and then she felt the impact and everything went dark.

* * *

The soft bell for the elevator while Natalia was in his arms brought Hudson to instant alertness.

Then he registered that it would be Gabriella leaving and he lightly shook his best friend awake. Her eyes opened groggily.

"She's leaving. Brie is leaving."

Immediately awake, she got out of bed. They found the note she'd left and stared at one another.

Natalia's toes curled. A rare "tell" of hers. She was nervous.

He stepped close to her and slipped his hand along the back of her neck. "We have things to discuss."

"I know."

"Right now, we need to reassure Gabriella."

She nodded. "Her note is a bit too cheerful, even for her. Do you think she'll still want to be our friend?"

"Yes."

"Let's meet her for coffee."

He smiled and nodded. They went upstairs and she took one of the spare outfits she kept in the guest room closet and went to shower. He knew he confused her when he stopped her from turning on the water.

Holding her hand, he led her to his bedroom. He put her outfit on the bed and continued into the bathroom. One arm held her against him as they waited for the water to heat.

Guiding her inside, he could tell she was off-balance. Hudson rinsed his mouth before he scrubbed his body, pretending they showered together like this all the time.

When in fact, it was the *first* time.

As he washed his hair, she seemed to shake from her trance and picked up his soap. He stepped from the shower and wrapped a towel around his waist so he could get her hair products from the guest bath.

She jumped when he opened the shower door and handed them to her. Bringing her forward, he gave her a quick kiss.

By the time she finished, he'd dried and pulled on boxer briefs. Having brushed his teeth, he was shaving.

She went to get her toiletry bag from the other bathroom and stood beside him, her damp hair curling the way he remembered from years ago, watching with a gentle expression on her face.

When he finished, he rinsed his face and dried it. Glancing down, he stared into her eyes, the unspoken question between them.

"I've never watched you do that before."

Then she reached up and wiped away a smudge of shaving cream he'd missed near his ear. He captured her hand and planted a kiss on the inside of her wrist.

He watched as she brushed her teeth, waited for her to rinse and dry her mouth, before he pulled her into his arms and kissed her.

When he broke it, he rested his forehead against hers. Her arms were tight around him, her palms flat on his back, and though they'd hugged often throughout the years, it felt different.

She planted a kiss on his jaw, nuzzled him with her cheek, and whispered, "I want to make sure she's alright. I'm worried."

He nodded and let her go.

Ten minutes later, they were dressed and exiting the elevator in the lobby. No one was at the concierge desk. Henry was missing from the front door.

As they stepped outside, it was obvious that something was very wrong. One of the catering staff shoved past them without a word and took off at a hard run down the street. Two women from housekeeping followed close behind with armloads of towels.

If Hudson remembered, the man was a medic in the Army. He watched him shove his way *violently* through a gathering crowd and drop to his knees out of sight.

He glimpsed Henry, directing people back. Carlo was speaking rapidly into his cell phone, a building radio in his other hand.

Everything inside him coiled tight with tension and in his life, Hudson's instincts had rarely been wrong.

"Natalia. Stay here."

"The fuck I will." Her instincts were usually solid, too.

As they neared the corner, an ambulance came to a rocking halt blocking the street. Paramedics were out and approaching a figure lying on the street within seconds. A third man followed with a bag.

The watching crowd was growing and Hudson shoved people out of their way without giving a damn.

He shouldered his way to the curb and caught Natalia as she took in the scene, gasped, and started to collapse at his side.

The shock of seeing Gabriella lying crumpled in the middle of the intersection as paramedics worked over her with rapid efficiency went clear to the bone.

Holding Natalia back, supporting her weight, Hudson shoved his panic down *hard*, ignored his automatic reaction to go to the woman they'd spent the night loving, and took in the conversations around him.

He watched and listened to people who'd witnessed what happened.

"She had the light…"

"The car built up speed…"

"That driver meant to hit her…

"He kept going…"

Hudson pulled his phone from his pocket and kept his eyes on the woman who'd become so important to them.

"Hollow."

"I need you to get traffic camera recordings for the last half hour. I need every car, every face in the crowd."

"Intersection."

"Fifth and Seventy-Second."

"They're real time. I'll have to hack to get a history. One hour. It takes some finesse." There was a pause. "What happened?"

"Gabriella Hernandez was struck by a car."

"Hit and run?"

"Yes. I want the license plate. I want the footage. I want all the connections I'm going to need."

Another long pause. "Consider it done."

* * *

"BP dropping…"

"Clear her airway…"

"Get these people back…"

In and out of consciousness, Gabriella drifted, getting snatches of conversation. Her body remained numb to her commands and words failed her.

"Get her up…get her up…"

"En route to Lenox Hill…"

Brie thought about her parents, her sister, her friends, and her life. She asked God for forgiveness for any hurts she'd caused, asked for Him to watch over the people she loved.

Before she slipped under again, she sent warm thoughts to Hudson and Natalia, hoping they loved one another as hard as they deserved.

"We're losing her…"

Chapter Fifty-Two

Hudson's next call was to Leonard. "Pick us up. We need to beat an ambulance carrying Brie to Lenox Hill."

"Yes, sir."

By the time they loaded Gabriella into the back of the ambulance, his car pulled to a stop on the other side of Fifth. He bodily picked up Natalia and jogged to it. He practically threw her inside and followed.

Leonard pulled into traffic before the door was fully closed. Using the skills he'd learned in some of the most dangerous war zones in the world, he weaved in and out of traffic in Hudson's Rolls.

He ran several lights without coming close to hitting people or cars. At one point, he drove them in reverse on a one-way street, spinning the car at the turn he wanted.

Hudson said nothing, made no more calls, and attempted to silence the screaming inside his own mind. His best friend shook painfully hard beside him and he held her tightly.

Leonard came to a hard stop at the hospital emergency entrance and Hudson didn't wait for him to come around, stepping from the car and pulling Natalia with him. The double doors opened and the woman at the reception desk sat back startled.

His demeanor had that effect on many people.

"My name is Hudson Winters. Do you know who I am?" The woman nodded slowly. "This is Natalia Roman. We have a close personal friend who was just involved in a car accident. She'll be here shortly.

I want people, the best you have, here in the next ten minutes ready to save her life. You get on that and point me to administration."

Her hand shook as she pointed down the hall.

Within three minutes of stepping from his car, he was standing across the desk of the hospital administrator. He restated his demands.

"There will be no delays while you check her insurance. There will be no racial profiling. There will be no bullshit of any kind or I'll make it my personal mission to take this hospital apart one person at a time."

The man sat down hard in his chair. "We can't *promise* to save her."

Hudson leaned over the top of the man's desk and growled. There could be no mistaking the deadly expression on his face.

"That's the *wrong* fucking attitude."

"You're right, sir. Absolutely. I apologize, Mr. Winters. Everything medically possible will be done to save her."

"Better."

He stood to his full height and left the office. He still held Natalia's hand tightly in his. Back at the front desk, the receptionist hung up her phone.

"Miss Hernandez just came in. They're prepping her for surgery. If you follow that hall, you'll find a waiting area just outside the surgical wing." She handed him two pieces of plastic. "Your passes."

The woman was willing to do *anything* to get him out of her space.

The waiting room was decorated much like every other. A few boring landscape prints, patient rights notices, and utilitarian furniture that was neither attractive nor comfortable.

For a long moment, the friends stood in the center of the room and simply stared at one another. By the time she broke, he had her tightly in his arms.

"Don't. Natalia, she's going to be alright."

For several minutes, he held her as she sobbed with her head on his shoulder and he whispered softly against her ear.

Every cell in his body felt murderous and he knew if the person who had *deliberately* hit Brie stood in front of him, nothing would stop him from taking a life.

* * *

As Natalia calmed, he gently stroked her hair. She took the handkerchief he offered and pulled herself together.

The skin around Hudson's mouth and eyes was tight and for the hundredth time during the life of their friendship, she marveled at his strength, but knew it came with significant cost.

Lifting her hand, she placed it along his cheek. "I know she's going to be alright. We'll fly in the best surgeons."

A kiss on the corner of his mouth made his hands tighten on her hips.

"You know who I suspect. She'll *hate* me. I should have protected her, Natalia. It was my responsibility."

"You're not God. You're the only one who holds yourself to such standards." The words were said softly in his ear and he pressed closer. "Brie will understand. She won't blame you because you're not at fault. She *will* survive this, she *will* heal."

Leaning back, she peered into black eyes that hid so much. "Those who love you, love you *always*, Hudson. It's love that forms deep roots and it's unshakable."

The word he said was spoken so softly she almost missed it. "Broken." She whimpered. "Broken on the street. I wanted to go to her but I didn't. I didn't tell her it would be alright." A frown formed between his eyes. "I didn't know if it would."

She pushed back her shock at the sight of tears slipping from the corners of his eyes and wrapped her arms tightly around his neck. He held her painfully hard and buried his face in her hair.

Never, in thirty years, had she seen him cry. That he *could not* hold back told her more than words that Brie affected him as strongly as she affected Natalia.

"We will help Brie get better, keep her safe, and continue to learn from her exemplary heart. We won't lose her, not now."

"Why can't I *love* her? I want to." His voice was ragged.

"I don't know, darling. I want to love her, too. That we aren't able to manage it is…confusing."

He nodded against her and took several deep breaths, lifting his head to look at her. "I love *you*, Natalia. I've never been deficient there, though I haven't always shown it."

"I've loved *you* for most of my life, Hudson. I don't regret a single day and you've *always* shown it."

She led him to the ugly sofa along one wall and they sat close, her hands wrapped around one of his.

"The first time I saw you, I knew you were going to be important to me. We were ten and you were different from anyone I'd ever met before. I know Brie would love to hear the story. She's so careful not to ask questions about our pasts but I know she's curious."

She settled comfortably against him and leaned her head on his shoulder. He kissed the top of her head. "We'll tell her."

"She already thinks you're Superman. Can you imagine if she knows what you fought through as a child? Darling, we might want to find her a nice man to love her before we share."

He gave a grudging laugh.

* * *

Hudson thought back to the day he met Natalia.

Sister Dana watched the three-year-old twins and kept an eye on Camille while he went house to house, looking for yard work and odd jobs. The elderly woman had been a godsend in their lives.

They wouldn't have survived without her.

Natalia was riding her bike out front when he knocked on her parents' door. She had pretty blonde hair and even with the distance, he could see that her eyes were bluer than anyone's eyes he'd ever seen.

Mrs. Roman was a kind and quiet woman who smiled easily. "My husband has been laid up with a horrible cold. It would be lovely to have the yard mowed so he doesn't have to worry."

Half an hour later, when he knocked again to tell her he was done, she handed him a crisp twenty-dollar bill and a glass of lemonade.

"It was only ten, ma'am. I don't have any change."

Natalia's mother shook her head. She had lovely blonde hair arranged in an elegant up-do. She'd been wearing low heels and a pretty dress.

At the time, he wondered why. His own mother spent her days in a nightgown. When Sister Dana could coax her out to eat, she slipped a robe on and stepped into soft slippers.

"You did a wonderful job; it was *worth* more than ten and I'm happy to pay what it's worth. What's your name?"

"Hudson, ma'am. Hudson Winters."

"Aren't you polite?"

"I try to be."

Natalia came to stand beside her mother, leaning against the door with her arms crossed. Close, she was even prettier than he thought.

"How old are you?" she asked him.

"Ten. How old are you?"

"Nine but I'll be ten soon. Do you have a bike?" He shook his head. "You're tall. I bet you could ride my older brother's bike. He left for college a few weeks ago."

"I-I can't play right now. I need to do a couple more lawns."

Mrs. Roman smiled warmly. "I've already taken care of that. I saw you were doing such an excellent job that I called two of my neighbors. Mrs. Dorsey," she pointed past him and across the street, "has a husband who travels for work. She's been looking for someone to help her around the yard."

The yard looked like it hadn't been mowed in weeks. He nodded.

"Just past her is Mrs. Connelly. Her husband passed last year and her son tries to make it up from the city to help but doesn't get here as often as she needs. She was hoping you might be willing to cut her grass and run a few errands for her."

"Yes, ma'am. I'd be happy to."

"She'll need you to go to the grocery. We thought you could have Tom's bike to get around. It has a carrier on the back."

Hudson looked at her carefully. Her eyes were kind, her expression gentle and open. As he met her gaze, he knew she *knew* who he was and what his circumstances were. It wasn't a big town. Word of his mother and her situation would have gotten around.

Instead of offering him charity, she was giving him the opportunity to take money he'd *earned*. Even at ten, he knew the difference and appreciated that she did as well.

He put his shoulders back and extended his hand. "Thank you, ma'am. I appreciate your help."

Her smile made her eyes sparkle as she shook hands with him as if he was a grown man. "You're welcome, Hudson. My Dale will be up and around in the next couple of days. I know he has a few projects to do before the weather changes. You'll stop by?"

He nodded and handed her back the glass.

"Wonderful. You go see the neighbors and when you're all done, Natalia will have the bike ready for you."

For the next few hours, he cut lawns, scrubbed outside garbage cans, and swept cobwebs off porches. The list of tasks they needed done would keep Hudson in regular work for weeks.

Mrs. Dorsey was a wonderful, plump woman who sent him home with another twenty dollars and a bag of fresh-baked cookies. Until he graduated high school, he was the only person who mowed her lawn, raked her leaves, or shoveled her driveway clear of snow.

When her sister and her family moved in across the street, she became another client that happily paid him for work their husbands didn't have the time or inclination to do.

Elderly Mrs. Connelly sat on her porch as he worked and sipped hot tea. When he finished, she asked if he'd sit and talk for a few minutes. She gave him several fives from her wallet and asked him what he planned to do with all the money he was working so hard to earn.

Her eyes had once been very blue, easy to see despite the cataracts that clouded them now. One hand trembled when she lifted her cup.

"Food for my family. I'll also pay a little on the gas so when it starts to get cold, we don't have to worry. The rest will be set aside for rent next month."

She stared at him without speaking for a long time, rocking softly in her chair. "When I was newly married, we were in the middle of the Great Depression. Have you learned about that in school?"

Hudson nodded. "I had two little ones and another baby on the way. Times were hard and everyone worked. Everyone pitched in to keep families afloat."

He didn't interrupt or fidget. Over the years, many people would remark on his ability to remain perfectly still.

"My husband worked almost twenty hours some days. I took in laundry and sold eggs from our chickens, canning from our garden, and made every penny stretch as far as I could."

Mrs. Connelly sipped her tea. "After the war, things were suddenly prosperous again. Work was easier to come by, building started up again, and food was once again plentiful."

Her rocker stopped. "No matter how well my darling Walter took care of us, I always kept a little back, saved what I could, and made the most of every penny. Hardship teaches a lesson you never forget."

"Yes, ma'am. It sure does."

She smiled. "You keep coming here to help me, Hudson. You do your part to keep your family afloat and when you're grown, you're going to be more successful than you ever dreamed."

"Yes, ma'am."

"Adversity makes you hungry. I think *you* may be hungrier than most."

Every week for many years, she paid him to do odd jobs around her home in addition to lawn work. He did her grocery shopping and often bought seeds with his own money so he could plant flowers around her porch in the spring.

They always spent a little time talking before he had to go home. It never failed to move him when she asked about his mother and his brother and sister. She knew Sister Dana from the soup kitchen where they both volunteered.

Mrs. Connelly was a good woman from the first day he knew her until the last.

When he returned to the Romans' home that first day, Natalia was waiting for him in the driveway. Beside her was a bike that looked brand new. His eyes widened.

"Before you say anything, my brother had this bike for *years*. He just took good care of it is all. Mom says you're to take it and she'll see you next weekend."

Hudson took in the slim girl. They were almost the same height but she was very narrow. Usually, girls didn't talk to him. He thought he maybe even scared them for some reason.

That was why he was shocked when she said, "We should be friends."

"I'm not, I mean, I don't have friends."

"Is it because of your family?" He bristled and she rushed on. "No, I don't mean it that way. I don't have friends either."

She shrugged and Hudson relaxed. "I don't like most other girls and I make boys nervous." She tapped her temple. "I'm super smart. Boys don't like that much."

"I don't mind that you're smart."

Her grin was huge and he noticed her front teeth were crooked. She planned to push the bike while he pushed his lawn equipment home.

Part of him worried about her seeing where he lived. Part of him figured if she withdrew her friendship *now* it might be for the best.

The neighborhood he lived in was less than a mile away but it might as well have been in another town. The differences were stark. Houses needed repair, yards were choked with weeds, and the few cars were rundown, if they worked at all.

Natalia chatted non-stop while they walked. He didn't think he'd ever talked so much at one time.

"I like your name. Is it special for something?"

"My-my dad's last race in college was on the Hudson. He was the captain of his rowing team and they won by a huge margin. My mom drove behind the school's team bus the whole way to New York."

He swallowed hard. "After they won, she said he picked her up and swung her around, that they couldn't stop laughing. He asked her to marry him and she said yes."

They walked a little way in silence. "Back at school, his friends were so awed that they'd won – they were supposed to place third or lower – that they started calling him Hudson. He graduated and moved back to New York to work with his family. He planned to come back to get her when she was done with school but then he died."

Natalia said quietly, "I'm sorry."

"My mom found out after his funeral that she was pregnant with me. Her family won't talk to her. His family blames her for his death."

"But, why?"

"He was killed in a plane crash going to see her." He walked up the broken sidewalk and turned at his house. They did the best they could to keep things up but he knew it needed paint.

"My mom is probably sleeping but I need to check my little brother and sister. Sister Dana probably made a snack if you want."

"I'd love a snack, thanks."

Sister Dana welcomed the young woman into their lives and Natalia fell instantly in love with Scott and Sylvia who toddled around looking adorable. After they ate oatmeal cookies and he put all his stuff away, he insisted on walking her back home.

"You don't have to, Hudson. It isn't far."

With a firm shake of his head, he insisted. "It's too far for you to walk alone." He gave her a rare smile. "You're my only friend and you're a girl. Terrible things happen to girls more than boys. I'll walk you home."

Only when she was safely inside with the door closed did he climb on his new bike and return to his house.

It was the first day of their friendship and it was rare, even after three decades, for them to go a full day without talking.

He used that bike day in and day out for *years* and the work Mrs. Roman and her neighbors paid him helped keep his family safe.

Elderly Mrs. Connelly changed his future.

Only Natalia knew that before she died, the old woman used the "nest egg" she'd been saving since World War II and paid for his college education. Her children didn't know about the money so no one questioned such generosity to a young man they'd never met.

She also left him several suits, ties, and accessories from her late husband with a note that said, *"To get you started. You'll be buying your own suits soon enough."*

Sister Dana, Mrs. Roman, and Mrs. Connelly were the three adult women who had saved him when he was too young to save himself.

Natalia had often saved him as a grown man.

When he started making money, he returned the favors he'd received by helping every person who had a part in keeping him alive.

The loss of Sister Dana a few years before had hit him hard. In all the ways that counted, she'd been his surrogate mother when Camille had been too broken to assume the role.

Until her death, he'd ensured she wanted for nothing.

Natalia's mother was still alive, living in Boca Raton since her husband's death. Hudson shared responsibility for anything she needed with his best friend.

Anonymously, he replaced the small stone that once stood on Mrs. Connelly's grave with one that was a work of art. An intricately carved marble angel held a plaque inscribed with the words, *"A devoted wife, mother, and friend. She always remembered her struggles and strived to help the hungry."*

There was no end to what he would have done to keep Camille and Natalia safe and happy.

His younger brother and sister had lived under his umbrella of protection from birth. Ensuring they had food, shelter, and clothing drove him as nothing else could have.

He often forgot they were his siblings and not his children.

Now Gabriella would find herself in a very small group. The love they wanted to give her wasn't the kind she needed, but they would give it anyway for as long as she would accept it.

First, they had to keep her alive.

Chapter Fifty-Three

Several hours after the accident, Brie was still in surgery and it was estimated that she would remain there for several more.

Hudson took his best friend home to shower and change. Natalia was exhausted and needed to eat. She insisted on being dropped at the club so she could make arrangements to cover her absence.

Leonard held the door and she started to get out when Hudson roughly pulled her back. A hard kiss, a harder hug, and he released her.

"I'll be back to get you in an hour."

She nodded and they waited until she was inside before pulling into traffic and returning to the building.

As he approached the door, he noticed that Henry was shaking badly. "Good afternoon, Mr. Winters."

"What is it?"

"Nothing, sir. I'll be fine. My apologies."

"Henry." A horrible thought. "Did you see her get hit?"

The older man tried to hold back a sob. "Yes, sir. I yelled but Brie didn't hear me. At the last second, it looked like the driver pumped the brakes but it was too late. The paramedics said Barry kept her alive. She'd have bled out on the street."

Thinking about Brie, he paused. "Henry, get someone to cover your shift for a week. You're badly shaken."

"It's alright, sir…"

"I insist."

"Thank you, Mr. Winters."

Nodding, he continued inside and gave Carlo instructions. "He needs to rest. If you or the others need time, I'll approve it."

"Thank you, sir. That's kind of you."

"That's good business."

"No, sir. That's humanity. Brie's influence. She'd be proud."

The words, coming from the first man he hired when he bought the building, affected him deeply. With a nod, he went to his home and found it was far too quiet.

* * *

When he picked Natalia up and returned to the hospital, she told him she'd called Brie's friends.

Riya and Tawny had to fly back from Florida with their men. After Riya broke down and Tawny started screaming about revenge, a levelheaded Max took the phone and she'd given him all the information.

They arrived after dark and the four men stayed behind while the friends went to ask for a status. None of them wanted to cause Brie stress or awkwardness that she'd have to deal with when she woke up.

The M's took Hudson aside. "What can we do?"

"I'm looking for him. He came on-grid long enough to hurt her. I'll find him. Brie will decide what is done to him."

Micah nodded. "There wasn't a doubt in our minds. What do you need help with in your *life*, mate?"

He couldn't hide his surprise.

"You might not have plants or a cat but fortunately, we're accustomed to the same world. What can we do to help?" Max pressed.

"The building staff who helped Brie. I gave them time off. They need more for what they did." He was unaccustomed to asking anyone for anything other than Natalia. The sensation felt foreign.

Max nodded with a small smile. "A good place to start."

* * *

Brie's family arrived that night. Eleanor Shaughnessy had contacted them per instructions in her employee paperwork.

Hudson and Natalia stepped back, unwilling to interact with them and muddy the waters when her life was in danger. His name alone would cause questions he wasn't certain how Brie wanted him to answer.

The day after the emergency surgery that saved her life, she was placed in a drug-induced coma.

Hudson bribed half a dozen members of the nursing staff to keep him posted day and night.

Lola rearranged his schedule and made sure nothing would take him out of New York until Brie was pronounced out of danger.

All any of them could do was wait.

* * *

Since the day Gabriella had given him a description of the man who conned her, Hudson had been searching.

If someone was *on* the technology grid, they were traceable, and Hollow was the best at following the electronic breadcrumbs.

Brie's thief had dropped *off* the grid. There hadn't been a sign of the man for more than six months.

He'd simply disappeared.

A few weeks prior, a strange prickle on the back of Hudson's neck caused him to arrange for Leonard to take Brie where she needed to go. The driver could and would protect his charges with his life. Part of him thought he was probably being paranoid but he didn't care.

The moment Brie was hit, her con man was back *on* the grid. From one camera, Hollow tracked him to the next and the next.

Forty-eight hours after a car struck and almost killed a woman who'd only ever been gentle and kind to the people in her life, Hudson's phone rang.

"Winters."

"Hollow. Can you talk?"

"Yes."

"Winters, you need privacy."

Darkness settled over his body. "I'm alone. Tell me."

There was a long pause. "You already *know*. You know exactly what I found out because you suspected." Silence drew out for almost ten seconds. "Fuck."

"I need to hear you *say it*, Hollow."

A heavy sigh and then, "The car that hit Gabriella Hernandez was paid for in cash approximately six weeks ago. With the make and model, I've located it on several traffic cams. In several, Miss Hernandez is visible in the same shot."

"He's been following her."

"Yes. We found the car. The license plates are bogus but the prints left behind when my guys towed it to their facility and searched it match Scott Truing's. He wiped the interior down but forgot the trunk and inside the door."

Hudson remained silent, processing the fact that the brother he'd loved from birth had tried to murder someone he cared about.

"We've been watching Christina for months but things didn't end well between them. Apparently, she was unaware of his plan to send Miss Hernandez to your place. She might know something. I'm going to shake her down."

"I'll handle that. Send me the address."

"Winters…"

"Send me the fucking address."

"Done."

He pressed his thumb and forefinger into the bridge of his nose. "How the fuck did I miss the fact that my brother is a sociopath?"

It was a rhetorical question and Hollow didn't answer.

"When he's found, I need him taken into custody, transported to a secure location, and held until Brie is strong enough to face him. Cost is unimportant."

"Consider it done."

"Hollow. If you can prevent it, don't hurt him."

"Understood."

* * *

The next day, Leonard drove them to an address in a car "borrowed" from a long-term storage lot.

The men wore jeans, work boots, gloves, and hoodies.

They parked at a meter, put money in, and entered the three-story walkup. Leonard carried a small bag in his hand.

Crouching, the man picked the six locks in under eight seconds each. As the knob turned, he sprayed the hinges with WD40. Inside, Hudson walked in the direction of television noise.

Christina watched with a cigarette in her hand.

The moment he stepped in front of her, she started to scream. Leonard placed his gloved hand over her mouth. He held her against the back of the couch with one hand as he took the cigarette with the other and snuffed it between two fingers.

"You'll remain silent other than telling me what I wish to know. If you don't, I will have you killed. Are we clear?"

She started to scream behind the glove.

Hudson turned, stepped back, and kicked the front of her television in. Turning back, he said calmly, "Let's start again. You'll remain silent other than telling me what I wish to know. If you're not clear, I will hurt you until you understand."

Walking to her purse, he dumped it on the coffee table. Pocketing her cell phone and wallet, he piled baggies of drugs to one side.

Leaving her where she sat and depending on Leonard to keep her contained, he searched her apartment.

He turned up more drugs and banded stacks of cash from several locations in her bedroom and bathroom.

As a man who'd done construction most of his life, he noticed irregularities in the way rooms were put together. Her refrigerator sat too far out in the room. The wall behind it backed to the bathroom.

No contractor would have wasted so much space when every square foot in New York City was prime real estate. He pulled the appliance forward, not expecting it to move without effort.

It was on wheels. A woman like Christina wouldn't be able to move the heavy old model otherwise. He glanced behind him and saw her thrashing, her eyes wide as she watched him. Muffled screaming barely reached his ears so he wasn't concerned about her neighbors hearing.

The extra section of wall had been added recently and an extension cord provided electricity to the fridge. Pushing, he found the small release and the piece of wall slid to the side.

"Christina, you've been a bad, bad girl."

Shelves inside the space held bricks of cocaine, pot, and hundreds of bottles of prescription medication. More cash, jewelry – much of which he recognized as gifts he'd had Lola buy her, and a box filled with passports and other ID blanks.

He walked back in the living room and sat on her coffee table in front of her. She was shaking, crying in a way that wasn't faked for once, and he signaled Leonard to let her go.

As she reached for a pack of cigarettes, his driver grabbed her long ponytail. "Slow. Don't make me nervous."

She nodded. "What do you want? I'll tell you whatever you want."

"Where is he?"

"I don't…" At the look on his face, she murmured, "I'm sorry."

"Let's start again. I realize your initial reflex is to lie. Where is he?"

She lit the cigarette with shaking hands. "He always underestimated you. I tried to tell him after I met you. I wasn't the first girl. The other one quit when he told her to hook up with you. Apparently, she told him she wasn't fucking with you and he shouldn't either."

There was a hard shake of her head. "I liked the deal I had going. He never warned me the last mark was told to go to your place."

"Focus. Where is he?"

She crossed her legs and tapped her foot. "Can I come back?"

"No."

"You can do whatever you want to me."

"Already did. No." He leaned forward.

She took a deep breath. "We have a place off-grid Upstate. In a tiny town of about three hundred people called Ellisburg. H-he goes by the name Noah James."

There was terror in her eyes. She knew the significance. His younger brother was using the first names of their biological *fathers* despite knowing that James Polton had *raped* their mother.

Rushing on, she whispered, "They don't even use credit cards much in the stores there. No cell services. We used it to lay low after each mark was fleeced. A mile or so outside of town, there's a road to the left that leads up. The cabin is at the top."

"Is he armed?"

"Heavily armed and using. He's been going through his share of the con profits for almost a year."

Hudson leaned forward. "There will be no misunderstanding between us. You call my brother, warn him we're coming, or anyone else gets hurt because of you and I'll have you killed."

She frowned. "Anyone *else*? I never hurt anyone."

"The last woman, Gabriella Hernandez. Scott ran her down in the street. She's fighting for her life."

Eyes wide, she stubbed out the cigarette and immediately lit another. "He was in love with her. Had her place bugged and heard her telling her sister that she didn't mind faking orgasms because he cared about her. Drove him bug-shit crazy."

Shaking her foot nervously, she stared through the window. "He said he was going to get her worse than the others. Make her pay. Fuck."

Hudson watched her face.

"No offense but have you been fucking her?" He said nothing. "After I got with you, I couldn't have sex with Scott anymore. He sent me over there but he was furious." She sighed. "Can I stand up?"

He leaned back, she stood, and turned enough to hide her face. "I know what I am. I use my body to get what I want. The first time I fucked you, he sh-shoved a cleaning brush inside me and called me a filthy whore. I bled from the scratches inside for a week."

Facing them, her smile was self-mocking. "It's the cost of doing the shit I do but that girl never hurt anybody. I hope she'll be alright."

"There's a very specific chain of events that led her to be on that corner when he ran her down. They all start with you and my brother. Anything happens to her and there isn't a hole deep enough for you to hide in. Are we clear?"

She nodded. "I don't want him near me. Not now. Take his money with you and keep him away from me."

Leonard followed as she reached into the hideaway cabinet and pulled out three large stacks of cash. Handing it to him, she said, "This makes us square. I don't want to see him again."

Arms crossed in the doorway, Hudson smiled. "I'll take your share of the profits from conning Gabriella."

"Fuck. Alright."

She handed Leonard three smaller bundles. He raised his brow. "I was *getting* the other one."

A fourth went on the stack and his driver placed them in the bag. He let her see the other items inside and she backed against the wall.

"I just thought that if she's with you, she doesn't need it."

"She's a friend. I reimbursed the others quietly. She won't take the money unless she knows it's from the people who stole it from her."

Christina couldn't hide her surprise. "That's some classy shit."

"Yes." He turned to leave and called over his shoulder. "We won't see each other again unless you've given me shit information."

They slammed the door and returned to the street. As Leonard started the engine, he grinned. "Rather convenient that the car we borrowed had a tool bag."

Hudson couldn't help but laugh. Then he took out his cell and relayed the information he'd received to Hollow.

"On it. I'll call you when I have him in custody."

Leonard dropped him in front of the building. "Give me about an hour to return the car, change clothes, and get back here, sir."

"Thank you, Leonard."

"Anytime, sir. I mean that. Brie's a good person. Soul deep."

With a nod, he went upstairs. He stared at the magnificent view but didn't see it. His highest priority was Gabriella's care and safety. After all, his brother had already tried to kill her once.

He called Natalia and filled her in.

She whimpered in pain. She'd known his brother since he was a toddler. "I hoped you were wrong. I so *wanted* you to be wrong."

"I want you to move into the penthouse."

A long silence. "Why?"

"Many reasons, Natalia. Some are urgent while others are preference. I'm having Scott picked up. I've already assigned security to Brie in the hospital but I need you here. Until I can remain calm enough to question him, I don't know what we're dealing with."

"What about Camille and Sylvia?"

"Mom won't leave the building. Sylvia isn't speaking to me right now."

His best friend was quiet as she thought about his offer. "I want you to be comfortable, to know I'm safe. I know that's important to you."

He heard her hesitation and every word Brie had said to them about being afraid returned to him.

"Gabriella's doctors plan to keep her under for at least two weeks. Possibly longer. The damage to her skull…"

Calming the pounding of his heart, he started again. "That's too long to spread my attention in so many directions."

"I understand."

"I've had someone watching my mom for months now. I wanted to know if Scott visited. If he tried to twist her up."

"I *know* you're not leaving Sylvia in the wind."

"Hollow is tracking her." He waited, prepared to pressure her.

"Alright. I'll pack some things and be over tonight."

He exhaled roughly but silently. *Thank you.*

"I'll send the car."

Chapter Fifty-Four

Hudson and Natalia's first night living together began awkwardly.

Over the past decade, when Natalia arrived at his place after dark, she was his submissive from the moment she stepped off the elevator.

This time, he greeted her.

One of the valets carried her bags to his bedroom, which made her eyes widen in surprise. He held her hand and led her to the kitchen.

When he handed her a glass of wine, she gave him a careful smile. He wondered if he was the problem.

"How do I relieve my tension without tying you up and taking complete control of you?" The question shocked her. "Why am I this way? Why do I subdue the one person I trust in all things?"

She set down her wineglass and stepped close to him. "You've earned your alpha status with intelligence and hard work. Both professionally and sexually. Your success has an unexpected burden, a small side effect. It's one you can relieve with me, that counters my own, and also provides you respite."

His eyes closed and she hugged him.

At his ear, she whispered, "You know I need the edge, the freefall. You don't *injure* me, and *never* disrespect me. You push me higher than anyone else has ever been capable and bring me back safely. Every time."

She raked her fingers through his hair and leaned back.

"That's the side you perceive as dark but there's the side of you that adores and protects women instinctively, that's angry when you can't protect us from every bad thing."

"I don't know if I can merge them."

"Hudson, both of those sides are *you*. They have *always* been. No matter how rough the sex, you always ensure my pleasure, care for me, and make me feel important to you."

His arms held her hard. "You're the *most important* thing to me, Natalia. Above family, above business or money, above my own life."

"*Hudson…*"

He took her mouth hard and she moaned, her hands clutching his hair. It went on for a long time and when he broke it, he didn't move away. He couldn't catch his breath.

"Not yet. My insides hurt."

She nodded and hugged him as tight as she could. They stood like that for a while. Then he led her upstairs.

In one-half of his closet, there were clothes in bags from her favorite designers. Shoes beneath, underthings in drawers. All the things he knew she particularly loved.

"So you don't have to carry things back and forth."

He showed her where all of her products were in the bathroom. "Lola called Dior and had them send everything on your profile. She got you the…other stuff you need, too."

"Still freaks you out?"

"Oh yeah."

"Noted." Stroking her hand down his arm, she wrapped her fingers in his. "Are you sure you want me sleeping with you at night, Hudson?"

He stared her down.

"Okay. I'll sleep with you."

Leading her down the hall, he stood in front of the empty rooms. "Make yourself an office and a changing room. You like space. I don't care about the design as long as it makes you happy."

Then he led her downstairs and ordered them food.

* * *

The two of them settled into a routine. It would have seemed odd to outsiders. Most of their business was conducted through their assistants with infrequent trips to their places of work.

After a single day of working across the hall from one another, they were finding random excuses to walk back and forth.

They would break for coffee and eventually one of them would order dinner. Sitting together at the rarely used dining table, they talked with an ease born of decades of familiarity.

Around ten at night, they would receive a call from one of the nurses that the Hernandez family had returned to their hotel.

Putting on casual clothes and sneakers, they would walk the few blocks to the hospital. They both felt it made them less conspicuous.

They held hands there and back. A unique experience for both of them but one neither thought to question.

Security would key them up and they would sit with Brie until dawn when they would kiss her goodbye and tell her they'd be back the next night and to stay out of trouble.

Natalia would talk to her. Hudson held her hand.

They ignored the swelling, bruising, stitches, bandages and casts, talking to her about the life she was going to have when she was better.

Sad words, talk of death, were not allowed.

Every word was based on the assumption that Gabriella was already on the mend and would be leaving any day.

* * *

During her fifth night in intensive care, a nurse was updating them on her progress a few minutes after they arrived when Brie began to seize. She coded twice before they were able to stabilize her.

Hudson and Natalia stood shell-shocked outside her room. They watched the doctors and nurses scramble around a woman who had been too still for too many days already.

The staff frequently glanced nervously at them in the hall and Hudson knew his threats were distracting them from doing their job.

"Focus on *her*! We're leaving."

A tiny piece of floating bone was lodged near her jugular and she was rushed into emergency surgery to remove it.

A cab returned them to the penthouse.

Ragged emotionally and physically, they quickly showered and climbed under the covers. Natalia sobbed and Hudson held her, stroking her back. Neither of them was accustomed to fear.

They'd never watched someone struggle to live.

He talked her through it, insisting that Brie would be well again, and the *force* of his belief eventually soothed her.

She drew strength and solace from a man who had always provided it.

Wrapped around one another, she slipped into a deep sleep and he watched her for a long time.

* * *

More than twenty-two years before, the day after Natalia turned eighteen years old, Hudson took her out to dinner.

He opened doors, pulled out her chair, and complimented her on how pretty she looked. With her fair skin, she was unable to hide her blushes over the course of the evening.

Afterward, he took her to see *Scent of a Woman* because she'd mentioned she wanted to see it. There were several points where she cried and he related strongly to the character of Slade, depicted by Al Pacino.

They walked their small town, her hand tucked in his arm, and she asked him if he'd like to learn to dance.

"Do you think I need to?"

"One day, you'll be a businessman who strikes fear in the hearts of your rivals." She glanced up at him with a cheeky smile. "Not only will it soften you to the ladies but no one will expect it."

"I don't think I'll ever have chances to dance. I'll work all the time, just like now."

"Nonsense. Powerful men attend balls and dinners thrown by other powerful men."

He considered her words silently. Finally, "Will you teach me?"

"Naturally. It's highly likely that I'll dance with you many times in the future. We'll make a striking pair as we move around the floor."

At his car, a used Chevy he'd saved to buy for a year, he held the door. "You know things I never think about, Natalia."

"That's what makes us so formidable, darling."

He liked it when she called him that. She liked that he never shortened her name. Some of her friends called her *Talia* or *Nat* and she hated when they did.

She slid into the front seat as if it was an expensive car – or even a nice one – and he closed the door. Behind the wheel, he glanced at her and was struck again at how lovely she was.

Natural blonde hair curled around her face to her shoulders and her eyes made his mouth dry.

"We should watch a movie at your house."

Three years after he started working for the Romans' neighbors, Hudson had enough to move his family a little closer to the acceptable side of town to a house with rooms for the twins and Sister Dana.

Every week, he did work on the place to make it more energy efficient or help it look nicer. It never needed paint, the doors were always level, and all the windows had screens.

He slept in a converted storage room over the garage. The stairs were on the outside of the house.

Without a word, he started the car and drove home. When he stopped in the driveway, he reminded her, "Wait."

Walking around, he opened her door and she stepped out. He held her hand going up the steps because they were steep.

Upstairs, she stood over his desk and asked him questions about several of his ideas when he brought her a glass of wine. She clinked their glasses together with a smile.

"I can't believe how easy it is for you to buy this." He shrugged. "You carry yourself like a grown man. They don't even question you."

There were several copies of the New York Times on the edge and she pointed at them. "You're still planning to move to New York?"

"I have to. One day, my father's family will see my name everywhere and they'll regret what they did to my mother."

"You're the most focused person I know, Hudson."

"*You're* the most focused person I know, Natalia. I'm so proud of you for being named Valedictorian. You worked damn hard for it."

She hugged him. "The only reason you've never beaten me is because you work so much. Harder than anyone I know, young or old."

It was two hours and three glasses of wine later that she crawled over his lap and kissed him.

He set her back. "Natalia. You've been drinking. I would never betray your trust. I value it too much."

"You've earned it. I'm pretty buzzed and playful but not *drunk* and you know I know the difference."

"Are you sure?"

She nodded and when he still hesitated, she said, "Yes, I'm *sure*." Hudson stood up with her and she gasped. "I always forget how strong you are." It made him smile.

He stood her beside the bed and took off her clothes, then his. There were condoms in the side table drawer and he took out several. Her eyes went wide.

"Are you still sure?" She nodded. "If you change your mind, I won't be even a little upset because you can."

Then she threw her naked, lithe body into his arms and he caught her. Their first time together was filled with more laughter than either of them thought was appropriate and they talked during about silly things.

Having dreamed of touching her for two years, he took his time and made sure she was ready before he slid inside her.

It was the most perfect memory of his young life and it carried him through when he wasn't able to have her.

* * *

When she was twenty, he'd picked her up from a party her friends had forced her to attend. She was feverish.

"Were you sick when you left the house?" She nodded. "Why did you *go*? You're going to catch pneumonia."

"They called me boring."

"Assholes. I'm taking you with me."

At his tiny apartment three blocks from hers, he made her tea and took care of her for the weekend. By Sunday afternoon, she was much better but he made her a hot toddy just to be sure.

Laughing hysterically a little while later, she straddled his legs, rolled a condom on his cock, and put him inside her. Sitting up, he held her tight and powered them over so she was beneath him.

Her laughter soon turned to sighs and the way she felt around him as he drove forcefully into her body would help him be strong as she drifted away again.

* * *

Eighteen months later, Hudson found out from Lola that Natalia was having plastic surgery, getting *implants*, after pressure from her loser boyfriend. One in a line of many.

He got there in time and plotted the beating he would later deliver to her boyfriend. The boyfriend would be lucky to survive it.

He'd had several lovers by then and he found himself holding back sexually with women he knew couldn't handle what he wanted. He dated them, took them to dinner, and fucked them as hard as he could without the edge he truly wanted.

Hudson wanted *complete* control.

Over their experience and his own. He wanted to warm the surface of their skin to increase blood flow and heighten the climax he provided. To tie them down, perhaps completely immobilize them, so they had no choice but to take what he delivered.

His personal need started at nineteen with a random book found on a forgotten shelf in a bookstore that no longer existed.

Images of bondage – combining control with sexuality – sank into his brain and never shook loose. Over the years, he visited clubs and found some were too extreme while others were mostly older married couples walking on the dark side.

He distrusted the women he dated with his secret since he already had far too much to lose if he confided in the wrong lover.

There was only one person he'd ever trusted.

The night he stopped her from getting surgery that was high-risk and unnecessary, he insisted she stay at his apartment. She came out of his bathroom after a shower, barefoot in panties and a t-shirt, toweling hair she'd only recently dyed deepest black.

It sometimes threw him off.

From his chair across the room, he watched her. Gradually, her movements slowed and finally stopped. She held the towel in one hand as she stared back at him.

"Come here."

He still remembered how her eyes widened at the command in his voice an instant before her nipples hardened sharply.

She made her way across the wood floor and stopped inches from his knees.

"I want to fuck you."

Her eyes were huge in her face. Her damp hair curled around her cheeks. "Alright." The word was said softly and he knew she was unsure of what he was trying to tell her.

"I need to experience something with you. If you don't like it, we'll never try it again. If you aren't happy, we'll have it between us." He took a deep breath. "If you *do* enjoy it, we need to talk."

She didn't speak, simply nodded. Her trust in him was written on her face as it had been the day he met her and walked her home to make sure she arrived safely.

He would always make sure she arrived safely.

Standing, he took the towel and slid her t-shirt up her body, tossing both to the couch. "Walk to the bedroom."

She turned on her heel without hesitation and entered his room. His bed featured a wrought iron headboard and he planned to tie her to it.

"Get on the bed on your knees. Grip the top rail."

He opened his closet and removed two ties. Approaching her from the side, her eyes flicked to his hands and back to his face.

"I won't hurt you. I would never hurt you, Natalia."

"I know." She faced the wall above the bed and held the rail until her knuckles were white. "I believe in you more than anyone else, Hudson. I just hope you don't think badly of me…after."

He didn't bother to respond to the statement. It was ridiculous to even consider that he would ever think badly of her. He accepted her unconditionally.

After securing her to the frame, he removed her panties. He took his time stripping away his clothes and watched her. She didn't move. From the bedside table, he removed lubricant.

He hesitated as he reached for a rubber.

"Are you still on birth control?" She nodded. "Can I take you without a condom?" Her eyes met his and she nodded again, slower this time. "If you should ever end up pregnant, I'll take care of you."

Swallowing hard, she turned back to the wall.

"Spread your knees."

She did and when he stood on the bed, she stared at his cock. Never in his life had he been so hard. The shaft jutted from his body, the head was almost purple, and his balls were drawn tight.

"Open your mouth."

Her eyes lifted as her lips parted and he fisted her hair. Holding her still, he started with shallow thrusts, gradually increasing the depth and force. When her eyes began to water, he slowed and pulled back.

"Breathe through your nose. I'll be more careful."

The first climax took less than six minutes. Being able to fuck her hot mouth had stolen control he hadn't fully achieved yet.

When he softened a bit, he thrust between her lips more firmly and she gained confidence in the act.

Over the years, she would perfect the art of taking his cock down her throat.

Pulling from her, he went to his knees and kissed her hard. She moaned against him and he allowed his hand to drift over both breasts, down her torso, to her pussy.

She was *drenched* and he broke the kiss.

"You liked that? You liked me fucking your mouth?"

"Yes."

"You're so wet."

"Hudson, *more.*"

Positioning himself behind her, he was still hard enough to enter. He pressed and she leaned forward to rest her head on her tied hands. He pumped into her wetness slow and easy until he hardened fully again.

Allowing his thumb to trace the pucker of her ass, he asked, "Has anyone ever fucked you here?"

"No, but I want to know what it's like."

He spent a long time preparing her ass with his lubed fingers while he casually stroked into her wet heat. When she was slick and warm, the tightness eased a bit, he scissored them inside her.

Natalia panted into the quiet room.

Hudson pulled from her body and went to wash his hands, returning with a small bowl of soapy water and a washcloth.

"It might hurt."

"I know."

"You haven't come yet."

"I'm letting it build. I do that when I'm alone."

Without another word, he climbed back on the bed and set his cock at her tiny hole. Carefully, he pushed forward and listened to the sounds she made until he was buried to his balls.

Leaning over her back, he whispered at her ear, "Your ass is squeezing my cock like a vise. Are you alright?" She nodded. "Tell me if you need me to slow down or stop."

He gripped her hips and pulled back, dripping more lube over his exposed shaft. Then he powered forward and she screamed. Instead of stopping, he set up a steady rhythm until she was moaning and pushing back to meet his thrusts.

"Feels so fucking good, Natalia. So fucking amazing."

"More."

With a deep breath, he took her harder and watched the muscles of her ass flex with each thrust.

Reaching beneath her, he stroked over her folds. Pinching her clit between his thumb and forefinger, she gasped.

"I'm going to come. Don't stop."

As he stroked and pinched the little bundle of nerves, she went over the edge with a muffled scream and shoved her body back to take his cock deeper.

There was only a slight hesitation as he gripped her firmly and fucked her harder than he'd ever taken another woman.

In moments, he was filling her with his come as her name echoed through the room. They stayed like that for a long time. Getting their bodies under control so they could think.

"Hudson?" He kissed her shoulder. "I liked that a *lot*."

It was the beginning of an understanding between them, often unspoken, that spanned sixteen years. He had fucked her in his car, what they called his "recreation" room, in public places, and at her club. Taken her mouth, her pussy, and her ass more times than he could count.

Forcefully, driving them both into orgasm with no limits, no conditions. She'd taken every act he'd ever committed in or on her body without complaint, begging for more.

She was the only person he could count on in every way. The only person who knew every sordid detail of who he was and where he'd come from and always picked up her phone to be whatever he needed.

* * *

In the hour before dawn, Hudson stared at Natalia's sleeping face.

Her eyes were swollen from crying. Her lower lip was red where she'd bitten it to keep from screaming when a nurse wheeled a crash cart into Brie's room.

He watched her, remembering every time she'd stepped up when others couldn't or wouldn't. How she took his moods and turned them around. The way only *she* could keep him from losing his mind.

When her eyes fluttered open, he kissed her and it was different from every kiss they'd ever shared.

Slowly, his tongue explored her mouth as his hands explored her body. He pulled the thin tank top she wore over her head and pushed the soft panties down her legs. If she tried to speak, to question what was happening, he kissed her again.

This was no time for words.

Her hands lifted to trace him. She rarely had the ability during sexual play. Short nails raked through his hair, over his nipples, down his back, and her touch sank to the deepest part of who he was.

He held her hard and the kisses, the discovery, went on and on.

Then she pulled him and he moved willingly between her thighs. She was slick, ready for him. The head of his cock found the heated entrance of her pussy and he slid just inside.

The skin of her back glided over his arms where he hugged her, connecting them as he worked his way inside a body that a day before he would have said was familiar.

Fully seated, they stared at one another for a long minute. Her breath panted between her lips and their hearts pounded furiously. Their skin touched everywhere possible.

Then Hudson *made love* to his best friend for the first time.

Pressed as close as they could get, his strokes were slow and deep. He never looked away from her face, watching her watch him. One hand slipped around to brush her hair from her face.

His thrusts continued. Accustomed to being taken hard and fast, her first orgasm built slowly. As it broke, the flush staining her breasts, chest, and neck, Hudson exhaled sharply and kept going, pushing past the tightness of her body milking his cock.

She sighed his name.

It could have been ten minutes or an hour but they maintained the full-body hug as he showed Natalia in actions what had always escaped him in words.

The second climax stole her breath and it was the sight of tears slipping from the corners of her eyes that took his control.

He gave her his kiss as he filled her with his seed and it was a moment unlike any that had come before. When the spasms finally settled, he continued to thrust lightly.

"I love you, Natalia." The words were different than every time he'd said them before that moment.

"I love you, Hudson."

"Look at me."

Her eyes were closed and she slowly shook her head. "I can't."

"*Look at me*, Natalia."

The blue of her eyes shimmered with her tears. He kissed the corners, her cheeks, and at last her lips.

Her fingers traced Hudson's brows but she didn't speak.

"I liked that a *lot*."

She made a sound that was a mixture of laughing and crying. Then they were hugging each other tight as he stroked her hair and whispered that it was going to be okay.

She didn't believe it yet.

He would convince her.

The touch of her hands on his face, in his hair, was different from every other touch and he knew, in that moment, that Brie had been right all along.

It was all about timing.

Chapter Fifty-Five

First week of April...

The first thought Gabriella had when she opened her eyes was that she'd never hurt in so many places at the same time.

"Gabriella...Gabriella."

The shock of hearing her mother's voice beside her an instant before the strongest woman she'd ever known burst into tears *scared her to death.* She tried to speak, to reassure her, and realized there was something over her face.

Full out panic. She was suffocating...

A nurse leaned over her and whispered, "Miss Hernandez, sshh, there's a tube down your throat. I'm going to remove it now. It's going to be okay."

She worked quickly and efficiently to loosen the tape and pull the plastic out. The gagging and eventual vomiting embarrassed her. The thin fluid went in her hair.

Confused and in pain, tears fell freely.

"The doctor is coming. There, there." The woman had a soft accent. With gentle hands, she wiped her face and helped her rinse her mouth. "We've been keeping a close eye on you today. The doctor said your vitals indicated you might wake up."

She tried to talk but nothing came out. After a small sip of water that burned all the way down, she tried again. *"Day...?"*

"You've been with us for almost four weeks." She knew the shock must have been written all over her face. "Don't worry. You're very much on the mend. You've quite the fan club."

She winked and cleaned the bile from her hair.

A warm and calloused hand stroked her head and she turned slightly to see her father. Cabral Hernandez was a champion to his daughters. Anything he put his mind to, he managed to accomplish. He'd instilled a willingness to work hard, every day, to accomplish their goals.

"My Gabriella. How we have worried for you." He bent to kiss her face all over then reached to pull her mother closer.

Still lovely in her fifties, Tallila Hernandez wiped away her own tears. She was brilliant and people in the business world tended to underestimate her because English was not her first language and she'd been born in a poor village with no running water or electricity.

She turned a firm look on her youngest daughter.

"What have I *told* you about letting anything happen to my little one? Hmm? You're one of my two most precious possessions. You can't allow even the tiniest scratch. Not the *tiniest*."

With their cheeks pressed together, she added in whispered Spanish, "You're *never* to scare me so badly again. I wouldn't survive losing one of my girls."

Izzy worked her way between their parents. "I go to the damn bathroom for five minutes and you *finally* wake up! Oh my god, Brie! You never do anything halfway."

Tears of relief poured down Isabella's face. She kissed her then rested her head on Brie's shoulder and sobbed brokenly.

Brie struggled to speak. "…*happened?*"

Her older sister pulled back. "You don't remember?" Brie shook her head. "A car hit you as you were crossing an intersection." She lifted her hand and kissed the back. "You've broken bones…everywhere. It was the internal injuries that worried your doctors."

"Walk...?"

"You aren't paralyzed, Brie. No, honey. They have you on constant drip to hold back the pain so you can heal. They put you into a drug-induced coma to let your body rest."

A hundred things flew through her mind but she was unable to capture any of them. She drifted back to sleep and wondered if Hudson knew about her accident.

* * *

The days passed like a dream. She often saw and heard people in her room but she had to struggle to stay awake, to focus, and her body demanded rest. Riya and Tawny may have come many times or it might have been one day.

Late one night, she dreamed she heard Hudson's voice on one side and Natalia's on the other, whispering that they needed her to get better. They kissed her and stroked her hands, the only places on her body that weren't casted or bandaged.

Hudson's voice was deep and warm. It made her feel better just hearing it. "You're strong, Brie. Fight." He kissed her cheek and added, "I'm so very sorry."

"Come back, Brie." She felt Natalia's tears.

She wanted to comfort them, angry that she couldn't open her eyes. "It's alright. Alright..."

The next day, she knew it had to be a dream. It was the first day she managed to stay awake for more than a few minutes at a time. She was shocked to learn she'd lost another week of her life.

Her mother held her hand. "Gabriella?"

"Yes?"

"Who is *this* Hudson Winters?"

She turned her head. "How do you know about Hudson?" Concentrating, she added, "He isn't the same man."

414

"This I know." Tallila's brows raised dramatically. "It would be impossible to not know about him since he is paying for your care despite our insistence that we are perfectly able to do so."

Brie was unable to hide her shock. "Hudson knows I'm here?"

For a long time, her mother said nothing.

Then she sat forward on the chair. "Gabriella. Hudson beat the ambulance to the hospital the day you were hurt."

"What? I don't understand."

"Your father and I didn't either. When we arrived that night, we assumed there would be papers to sign and insurance to present. The hospital informed us that your entire bill was being covered by Hudson Winters." She shook her head. "We were confused. More so when we realized you work in his building and live in an apartment he owns."

"Long story. He felt responsible when I showed up at his home."

There was a long silence and then her mother nodded. "His mother was kind enough to let us in when we went to pick up a few personal things to bring for you. Camille said so many lovely things about you."

"Camille is strong, like you, Mom."

Then the pain medication shut her off like a light.

* * *

It was dark when she startled awake. The jarring movement aggravated the broken vertebrae in her neck, the broken ribs, the fractured pelvis, the broken bones in her wrist and both of her legs.

She managed to muffle the whimper of pain.

Her head was pounding against her skull. When the doctor showed her the x-rays, she was reminded of a boiled egg that had been dropped. It was the worst of her injuries. The one that would take a very long time to heal.

She was lucky the driver hadn't killed her. Lucky she wasn't paralyzed. Grateful she still had brain function and remembered how to tie her shoes, create a logo, and cook.

Gabriella knew she remembered these things because she quizzed herself on them constantly when she was awake.

"Hello, little sister." She tried to smile at Izzy through the pain. "You don't have to pretend. I know you're hurting." Smoothing her hair, she whispered, "I can't wait to be able to do your hair."

"Am I in a different room?"

Her sister grinned happily. "You're in the long-term ward now. Officially stable and out of immediate danger."

"When can I go home?"

"Patience. That won't be for a little while." Meeting her eyes, she asked, "Are you involved with Hudson and Natalia?" Brie's eyes shot open and met her sister's in panic. Isabella smiled. "I don't *care*, Brie. You're a grown woman with a huge heart. You deserve to find happiness wherever you can."

She leaned on the railing. "He's very abrupt, your Hudson."

Turning her head, she said, "He isn't *my* Hudson, Izzy. One day, he and Natalia are going to look at one another and it'll suddenly click that there's only one person for either of them. It will be beautiful."

"Do you know he and Natalia visit you every night?"

"I didn't dream it." She smiled. "That makes me happy. I adore them. You will, too."

"One of the nurses calls to let them know Mom and Dad are gone and they show up twenty minutes later." Her smile was huge. "That's how I busted them. I overheard the night nurse telling them our parents had returned to their hotel so I waited."

"I don't, I don't remember."

"You get heavier medication at night. It doesn't stop them from coming, from talking to you."

"I wish I'd known."

She looked at her watch. "Are you awake? Really awake?" Brie nodded. "Good." She leaned over and kissed her cheek. "I'm so glad you're alright. I was out of my mind with worry."

"I love you."

"I love *you*, Brie. You scared years off my life."

"Off all our lives," a deep voice said from the door. Brie glanced passed her sister and saw Hudson and Natalia standing in the threshold.

"I'll see you in the morning, little sister." Isabella kissed her, stood, grabbed her bag, and left the room.

They wore jeans, t-shirts, and sneakers. She'd never seen them in outfits that wouldn't be appropriate at any board meeting.

"You look so *young* in those clothes." Her voice was shaky but she couldn't seem to stop it. "I've been sending you positive thoughts. Did you get them?"

They approached the bed on either side and took her hands.

"That explains so much. You're like a magical fairy, darling." Natalia's were brilliant. "You're *awake* for the first time while we've been here. Your eyes are so clear, Brie." She leaned over to hug her carefully and then she was crying hard. "I've never been so worried."

"Don't cry. I'm going to be fine, the doctors said."

Natalia leaned back and stared at her, cool fingers curved along her face. "The one thing I want to tell you, while you're awake, is that I think you're one of the best people I've ever known. You could have died and you wouldn't have known how important you are."

Hudson squeezed her hand and she looked at him. His face was tense. To an outside observer, they'd think he was angry but she'd spent months watching him, sketching him, before he ever kissed her. She knew his face better than she knew her own.

He was afraid.

"Something happened." There were few things that could frighten a man such as him.

He put one palm above her head and leaned over her body. The palm he slid along her face and into her hair was so *warm*. Her eyes drifted closed for just a moment to absorb the sensation.

"Don't move yet. I'm freezing."

"It's the pain medication, darling." Natalia stepped to a cabinet and pulled out a thicker blanket that she laid over her body. "Better?"

"So much." She stared up at Hudson. "Whatever it is, whatever happened, I want you to know that it will change nothing. I consider you one of my best friends, a man I care for and respect. Tell me."

"I messed up, Brie." His voice was so quiet she barely heard him.

"You're human. Despite the fact that your cock is god-like. Sorry, Natalia. I mean, hard all the time. No wonder Tawny noticed."

They laughed and Brie knew that no matter what, it was going to be okay. There would be a little time of pain, she felt it coming, but these two people were harder on themselves than anyone else could ever be.

Hudson cleared his throat and leaned back. Natalia's hand tightened around hers and it was clear the other woman was sharing her strength.

"The day I met you, I'd been seeing someone. She lived with me. I knew what she was but I ignored it. She served a need and had her place. I never imagined she'd use the resources I gave her to assist in running a long-range con."

Her eyes went wide. Hudson's *girlfriend*…

"Wait. I threw her out that night and confiscated the stash of fake IDs of the other women she helped rob. I've compensated every single one except you."

"You didn't tell the police."

"No, I didn't."

"You were embarrassed." The look on his face confirmed that was part of it. A man like Hudson would be livid that someone close managed to fool him. "There's more."

He nodded slowly and she knew the rest was worse. *This was what he was afraid to tell her.*

"I've had her movements tracked since the day she left my apartment. I needed to know who her male accomplice was. Then I could determine whether turning them over to the police was my best option, or if I should handle it myself."

"You know the identity of the man."

"The day you described him, I suspected. I didn't *want* it to be true, Brie. I tried to find a hundred explanations. Another answer, *any* answer but that one."

It was someone he loved.

* * *

Gabriella thought back to conversations she'd had with the pretend Hudson. There were times she would have sworn he was angry and he would laugh it off, using his charm to divert her attention.

Something in particular once set him off more than any other.

It involved her sister Isabella.

Brie had stopped at the store after her shift at the winery and he pulled in beside her. He always rented an expensive car when he came to visit but what he drove didn't matter. She was happy to see him.

The man she knew as Hudson smirked at her car. "When are you going to buy something nice, Brie? That car is a clunker."

It was odd for those to be the first words out of his mouth when she got out and walked to him. They hadn't seen each other in months.

"I've had this car for years. I don't know what I want yet, what I'll need when I eventually move out on my own. I might not need a car at all." She shrugged. "I figure this one still runs."

"Your sister drives an Audi."

"Izzy *loves* her car."

"Your parents should step in and help you once in a while. You're the youngest. You work a lot harder than she does. Everything is easier for her. It isn't right."

For a moment, actual animosity seemed to bleed into his voice and she didn't understand.

He didn't know her family.

He always found an excuse not to meet them.

Her smile was careful. "I *chose* the winery. I have no interest in the fashion portion of my family business. That was perfect for Izzy. Our parents do lots of things for both of us."

She put her hand on his cheek.

"We *both* work hard for our paychecks. It's all part of Mom and Dad's plan to have us ready for the world. She spends most of her earnings and I save most of mine, but it doesn't change that we have to *earn* what we make. My sister is awesome."

Looking at the conversation now, Brie recalled how her "boyfriend" had assumed a mask after his outburst.

He made an excuse about his behavior. An excuse that casually mentioned an *older brother* he didn't like very much.

* * *

"It was your brother. He pretended to be you."

Hudson closed his eyes. "His name is Scott."

So many things suddenly made sense.

The pain written on both their faces made her heart hurt. She tried to imagine what it would be like if Izzy had done something similar to her and wished she was able to hug them.

Nothing would have made her take her eyes off Hudson. Something was pushing at her mind, wiggling around and making her head swim.

"He found out I was still in New York." She closed her eyes. "He figured I would have gone back to my family after causing you untold embarrassment."

"You're the only one who ended up in New York. The others were robbed in less than six months. I don't know why you were different."

Opening her eyes, she stared at the hard set of Hudson's jaw.

"He never thought I'd stay here. There's no way he figured that you would help me. His plan hinged on you doubting my story and me being weak, naïve, and ashamed. I messed things up for him."

Hudson nodded again.

"I ruined the game." She shook her head. "I spent a fortune on a private investigator and had no idea I'd already gotten him caught."

"I can't tell you how sorry I am, Brie."

"He blamed you for everything he didn't have and he blamed me for messing up his con. He was furious with both of us."

Hudson remained silent, allowing her to make the connections.

"The man I hired called me two weeks after my surgery to say he was tracing a strong lead. There was no way your brother could touch *you* and he would have known that." She swallowed around the lump in her throat and it was painful. "He tried to kill me. Didn't he?"

"Yes."

The truth was what she expected but it still hit her hard. It destroyed her emotionally to know that a man who'd touched her body and said the word *love* to her many times had tried to *kill* her.

She lifted the arm without leads, the one that was casted from her thumb to mid-forearm, and pressed her eyes in the bend of her elbow.

"What is *wrong* with people?" She let herself cry. "I'm so tired, damn it. I hate being stuck in this fucking bed."

After a long time, she lowered her arm and allowed Natalia to wipe her face. Tears made her blue eyes shimmer. Hudson looked fierce.

Her thoughts raced and for once, she wanted them to be quiet.

"The man flew thousands of miles several times a year. He lied and pretended to love me, all while planning to screw me worse than the mediocre sex I was getting."

The laughter that bubbled up in her chest was cold. "How could you bear to *touch* me, suspecting your brother fucked me first?"

His eyes drilled into hers. "You may have had *sex* with my brother but I can guarantee I was the first man to *ever* fuck you."

Nothing less than the truth. She sighed. "I'll give you that one."

"I *will* make it right."

"You didn't *do* anything. It isn't your responsibility to fix what you didn't break, Hudson. You have your own shit to deal with now. It's horrible in its own way, worse than mine, I think. It was something I didn't want for you."

"It goddamn well is my responsibility. I can't take away your accident or the pain you're going through. I can't change the fact that I thought could protect you until I found Scott."

His fingers slid along the curve of her skull gently. "I'll take care of you now. I'll protect you. I'll help you through all of this to the other side." He gave her a small smile and it looked stunning on him.

"I *do* love you, Gabriella. Not in the way you need, I know, but less than a dozen people in my entire life have made me feel love. You're the only one I didn't see coming."

She stared at him for a long time and then looked at Natalia equally as long. The smile that broke over her face couldn't be helped and she wouldn't have held it back anyway.

"Y-you *see* it. Finally, you *finally* see it." Tears slipped from the corners of her eyes and she smiled through them. "Nothing else matters. It's all going to be okay now."

Natalia laughed through her tears, covering her mouth. "Only you, darling. You're a fucking original."

"I can't hug you. Hug me so I can pretend." She bent and slipped her arms so carefully beneath Brie's body. "You sparkle in love, Natalia. Somehow, you're even more beautiful."

As the nurse entered to administer her pain medication, Hudson leaned over her body and kissed her forehead and the tip of her nose.

"You have a long road ahead of you. We're going to force things on you that you'll fight because you're one of the most stubborn people I know. I need you in top form, so you feel like you have a chance, even though I'll still win."

"Arrogant."

"Always."

Then she felt the drag and couldn't keep her eyes open. The darkness rose up to wrap her inside it and her last thought sent her there with a smile of pure joy.

No matter what happened to bring her here, what she'd gone through, she'd been the bridge she was always intended to be.

Hudson and Natalia were in love.

Chapter Fifty-Six

The first day Riya and Tawny visited while she was coherent, the redhead scared the *hell* out of her poor mother.

Busting in the room, she yelled, "Bitch! Don't you *ever* scare us like that again or I'll slap that pretty ass that makes me stupid jealous!"

"Hello, Mr. and Mrs. Hernandez. I'm Riya Scottsdale-Chadwick and this is my friend with no filter, Tawny Ratliff. I forgot her medication this morning. My apologies."

In Spanish, her mother whispered to her father that their daughter's friend was crazy and Riya assured them – also in Spanish – that she certainly was but ultimately harmless.

Oblivious to the smoothing of ruffled feathers going on behind her, Tawny approached the bed with a deck of Uno cards.

"I'm whippin' your ass this time and I don't feel the least bit bad that you're hurt. I take my breaks where I can get them." Tilting her head, she added with a sigh, "Your hair is fucked up. I see a spa day in your near future."

Then she started dealing cards.

Late that night, after her parents returned to their hotel, the door to her room opened and Riya snuck inside, her men behind her. Zach was holding Tawny against his chest, his hand over her mouth as Quinn had a fit of quiet hysterics.

"The guys wanted to see you so bad. We didn't want to freak out your parents. One dose of Tawny was enough for a little while."

Max and Micah walked to one side of the bed, Zach and Quinn on the other. She looked back and forth at them.

"I'm recovering, you know. All this pretty in one place is just too fucking much. I'm only human and Tawny carries a switchblade."

Poking her head around Quinn's shoulder, she said, "I'd totally lend them for fuckery. They're *very* good and you and me are tight, Brie. You'd feel like a brand-new woman. No shit. Orgasms for *days*."

"Um, never again. I love your guys and I can't have that image in my head. I'm healing!"

"She says she'd lend them but she's a fucking liar," Riya interjected. "She's more likely to climb in bed with you *herself* than let either of them take off a single sock in preparation."

"Fuck you, wait, that's kind of hot." Her men couldn't help but laugh and the M's just shook their heads.

"No." Brie didn't need *that* image in her head either.

They attempted to keep the noise down but when Hudson walked in looking furious with Natalia behind him, she knew he thought they were disturbing her.

He took a breath but before he could say a word, she smiled. "Now *all* my best friends are here. This is better."

The fight went right out of him and one side of his mouth lifted.

Natalia hugged his waist before approaching and leaving kisses on Brie's forehead. "You look good today, darling."

"I know that's a lie. I can *feel* the knots in my hair. They'll probably have to shave my head when it's all done."

"Nonsense. I'll take you to see a friend of mine and she'll get you fixed up right and tight. I've known her since college."

Tawny put her hands on her hips. "I was going to take her to my person. I want to see that rat's nest tamed."

Staring into Brie's eyes, Natalia winked. "We have the *same* person, Red. I'm the one who sent you to her."

"Right. Brie will fucking *love* Bibi. No shit. Girl's day! Think we can sneak her out? Bring her right back? With less dreads action?"

Hudson stepped around Natalia and kissed Brie's head. "You have lovely hair, even now."

"Thanks. Love that tie. What's going on with you?"

The two of them chatted while the other people in the room stared on in surprise. He straightened her leads, pulled her blankets higher, and held a glass for her to take a sip of water.

One of Natalia's hands rested around Brie's fingers, her other was wrapped around Hudson's.

Riya's happiness was easy to read. "You did it," she mouthed.

Brie winked.

* * *

It was several days before Brie thought to ask Hudson a question she should have asked first. "What if he tries again? To hurt me?"

"Impossible."

"Why is it impossible?"

"Scott is sitting in an apartment which he is unable to leave. There are armed men stationed with him as well as outside the door and in the lobby. Much like a safe house. Only, in this instance, the person being kept safe is you."

"Why?"

"You deserve the right to confront him. Without police, without lawyers. He took your pride, he stole from you, and he tried to kill you. Every day you're unable to leave this bed, he'll be unable to leave that apartment. Consider it tit for tat."

"It could be *months*, Hudson."

Hudson shrugged. "The apartment lacks for nothing and it's far better housing than he'd receive if I turned him over to the police. I gave him the option. He chose wisely."

"What about your mother? Your sister?"

"They have permission to visit him. So far, they've chosen not to." His fingers slipped soothingly over her brow. Her headaches were brutal some days and she worried that she would always have them.

"Thank you for understanding that I *will* need to see him. I need him to explain." She paused. "This can't be easy for you and I'm so sorry. You're kind to think of me."

"Only the women in my life have ever thought me kind."

Brie grinned. "Then it's good you surround yourself with women."

Strong arms slid carefully beneath her. Through the bandages around her torso and the hospital gown, she felt the warmth of his skin. He pressed his cheek to hers.

"I need to hug you. I don't want to hurt you."

"You aren't."

"I can't believe you forgave me. I'm glad we're still friends."

"You didn't hurt me, Hudson. As for being your friend, that's completely selfish. There's no better street fighter at life than you. Well, other than Tawny but she's so easily distracted."

He chuckled, kissed her temple, and carefully let her go.

Natalia kissed her other cheek and she was swept back to the moments they'd held her between them.

So many beautiful memories.

* * *

The days passed slowly and Brie found herself missing a mish-mash of things. Her little statue, the café where she liked to sketch, and laughing unreservedly with Riya and Tawny.

People from the building stopped by to visit, Lola and Leonard, and her neighbors from her apartment.

Unaccustomed to so little activity and without the mobility to draw for extended periods of time, she was bored unless she had company.

She harassed her doctors daily about when she could go home.

In the middle of her third month, after consulting with several specialists, her parents considered returning to Washington.

One or the other of them had been with her every single day since her accident.

Not only did she know they had active lives to get back to, their constant presence was driving her bat-shit crazy.

They went back and forth for several days until Izzy finally threw up her hands and shouted in Spanish, "I'm capable of looking after my little sister!"

Pressing her fingertips to her temples, she added more calmly, "Brie is going to be in worse pain during rehabilitation than she is now. You know she'll try to hide it so you don't worry."

Her mother petted her hand.

"I'm staying at her apartment and I can work remotely here like I've been doing. New York is a fresh infusion of fashion on a daily basis so this might move our design arm to the next level."

"You'll stay *here* with your sister?" Their mother was anxious, worried, and being pulled back to the West Coast by their various business interests. "Until she's better, yes?"

"I won't leave New York until Brie is released completely from medical care." Isabella was reaching the end of how much time she could handle their parents.

"You'll call me *every* day. More if there's a problem." Izzy nodded. "You must let us know if we need to come, Isabella."

"I know, Mom."

The older woman released a heavy sigh and both her daughters could see the exhaustion weighing on her.

Her parents built their empire hands-on and as a result, it required a strong dose of regular involvement from the founders.

"Mom?" Tallila moved nearer. "I'm alright now. All that's left is the exhausting and painful road back to normal."

Hands that were surprisingly strong gripped her face.

"It's when you almost lose something you love more than you love yourself that you see the mistakes you've made like road signs *behind* you."

"You're a wonderful mother. I love you."

"When you're better, when you're back to the cheerful, happy girl I know, I hope you'll consider moving back to Washington."

Brie opened her mouth to object.

"Wait. Not our little town. You've grown out of it. I thought perhaps Tacoma or Seattle. Far enough to make you feel independent but *closer*, Gabriella. There's no pressure. Something to think about."

For a long moment, she considered the implications of moving back to the West Coast. "I promise to consider it carefully, Mom. Right now, I have to focus on recovery."

Tallila's eyes lit up. "That's all I ask."

She was gathered in a careful hug that warmed her from the inside out and there were tears on her mother's cheeks when she pulled back.

"I'll make sure you and Izzy have everything you could possibly need before we take a flight back at the end of the week." Glancing at her oldest daughter, she gestured her closer.

"I need to talk. Give me a moment to gather my thoughts."

Clearing her throat, she said, "When your father and I set up your inheritance, we thought to use it as a control if you were doing bad. They were created when you were just a baby, Gabriella. You were barely three, Isabella. The way we looked at you then was different."

There was a small shrug of her delicate shoulders. "You took cookies from the jar, told little lies, all insignificant things. You were good girls always, bright, and hardworking unlike most people your age. We wanted to protect you so we held you in our hands like butterflies."

Tears slipped from her eyes. "It wasn't until this horrible thing that we realized we'd closed our hands into fists, crushing the natural beauty and goodness you've had since you were born."

"Mom…"

"The way you fought when you came here and built a life. How you've stayed by your sister's side, working well into the night so you don't fall behind. It's only now that we realize, you *are* the women we always hoped you'd be. It happened right in front of us."

Swallowing hard, she patted Brie's hand and squeezed Izzy's. "Your father and I had the attorney meet us at our hotel a few days ago. We released the money always meant for you. I'm sorry it took so long."

Then the three of them were sobbing, her mother and sister bent over and doing their best to wrap her in a hug.

Their father entered the room with a tray of coffees and frowned. "What did I miss?"

* * *

Three days later, Brie's parents returned to Washington. The long and highly emotional farewell took everything she had. "Thank you for being here so long, for being here when I woke up."

Her father kissed her cheeks. Cabral stared down at her for a long time before tracing his finger over her temple.

"The bruising is finally disappearing. This pleases me, Gabriella." He leaned closer and rested on the rail of the bed. "You're not to endanger my little mouse again. If anything happens to you or your sister, everything we have is worth nothing. Do you understand what I say?" She nodded.

"A car will drive you securely from now on. There will be no arguments about this."

She stretched her inner independence and thought she could handle the leash her parents needed for a little while. "Alright, Papa."

Izzy's eyes widened behind Cabral's shoulder. Then she grinned and mouthed, "Pick your battles."

At her ear, her mother whispered, "The *girls* look like they fit you now. One less pain for your body to bear while you heal."

Then they were gone and she cried herself to sleep.

The road to recovery would be long but she would travel it smiling.

Chapter Fifty-Seven

Third week of May…

It was early in the morning when the orderlies came to transport Brie to the ambulance waiting downstairs.

She was being transferred to a long-term residential rehabilitation facility and the thought made her incredibly depressed.

As someone used to walking, to being active whether she was working or not, the constant stillness frustrated her.

Izzy followed in Hudson's car.

The paramedics chatted with her while they drove and she thought they had nice faces. When she could sit up properly, she would sketch them. She missed her art desperately.

A small window in the rear door made it impossible for her to watch their progress. Then they were backing up and she was being unloaded from the back like a package.

Up a small ramp and then she was in a huge elevator obviously used for freight deliveries.

The color of the walls and shape of the lights in the ceiling of the car made her frown in confusion.

"Where am I?" she asked as the doors opened.

A voice behind her said, "You're home, Gabriella."

It was impossible to turn her head enough to see Hudson so she had to wait until the paramedics turned the bed.

"What are you talking about?"

"Remember when I told you to keep your strength up to fight me but I'd win anyway?" She nodded. "I won."

Then she was pushed through the doors of one of the single-story apartments and she was even more confused.

Natalia rushed from a room with a huge smile. "There you are, darling." She bent over the bed to kiss both of her cheeks. "You're going to love it and we tried not to go crazy. You have to pick all the paint colors because you're the artist."

"Wait…what?"

On her other side, Hudson said, "It legally belongs to you."

She blinked, her head dizzy. "You gave me an *apartment?*"

"Yes."

Brie stared at him, her head pounding. "You can't give me an apartment."

"It's my building. I can do what I like."

Mouth opening and closing like a fish, she sputtered, "Hudson…"

"Hush. You can yell at me later."

"We asked for Lydia to come back since you got along so well. She's going to get you settled and introduce you to the other two nurses and the physical therapist who'll be working with you."

"Here? I'm going to recover *here?*"

"Completely. There's a gym equipped with everything the specialist we consulted said you would need." She smoothed a cool hand over her cheek. "You aren't to think or worry. Now is not the time."

"I don't, I'm…"

"Yes, darling. We know. You get settled in and I'll be back in a couple of hours with a good friend of mine who's been dying to meet you."

Then they kissed her face and left.

Blown away, she smiled at Lydia's friendly and familiar face. "I made cake. I have so many videos to catch you up on."

It made her laugh. The entire situation was surreal. She was afraid to even look around.

Had Hudson really given her an apartment?

The other members of the medical team were wonderful and bustled around, getting her moved from the hospital bed to an enormous wheelchair. She thanked the paramedics as they waved goodbye.

"How about a soak, Brie? Now that your casts are off, I'm sure you'd love to scrub the grime off with a real bath."

Even the *thought* of a soak made her moan.

"That's what I figured." They showed her how to use the special lift that helped her get in and out of the tub safely. "You've been on your back for three months. It's going to take time for your bones and muscles to come back. Baby steps."

Nodding, Brie leaned back in warm water that had never felt so good. Glancing down, she grimaced at the scars.

Gone was her flawless skin. The tender scar along her scalp was almost six inches long. There was another along her neck and many scattered over her torso and legs.

Izzy appeared in the doorway. "Stop staring at the scars. Natalia said Dr. Geldin will make most of them a distant memory."

"I can't believe I'm recovering here."

"You *live* here now, Gabriella. Hudson honest-to-god signed over ownership of this place to you."

It was insane. She knew what these places listed for and there was no way she could let him just *give* her one.

"I'm staying here with you for a couple of days to make sure you're settled but I'm living in your old apartment." Part of her started to panic. "Calm. All your stuff is here."

"So much information to process."

"Soak, relax, and then you get to dress in soft clothes that belong to you instead of that shitty hospital gown."

Then she blew her a kiss and left Brie alone. She was so overwhelmed that she fell asleep.

* * *

It was Natalia's voice that brought her awake. "Let me help you, darling." She covered a soft scrubby with a delicately scented body wash and started at her feet.

The motion felt good but she was embarrassed.

"You don't have to do that for me, Natalia."

"I worked as a home health aide in college. If anyone deserves careful attention with someone they know, it's you. Don't worry."

"I'm so scarred," she whispered.

"You have a few but Abraham will take care of most and the others will be less apparent. You survived so much trauma, Brie." She frowned. "You've lost too much weight. We'll gradually put it back."

"No thanks. I found a diet that finally worked."

"Stop that. You're a beautiful woman at any size."

She worked her way over the front of her body and helped her sit forward so she could wash her back. Draining the water that was murky with plaster dust from her casts, she refilled the tub.

"One more pass."

Repeating the same process, she scrubbed her body a second time and rinsed her thoroughly. Lydia came in to help her dry and dress in a soft sport bra, t-shirt, and yoga pants.

She felt much better sitting in the wheelchair. They pushed her into the living room so she could see the city.

"I've missed it."

Natalia crouched beside her. "Lola helped me frame your painting. We're doing the building commemoration ceremony in a few weeks. It was pushed back so you could be there. It's perfect, Brie."

"Do you think he'll like it?"

"He is going to *love* it. The size of your heart humbles me."

She started to say something else when a boisterous voice said from the door, "Natalia, is this the pretty girl I'm playing with today?"

"Hi, I'm Brie." Grinning at a strikingly good-looking woman who looked close to six-five, she tried to maneuver her chair in that direction.

"Uh uh, I'll come to you, honey. Aren't you just adorable?" Pulling up a chair from the dining table, she sat directly in front of her. Everything about her reminded Brie of brown sugar. The shade of her hair to her eyes and freckles.

"I'm Bibi. I've been *waiting* to meet you. Today, I'm going to get those knots out of your hair without putting any stress on your skull. When it's clean and silky, we'll braid it to avoid tangling."

"Thank you. You have the most gorgeous skin. I *love* your freckles."

For a long moment, she stared into her eyes. Reaching out, she picked up her hand and held it in two much bigger ones.

"You were so right, Natalia. She fucking *glimmers* with goodness. I was lucky enough to meet another soul like yours years ago, Brie. It's rare." Her smile was brilliant white. "By the time I leave, you'll feel so much more settled in your skin."

It took three hours and two deep conditioning treatments to get the tangles out of Brie's hair. To rinse, Bibi palmed her entire skull and supported the weight of her head over a portable sink that her chair backed right up to.

More conditioner that relaxed the curl tightness and she plaited the length into a loose braid.

"Eyebrows then I'm doing your fingers and toes."

In no rush, the two of them chatted non-stop while Natalia and Izzy sat working quietly on their laptops. Gathering her equipment on a valet cart in the late afternoon, Bibi pronounced her gorgeous.

"So are you. I think you glimmer, too."

A careful hug was followed by kisses on both her cheeks. "You'll come see me when you're all better?" She nodded. "Focus on your rehab, call me every couple of weeks to come by, and I'll look forward to showing you my shop when you're up and around."

To Natalia, she said with a wink, "I'll see you in a few weeks."

She left whistling and Brie murmured, "I love her. Thank you so much for introducing me, Natalia."

At her side, she bent and kissed her forehead. "I knew you'd get along. Now a short rest."

* * *

It took Brie two weeks and buckets of sweat to get to a point where she could get from the bed to her chair and back again, on and off the toilet, and to maneuver through the rooms without assistance.

After another week, she could use a walker if it was early in the day.

Daily physical therapy left her drenched and sobbing but she tried not to complain. The pain in her legs and hips was brutal but she knew it was necessary if she ever wanted the opportunity to walk the city streets again.

Progress was slow but it was measurable. Her friends, co-workers, and sister came often to visit after she rested in the afternoon.

The apartment had three bedrooms, an office, and a gym. The living spaces were similar, though slightly smaller, than the penthouse Hudson and the M's lived in. She loved the open space, the huge windows, and the access to the people she was closest to.

She started sketching again, initially frustrated at her stiffness. When Izzy saw what she was working on, she contributed some ideas and the finished product was gorgeous.

* * *

One evening, Brie sat in her wheelchair, the special desk across the top, sketching in front of the big windows facing the city. She had the same view Hudson did from his home above her.

The thought made her smile.

Lydia opened the front door and the man she was honored to call her friend – one of the best she had in her life – stood on the other side. "Hudson. Where's Natalia?"

"She's hosting a birthday party at the club. There were last minute preparations and she's been there for two *days*."

"Absence makes the heart grow fonder, Hudson."

"It also makes the cock grow harder," he said deadpan and she cracked up laughing. "I'm climbing the walls. She won't let me see her until tonight. I *distract* her."

"Hudson, sit and talk with me. Catch me up."

Sitting at the dining table beside her, he told her about several business deals he was working on and finally, his voice trailed off. Her smile was gentle. "You mean personally."

"Yes. How do you feel?"

"Afraid. I don't like it one fucking bit."

"Tell me why."

"I don't…communicate well. I worry she doesn't know things I want her to know."

From the back of her sketchbook, she pulled the drawing she'd done for him. His eyes widened as he took it from her hand. Then he laughed. "So simple. How grateful I am for you, Brie."

She stared at him. "That isn't the only thing she needs. I've done a lot of research sitting around, bored out of my mind."

Tilting her head, she said quietly, "You would have bought her something long ago. You might not have been able to verbalize what you wanted, or even understood how you felt for Natalia, but those feelings have *always* been there."

Their eyes met. "A collar."

"You have one for her."

"I bought it after the first night that everything changed between us sexually. Our dynamic was different."

"How long have you had it?"

"Sixteen years."

"Why haven't you given it to her?"

"I waited for her to give me a sign."

Rolling a bit closer to a man who was so powerful yet so fragile when it came to one woman, she took his hand.

"In every area of your life, you maintain control. Even your interactions with Natalia have followed a certain pattern from the beginning." He frowned.

"She *needs* you to take control in this because she's accustomed to you leading, Hudson. You're the only person she allows to do so."

His lips parted and she watched the realization take hold. "Fuck."

"At least you've had *that* during the course of your friendship. It would have been horrible if the two of you had been hard up for so long."

His laugh was accidental and she liked the way it transformed his face.

"I think you have somewhere to be, don't you?"

Leaning forward, he cupped her face in his hands. "I love you. Thank you for making everything easier."

"Thank you for being my friend, Hudson."

He kissed her forehead, her cheeks, and ended with a light kiss on her lips. "It will be spectacular watching you receive all the love and appreciation you deserve one day, Gabriella."

"Don't keep her waiting anymore. Tell me all about the party in a couple of days."

With a nod and one more kiss to the top of her head, he strode for the door. She watched him go; filled with joy for the love they finally recognized, and acknowledged that her happiness was bittersweet.

Talk of her finding love seemed foreign because she only related to it about other people.

Forever an optimist, she knew it was still possible. She wanted it but she would never settle for less than a man placing all he was in the palm of her hand and knowing with every cell in his being that she would keep it safe.

In the meantime, she'd vicariously enjoy the love Riya, Tawny, and Natalia had found.

Someday, maybe it would be her turn.

Chapter Fifty-Eight

Upstairs, Hudson changed into the clothes Natalia had left for him to wear to the birthday bash for one of her favorite members at *Trois*.

He grinned as he dressed in the ribbed tank top, dress shirt, retro pinstriped suit, and suspenders. He wore classic wingtips on his feet. As requested, he slicked his black hair back with gel.

Laughing at himself but more excited about an event than he'd been in a long time, he walked into his office.

From the safe, he took a black box. Inside, resting on black velvet was a custom platinum chain made of thick links. There was a teardrop shaped sapphire in the center.

Closing it and relocking the safe, he slipped the box into his suit jacket.

In the car, he smiled at Leonard and then his mind became distracted, wondering what Natalia would be wearing.

He called his assistant. "Isabella Hernandez should have work space in the building. I know she's working remotely right now. We can provide her better resources. Brie will need space as well."

Lola laughed. "I have the perfect offices for them on our floor. It will be fascinating to have other people around who talk."

"I *talk*."

"My *desk* is more talkative. Your will shall be done, my liege."

"Have I told you lately that you can be a bitch?"

"Mm, compliments are unnecessary. Alright, I have no time to play.

My boss gets downright *cranky* if his plans aren't implemented instantaneously. I'm out."

Lola hung up on him and he couldn't help but grin.

The car pulled to the curb as the sun was beginning to set. It lit the front of the building beautifully.

Valets for *Trois* were turned out in classic 1930's wear and Hudson told Leonard to take the rest of the night off.

"I'll call you tomorrow afternoon, no earlier than three."

"Yes, sir. Thank you."

There was no way he'd be able to wait until they returned to his – *their* – penthouse. The moment the last guests left the club, he planned to fuck his woman for twelve hours straight.

Melody's fortieth birthday party was a burlesque theme and *Trois* was decked out for the occasion. Satin swatches in burgundy and black were woven through the carved concrete bannisters out front.

The security guard nodded at Hudson as he held the door.

Natalia turned to speak to one of her staff and he stumbled to a stop. She towered over the young server who was similarly dressed but currently barefoot.

"Was Etta able to fix the strap?" The woman nodded. "Excellent. Remind me to order you a new pair. You're damn lucky it didn't give way coming down the stairs."

They chatted for a moment and the girl walked away with a smile.

His best friend was costumed for the evening in a blue and black lace-up corset and satin tap pants with thigh-high stockings on garters that lead to retro black tap heels. Her legs looked a mile long.

As gorgeous as the outfit was, it was not what held his attention, knocking the breath from his body and all thought from his mind.

Natalia was blonde.

Her natural color was accompanied by the curls he'd always loved. Tiny, jeweled clips pulled it back and made the blue of her eyes radiate from her face.

At that moment, she glanced up and their gazes locked.

She self-consciously touched her tresses and he assumed his expression as he walked toward her told her exactly what was on his mind. He didn't stop until they were close enough for the fabric of her corset to brush his chest with every breath.

It had been many years since Hudson had seen her unsure of her appearance. In the last few months, he realized that clothing was armor she used to insulate herself from the rest of the world.

"Hudson, I…"

"Ssh. Let me look at you." He reached up to stroke his fingers through the honey blonde hair he'd all but forgotten. "You're beyond beautiful, Natalia. Always so fucking *beautiful.*"

In the main foyer of her club, in front of her employees and a few guests, he kissed her. It was the first time anyone close to them, other than Brie, had seen them touch intimately.

There was more than one gasp.

His heart made the same sound as he publicly *claimed* the one woman who had held his heart in her competent hands for most of his lifetime.

One hand slid beneath silken hair to cup her nape and hold her in place, taking her breath and giving it back. His arm circled her waist and he distantly heard the clipboard she'd been holding hit the marble.

Delicate hands moved over his chest and wrapped around his neck as Natalia took the last of his heart and handed him hers in return.

Time lost meaning and when he broke the kiss, the air around them was still.

"I love you. With every cell in my body, with every ounce of emotion I possess, with all my strengths and my flaws. You are *mine*. I stake my claim. Do you accept me, Natalia?"

There was a slight pause as she stared deeply into his eyes.

Then she whispered, "I love you. I offer you my most precious belongings. My body, my mind, my heart, and my soul. To do with as your will and passion dictates. I accept your claim, Hudson."

To people such as them, the words were as significant as wedding vows. The importance was not lost on her staff and as he scooped her into his arms, they clapped and cheered behind them.

He carried her to her office, kicked the door closed behind them, and set her on her feet. He pinned her to the wall as he reached behind her to turn the lock.

One long leg wrapped around his hip as he ground his cock against her. Touching his forehead to hers, he worked to steady his heart and his breathing.

"I'm sorry I waited so long."

"You waited just the right amount of time, Hudson."

He took the necklace from his jacket and she covered her mouth as tears filled her incredible blue eyes.

"If I had to ask, I didn't deserve you."

"You *always* deserved me, darling."

Attaching the collar around her neck, the stone fell at the hollow of her throat, as he'd known it would.

"Natalia?"

"Yes?"

"It might take time to get used to the blonde. You've never sucked my cock as a blonde."

"We should correct that oversight then."

He smiled and took a step back. Shrugging off his jacket, he dropped the suspenders from his shoulders as his hands went to the closure of the slacks.

She smiled and stepped from the wall with her shoulders back.

"On your knees."

Epilogue

Last week of July…

Harper Delkin took a long pull of his scotch. He'd been personally invited to the exclusive party by Winters' assistant.

If Lola called, you damn well cleared your calendar.

The gala was to commemorate the one building the real estate mogul had worked slowly, methodically to acquire for more than ten years. It was a personal milestone.

There were many people he recognized and more than a few he didn't. He'd already talked with Bishop. Chadwick and Scottsdale had given him advice on an investment he was considering but quickly lost interest in all talk of business when their woman appeared.

Winters circulated with a *blonde* Natalia by his side. The necklace she wore was priceless but it symbolized far more than wealth. The sight of it validated the rumors he'd heard. Apparently, the man had acquired another priceless treasure recently.

He'd been slow as hell about it.

Since college, the two of them had often been mistaken for one another. In the black suit with a tie that matched Natalia's eyes and dress, Winters could have been his brother. He was his oldest rival.

A man some would call his friend.

In his professional life, Harper had never seen a man more driven to succeed. He respected the trait above all others.

His eyes roamed the room, taking in some of the biggest power players in the world. He was considered one of them.

A woman drew his attention more than once. She sat at the far end of the room in a large leather chair.

The bodice of her blue-black gown hugged her curves and flowed out over her feet. Occasionally, she shifted her leg and he'd glimpse the tip of a matching peep-toe heel.

He took in her glossy black hair, hanging loose and curly down her back, golden skin, and dark eyes that sparkled as she talked.

Harper wondered who she was.

Admittedly lovely, she didn't circulate. People approached her to talk, gathering around her like she was fucking royalty. She was animated, openly friendly, drawing men and women alike.

She reminded him of his dead wife. As if she was entitled in some way.

He'd been watching her off and on for two hours when Natalia stepped up on the stage of the ballroom and rang a small bell to get everyone's attention.

It was clear that Winters was unaware of what she was doing.

"If everyone could give me your attention for just a moment. Darling, will you join me?"

Winters made his way to her side, his hand sliding along her waist and firmly sealing their sides together. The move made Harper smirk.

He will have no doubts regarding who she belongs to.

Natalia smoothed her hand over the breast of his jacket and smiled warmly. He pressed his face to her cheek. She cleared her throat.

"This building was particularly important to Hudson. He worked for years to acquire it and it became possible just a few months ago. Someone dear to us saw the significance to him instantly and created an extraordinary gift to mark the occasion."

She motioned to two men who entered carrying a large covered canvas that was taller than they were. They walked to the stage while a third man rushed ahead to set up an enormous easel for them to place it on.

"A commemorative painting by Gabriella Hernandez."

The men lifted the linen and revealed an exquisite depiction of the building where they stood, done in oil.

Several of the guests audibly gasped.

Even from more than twenty feet away, the detail and talent were clear. The layers made it appear almost three-dimensional.

There was no mistaking the impact the art piece had on Winters the moment it was revealed. Harper had never seen such emotion on the man's face.

He moved to stand in front of it, staring at it for a full minute. Then he turned to kiss Natalia, murmured to her, and stepped off the stage.

Walking purposefully through the room, around his guests, he headed directly to the young woman in the leather chair.

Then Hudson Winters – one of the most dominant men he'd known in his lifetime – *knelt* at her feet in a five-thousand-dollar suit.

He spoke quietly to her, taking her hand between both of his. When he stroked the back of his knuckles over her cheek, she started to cry and he kissed her lightly.

In no hurry, uncaring that there were a hundred other people in the room, he whispered at her ear and made her smile. With a small nod, she hugged him and he stood.

As he turned, their eyes met across the space. Winters' black eyes delved into his own pewter ones and neither of them blinked.

The woman's hand was still in his and Hudson glanced down at her with a gentle expression. Then he kissed the back and placed it carefully in her lap.

The message was clear. The woman was incredibly important but Winters did not claim her as his own. He returned to Natalia's side and pulled her away from the party.

Harper continued to watch the artist, fascinated at her animated conversations with the other guests.

An hour later, she tugged a messenger bag from the other side of the chair she sat in and withdrew a small sketchbook. In the middle of a party, the girl began to draw. His youngest brother was a creative type and he knew they could be eccentric but it seemed unusual.

He made a decision.

At functions such as this, where he could be photographed or overheard, the bodyguard standing just behind him remained silent.

"Elijah." He felt the man draw near. "I want to know all there is to know about Gabriella Hernandez."

From his peripheral vision, he watched as Elijah moved into a level position at his side. "She's lovely, enchanting even."

Frowning, he said, "Probably a hustler. Winters' taste in women other than the magnificent Natalia has left much to be desired."

"What about *my* taste in women, Harper?" He turned his head and met Natalia's brilliant blue eyes. She was *pissed*.

Absolute silence was something he should consider himself.

"Brie is not a *hustler*. If you were to line up the people in this room, she would be the kindest, most selfless of us all."

Stepping close, she murmured, "Despite your history, your money, and your power, Gabriella is too good for you."

He didn't blink but a ripple of shock traveled through his body. He'd never seen Natalia angry. The woman didn't rattle in any situation.

She started to turn, paused, and said over her shoulder, "You've been watching her all night. I came to ask if you wanted an introduction. Both of you. Now, you can go fuck yourself."

Then he and Elijah watched Hudson's woman walk into the crowd, mingling with the guests, a cool smile on her face. Eventually, she appeared at Brie's side and perched on the arm of the chair where the young artist sat.

Brie looked tired or ill, reclining against the back with her long dark hair flowing around her.

Twice, Natalia smoothed her brow and spoke soothingly, as if to calm or reassure the woman in some way.

Moments later, Hudson appeared and spoke to her. Brie shook her head but he bent and lifted her into his arms. She rested against his shoulder as he carried her through a side exit.

"Follow."

Elijah reacted instantly, walking into the crowd. Harper watched him go, the fluidity of his movements a thing of beauty.

Gabriella Hernandez was a woman under the protection of one of the most powerful men in the country. She was not a lover, relative, or business associate.

Harper Delkin wanted to know why.

Hudson's Vow

I love you.

With every cell in my body.

With every ounce of emotion I possess.

With all my strengths and my flaws.

You are *mine*. I stake my claim.

Do you accept me?

Natalia's Vow

I love you.

I offer you my most precious belongings.

My body, my mind, my heart, and my soul.

To do with as your will and passion dictates.

I accept your claim.

Security

A Barter System Universe Short Story

Over the sixteen years he'd known her, half of them had been filled with love and the other half filled with a deep and sincere respect.

His love had haunted his nights and destroyed his peace of mind for almost a decade.

She only had eyes for one man and it was not her employee.

Finally, the hold she did not know she had on him lessened and he breathed a sigh of relief, free at last to focus and interact with other women in the world.

Six weeks before, a new woman walked into his life and into his heart without a single moment of warning so he could protect himself. Very different from his first unrequited love, she was pretty but not beautiful, smart but not brilliant.

Her magic was in her smile. She smiled with her entire body and it lit her from the inside out. Genuinely kind and exceedingly generous, he watched her with the rest of the staff and fell deeper in love every time she laughed.

He was not a man who spoke of his feelings and being raised in the frozen tundra of Siberia had made him hard and unable to hold conversations others took for granted. Thankfully, his English was better than it had been twenty years ago.

He saved most of his earnings just in case he ever ended up a married man. He wanted to have everything necessary to provide for a wife, maybe even children, someday.

Passing forty-three years of life without such a miracle made him doubt the possibility more by the day.

He wondered at his purpose, why fate had seen fit to place him near women his heart opened for without the ability to tell them.

It seemed cruel.

He checked all the doors and smiled at his boss as she left on the arm of her new husband. The man was worthy of her and nodded as he held the door.

Only when they were safely ensconced in the man's car did he turn back to the foyer, prepared to make one more round of the old mansion before heading to his quiet apartment.

A sound reached him as he touched the door to the main ballroom and he paused. Hearing it again, he turned and followed it. Down the hall, he waited for another. When it came, he approached the door to one of the specialty rooms used by guests.

No one should be in the club.

Pushing it wide, the scene before him filled him with rage. An older man, one of the first members, held her against the wall. His forearm pressed against her throat as tears streamed down her face. She was desperately trying to fight but made no progress.

Her eyes met his over the man's shoulder and she didn't need to say a word.

Without hesitation, he bodily lifted the man from her, slamming him to the hard floor, bouncing his head off the surface. Kicking him to his stomach, he removed cuffs he'd never had to use in this building from his low back. The man was out cold.

Only when he was secure did he turn his head to look at the woman he loved. She'd slid down the wall and sat weakly on the floor. Her clothing was ripped and she had bruises on her face.

Despite the circumstances, she tried to smile one of her beautiful smiles through her tears and shakes that were noticeably worsening.

He shrugged his suit jacket from his shoulders and wrapped it around hers.

"Thank you, Stav."

"You're welcome, Vita." He stood and took her with him. "Come. I'll keep you safe."

"I know."

© Shayne McClendon

Unpretty

A Barter System Universe Short Story

Natalia Roman ignored the butterflies and full body chill as she sat in the exam room in nothing but a paper gown.

I can do this.

For weeks, her boyfriend slowly pushed her to this moment. Gently at first. More firmly over the last few days.

"I love you just the way you are but wouldn't *you* be happier if you had more going on up top? You'd push your hotness level up, babe. I bet it makes you feel like a *totally* different woman."

As a teenager, she never obsessed over her body. She was naturally tall and lean, which suited her just fine.

Natalia enjoyed being active and breasts, she often thought, seemed like a hindrance. Never growing past an A-cup didn't concern her because she didn't think about it.

Until she was told by her first boyfriend that she looked like his little brother without clothes on.

From then on, she wore padded bras. When her best friend asked about it, she told him they were pretty.

Hudson Winters wasn't convinced. The man seemed to know her better than she knew herself and he eventually got the real story. The boyfriend walked into class with a black eye the next day and broke up with her.

She was secretly relieved.

As a freshman in college, a man she dated for a while insisted on having the lights off. She asked him why and he said, "Then I can imagine you with tits."

Experimenting with women was a relief to her self-esteem. They liked her body, wanted her all over them, and appreciated being able to touch her with no conditions.

Then she met Gray Dodd when she was twenty-three. Grand gestures and PDA were his style, though it was rarely her own. She wasn't in love with him but considering her history, he seemed to be an improvement.

Three months ago, he came to pick her up and she opened the door in a towel.

He perched on the edge of her bed while she finished getting dressed and when she slipped on her padded bra and panties, he came to stand behind her in the mirror.

"Why do you wear these?" he asked her as he cupped the lace.

"They make me feel pretty."

"No, I mean the padding."

"They make me feel pretty."

"Why don't you just get a pair?" Shocked, she hadn't replied and he added with a shrug, "I'm not saying you need them but if you want tits, why don't you buy them?"

He kissed her behind her ear and went to make himself a drink. She stared at herself for a long time and wondered…

She shook her head at her ridiculousness and she put it out of her mind.

After sex one night, she was getting dressed to leave when he said, "So, are you going to do it?"

Confused, she turned to him with her top in her hand.

"Get a boob job?"

"No. Why would you bring that up after all this time?"

"I thought you were thinking about it."

"No."

"Why not?"

Slipping the shirt over her shoulders, she hurriedly buttoned it. "Surgery is risky. I'm a bleeder."

"So…you're scared."

With her shoulders back, she put her hands on her hips. "Hmm, I'd call it cautious. Hemophilia makes surgery especially dangerous for me."

"You won't die from a boob job."

"You wouldn't be the one taking the risk though, would you?"

She stepped into her shoes and he bounded from the bed. "Wait, Talia." She hated when he shortened her name. "I didn't mean to make you mad. I can tell you're insecure about it, that's all. I want you to be happy." There was a pause. "I love you."

Eyes wide, she took in the information and didn't know how she felt about it. She didn't even know what love *was*. Unlike most of the women she knew, she'd never been in love. She never said the words to anyone other than her family and Hudson.

Saying them felt like lying.

There was no doubt in her own mind that she wasn't normal. She didn't have any interest in being a wife or mother. Could care less about a wedding or having a man underfoot. Her mother worried that she would end up alone.

Sometimes, she wondered the same thing.

"I love you, too."

"I'll see you tomorrow?"

She nodded and left but this time, his words stayed with her. For the first time in her life, she was self-conscious.

Gray wore her down and she admitted that she let him. So here she sat in a sterile room.

The door opened and an older man walked in. "Hello, little one. I'm Dr. Geldin. You can call me Abraham. What can I do for you today?"

Carefully clearing her throat, she replied, "I'd like implants."

For a long moment, the doctor glanced over her body. "Why is this?"

"Why do I want implants?"

"Yes. Why?"

"To have breasts."

"You have breasts, little one. They suit your narrow frame. You are lovely. Why do this?" She couldn't answer because the words would have shown how weak she was. "Do you do this for a man?"

She nodded slowly.

"A man who doesn't appreciate the symmetry of your body is a fool."

The door behind the doctor slammed open and hit the wall. Hudson stood in the threshold and his expression was livid.

"You're not *touching* her."

Dr. Geldin smiled and Natalia found it odd considering her best friend looked beyond psychotic at the moment.

"I agree with you, young man. She's ideal exactly as she is." He stepped closer to Natalia and lifted her chin. A long scar snaked behind her ear to her shoulder from the branch she'd landed on when she fell from a tree at twelve. "However, I can treat this if you like without any surgery at all. Wouldn't that be nice?"

She smiled at him. "Yes. I'd like that."

"Good! We agree! My nurse needs to do a small skin patch test to make sure the solution doesn't bother your skin. It will take three visits, okay?"

"Okay."

"Visit with your friend and you can get dressed. Leave the gown over your bra."

"Thank you, doctor."

"Ah! You look even prettier now than when you came in. This decision sits better on you, I'm thinking."

He left and closed the door. Hudson wore a suit and she remembered that he'd closed on his second commercial property today.

"Did you get the warehouse?"

"I did."

"Everything went smoothly then?"

"You won't risk your life for a fucking *man*, Natalia. Do you not remember that you almost bled to death when you got that cut? It didn't even seem that bad when it happened but I thought you would die before I could get you to the hospital."

He walked closer and cupped her face in his hands. "You would *willingly* go under the knife for a man who doesn't appreciate how beautiful you already fucking *are?*"

"It was stupid."

"Very fucking stupid."

"You'll stay with me?"

"You know better than to ask. We're having dinner."

She met his eyes. "What about Tonya? She hates me."

His brow quirked mockingly. "She told me she loved me and I broke up with her."

Natalia started laughing and he joined her. Suddenly everything was alright in her world again.

* * *

Hudson took her for steak and red wine to celebrate. After he ordered, he stated, "Your iron levels are shit. Eat every bite."

"Yes, my liege." He grinned and they settled into old conversation that was warm and familiar to her.

When she hit puberty, she was diagnosed with a rare blood disorder that she'd inherited from her father. The amount of blood she lost every month was frightening.

The chance that she would ever get pregnant was slim to none and that was just the way she liked it.

Kids scared the shit out of her. There was no doubt in her mind that she would make a horrible mother.

After dinner, they strolled the city. They ended up in front of the first piece of property he purchased. A light in a third-floor window made her smile. "Your mom is still up."

"She reads late. Come on."

"I was going to head home, Hudson."

"Tonight, you're staying here." Without another word, he took her hand and led her inside. Little by little, he was renovating the old residential space.

He planned to turn it into apartments.

She was awed by the changes in the foyer. "Oh my god! You've done so much work since I was here last!"

"You haven't been by in months."

That made her laugh. "Hudson, you suck at reading the emotions of the people around you. Tonya used to grind her teeth when I stopped by. Drove me fucking nuts."

Her best friend shrugged as he headed to the second floor. "I saw it. I just didn't care."

Perfectly Hudson behavior and she wouldn't have him any other way.

The apartment he converted for himself had undergone even more changes. She walked the space slowly, taking it all in. "I can't believe you were able to bring these floors back."

"Hardwood wants to shine. You just have to rub it right."

"Sounds like men I know."

His laugh filled the space as he shrugged off his jacket and loosened his tie. "I remodeled the bathroom. You can shower and grab one of my t-shirts in the bottom drawer."

"You want me to stay?" Normally, they were drunk when they fooled around. Right now, she wasn't even buzzed.

Turning, he put his hands on his hips. It was hard to tell what he was thinking. "Yes. You're staying."

"Okay. You talked me into it."

She gave him a wink and walked to the bathroom confidently. Inside, she was a nervous wreck. There was a tension between them tonight and she wondered if she could tell him some of the thoughts in her head.

It was a topic that had the power to embarrass her. Natalia was not a woman who experienced such things.

There was something she wanted, maybe even *needed* sexually. She didn't trust Gray or any of the relationships that had come before him to give it to her safely.

The last time she'd fooled around with Hudson was a few weeks before Gray and Tonya entered their lives. They'd been completely wasted, stumbling up the stairs, whispering too loud, and holding one another up.

Just inside his door, Hudson slammed her up against the wall and took her harder than anyone had before or since. Harder than any other lover seemed capable of accomplishing.

Her panties hadn't survived the encounter and they were still fully dressed when he pushed her over the peak and followed.

The next morning, she stared at the bruises on her inner thighs and it made her breathe too fast. The tenderness of her scalp where he'd gripped her hair made her heart rate speed up.

Just remembering the experience made her wet.

Since that night, there hadn't been a day when she didn't think about it. She often masturbated to the memory. Sometimes, she imagined she was tied up when he took her. Occasionally, she pretended she was wearing a blindfold.

Always, it made her come harder alone than she could with a lover. Any other lover but him.

She took her time showering and left his bathroom barefoot, in panties and a t-shirt, toweling her hair. From his chair across the room, she saw him watching her. Her movements slowed and finally stopped. She held the towel in one hand as she stared back at him.

"Come here."

The command in his voice made her nipples harden sharply. She made her way across the wood floor and stopped inches from his knees.

"I want to fuck you."

She knew her eyes were huge in her face because *once again* she seemed in harmony with her best friend. Her damp hair curled around her cheeks and tickled her skin.

"Alright."

"I need to experience something with you tonight. If you don't like it, we'll never try it again. If you aren't happy, we'll go on as we have with this between us." He took a deep breath. "If you do enjoy it, we need to talk."

She didn't speak, simply nodded. She trusted him with every cell in her body and that meant in every aspect of their lives. He'd been there for her too many times to doubt him. Natalia *mattered* to him and she *knew* he would always keep her safe.

Standing, he slid her t-shirt up her body and tossed it to the couch. "Walk to the bedroom."

Without hesitation, she returned to his room. His bed was on a wrought iron frame that hadn't been there the last time she'd stayed with him. That night, they slept on his mattress on the floor.

She knew without asking that he planned to tie her to it. Everything inside her went hot at the thought.

"Get on the bed on your knees. Grip the top rail." He opened his closet and removed two ties. Approaching her from the side, her eyes flicked to his hands and back to his face. "I won't hurt you. I would never hurt you, Natalia."

"I know." She faced the wall above the bed and held the rail until her knuckles were white. "I trust you more than anyone else in my life, Hudson. I hope you don't think badly of me...after."

He secured her to the frame and removed her panties. He took his time stripping away his clothes and watched her. She didn't move but soaked up the sexual tension as he made her wait.

From the bedside table, he removed lubricant and she noted his hesitation as he reached for condoms.

"Are you still on birth control?" She nodded. "Can I take you without a condom?" Her eyes met his and she nodded again, slower this time, wondering if it would feel different. "I'm clean and if you should ever end up pregnant, I'll take care of you."

Swallowing hard, she turned back to the wall.

"Spread your legs."

She did and when he stood on the bed, she stared at his cock. He was rigid. The shaft jutted from his body, the head was almost purple, and his balls were drawn tight.

"Open your mouth."

Her eyes lifted as her lips parted and he fisted her hair. Holding her still, he started with shallow thrusts, gradually increasing the depth and force as he fucked between her lips.

When her eyes began to water, he slowed and pulled back. She knew he felt bad, that he thought he hurt her.

"Breathe through your nose. I'll be more careful."

The first climax took less than ten minutes. Years later, when he perfected his control, he could easily last for half an hour. Longer than any man she would ever fuck. When he softened slightly, he thrust between her lips more firmly and she gained confidence in the act she hadn't performed often.

Over the years, she would perfect the art of taking his cock anywhere in her body.

Pulling from her, he dropped to his knees and kissed her hard. She whimpered against him and he allowed his hand to drift over her nipples, down her torso, to her pussy.

She was *drenched* and he broke the kiss.

"You liked that? You liked me fucking your mouth?"

"Yes."

"You're so wet."

"Hudson, *more.*"

Positioned behind her, he was still hard enough to enter her. He pressed and she leaned forward to rest her head on her tied hands. He pumped into her wetness slow and easy until he hardened fully again. Time lost all meaning. Nothing mattered but what was going to happen next.

Allowing his thumb to trace the pucker of her ass, he asked, "Has anyone ever fucked you here?"

"No, but I want to know what it's like." It was the truth. For the first time, she felt as if she could have her questions about the forbidden answered. She wasn't going to allow the chance to pass her by.

He spent a long time preparing her ass with his lubed fingers while he casually stroked into her wet heat with his cock. When she was slick and warm, the tightness eased a bit, and he scissored them inside her.

Natalia heard her own pants into the quiet room.

Hudson pulled from her body and went to wash his hands, returning with a small bowl of soapy water and a washcloth.

"It might hurt."

"I know."

"You haven't come yet."

"I'm letting it build. I do that when I'm alone."

Without another word, he climbed back on the bed and positioned his cock at her anal star. Carefully, he pushed forward and she tried – and failed – to hold back her moans until he was buried to the hilt.

Leaning over her back, he whispered at her ear, "Your ass is squeezing my cock like a vise. Are you alright?" She nodded. "Tell me if you need me to slow down or stop."

He gripped her hips and pulled back, dripping more lube over his length. Then he powered forward and she screamed. Instead of stopping, he set up a steady rhythm until she was moaning and pushing back to meet his thrusts.

"Feels so fucking good, Natalia. So fucking good."

"More."

With a deep breath, he took her harder. Reaching beneath her, he stroked over her folds. Pinching her clit between his thumb and forefinger, she gasped.

"I'm going to come. Don't stop."

As he stroked and pinched the little bundle of nerves, she went over the edge with a muffled scream and shoved her body back to take his cock deeper.

There was only a slight hesitation as he gripped her firmly and fucked her harder than she would have thought was physically possible.

In moments, he was filling her with his come. Her name echoed through the room.

They stayed like that for a long time. Getting their bodies under control so they could think.

He kissed her shoulder and she knew he was afraid to show her his reaction because he was too quiet. She smiled against her arm and wondered what other adventures the two of them would find together. He would accept her, the *real* her, just as she would always accept him.

"Hudson?" She paused and said warmly. "I liked that a *lot*."

© Shayne McClendon

The Barter System Series

Read the entire series now!

The Barter System Prequels

The Barter System (Book One)

Hudson (Book Two)

Backstage (Book Three)

Liberation (Book Four)

Radiance (Book Five)

The Barter System Companion – Volume 1

The Barter System Companion – Volume 2

About Shayne McClendon

If you're looking for stories that tug at your heart, make you laugh out loud, and sometimes make you cry so hard you need a giant box of tissues…look no further than books by Shayne McClendon.

She's a prolific author (more than 8 million words and counting) known for dramatic, steamy, enthralling fiction that will grab you and not let go until the last page.

A nomad at heart, Shayne currently lives in America's heartland with her dog, cats, and two grown children.

She listens to the voices in her head because their ideas are (almost) always awesome. Coffee consumption is too high, amount of sleep is too low, but the words always feel just right.

Be sure to like her <u>Always the Good Girl Facebook page</u>, or visit her at <u>Always the Good Girl</u> and join for your free story!

Shayne currently has more than two dozen books that range from heart-wrenchingly romantic to captivating non-stop heat. Explore them on the next page!

Also by Shayne McClendon

Dramatic Romances
Completely Wrecked
The Hermit

Sports Romances
Love of the Game
Hart of the Matter

Country Romances
Yes to Everything
Somebody
Gravity
Break Down Here

The Barter System Series
The Barter System
Hudson
Pushing the Envelope
Backstage
Liberation
Radiance
The Barter System Companion – Volume One

The Great Outdoors Series
Sunny's Heart
Permission to Come Aboard
Permission to Land
Special Delivery
Embrace the Wild

Short Story Anthologies
Quickies – 2014 Edition
Quickies – 2015 Edition

Romantic Comedies
Always Delightful

Special Acknowledgments

For my friend and longtime personal assistant, Jana who never lets me fall on my face.

For Rhonda and Sheryl who are changing the way my words are presented one book at a time. You've given me incredible peace of mind. Thank you.

Without the help of these women, I'd fail.

All the love in the world,
Shayne

Proof

73660411R00265

Made in the USA
Columbia, SC
14 July 2017